KNOT HER Shot

a novel by

Ari Wright

Published and formatted by Blue-Eyed Books

Knot Her Shot, MVP: Most Valuable Pack Book 2

ISBN: 9798989007264

ebook ISBN: 9798989007257

Cover: Quirky Bird Covers by Staci Hart

To all the thirsty babes in my DMs begging for more.
This one's for you.
Get it, girl.

the cheat sheet

WHAT IS *an omegaverse?*

An **Omegaverse** is an alternate universe wherein humans have evolved a biological hierarchy based on three individual designations: **alphas, betas, and omegas**. In an Omegaverse, every person falls into one of those three categories (or "designations") by the time they reach adulthood. Their **designation** then determines certain elements of their physiology, psychology, and physical appearance. The humans in this Omegaverse are not shifters.

Alphas are large, strong, dominant, possessive, and territorial. While civilized, they often struggle with the urge to use force or exert their dominance over others; particularly fellow alphas. Optimized anatomy makes them physically superior in many ways, including reproduction.

Male alphas have a "knot" at the base of their penises. This **knot**, much like the penis itself, becomes engorged when they are aroused and expands to its full size upon completion, "locking" an alpha into his partner. Female alphas have a "lock" inside their vaginas that perform a similar locking maneuver on their partners.

Alphas are biologically compelled to find compatible partners based on individual scents. They also tend to form **packs** with others. Omegas often become the center of packs because they are the only designation capable of creating **bonds** between others. There is rarely more than one omega in a pack. Once a pack bonds with an omega, all of their scents alter subtly. This shift helps protect bonded omegas from unwanted advances.

Betas remain the most similar to everyday humans. They do not have intense scents or the same biological compulsions that alphas and omegas share. Many beta-beta relationships resemble traditional monogamous partnerships. Because they cannot bond among themselves, they often choose to marry instead.

Omegas are smaller and softer in stature, naturally submissive, wary of violence, fearful, emotional, empathetic, and magnetically attractive. Omegas' bodies are built to endure the demands of an entire pack of partners, emotionally and physically.

Omega biology draws alphas in. When omegas are aroused, their bodies send nearby alphas a signal by **perfuming**. Omega perfume is a concentrated hit of their specific scent, intended to lure an alpha to their aid.

Alphas and omegas each have distinctive scents. Their bodies produce these scents at all times, but they are particularly strong when the individual is sexually aroused or emotionally distressed. Alphas and omegas can have very intense, all-consuming physical and emotional reactions to each other's scents. While uncommon, the phenomenon is called **scent-sensitivity**.

Scent-sensitive alphas and omegas are referred to as **mates**. By some twist of fate or biology, they are near-irresistible to one another. Separating from their scent-sensitive mates would cause an omega extreme pain and distress.

Omegas experience **heat cycles**. These "heats" are spurred by the biological imperative to mate/bond with an alpha (or group of alphas) who will provide for and protect them. When an omega goes into heat, he/she will experience intense physical pain unless they are knotted by their alphas regularly. Heats send omegas into a state of limited lucidity that is known as a **heat haze**. This haze makes them extremely vulnerable and unstable.

Omegas can take **suppressants** to lower their hormone levels.

Suppressants help make the pain of heats tolerable for omegas who do not have alphas. Unfortunately, over time, suppressants become less effective.

Unbonded alphas who encounter an unbonded omega can experience **rut**. Rut is a condition wherein an alpha loses his/her mental faculties and gives in to the biological imperative to knot/lock an omega. Rut is often dangerous for omegas.

Omegas **nest** in order to feel secure. An omega's nest should be a soft, round place that feels low to the ground and dark. Omegas take great pride in building their nests to their individual tastes and their alphas' approval. It is their alphas' duty to provide this space and the resources to outfit it.

Courting is the process by which alphas can press their suits with an omega of their choosing. It is generally a task undertaken by the entire pack in pursuit of their one chosen omega.

penalty box

(content warnings)

welcome to the **MVP** omegaverse

I'm so glad you're here!

Knot Her Shot is the second installment in the *MVP: Most Valuable Pack* series. If you haven't read Book 1, please don't worry, this is intended to be read as a *complete standalone*!

This is a why-choose Omegaverse romance. It includes lots of knots, tons of spice, and absolutely no choosing!

If you don't like rowdy alphas, swoony mates, and group sex scenes (including packmates lending each other a hand), this may not be the HEA for you <3

Content Warnings: orphans/loss of a parent, past/childhood neglect, dyslexia, depression, pleasure Dom/sub relationship, double penetration/DVP, dubious consent, primal kink.

knot her shot playlist

Chinatown — Wild Nothing
Too Well — Reneé Rapp
Never Be Like You (feat. Kai) — Flume
Big Energy — Latto
The Champion — The Score
Love Me Harder — Ariana Grande, The Weeknd
Into It— Chase Atlantic
Adore You — Harry Styles
Over and Over Again — Nathan Sykes, Ariana Grande
Too Sweet — Hozier
Cravin' — Stileto, Kendyle Paige
This Love (Taylor's Version) — Taylor Swift
Strangers x Midnight City — Sevven
Radio — Lana Del Ray
Dizzy — MISSIO
Runaway (U & I) - Svidden & Jarly Remix — Galantis
Turn The Music Up — NF
Twisted — MISSIO
Clocks — Alex Baker, Sahara Moon
The Difference — Flume, Toro y Moi
Lovers— Anna of the North
ANGEL — Toby Mai
More Than Enough — Alina Baraz
Home — Good Neighbours
How You Get the Girl (Taylor's Version) — Taylor Swift

To listen along, check out Ari's Spotify!

prologue

Ten Years Ago

THIS IS FINE.

Nothing to see here.

There are a lot of things you can tell yourself if you're willing to listen. I'm not sure if the fact that I believe my own nonsense means I'm a genius convincer or a gullible loser who will believe anything.

Can it be both?

At the moment, I'd say I'm walking a tightrope between stupidly romantic and just plain stupid.

And I'm slipping.

No, literally. My foot is slipping and if I let go of my bunk room's windowsill, someone is going to have to scrape me off the sidewalk two stories down.

Once the sun comes up.

Maybe it would have been better to do this in the daylight.

Oh, but the sunrise is so much *prettier* than the sunset. All the soft baby pinks and violet blues and frothy clouds. My window faces a tree that blocks out most of it. I just want to see if I can glimpse the horizon if I climb a *little* higher up...

Carefully planting my bare foot against a roof shingle, I rebalance the book under my left arm and size up the stretch to the closest eave. Sandpaper texture scratches my toes while the cool morning air settles over my arms. I have to extend every muscle in my spine to reach the next ledge, carefully easing my way around the corner of the roof.

I'm pretty sure if I just skirt around to the side of the house, there's a dip between two dormers—

"What are you doing out here?"

My life flashes before my eyes in a dismal blur of government-issue greige. I startle, nearly losing my grip on the corner of the roof.

"*EEecht!*"

Ignoring my squawk, a big hand snatches my wrist just before I lose my balance. "Are you *crazy*?" the guy mutters. He drags me into the valley between roof segments before dropping my arm.

I scramble back from him, pressing into the shingles, eyes bugging with fear. "W-wha—Who—Wh-why?"

He's one of the older kids in our group home. Almost the shape of a man, but too gangly and full of the kind of restless fury that only comes from being caged in an orphanage.

That's what happens to us, I've realized. We either grow fearful... or furious.

I'm afraid this guy is in the second category.

I'm afraid I'm in the first.

Dark brows lower over his eyes. "Don't freak out," he

mumbles, shifting back. "I don't give a fuck why you're up here. I was just saying; you're crazy."

Normally, I'm mousy. Sensitive. Skittish. I've been called a lot of things, but never crazy.

I'm typically too busy trying to follow all the rules and keep everyone happy to make much headway in the "crazy" department. Though, I suppose, climbing up onto the roof alone, in the dark, doesn't exactly scream, *"sensible."*

A big hand waves in front of my face. "Focus, butterfly. You could slide right off this thing."

I realize I've totally spaced out and duck my chin, hiding the way hot blood blazes under my cheeks. "Right. Sorry."

He shrugs his shoulder. It's massive, even in his ill-fitting hoodie. If he hasn't designated as an alpha yet, I bet he will one day soon.

An oddly serene silence settles between us. A thousand different things to say play through my head before I rewind his earlier remark, quirking my eyebrows at him.

"Butterfly?"

The first strains of dawn touch his face, barely illuminating the half-smile that twitches on his lips. He nods at my hair. "Your clip."

For fluff's sake. I have my oh-so-childish, completely mortifying butterfly clip nestled in my hair.

It was the first thing my fingers touched when I rifled through my shoebox of accessories in the dark. I didn't want to linger and wake my roommates, so I grabbed it to hold my bangs out of my eyes while I scaled the roof.

I forgot it has little springs to give it movement. Now, as I cringe, pink, sparkly wings flutter against my curls.

Gads.

The almost-alpha keeps smirking as his eyes drop to my book. "I've heard you up here the last few mornings, but I didn't realize you were hosting a book club."

My giggle sounds nervous. I squash it and sniff. "If it were a book club, there would be snacks. And probably other people."

He leans back on his palms and shrugs again. "I'm another person."

I blink at him, convinced that I must be missing some sort of joke. "You... are."

That quick not-quite-a-smile twinges up again. "Then I guess all we need now are snacks."

chapter one

THIS IS FINE.

Nothing to see here.

Grunting, I lean back and tug on the enormous canvas bag of coffee beans blocking our aisle-way. The sack inches across the floor of Proper Coffee while I stagger backward, using all of my strength to pull it around the bar.

Good Lord.

Is it time to go home yet?

Nope. It's not even eight a.m. And everyone is staring at me.

Fantastic.

My manager is a young beta guy who almost never looks up from his TikTok feed. His thumb rolls over the screen hovering under his hooked nose. His voice sounds bored. "You good, Remi?"

Me?

Oh, I'm *great.*

My hands are raw from towing big canvas bags, and my fingers are numb from the weight of the latest one. Not to mention the pinch in my lower back. Or the fact that I haven't taken a full breath in about eight minutes.

"Yep," I pant, yanking harder. "All." *Tug.* "Good." *Tug.*

You know, given how often I conceal the truth, I really am an appallingly bad liar. How does anyone believe me? I wonder as I straighten and catch my reflection in the mirrored wall behind the espresso machine.

Staring at my face, all I see are fibs. In the layer of concealer caked under my eyes; *see, I'm not tired.* In the cream blush blended into my too-sharp cheekbones; *look, I'm glowing with happiness.*

None of it is honest, but the smile on my lips is particularly egregious. Slicked with some sort of tingly lip-plumping gloss. Wide, white, and positively thrumming with dopey doe-eyed optimism.

Pretty, though.

Just like the apartment I left before dawn, I'm a collection of cleverly disguised shabbiness. Pink paint smoothed over the craggy walls. Jars of fake flowers to cover water-rings on my second-hand furniture. Scented candles to mask the slight sourness of mildew. Thin curtains and bright sunlight to fill the cracks in the ceiling.

If no one ever looks too closely, I look nice, too.

An innocent, big-eyed, fine-figured omega. Whistles on the street, leering eyes across the counter at the coffee shop, phone numbers inked into receipts and drink sleeves, and—in one especially audacious case—my own wrist.

Which is why I now have on the baggiest joggers I could find in my size and an old hoodie that swallows me whole. Wouldn't want anyone to, you know, *see* me. And heaven forbid someone catches a whiff of my omega-ness under the layers of de-scenter I spritz on each morning.

I usually wear a hat, too, but that fell off somewhere back by the storage closet. And I think I might just leave it there.

Not that I'm too exhausted to go grab it.

Which is another lie.

Put it on my tab, universe.

THE SUNSHINE SLANTING through the shop's front window shifts from soft morning light to a harsh afternoon glare. The extra sun helps the small brick space's overall aesthetic, but it hurts my eyes a bit. Omegas tend to prefer softer lighting and dim rooms.

We used to have curtains—but they were removed when the shop came under new management. Along with the hand-made pastries I used to bake in the back; the comfy armchairs people used for reading; and the previous shift leader—an eighty-year-old grandma called Nan.

Apparently, this new company has no interest in anything soft or homey. Even grannies.

I'm still sad about losing my baking outlet. Aside from the occasional batch of cookies, my kitchen at home is too small to make anything worthwhile. After four years here, I had gotten used to using Proper Coffee's industrial kitchen for my more ambitious experiments.

Now, that space is used for storing the shrink-wrapped baked goods that come in on a truck every other Thursday.

I may not have any formal education, but I'm not stupid. I

can see the writing on the wall. And when a group of suited-up alphas comes waltzing in, each of them squinting around the room and tapping at tablets, my stomach sinks. They're here more and more, lately, which means they must not be happy with the way their investment is working out.

The men march right past the counter, heading to the back of the shop. I make a face at the latte I'm preparing, silently thanking the Lord that this place still uses decent industrial scent-neutralizers, so I don't have to smell any of their alpha stink. Or worry about any of *them* scenting *me*.

It's never been an issue before, but it's become a problem lately. Ever since I had yet another solo heat over Thanksgiving, my hormones have gone from unpleasantly insistent to downright *demanding*.

I know I'm only twenty-four, and everything, but I think my biological clock may be broken. Because its alarm has been *blaring* at me for months, a shrill reminder that I need things no one is giving me.

"Hey, sexy!"

I jump, whirling and pressing a hand over my thrumming heart. When I see it's my best friend, Meg, grinning at me from the other side of the counter, I shake my head.

We used to have a bell on the door to prevent this sort of thing. Guess that's not necessary, either.

"What are you doing here?" I hiss, whispering and glancing at the back door. "I'm working!"

Lord, if one of these uptight alphas sees me goofing off and fires me, I'll truly be hopeless. It hasn't been easy, being an omega on my own, with no access to education and no family support. If I lose my income, I'll be right back in the same group-home situation I came from.

Meg tilts her head, sending her kitschy orange-heart sunglasses listing to the left. Her blonde brows snap into a frown. "It's Saturday. You're coming over for dinner, right?"

Oh. Right.

Above the mirrors, our clock tells me it's well past four. I've been here since five a.m. and haven't eaten a single bite of food. Maybe my stomach's seething has less to do with my agitation and more to do with not eating.

Also, I was supposed to be off at two.

It would have been nice if the manager had noticed.

I untie the plain black apron tied over my baggy clothes and start to slip out of my hoodie, too. It's big enough to tent me, which is exactly why I've always loved it. Underneath, though, I'm dressed for an afternoon at Meg's place.

Calling it a "house" is like calling the Mona Lisa "a painting." Really, it's more of an *estate*. Much too modern and masculine for my taste, but still something a magazine could easily feature on its cover.

Which makes sense, since all of the alphas who live there have, in fact, *been* on magazine covers.

It's easy to forget Meg is sort of famous now. Aside from being beautiful, she doesn't even look the part. Currently, she has on a simple black bikini with a strapless romper over the top. And even though she's the center of the most famous pack in professional sports, she's still the exact same person she's always been.

She picks up the hoodie with her thumb and forefinger, making a face at it. "What, were they out of car covers?" Her eyes light up. "Or did a guy leave this at your place?"

I almost laugh. Ironically, I spend most nights snuggling with that old sweatshirt because there *isn't* anyone around to witness it.

I am surprised Meg's never noticed, though. I've had it for years.

To be fair, I used to be fanatical about hiding it. My omega instincts insisted we kept it tucked away in whatever makeshift nest we used that year. But lately, wearing it to work has been the only way I feel safe here.

"It's mine," I fib, adjusting the frilled strap of my eyelet tankini top with a shrug. "I... found it."

The second part is not technically untrue. I did find it one morning, sitting outside my door at the group home I used to live in. Meg probably doesn't need to know where it came from.

Ever since she found her pack, she's become obsessed with finding one for me, too. Any mention of alphas—even if they're ones who no longer know I exist—sends her into matchmaking mode.

I've lost track of how many times she's tried to parade me in front of her alphas' football team. Before, I might have let her. But ever since I started feeling so jumpy and *needy*...

Geez.

I can't breathe just *thinking* about being alone with some random pro-athlete alpha.

Meg narrows her blue eyes, bending forward to skim her button nose over the hoodie's hem. I squash a beat of smugness, knowing she won't get anything other than my scent. Any other smells wore off a long time ago. With a sigh, my best friend sets the sweatshirt aside, already bored.

One of her alphas must reach out to her through their bond. Probably Declan, if the way she rolls her eyes is any indication. She'd never dare roll her eyes at her pack's leader, Ronan.

Watching her have her internal argument, I can't help but smile. It's strange; while I know I definitely want what Meg has, I can't begrudge her any of it. She's the only family I have, and I want all of this happiness for her.

I just want to cry at the same time.

The feeling isn't new, for me. I spent years in government care, watching whichever friends I managed to make find their forever families. No one ever wanted to keep me, but I still tried to be happy for the ones who were chosen.

My best friend reads my face, her own scrunching with concern. "Are you okay? You look worn out."

Really, I haven't slept through the night in months. My last heat left my nerves a frazzled mess. And I'm beginning to wish I could avoid the rumpled mini-nest I made for myself in the bottom of my closet.

I force a bright smile. "Mmhmm, fine!"

Meg's brows drop into an unimpressed glower. "Remi. C'mon."

Hey, I told you; I'm a *terrible* liar.

"Seriously," I insist, doubling down, "I'm good! Let's get going before anyone notices I'm leaving."

Meg narrows her eyes, pissed. "Are they still being dicks? You know we can get you another job, Remi. Anything you want. You don't have to come here anymore."

Irrational panic rises inside of me. I know she's right, but I also know that this is the only place in the world that's been consistent for me.

I can tough it out. After all, it isn't as if I have anything else going on.

"I'll keep that in mind," I tell Meg, bending to gather my things from behind the counter. I tap at the iPad there, punching out and accepting all sixteen dollars of tips I earned that day.

Thrilling.

"Declan's making dinner," Meg mutters, looping her arm through mine. "So I hope you're not too hungry."

I herd her toward the door, feeling antsy. I've got to get *out* of here. "Who's driving?"

She knows I don't have a car. And I know she rarely chauffeurs herself these days. A peachy blush warms her face. "Ronan's waiting in the Rolls."

"Don't you mean 'Daddy?'" I tease.

She snorts her denial. "*No*."

So, I may be a liar.

But aren't we all?

chapter **two**

I KNOW you have no reason to believe me at this point, but, I swear, I'm really not a jealous person.

However, watching my best friend nuzzle noses with the country's premiere quarterback-slash-heartthrob? Knowing they're mates? Seeing the utter contentment and joy all over both of their faces?

If envy turned people green, I'd resemble the lime floating in my margarita.

Declan Howard lingers over Meg for a long moment before tossing her a cocky grin and standing up straight. He skirts his eyes over to me, letting a bit of chagrin into his expression while he moves toward the grill.

"Sorry, Remi. Had conditioning early this morning, and I didn't get to see Meg before I left."

I wave him off, trying not to let my phony smile pull too tight. "You guys are adorable," I say, then gesture around their lavish lanai. "And this *is* your house."

Meg snorts, adjusting her bikini top. Looking at her, I realize my pastel sundresses and frilly swimsuits contrast with my darker complexion every bit as much as Meg's black straps stand out against her paleness.

I didn't know my parents, but the ethnic ambiguity they passed on to me created a surprising mix of traits. Brown skin with hazel-y blue eyes. Black hair that's curly, but fine. Not to mention my designation, which is rare enough on its own since only one-in-ten people end up becoming omegas.

"I'm glad you're cool with the PDA," Meg mumbles, grimacing. "Because I also missed Theo this morning, and if the vibes he's sending through the bond are any indication—"

A loud whoop cuts in as her enormous tight-end alpha tears out of their house and bolts right to her.

Naked.

Well, *basically* naked. He has boxers on, I think, but it's all sort of a muscular blur of hairy, blond energy.

"Theo! Don't you *dare*—"

Meg squeals as he hauls her into his thick arms and spins her in circles. It only takes two lumbering steps for him to reach the pool's edge, plunging them both into the aquamarine water.

I watch the evening sunlight reflect on the surface, feeling all sorts of wistful. The truth is, I'm happy for my best friend. She's an incredible person who deserves all of this happiness more than anyone else I know.

The truth is, I am also sick to my stomach with how much I want what she's found.

It's been eight months since she met her pack, and I've mostly moved through my negative emotions. There were times when I struggled, constantly thinking it wasn't *fair*. Meg never wanted alphas of her own or life as the center of a pack, yet that's exactly what she got. Whereas I *always* wanted my own alphas, my own family—

But no one ever wanted me back.

"Hello, Remi!"

I recognize Dr. Archer Monroe's voice before I squint my eyes open and find him standing at the end of my lounge chair. Ever the respectable man of medicine, he has a layer of sunblock on his dark skin and a perfectly appropriate pair of red swim trunks to cover his lower body. The upper half remains frightfully bare.

Meg is a great friend, so I doubt she's ever told her alphas that they're basically the first men I've ever seen partially-naked in person. It's overwhelming for me, visually; but thankfully, their bonding eliminated any possibility that I might find one of them attractive in any meaningful way.

Now, whenever one of them is close enough for me to smell, I pick up on Meg's underlying signature, and my body gives a big, fat *no thank you*.

Smiling back at Archer, I lift my hand in a shy half-wave. "Hi!"

Why am I so awkward?

Ever since Meg moved in here, visiting her feels like going to a friend's house in middle school and not knowing what I should say to her parents. Especially when Ronan is around. Because that alpha is *all kinds* of intimidating.

"Thank you for letting me come over," I blurt next, repressing a cringe.

Lord, I even sound like a middle schooler.

Always kind to a fault, Archer smiles wider. "Of course. Having you here makes Meg so happy; we love that."

He shuffles the books tucked under his arm and sets one at the very end of my chair, careful not to touch me. He clears his throat before fibbing, "I found this extra copy in my collection upstairs. I don't need it back."

He truly is a nice man. When he discovered I love to read and noticed that all of the books I brought poolside were from the local library, he began casually offering me copies of things he'd "finished" with.

It wasn't until I found a very recent price sticker on the inside of one of their dust jackets that I realized he'd specifically bought two copies so I could have one.

...And it wasn't until I mentioned it to Meg that I realized *she* masterminded his charity.

She does that sort of thing now that she can. Slipping cash into my purse when she thinks I'm not looking, picking up checks for meals, buying me an absurd amount of Christmas gifts.

I know she only does it because she loves me. We've shared everything with each other since we met—she doesn't see why her new family and their wealth should be any different.

There's probably some way for me to explain how small it all makes me feel—but then she would feel bad. Plus, if the measly tips I made today are any indication, I'm not exactly in a position to turn down financial help.

Archer accepts my thanks for the "extra" book and pulls a nearby lounger to the pool's edge. Meg and Theo chase each other around the shallow end, playing a ridiculously mushy version of Marco-Polo until Theo finally gets his arms back around her and lifts her up to his packmate.

Meg situates herself against Archer's side, grinning when his lips graze her forehead. Their eyes meet in a pointed way that tells me they're communicating internally. I don't catch on to Theo's involvement until he makes a nervous coughing sound.

My best friend shoots him a look. "Theo," she calls, just a touch too shrill, "I've been meaning to tell Remi about that thing your sister is doing. What's it called again?"

Despite the fact that this is clearly some rehearsed skit, the big alpha stammers for a second. "It, uh, um, it's called Forever Matched?"

My stomach twists at the name. A whine bubbles at the base of my throat. I stab it as quickly as I can, hoping no one heard.

Archer is much better at playing along. His answering, "Hmm," manages to sound genuinely ponderous. "I've heard of them. Very reputable scent-matching service. They have the highest global success rate—if I'm not mistaken."

Archer is *never* mistaken.

Theo flips his dripping man bun off the top of his head, nodding too earnestly. "That's what Emma said. Like, three of her sorority sisters have found packs through them."

Meg fiddles with the drawstring on her doctor alpha's swim trunks, very carefully *not* looking at me. "What do you think, Remi? Would you ever use a service like that?"

Feelings fly through me, too fast for any to sink in. There's a stab of betrayal—because *of course* Meg knows that a professional scent-matching service is the *last resort* for omegas—and a flash of dismay.

I narrow my eyes at her. "You know how I feel about it," I tell her, prim. "Besides, those services cost tens of thousands of dollars."

She drags her gaze up to mine, flinching in a guilty wince. "Rrriiiight... but, just for the sake of argument, if cost wasn't an issue—would you do it?"

I mean, if cost wasn't an issue I'd be on a private jet to a spa on the Amalfi Coast.

But I'm a barista.

Last week, I ate microwave rice out of pouches four nights in a row.

It's an effort not to glare. Meg, of all people, knows how hard it is to be omega without a pack. I may not have the same heat issues she did—*yet*—but it still isn't fun to be in agonizing pain for days at a time and handle it all by myself.

Meg knows I just went through a terrible heat over the holidays. She knows I need a pack and have always wanted to find one the old-fashioned way. Am I really so pathetic that she feels like she needs to push this on me now?

"I don't know," I tell her, hiding my frown behind my drink. "I would have to think about it."

But I know I won't.

Because the fact is, what I want can't be boiled down to numbers or lab samples.

I want a *home*. And I'm not sure there's an equation for that.

chapter three

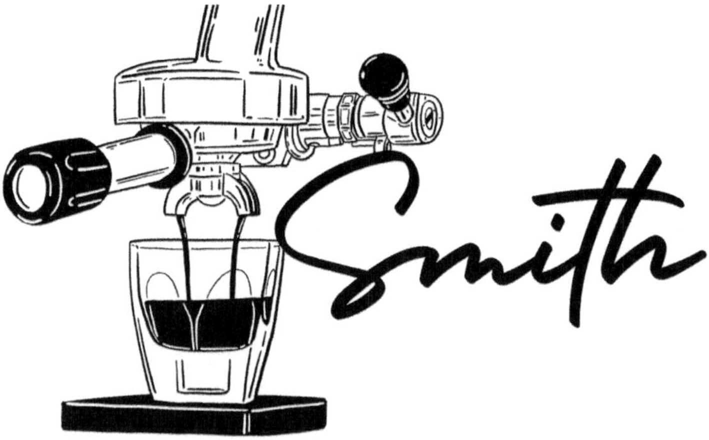

WE ALL AGREED.

I *thought* we all agreed.

Monday morning. Eight a.m.

But it's eight-twenty, and my cup is the only one on the counter.

I stand there, staring at it. Thinking about how this is a perfect metaphor for my whole life.

A sad cup of jizz—sad because I filled it to the brim with my backed-up balls—sitting alone, in the house I bought, on the countertop I chose and had installed. Next to my phone, which has buzzed ten times in four minutes.

The cup is from the clinic I selected. For the specific scent-matching company I researched, applied to, and landed a highly coveted slot with.

All my work. Hours and hours of it.

And all these two jack-offs had to do was—

Well.

Jack off.

If they can't even come through for *that*, then what in God's name are we even doing?

Noise interrupts my brooding. I know without looking up that it's my youngest packmate, Damon; because Cassian never makes noise. Despite being a professional hockey goalie who's built like a brick house.

Damon comes shuffling into the room, wearing nothing but those tight briefs he likes so much. He scratches his sack and presses the heel of his other hand into his left eye socket, grunting.

"Morning, Big Hoss. What's with the weird moisturizer sample?"

I blink at him, refusing to believe he actually ignores me this thoroughly. My phone starts up again. "It isn't moisturizer."

He shrugs, reaching into a cabinet and coming up with a box of chocolate breakfast cereal. Without bothering to find a bowl, he shovels a handful right into his mouth.

"Is it milk?" he chews. "Because I could use some."

My eye twitches. I roll my lips together, trying my best to remember all of the parenting books I read fifteen years ago, and their tips on how not to absolutely strangle spoiled, useless brats.

Granted, the spoiled useless brat is twenty-six now. And I've never really been a parent, just a pack alpha.

But God help me, some days I wonder.

True to form, Cassian appears from somewhere mysterious, fully dressed, without making a single sound. Until he grumbles, "It isn't milk."

He sits at the breakfast bar, three feet away from my sample cup, and pulls a paperback out of the interior pocket of his athletic jacket. I watch him, too infuriated by his apathy to even form words.

He's Cassian, though. Which means he sees everything without even looking at me. His fingers turn a page, the motion deliberately casual. Belying the irritation underscoring his voice. "I told you; I'm not doing that."

I silence my phone again and repress the urge to strangle him, repeating my most common mantra where dealing with my pack is concerned.

Control, control, control.

Damon's posture stays loose. He looks at both of us, ice-blue eyes wide. "I have no idea what either of you are talking about."

Cass and I answer flatly, in unison. "We know."

Ignoring Damon, I focus on my stepbrother. "We talked about this," I say, forcing calm I don't feel. "Jobs, house, omega. You agreed."

His features don't even flicker. His eyes continue scrolling across the page in front of him. "I agreed that it made sense. I didn't agree to *do* it."

For fuck's sake.

Damon's eyebrows push together. "Omega—?" He drops his gaze to my sample cup. "*Ohhhhhhh.* Oh, fuck! Was that today?"

I speak through my teeth. "It's on the calendar, Damon."

He turns toward the whiteboard pinned on the side of the refrigerator and frowns like he's never seen it before.

Jesus Christ.

I force an exhale through my nose, willing myself not to have a stroke. "Did you *read* the calendar?"

Of course he didn't.

This is probably the first time he's ever even *looked* at the damn thing.

His shoulders pop up in a dismissive shrug. "All right. Shit." He flashes the smile that always seems to get him out of trouble and pulls his phone... out of his underwear? "Just give me five minutes to crack one out. I've got, like, six unopened nudes in my IG messages."

Yeah, I bet.

The worst thing is, for most guys, those messages would be the direct result of Damon's position as the star forward for the Orlando Timberwolves and the millions that come with it.

But for him?

Not a problem. Damon's never needed a hockey career or money to get nudes.

And now he has *both*.

I'd appreciate the irony if my balls weren't so sore.

I toss him the sealed, empty cup I found sitting on his bathroom counter. "Here. Five minutes."

He flips his phone, flashing a whole lot of naked skin. With a chuckle, he strides off down the hall. "I'll only need three!"

I rub my palm over my forehead, muttering, "He really shouldn't advertise that."

Cassian turns another page, pointedly ignoring me.

To the untrained eye, it would seem like he has no dog in this hunt. But I know him as well as I know Damon; and he's invested.

Usually, by this time, he's on his way to morning skate because, unlike Damon, he hates to be late. If he didn't want to be around us, he could leave now or go back up to his room. The fact that he's even sitting here, in the kitchen, means something.

It took me a long time to learn that Cassian says just as much with his actions as most people say with their mouths. More, on occasion. Like me, he rarely does anything random and this is a message, too.

I don't want to be here, the book in front of his face says.

But I care about what you want, too, his ass in the stool adds.

I sigh. "Cass—"

He lowers the book, slowly revealing a scowl. The familiar expression stabs my center. I can picture a younger, surlier version of it on a younger, surlier Cassian. Back when we lost our parents —and everything went to hell.

He's smart enough to play on my guilt by using the same expression now. Because Cassian is easily the smartest guy I know.

I could try to appeal to his conscience. That's how I got him to agree to this whole thing in the first place. After years and years of refusing to date, I only wore down his stubborn commitment to being a loner with guilt. Specifically, the fact that if *he* won't accept an omega, *we* can't have one either.

When he couldn't argue with that point, he agreed to make this one single contribution to the search process.

A plastic cup of jizz.

Hell, I'd settle for a tablespoon at this point.

My thumb mashes my phone again, silencing yet another alert. "Cassian. This is important."

I can't explain why. Only that some indistinct sense of need has been prowling under my skin for months, now. And if I don't find some sort of outlet for it? I'll go insane.

Besides, this is a foolproof plan. Forever Matched is the most selective scent-matching service in the country. When their algorithm finds us an omega with a high match percentage, I'll know for a fact that I've made the right call for our pack.

Even if Cassian hates me for it.

Our gazes clash—his forest green to my dark brown. I shove a wave of dominance at him, flexing my pack alpha influence.

Don't make me make you.

With a mutinous glare, Cass sets his book aside. Looking like the entire world is pinned right between his wide shoulders, he lumbers over to the refrigerator and rummages for a moment before producing his cup.

Filled up. Marked with today's date.

The bastard had it this whole time.

He sets it on the counter without a word, snatching his book to make a silent, fuming exit. Two minutes later, Damon flies back in, sliding on his socks, proudly adding his contribution to the line-up.

"What do we do now?" he asks, watching me stare at the row of cups.

We won't do shit. *I* will put on rubber gloves, pack up the samples, and take them where they need to go. Because someone has to.

And I'm the one who does the things no one else will do.

"Turn it in," I say, striding from the room to answer my next phone call. "When they match us, we'll have our mate. Numbers don't lie."

chapter **four**

I USED to like the scent of coffee.

Now, as I step back into Proper Coffee after a quick (eight-minute) lunch break, the smell just makes me nauseous.

Carefully covered with de-scenter, my usual baggy clothes, and an Orlando Ospreys cap, I edge around the cluster of suit-clad businessmen muttering to each other. Several glares cut my way. My Omega quivers, a flare of urgency sending a bunch of odd sensations through my body.

The presence of so many alpha pheromones—even when I can't smell them—makes me edgy and needy in the most humiliating way. I don't want to perfume for any of these strangers, but my body is dripping slick, and my pulse throbs between my legs.

When I whine quietly, their boss scoffs and snarls, "There's a line, in case you didn't notice."

What *I notice* is my manager once again staring at his phone while customers pile up at the register. Ducking my head, I hustle over, doing my best to ignore the shooting pains that streak up the backs of my legs.

I've been on my feet for another eight-hour shift today. At least I remembered to have a granola bar this time.

I'm beginning to realize that, while I may be an excellent caretaker for friends, former roommates, and hapless fellow employees, I'm really not very good at taking care of myself.

If I could afford therapy, that might be worth unpacking.

I take a few orders before one particularly creepy alpha tries to reach over the counter and grab my arm. My manager finally steps in after that, thank the Lord.

I'm grateful the man didn't actually get his hands on me. That's the best part of working as a barista—there's always three feet of bar between me and whoever I have to deal with.

And today? I need it.

"This is supposed to be *iced*."

A splash of hot coffee splatters from a to-go cup as one of the investors' suited alphas slams it onto our service bar. I rear back, only narrowly avoiding a lash of steaming liquid to the face.

The aggression in his voice sends a tremor down my spine. I shrink down a bit and pick up the offending cup, spinning it to read the label on the side. Our system prints the stickers out automatically when it rings up an order. Whoever prepares the drink just reads whatever the ticket says and fulfills it.

Large lavender latte, it reads in clear block letters.

The word iced is nowhere in sight, which explains the mistake. I didn't ring this up, which means my manager probably keyed it in wrong.

No big deal, right?

Wrong.

A strike of alpha dominance has me close to hyperventilating. I can't even look up from the sticky floor; I have to lock my muscles in place, so I don't hide behind the counter.

"I know you're probably not *aware* of this, but *some* of us have shit we need to do," the man sneers. "We don't have all day to deal with your fucking incompetence!"

My shoulders hunch up toward my ears. I cringe away from his voice, the hostility sending me back a step. "I-I'm sorry, I didn't know you wanted it iced. The sticker is wrong. See here?"

With a shaking hand, I start to lift the cup toward him, turning it to display the label. Behind me, a coffee grinder starts up, blotting out the overwhelming whir of chatter and blend of strange almost-scents in the neutralized room.

The jerk across from me rips the to-go cup from my hand and thumps it back onto the counter.

What in the—

Shock snaps my head up, nearly sending my Ospreys cap to the sticky floor. The lid pops off the top of the latte on impact, revealing a battered version of the foam smiley face I had secretly hidden inside the drink and sloshing half its contents all over me.

So much for silently wishing my customer a happy day.

"I don't give a fuck what your excuse for being *pathetic* is." The coffee grinder subsides just in time for me to hear him bark, "*Remake it.*"

My legs tremble, absorbing the impact of the command. I choke back a fearful whine, my scent shifting. Luckily, no one can smell me under my de-scenter and the rich aroma of the coffee currently in the grinder.

Because he barked instead of asking, I don't have any choice but to scurry away and remake the alpha's drink. When I return less than a minute later, he snaps the cold cup out of my hand without so much as a thank-you.

Not for the first time, I wish I were more like Meg. She would have called him a prick, poured the new latte all over his monogrammed sleeves, and quit on the spot. But I've never been any good at standing up for myself. And—even worse—I actually feel *scared* here.

That never used to happen. I *loved* this job. Now it's just... ruined.

I lift the hem of the stolen hoodie to my face and use it to swipe at my wet eyes, mumbling to my manager about taking a break. He waves me on, rolling his eyes when he sees that I'm crying again.

I've always thought of myself as a quintessential omega in every traditional sense of the word. Meg fights parts of our designation, but I've never minded being softer and more emotional.

Lately, though, I feel as pitiful as everyone seems to think I am.

I'M on my second plate of toffee-nut cookies before I stop sobbing.

It's been a long day. In the midst of an even longer week.

I was already strung out on anxiety and feeling generally overwhelmed before one of the new investors at Proper Coffee barked at me, telling me I was taking too long to fulfill mobile orders and causing the whole counter to get backed up.

"Faster, or I'll find someone who can actually do *your job."*

Meg would have told him that, technically, none of this *is* my job. I was hired for a position that doesn't exist anymore, making the homemade baked goods we used to sell.

I'm too afraid to speak up, though. What if they decide I'm not worth keeping now that they've decided to peddle stale, generic pastries instead of mine?

Instead, I took every knock their boss threw at me, hunching and lowering my eyes every time I was barked into submission.

My quivery nerves eventually gave out, though, and I wound up choking down whines and swiping tears out of my eyes for most of my shift.

It was a relief to get home and have a proper breakdown. But even an hour spent crying on the floor of my closet-nest isn't enough to make me feel anything, other than terribly alone.

I haven't stopped thinking about Meg's thinly veiled offer to sign me up for a scent-matching service. The fact is, I need to find a good pack as soon as I can. My suppressants won't work forever. And the thought of having to go back to a heat clinic terrifies me.

As much as I wish I had a fairy tale like Meg's, most packs are not scent-sensitive like hers. Of the ones who are, even fewer meet by chance. Most use scent-matching companies... and Forever Matched is the best of the best.

Am I crazy to turn this offer down?

Should I get over all of my silly hopes and dreams and face reality? Or is that settling?

I hate being my best friend's charity case. Before I turned eighteen, my whole life was trash bags full of donated clothes; Christmas gifts given to me by church charities; treats passed over by strangers with pitying smiles.

I don't know why this feels so similar, but it gives me that same clench of humiliation in my gut. Embarrassment that I'm in this situation in the first place... and *heartbreak* that I know exactly why.

The fact is, finding people who want me has always been hopeless. I mean, it sort of makes sense; my own mother surrendered me at birth. If she didn't want me, what use was it trying to convince strangers to take me?

Still, I spent years spinning plates on my nose, doing everything I could be loveable to the families that considered me. Nothing ever worked. And the only alpha I've ever had a connection with made it clear I was firmly in his friend zone—and barely there, at that.

Thankfully, my body never had a chance to betray my attraction to him. The same day I found the sweatshirt in front of my door, my designation came through, and I was promptly "re-homed" to a facility for single omegas without family or guardians.

Meg was my roommate. Sometimes, I wonder if the universe knew I needed a distraction—and the reassurance that there were, in fact, more pitiful new omegas than me.

The poor girl didn't know anything about our designation. I leaped at the opportunity for a new mission to divert me from my misery. Projects were one of the many coping skills I honed over the years. Sometimes, I feel like I have dozens.

See a happy family walking down the street and feel a pang in your gut? Sing a happy song to yourself.

Need a way to get through holidays when you have no one to spend them with? Try that new baking technique that will take hours to perfect.

Feeling lonely and depressed in your new apartment all by yourself? Paint the walls pink.

Trying to forget your mortifying crush on a hot almost-alpha and the way his borrowed hoodie made you perfume for the first time? Give the new girl a lesson on slick-absorbing panties.

I pull my borrowed (stolen) sweatshirt over my face, huddling down into it. Pretending it's a blanket and not a relic of all the things I used to think I could have.

How much longer am I willing to live like this?

And what happens when I can't do it anymore?

chapter five

DAMON

THERE'S a moment at the beginning of every game.

The lights go out. The music swells. And some disembodied voice says *my* name.

It shouldn't be me. I shouldn't be here.

But that's the thing about me: even when every odd is stacked against me? I'll make it.

When I realized I hated living with my biological parents? I somehow charmed my way into people's houses for a weekend, a summer, a semester.

When I realized I'd never pass my high school classes on my own? I happened to date smart girls who helped me get by.

When my grades still weren't good enough for college, and I had to find some other way to make money? Well, thank God I was good at hockey.

Better than good.

Because here's the other thing about me: I'm lucky as fuck.

I know, I know. My parents were assholes. And I was poor. And my grades sucked.

I'm talking about *after* all that shit. Or maybe *because* of it. I don't *know*, but sometimes, I wonder if the universe finally noticed how much horseshit it had dumped on my head and decided to level things out.

How else do you explain the fact that, in the midst of all my high school couch-surfing, I somehow wound up becoming friends with Cassian? He had been playing hockey all his life, starting back before he lost his parents. And he was the one who recognized that I had the ability to play, too.

It was the first thing that I ever won an award for. The only thing. Because the more I played? The better I got.

Just in time for the major league scouts to pick me up.

Which happened about a year before hockey took off in the US.

See? Lucky.

It was all pure good fortune, including the part where I had Cass's big, grumbly ass to keep me in line. It's always been like that with us. I can't see three feet in front of me, but Cassian has an iMap of The Big Picture projected in his frontal lobe at all times. I run around doing whatever gets me hard, and Smith spends his whole life making lists—as if the minutia of his daily to-dos will actually fucking change something.

But Cassian?

He just knows what's what.

It's how we became friends in the first place. We were always the first two freshmen in our high school's gym each morning. He was there to work on his muscle mass—I was there to get free hash browns from the lunch lady.

It didn't take long for us to figure out we were basically polar opposites in every respect except for one: we both wanted to be athletes.

Cassian was methodical about it. He worked from a set regimen of exercises and a specific high-protein high-calorie diet. When he wasn't working out, he had a book in front of his face and a grumpy scowl covering whatever the book didn't.

Meanwhile, I liked to skate by the easy way—a charming smile, a well-timed joke. Some flattery, some vague reference to plans I'd never actually pursue.

Whatever my training lacked in planning, I tried to make up for with enthusiasm. It helped that the gym was the one place where I actually felt successful; I could always do another lap, another rep, another workout, even when the other guys were about to pass out.

And don't get me wrong—I play hockey. I love a good fight. It's fun getting my hands dirty and absolutely pummeling the shit out of my opponents.

But Cass is built different. His determination and rage come from a totally different place. And he's in control of it.

Until he isn't.

And then? God help you.

The guy I'm matched up against in our season opener reminds me a bit of my silent-but-deadly packmate. I've never met this dude before, but he's glaring at me like I fucked his girlfriend.

Which... is a distinct possibility.

Especially if she's a puck bunny. Because Lord knows I've hit that shit in every city from here to Seattle.

Hell, who am I kidding? Canada, too.

My opponent skates backward as I fly down the side of the rink, closing in on the goal. Our latest recruit—another forward —sails down the opposite side of the ice. He's older than the average rookie, but still young enough for me to feel old as shit every time I think about it too hard.

The kid has a Basset Hound's name—*Gunnar*—but he can fucking *play*. With one eye on the shot clock, I pick my moment. At the last moment, I flick my stick and send the puck flying straight across the rink. He slaps it. The flashing buzzer sounds as the clock runs out.

Fuck *yes*.

I bump shoulders with the defender who's been glaring a hole in my helmet, shooting him a shit-eating grin. "Good game, bro."

Which is probably stupid. Because two seconds later, we're both on the ice, pounding each other's faces through our gloves.

Cassian hauls me back by my jersey and shoves me into the boards. I hear Gunnar laughing while my packmate mutters, "We *won*, Damon. For fuck's sake."

I let them tow me to the edge of the ice and pull me into the tunnel, then I tug my helmet off and swipe at my split lip.

Motherfucker.

Smith will be so mad if I have a black eye and that matching service thingy calls us in. *If* they ever call us in. The odds Cassian spat at both of us made the whole thing sound like a pipe dream.

Although, like I said: I'm extra lucky. In fact, this whole thing is very on-brand.

If anyone is going to find their soulmate from a cup of jizz, it's me.

At this point, I'm not sure what's scarier—the idea of *actually finding* our omega, or the implosion Smith will have if he can't check this box off. He's obsessed with that shit.

It started when he was seventeen and their parents had their accident. He thought organizing everything into a list was the best way for him to get his shit together and take care of Cassian.

It wasn't that simple, obviously, but he never let the damn thing go. Even when the list changed and grew, forming sub-lists and sidenotes. Didn't matter. He just worked harder, did more.

Once he got his degree, he expanded his company. Once the

company expanded, we made more money, and he had to learn about using it. Once he had our accounts secured, he started in about property. That led to our new house and two years of renovations, none of which ever got finished.

Now he wants us to have an omega? For what? So he can add ten new lists for all the shit he or she will need?

Poor bastard's just chasing his tail if you ask me.

I mean, no one *did*, but still.

It's ironic. Smith's been beating his head against the wall, trying to get Cass on board; if he was looking for an ally, he could have just asked me.

Most of the women gathered around the locker room entrance are betas, cloaked in scent sprays meant to mimic omega perfume. My dick perks up with a lazy sort of interest, and I almost roll my eyes.

Come on, Big D. You know this isn't what we really want.

To be fair, *I* don't know what we really want. I just know that every girl bouncing their titties at me looks the same, somehow.

None of them actually *do*... but... they do. You know?

Jesus. I need a shower.

Gunnar is more than happy to scoop up all my chips. He flashes them a grin and offers a cowboy's gentlemanly nod. It matches his accent. "Evenin' ladies."

They eat that shit up. Which is fine by me. I got my shots in, and we won, so, you know, let the new kid eat cake. Or pussy. Whatever.

"Mathers!"

That would be Coach Rolly, ready to hand me my balls for that scuffle after the final buzzer. Which is fair. My eye is swelling up already. We'll have to get ice on it to make sure I can still play in the game we have in two days.

If I can't score for us, I'm basically useless. To the team and my pack.

It will be fine, though.

Like I said— I'm a lucky bastard.

chapter six

CASSIAN

DO NOT DISTURB.

Whoever invented that feature should be given a Nobel Peace Prize.

Truly. Name one thing that's brought more actual peace to the modern era.

With my phone silenced and Damon already crashed in his room, sleeping off Coach's shouty ass-kicking , it's a perfectly quiet Thursday night in our pack house.

Smith is out, somewhere. At the office? Working, probably.

God forbid he stop and look up for half a second. I wonder what he's so afraid of finding if he does.

With a sigh, I step out of my nightly shower, leaving my spent cum and mild disgust to slither down the drain. If it were up to me, the daily stroke-off session wouldn't be a part of my routine.

Doctor's orders, though.

Professional athletes aren't allowed to take rut-blockers. Apparently, for those who also aren't sexually active, unchecked alpha hormones can build up and increase the odds that a random omega would throw us into rut.

Which sounds like a nightmare. For them. And me.

Instead, I spend every night standing under the steamy spray of my shower, roughly gripping my dick and knot while I imagine a set of much softer, gentler hands.

At least it's over. For now.

The whole house is half-finished—maybe more like one-fourth-finished—but I finally have a towel rack and a bathroom mirror, at least. Grumbling under my breath, I swipe my hand through the condensation fogging it.

Appearances are more Damon's thing. Still, I glance at my reflection, feeling obligated to at least check it, occasionally. Just in case I've actually become the beast I feel like on the inside, sometimes.

But no. I still have a straight, human nose. A scar sliced over my left eye. A clean-shaven chin with a cleft in it.

No forked tongue or fangs.

My hair is probably too long, though. Smith always mutters about it, saying it's no wonder everyone on my team calls me "Beastly."

I got the nickname halfway through high school. When I think about the way I acted on and off the ice, it was probably deserved.

I keep most of my frustration to myself these days. Beating the punching bag in our home gym to a pulp. Running for an hour every morning. Doing sit-ups until I can't breathe. Doing my lonely jack-off session every night because I literally have to.

Jesus.

If any of my opponents spent half a minute in my head, our defenders wouldn't even have to block them. They'd just run away, screaming.

Not that I really care. It's been years since I felt attracted to anyone, including omegas. Even then, every one of them somehow left me more agitated and unsatisfied than I was before we met.

They all chafed. Too stiff in the collar. Too tight over my shoulders. A pinch at my inseam.

Eventually, my Alpha sort of gave up, grunting in annoyed distaste anytime someone brought the subject up. It's hard to get an exact read on the instincts, but the impulses feel a lot like, *"Really? This mediocre shit?"*

As if he just can't be fucked to pay even a speck of attention to, you know, an alpha's *biological imperative.*

I've read every book on the subject, but none of them offer any answers. I didn't reject my mate or get rejected; those are the only documented reasons for "Alpha Apathy."

So, I decided to keep my issues to myself and let the guys have their "scientifically matched" omega. Because I might not be the most charming guy, but I'm nothing if not a team player.

Every alert on my phone agrees. The screen lights up the second I switch Airplane Mode off, filling with a string of notifications. Half of the alerts are texts from teammates. They're all nice enough, congratulating me on another shut-out. A few have links in them.

They all lead to similar articles, videos, and social media posts. *Raised by Wolves?* one jokes, along with a picture of D pummeling the shit out of the opposing team's defender.

It's a play on words, since whatever idiot named our team chose the Timberwolves as our title. And, now, according to this Sports Network article:

"Are these wolves rabid? The Orlando-based Timberwolves, poised to be one of the wild-card contenders in this year's NHL playoffs, seem to be in need of some house-breaking first. Star forward Damon Mathers is pictured below, engaging in a little after-game grudge match with one of the League's top-rated defenders. Mathers may be a veteran player, but his unsportsmanlike behavior is less like a Timberwolf and more like an untrained puppy.

Speaking of rookies, the Timberwolves recently signed a new forward to train under Mathers. Coincidence? Or careful planning by their team's staff? Either way, Gunnar Sinclair, 22, is now contracted to the Orlando hockey team for the next three years. Which may be a problem for their veteran star, whose contract is set to expire at the end of the season."

Fucking media vultures.

Perpetually trying to make petty drama where none exists. I swear to God, they stand around the hallways after games and listen in. Or one of them is sleeping with someone on our staff.

With the way the rest of the team is managed? It wouldn't surprise me.

Not much does, anymore.

I'd probably be more pissed if I were actually worried. Maybe it's the apathy that colors everything around me in shades of gray, but I can't find it in myself to get it up for this, either.

For one thing, Damon is one of the best players in the League. Our pack is the only reason he's on the Timberwolves instead of being off with a more elite squad. He wanted to go where we could both get contracts. At the time, he was a better player than me. Selling us as a pair was more like selling *him*, but with an added goalie bonus.

My stats are some of the best around, now. And as the years have gone by, Damon's gotten more reckless. Less professional. His penalties alone are ridiculous.

But he scores when it counts. He wins games.

And, more importantly? People love him.

If this comes down to some sort of popularity contest between him and, well, *anyone*? Damon would win.

We probably have nothing to worry about. And the more I scroll through the articles, the more I think they're all flash, no substance. Just social media proving, once again, that it's the scourge of society.

Turning away from my mirror's foggy reflection, I tug on the first T-shirt and pair of sweats I find, picking them out of a pile of laundry I'm fairly sure is clean. Smith would have a fucking coronary if he knew I don't put any of my clothes away, but I don't think I can remember a time he's ever come in here.

We each have our own rooms, which is a luxury I'm still not used to after years of sharing rooms and sleeping on cots. Maybe that's why I chose the smallest one.

The house has six. The largest is huge and attached to a nest—clearly meant as an omega suite. None of us have dared to touch it with a ten-foot pole.

Which means, if we get an omega, he or she will have some serious work to do.

Smith took the primary bedroom, situated on the opposite end of the long upstairs hallway. He has the most space and the least amount of stuff. So, basically, an empty, serial-killer-clean room three times the size of mine.

Damon took the bedroom just at the top of the stairs, in the center of the hallway.

Right in the middle of everything. Of course.

It also happens to have the largest attached bathroom, apart from the omega's—plenty of space for all his skincare and manscaping needs.

I picked the one between him and Smith, though their locations didn't really factor much into the decision. Truth is, I wanted the bookshelves built into the walls and the small balcony across from the entrance.

The room is probably meant to be a study of some sort,

because it has two whole walls of shelving, complete with creaky sliding ladders I won't ever need, being well over six feet tall.

I suppose, if we actually finished renovating the house, we would eventually refinish everything in here. As it is, the wooden built-ins are as faded and scuffed as the oak floor. The balcony doors stick, tacky from a dozen coats of gloppy white paint over half a dozen decades. And the ceiling is a craggy off-white that collects sinister shadows in low lighting.

The room is tired and neglected, with just enough potential to make it sad.

Perfect for me, actually.

And this house? It's a collection of torn-up, hollowed-out spaces that don't really fit together.

Which might just be perfect for all of us.

chapter seven

MY RIDE PULLS UP to the front of Forever Matched with five minutes to spare.

I smooth my hands over my lap, grateful that the silky pink fabric of my dress hasn't wrinkled. My hair is just as smooth, the black curls straightened and re-curled into perfect loose spirals, partially clipped off my face. Along with my usual makeup and the bright smile I've perfected, I hope I look like a girl eager to set up her future.

Because I am, I tell myself.

Who even knows whether I'm lying anymore?

Meg's voice echoes in my ear, slightly distorted by my broken, old AirPods. "Are you there?! What does it look like?!"

My stomach is a jumble of jittery excitement and nauseous dread. When I peer out at the imposing, white office building looming over me, fear edges out the thrill.

"It's, uh, big."

"That's what she said."

"Megera Ash."

"Remi Skyes."

I smile despite myself, gathering my cardigan and purse. "I'll call you after."

"Don't do anything I wouldn't do!" she chimes.

"Like going home with a group of alphas I don't know?" I return, teasing her. "I would never."

The call clicks off as my Uber pulls away. I blow out a deep breath, staring up at the impressive facade in front of me.

What on earth am I doing?

One moment of weakness, and now I'm here?! A girl should never make decisions while she's sitting on the floor of her closet, wedged between a plate of cookies and her vibrator collection.

The omega urge to run and hide kicks and thrashes inside of me. Years of people-pleasing, and a pathological fear of disappointing anyone are the only things keeping my feet rooted to the sidewalk.

I made an appointment. I can't just not show up...

Thankfully, the second I step inside, it's clear this place was *made* for omegas. The lobby is a small, round alcove. Flowering plants and overstuffed chairs fill the dome-like space, giving the room a cozy feel despite the bright sunlight filtering through its skylights.

The second I enter, ten different scents hit me all at once. A prickle shivers over my skin while I adjust, my mind racing to catch up to the adrenaline blasting through my veins.

Oh, right. No neutralizers in here. They want alphas and omegas to scent each other.

I'm grateful the woman at the front desk is a scentless beta. She takes my name and smiles, typing a few words before she offers me a wide selection of beverages—from champagne to kombucha. There's barely enough time for me to settle into a seat with my freshly brewed tea before one of the doors behind the desk opens.

A female alpha in a mint-green pantsuit steps through it, already beaming right at me. "Miss Skyes?"

I've always liked female alphas. Male alphas tend to be openly aggressive, but their female counterparts often channel their inherent dominance wisely. Usually, they're extremely organized and diligent in their care of others. Their no-nonsense authority was a common influence in the group homes I grew up in.

She watches me stand and carefully collect my bag and teacup, waiting patiently while I gain my balance before offering her hand.

"I'm Celine," she says, grinning. "I'll be the one working with you today."

The faint scent of eucalyptus rises off her chest, tinged with the distinct edge of *nope* that tells me she's already bonded. I notice a claiming mark along the side of her neck, nearly hidden behind her smooth blonde bob.

Her smile grows as she reaches up to gesture at it. "You'll see that I'm a big believer in our system. It's how my pack met our omega. That was ten years and three kids ago, and I'm still obsessed with her." She laughs lightly, "At least, she'd say so. I'd prefer to say I'm madly in love with her."

Obsessed sounds like a word Meg would jokingly use to describe her guys. I grin at the thought, pleasantly surprised not to feel a twinge of envy at the thought of happily bonded packs. In its place, there's a hum of anticipation.

Maybe—maybe this will work.

Oh God.

What if this works?!

Celine's grin turns knowing as she senses my budding eagerness. "Right this way, Miss Sykes. Or do you prefer Remi?"

She isn't holding a folder or cheating off a tablet—she actually knows my name. As someone who's been shuffled through every branch of government childcare and more free clinics than I can count, I'm already impressed.

"Remi," I demur, nervously fiddling with my purse strap.

"Remi." She smiles again, waving over her shoulder. "Follow me."

We walk down a standard white hallway and find ourselves in... a suite? It definitely doesn't feel like an exam room or a place for corporate meetings. Instead, it's a comfortable, luxurious space, reminiscent of a hotel room.

There's a neatly made bed off to the left, surrounded by a canopy and flanked by two small storage tables. On the right, a seating area with two armchairs and a loveseat takes up more than half of the room. Celine leads me to that side and lets me settle myself into the leather loveseat.

From the coffee table, she produces a tablet and an electronic pencil, deftly tapping at the screen while she sits back with all the confidence of an alpha in her element. After a moment, she sets everything in her lap and smiles over at me.

"All right, Remi, I'm sure you're curious and little nervous about how things are going to go, so let's go over it. First, I'm going to review the intake questions you answered."

She gives an amused look. "Some of these questions may seem pretty invasive, and you're free not to answer. But remember, we're trying to create a complete picture for your future pack, so there's really no need to be embarrassed. I can guarantee they'll want to know everything about you!"

I can't help but smile at that thought. "Okay."

"Okay," she repeats, nodding firmly. "Once we're done chatting, we'll collect your scent sample. It's a simple swab."

She flips the tablet back open, already poising her pencil over the pad. "First up—favored scents."

She calmly raises her eyes to mine, waiting for me to realize she's asking me for my favorite alpha scents. I'm lucky my darker complexion mostly hides the blood rushing to my cheeks, otherwise I'd be bright red.

"I..." Years of people-pleasing kick in, and the urge to be amenable is overwhelming. "Anything is fine."

Celine frowns, the expression unwittingly fearsome. "Remi, that just won't do. We are here to find your *perfect matches*. Possibly, if we're lucky, *scent-sensitive mates*. If we want any chance of that, you have to be completely honest with me, okay?"

Little does this nice lady know, I can't even be completely honest with myself.

I swallow past a dry throat, nodding. She smiles again. "Good. Trust me, I've heard it all before. Nothing you say will shock or offend me."

Forcing myself to relax, I blow out a tense breath and sink back into the loveseat. "I like food scents the best," I admit, hiding behind the rim of my teacup. "Sweet stuff mostly. And, um, coffee."

Her brisk, businesslike nod reassures me I'm not a freak. "Excellent. And any alpha scents that make you uncomfortable?"

Too many.

Growing up in group homes, being shuffled from foster home to foster home... there are far too many alpha scents I could never feel safe around ever again. A whine rises to my gullet as I repress a wave of unpleasant memories.

Celine waits, professional as ever, until I finally peep, "Nothing industrial. Leather, metal, oil, smoke."

She nods, reading the same response on the questionnaire in front of her. "And do you prefer a pack of all alphas? Or alphas and betas? And how many packmates?"

My eyes fall to my crossed knees. "Anything is f—"

Celine clears her throat, disapproving. "Remi."

I wince at being caught in another fib. The truth is, after years vying for scraps of affection in foster homes, I wouldn't want to share my alphas' attention with anyone else. If I find a pack that somehow actually wants *me*... I want to be the center of the pack.

"I-I think I'd prefer all alphas." I feel another flush move unseen over my face as I think about my heat needs; namely, the number of vibrating alpha substitutes it takes to survive on my own. "I'd need at least two—if they're... *athletic*."

Celine's pink mouth twitches. "Or perhaps three or four would be better?" she suggests, all tact.

I cringe with my whole body. "Probably. Three sounds good. No more than four..."

I expect some form of judgment. At least a raised eyebrow. I'm basically admitting I need three grown alphas to keep me satisfied...

But Celine smiles again, pleased with my honesty. "We'll omit any packs that include industrial scents and limit our search to all-alpha packs of three to four."

"Excellent," she goes on. "Now, heat history and preferences. How many heats have you had, Remi?"

"Um," I squeak, counting. "Three a year since I was sixteen. So, more than twenty?"

The alpha levels me with a look of deep concern. "All on your own?"

I don't know why her sympathy makes me want to cry, but I have to swallow down a thick wash of sadness. "Yes. I use medication to dull the pain, and suppressants to keep me lucid and safe at home."

She seems to sense I'm not finished and waits for me to go on. I swallow hard, forcing my voice not to shake. "A few years ago, one of the doctors at the free clinic recommended I do an unsupressed cycle, to help ensure the suppressants' continued success in the future. I ended up going to a heat clinic and—"

Remembered sensations sweep through my body. Shooting pains from my elbows—chafed from hours of presenting. The shivery claustrophobia of my small, sterile cage. Rough hands on my hips, bruising. Squelching soreness in my core.

"—it wasn't for me," I finish weakly. "I've taken care of myself ever since."

Grief darkens Celine's eyes. "Not for much longer, okay? I promise we'll find you just what you need."

She seems so sure. I try to absorb that certainty and let it soothe me. "Okay. What's next?"

"Next, we'll collect your scent sample and put it into our system, along with all of this personal information. If there's a match, it will pop right up, and we'll call them in!"

My heart seizes in my chest. "Call them... as in, right now? Today?"

"Yes, right now. Today." She smiles, the expression knowing. "My guess? They'll rush right over."

chapter **eight**

"THIS. IS. AH-MAZING."

You know, sometimes, it really seems like my best friend just likes to watch the world burn.

"Meg!" I hiss into my phone, pacing. "You never told me they were going to match me *today*! For fluff's sake, I didn't shave my legs!"

She snorts. "Is there a sink in that suite?"

"MEG!"

"Okay, okay," she chuckles. "I admit, I didn't research the

exact timeline. But listen, it's going to be fine. What's the worst-case scenario here? She plugs your info into their system, and you leave with scent-matched alphas who are scientifically guaranteed to adore you?"

Well, when she puts it like that.

Still, though. Two days ago, I wasn't even sure I *wanted* "scientifically matched" alphas. And now, a group of them might be barreling toward Forever Matched *as we speak*?!

If I hyperventilate in this room, I hope Celine won't be too mad. Or get in trouble.

She's going to hate me, isn't she?

"Remi," Meg says, softer. "Stop all your people-pleasing nonsense and talk to me. Do you *want* to leave? You know I'll jump in the car and come get you right now."

"I'm scared," I admit, dropping down into the loveseat.

Meg hums. "I was, too. That's normal, I think. But if they're right for you, they'll make it all better. I can't explain how it works, it just... does."

I don't have the heart to point out that she's unique. Most matches aren't as strong as hers. Scent-sensitivity is rare. I know that my chances of finding it are already way higher just by being here, though.

"If she comes back with a match, just ask Celine if you can postpone the first meeting," Meg chips. "I'm sure they allow that."

I'm nodding—stupidly, since she can't even see me— when the door to the suite sweeps open again. It's Celine, beaming, with a folder in her hands.

HERE'S the thing about the best-laid plans...

Celine crosses her legs, sitting opposite me once more. She watches my face carefully as she sets the folder on the coffee table and flips it open.

My back instantly goes ramrod straight.

A slight smile crosses her features. "Hmm. I thought so."

I barely hear her over my own pulse. An erratic pound fills my ears while I stare down at the unassuming folder, not understanding what's happening.

There are... alpha scents? *In* the folder?

From where I'm sitting, I can only sense the combined aroma of a pack. Brown sugar sweetness and dark chocolate, undercut by something deliciously bitter and masculine. A whine climbs up my throat, and Celine's smile grows.

"Here," she says, picking up a stack of notecards and handing them to me. "These are samples from the alphas. Tell me what you think."

But I *can't* think.

Ah!

My lungs stutter the second I inhale, spasming as painfully as the desperate emptiness in my core. All the muscles south of my waist clench and gel, the sensation a melting, aching sort of pleasure. I whine so loudly that the sound echoes back at me, tingling over my hard nipples to sink into the frantic beat behind my breasts.

Oh my God.

Oh my God.

Their scents are a maelstrom of pleasure and pain. Or maybe just pleasure, so strong my nerves sizzle and snap like they've been singed.

Frantic urgency sweeps through my body. I pant from the force of it, trying my best to think through the haze tunneling my vision.

It's hard to wrestle control of my faculties away from my Omega. As far as she's concerned, she's scented her mates, and she wants me to *move my butt.*

I reel myself back in, forcing deep breaths so I can think long enough to at least distinguish what I'm smelling.

The pack alpha's scent hits me first. The rich, delicious bitterness of strong coffee. It's the strongest of the three, but only just, edging over the others for only a few seconds before they all meld back together.

The coffee is layered over dark, melted chocolate. Aromatic hazelnuts. Luxurious smoothness and flaky salt and nutty, buttery *perfection.*

It's already everything I could ever imagine and more, but then I catch the last scent in the trio. My mind goes blank while I sway, dizzy.

A blend of warm autumn spices, it naturally complements the dark chocolate and toasted hazelnut. But this alpha is almost... sweet? Not too sweet, but there's definitely brown sugar, nutmeg, allspice, some sort of earthy undertone—

Oh my goodness.

It smells like pumpkin bread.

They all go together perfectly. My vision feels blurry. And no matter how much oxygen I pull into my body, my chest feels like it's caving in.

"Remi!"

Celine's voice is jarringly firm. Dazed, I realize she's probably been calling my name for a couple minutes. Her serious tone finally manages to cut through my haze.

"Remi," she says again, smiling slightly. "Did you hear me?"

I shake my head, surprised it doesn't wobble right off my neck. Her grin grows. "This is the Pierson pack," she repeats. "And you have a match quotient of 98 percent. Do you know what that means?"

My voice shakes. "N-no."

"Most believe scent-sensitivity begins around 95 percent, but, of course, there's no way to guarantee the math."

Because no one can *prove* scent-sensitivity, biologically. It just *is*. Like wind—something anyone could feel, but no one could quite describe the shape of.

Exactly like *this*.

Celine's eyes bore into mine, impressing the importance of her final statement. "Which would make these alphas your mates."

chapter nine

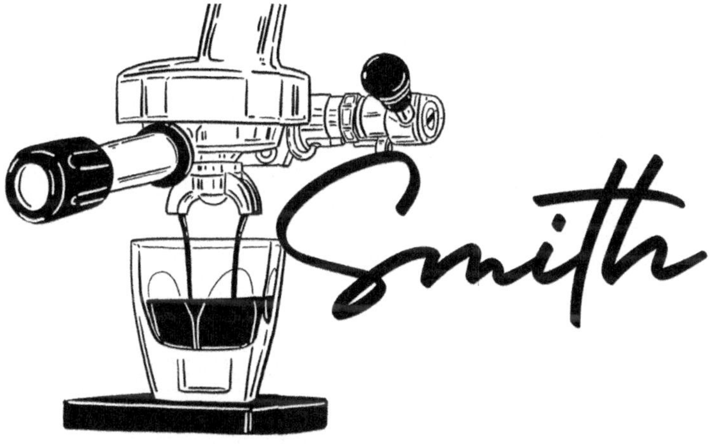

IF I HAD a hundred dollars for every time I'm interrupted by a second call while I'm already on one, I probably wouldn't have to work this hard.

I've been in the car half the day and on calls for all of it. At least when I'm driving from one building site to another, I can use Bluetooth. Otherwise, I might develop some sort of repetitive strain injury from holding this goddamn phone all day.

That would be pathetic, honestly, but not all that surprising. I should probably workout with the guys more often, but there's never enough time. Or the right time. Somehow, the days seem to slip by faster and faster, but they also pile up.

And I'm *tired*.

Down to the bottom of my bones.

But this thing keeps happening whenever I try to rest—where my mind pings restlessly, and the guilt that lives under the pit of my stomach rears up. Then my "rest" is fucked, anyway, so I get up and get more shit done.

Last night, on top of all my work shit, I also got out eighteen emails from Cass and Damon's agents. Freaking the fuck out about Damon being a dumbass and getting into some fight after the game.

For a minute, the messages blasted me into the past, when I was still in my mid-twenties, trying to finish a degree and work ten-hour shifts while saving up to get our pack on its feet. The guys used to get hauled in for shit all the time. School faculty, coaches, gym teachers.

Damon cheating on tests. Cassian beating up punks in parking lots.

Jesus Christ. We're all grown men, now. I thought those days were behind us, but apparently not.

I've been meaning to talk to Damon about his penalties this season. The same way I've intended to speak to Cassian about his worsening depression symptoms. There never seems like a good time, though, when we only pass each other occasionally in the mornings.

We probably should have discussed the Forever Matched shit more, too. After we decided it was the best way forward, we never sat down to hash out what, exactly we were looking for.

Hell. I don't even think I know.

Maybe there will be time when the season is over, in May. Although, fuck. May is overbooked on demolitions and rebuilds. Or June. Someone's birthday is in June. It isn't Cass. He's December. I thought Damon was in September—

Dusting construction debris off the pants of my navy suit, I fold myself back into my Range Rover. Just two more places to stop, and then, maybe, I can get dinner for all of us on the way home. We could sit down and talk this through.

A beep interrupts the latest update with my lead contractor at my newest build site. Annoyed, I click off one call and answer the unknown number.

"Pierson."

The voice on the other end is professional and crisp. "Mr. Smith Pierson?"

"Yes."

"This is Forever Matched."

My entire day screeches to a halt. I freeze, my hand falling from the gear shift. "...yes?"

"We have a match for your pack. A female omega. She's here now, actually. Would you like to come down and meet her?"

chapter
ten

DAMON

WHO THE HELL thought *I* was mature enough for this?

Well. No one, actually.

I just happen to be the closest, according to Smith. He called me in an angry panic, demanding I rush over to Forever Fucked or whatever it's called.

I still can't remember when I walk in the front door. All I know is that I'm nervous in a way I never expected to be, and I have to keep wiping my damp palms on my gray joggers.

Shit.

It would have been nice to have some *notice,* so I could have looked at least a little put-together. But when they called, I was in a session with my personal trainer, trying to sweat out a shitty morning practice where Coach kicked my ass.

Like everything Smith picks out, this place is nice, with a capital N and a dollar sign where the C should be. The instant I walk in the door, not going home to change feels like a mistake. I had time to shower after my workout, but between the sweats and the bruise over my right eye, I'm most definitely not at my best.

Will that matter?

Do I care?

Yeah, I think I actually *do.*

Especially when I take my first breath of sweet-soaked air.

What. Is. That?

There's no one at the front desk in this place, or maybe they're just on a break. Either way, I can't wait for them to come back. I have to follow the hum that suddenly crackles through my blood, pulling me to the door on the right side of the reception area.

I throw it open and charge through, only to collide with someone crossing from one room on the left to a different one on the right.

"Oh shit," I curse, "I'm so sorry."

I've got to stop bumping into people. I already have a black eye and a gnarly bruise on my jaw. The last thing I need is to ruin my face permanently. We all know it's the best thing I've got going for me, aside from my slap shot, and—

I blink down at the small person who just recoiled from our collision. It's a woman. Small and dressed in pretty pink.

And completely frozen, staring at me.

For the most part, I'm not a huge fan of mute staring. It happens a lot with fans—ever since I got signed and had a few videos go viral on TikTok. Normally, I prefer the people who just bustle right up to me and shove their boobs and a Sharpie into my face. The lurkers usually feel awkward, at best.

Not this little thing, though. The way her blue eyes turn to saucers is actually adorable. And, you know, I *did* run into *her*.

I smile. Open my mouth to say hello.

But the whole world evaporates into nothing the second I breathe.

Holy. Ever-loving. Fuck.

Omega.

It's weird, having one single moment when I suddenly understand so many things about myself and the universe all at once.

This is it, though.

This is *everything*.

What was I doing before? Must have been stupid. Nothing else could possibly matter this much.

My whole existence just... turns. Flips. Focuses. Until the rest of the world feels like a blur.

And *she's* crystal fucking clear.

Does my brain even work anymore? I can't seem to discern *what* she smells like... only that it's absolute world-ending perfection.

Every receptor in my mind lights up and pulses. My mouth waters, teeth aching to bite. Claim. Clamp down on her neck while I sink my knot into her tight little body and stay buried in that flawless skin forever.

What am I going to do first: pick her up and purr for her or get on my knees and show her the way she'll sit on my face every morning?

Jesus, Big D. Get a grip.

This is a *literal stranger*. And I just mowed her down.

Her hand floats up, absently pressing to the small swell of her chest. She blinks, two hazel-blue eyes beaming up at me from a face with dainty features and an upturned nose. All of it just as gorgeous as her warm brown skin.

I've never seen eyes like hers. Blue and brown and gold, spinning pretty patterns. And... leaking tears?

Is she *crying*?!

I think *the fuck not.*

Unable to stand for it, I curve my shoulders forward, forming a protective barrier between her and the rest of the world. All of my instincts turn on a dime, shifting from carnal claiming to comfort.

"Hey, pretty girl," I say, as softly as I can. "I didn't mean to scare you. Are you okay? Did I hurt you?"

She shakes her head, the movement slow and dazed. "No, I—I'm sorry. I just..."

I realize we're not alone when a female alpha clears her throat pointedly and curls a hand around the pretty girl's bare shoulder. "We were just moving to a meeting room. Remi's alphas are on their way."

Remi.

I like that. Short and sweet, just like her.

Off the ice, I'm not usually aggressive to other alphas, but I hate that this one is touching the little omega standing in front of me. Especially since she seems overwhelmed. I suppress a snarl, glaring at the female alpha.

"She's clearly upset," I husk, trying to keep the growl out of my voice. Turning back to the omega, I have to ball my hands into fists to keep from reaching out to touch her.

"Whatever it is, it will be okay," I say, knowing my words may be bullshit, but also knowing I have to make this better, somehow. "Is there anything I can do to help?"

She blinks, obviously startled. Can't say I blame her there. *I'm* startled. Especially when I notice that her gaze snags on the big purple circle around my right eye. She winces, and one of her hands flinches up, as if to touch it.

"Are *you* okay?" she asks in a small voice. "That looks like it hurts a lot."

Actually, *it does.* But no one else bothered to ask.

"Yeah," I reply, dumbfounded. And getting dumber with every pull of sweet-soaked oxygen. "It was my own fault, though."

She frowns, and even that face is beautiful on her. All ponderous and pouty.

"Let me guess—you make a habit of running into people?" she asks with a scolding twitch of her eyebrow.

An uncontrollable grin stretches over my face. "I sort of do, actually. I'm a hockey player. We like to ram into each other. Like bumper cars on ice."

Her second brow joins the first, casting me a dry look of disapproval. "Hmm. Looks more like you made someone mad and they punched you."

Holy fucking shit. She's *so cute.*

And, you know, *correct.*

My well-deserved bruise smarts when my face splits into another involuntary grin. "You callin' me a liar, pretty girl?"

She sniffs, giving a clogged little giggle sound that goes straight to my heart.

And maybe my cock a little bit, too.

I'm only human, okay?

"I would never," she says, but there's a little slyness to her eyes that I love.

Her focus drops to her feet. They're as dainty and adorable as the rest of her body, clad in pretty silver sandals. Sympathy and a surge of protectiveness rise inside of me. My inner Alpha lunges like a dog on a leash, trying to strangle himself to get to her.

Jesus, fuck. Down, *boy.*

For all I know, this girl belongs to some other asshole. But I can't just walk away from her. I need to make sure she's going to be safe.

And it's just that—a *need.* One that pounds in my blood, my ears, my brain. Whatever else I do, I must make sure this sweet thing is okay.

The female alpha stops staring daggers at me, her frown turning puzzled. She shifts the tablet in her arms and taps at it. "You said you play hockey?"

I nod, unable to look away from Remi's face a second time. Even when the other alpha chuckles to herself.

"Ah. That explains it," she chirps, flipping the tablet closed. "Remi, this is Damon. He's the star forward for the Orlando Timberwolves. And he's one of your alphas."

Because she's all I see, I notice every flicker on the little omega's face. The way her eyes go round and her lower lip quivers. For one heart-stopping second, I think she might cry again.

But then she smiles.

It's a wobbly, watery thing. But it hits my heart like a flaming arrow.

And I am *all the way in*.

chapter **eleven**

THERE ARE RULES FOR OMEGAS.

A lot of them aren't official. No one will put you in jail if you break them. But no one will care if something terrible happens to you, either.

Omegas shouldn't walk home alone. Omegas should wear descenter. Omegas should find good alphas to claim them, so they aren't as appealing to unbonded alphas.

And if an omega follows all of these rules and still somehow sends an alpha in rut? Well, that's bad luck. Biology is just a fact of life...

So, there are rules. And, generally, I'm a person who follows the rules. Likes them, even.

But *this* alpha?

He makes me want to break every rule I know.

I don't think I've ever met a single other person who's as handsome as he is. Black hair cropped short on the sides and left in tousled disarray on top of his head. Full, sculpted lips. High, prominent cheekbones, and an angled jaw wide enough to balance out his Roman nose.

I don't know where to look first. After a dizzying bounce, I land on a set of aqua-blue eyes. They're so gorgeous, it's easy to forget the purple splotch covering one of them.

His scent doesn't help my memory. The blend of warm autumn spices is mind-bending. It takes me a moment to match him with the scent card Celine gave me.

Good Lord.

This model-beautiful, broad-shouldered, pro-athlete alpha smells like pumpkin bread.

That makes me want to smile, but my body has other ideas. Goosebumps break over my skin as my knees wobble. I'm grateful I have both hands pressed to my chest; my arms hide the way my breasts peak, nipples stiffening, while my lungs shudder around air that *tastes* like him.

A whine sails right out of my mouth. The exuberant smile drops off his face, leaving him slack-jawed as he stares down at me. Giddy vertigo bends my mind as his scent swells, growing warmer, pressing all around me.

A rumbly sound echoes behind his navy T-shirt, but he quickly catches the maybe-growl-maybe-purr and coughs over the rest.

"Sorry," he apologizes, his voice a full octave deeper. "I'm just —Am I…? You *feel* this, right?"

I *feel* like my legs won't hold me up much longer.

Turns out, I'm right.

AS MY CONSCIOUSNESS RETURNS, I'm utterly heartbroken.

I'm *asleep*?

I knew all of this had to be a dream. That alpha was far too beautiful to be real.

Loss echoes through my middle, and I whimper, not wanting to open my eyes and lose the illusion. Based on how warm I feel, I'll probably crack my eyelids and find myself on the floor of my closet, wrapped in my oversized hoodie again.

Only... sweatshirts don't vibrate.

Oh, fluff.

Did I leave one of my alpha substitutes on the floor of my closet-nest and roll on top of it?

That is just humiliating on way too many levels.

I cringe automatically, recoiling into something solid that *moves*. A deeply unattractive squawking sound leaves my lips as my limbs twitch in all directions.

A dark, warm laugh has me whipping my head to the side, where I find myself face-to-face with the alpha from my dream.

Damon.

He's real?

He's here?

He's... holding me?

Fond amusement lights his aqua eyes while they drink in my shock. "Hi, pretty girl," he says softly, smiling. "You went down hard. Are you okay?"

Went...down?

I went down on—

Oh. He means I *fell* down.

Good Lord. I'm turning into Meg.

His features soften the longer we stare at each other. One of his huge, calloused palms comes up to brush my hair over my shoulder, rubbing my back gently. "Remi?"

I need to get myself together. If he thinks I'm scared or too timid, he might decide he doesn't like me enough to introduce me to his packmates.

Is he their alpha?

He certainly seems strong enough, though he doesn't have that steel, weighty dominance that usually smacks me in the face when a pack leader walks into a room. His energy is more... *electric*.

Even so, I should be trying to make the best impression possible. My lower back bows forward while I attempt to straighten my posture and paste on a pleasing smile.

"Yes," I answer, "I'm"— *hopelessly awkward* —"just fine. But I'm sorry I fainted."

Damon's smile comes easily, stretching his plush lips over perfect, white teeth. "According to Celine, it happens all the time. That's why the couches in these meeting rooms are big—room for us alphas to make our omegas comfortable. I guess passing out is common for omegas when they meet their—"

I feel a spark ignite in my middle. "Mates?"

His blue, blue eyes never leave mine. "Mates," he repeats.

The purr in his chest gets louder, unwinding the last bit of tension twined around my lungs. When he feels me relax, his features soften. For a moment, when his focus flickers to my lips, I think he might try to kiss me.

But his attention darts to the corner of the suite, one eyebrow quirking over his bruised brow bone. "Celine also mentioned that there are cameras in here. Multiple times." A spark of mischief touches his expression as he bends closer. "Apparently, I don't look very trustworthy."

He doesn't. Especially with that sexy-as-sin look in his eye. But every neuron in my brain pumps out geysers of oxytocin, telling me he's *safe*.

For the first time in as long as I can remember, I feel

protected. His arms flex, our hug heartrendingly tender as he holds me in his lap.

I carefully trace a finger along his black eye, biting my lower lip. "I can't imagine why..."

He grins, his pumpkin-spice scent thickening. *Hmm.* This alpha likes jokes and playfulness.

Okay. I nod to myself internally, frantically taking mental notes. *I can do that.*

It's going to be essential for me to learn all of them as quickly as I can. The faster I make myself useful to them and the happier they feel around me, the more likely they are to want to keep me.

chapter **twelve**

CASSIAN

IT STARTS when I get out of my car.

There's a current in the air. Snapping, crackling, pulling me closer to the unfamiliar building housing Forever Matched.

If I looked down and found a steel tether sprouting from my middle, I wouldn't be surprised. It would make sense, given the insistent *tug* I feel. Every time I inhale, the air seems to seep right out of the bottom of my lungs, adding to the sensation yanking me toward the double doors.

The second I step inside, I know.

This is why my Alpha had no interest in any other omega. Because somewhere, out there, we knew *this* was waiting for us.

Cake batter, honey, and lavender, all baked into warm, heavenly perfection.

Softness and sunrise and the sweetest edge of ecstasy.

Omega.

Everything inside of me lurches. I barely have the wherewithal to hold myself in check, collaring the beast inside of me trying to snap its binds. He fights at the stranglehold, pushing pure need into all of my pulse points.

Rut. Knot. Bite. Claim.

I freeze, locking myself down as every urge that's been dormant for years surges to the surface. The world is a blur, fading into background noise as my eyes finally focus, taking in the quiet, calm lobby laid out in front of me.

There's no one here.

Am I... crazy? Have I had some sort of break with reality?

Maybe. Because there actually is a beta woman at the front desk. I hear her speak to me, but I can't see her. My eyes are locked on the door to the right, as if I can somehow see through it.

The woman keeps talking, ignorant to the fact that my ears are buzzing with urgency. When she gestures to the same portal I can't stop staring at, I practically tackle the goddamn thing out of my way, bursting into a hallway where a well-dressed alpha woman waits with her arms crossed.

Instead of offering resistance, she waves me toward a room and casts me a *well get the hell in there* look.

My mind races, trying to process the perfume in the air. Is it *real*? Am I in control? God, what if go in there and hurt them?

I hate the answer my body gives me. Because it *does not care.* Nothing short of dropping dead will stop me from getting to the omega filling the air with gentle lavender and bubbling honey.

The door disappears. Did I open it? Melt it with the heat pouring off my body?

Who gives a shit?

I step inside the plush hotel-like suite, finding my most self-involved, least-emotionally-mature packmate cuddled into the sofa with a small omega bundled in his arms.

The way he's holding her, I can't see her face right away. But her sweet, honeyed scent strokes its way into my lungs, curling there until my nerves vibrate in pure pleasure.

Holy fuck.

Was that a *purr*?

I swear to God, I've never made that noise before.

They both startle at the sound, turning in unison to look at me.

Damon could be a piece of furniture for all that he fades into the background. My eyes loop over the omega's face, desperate to drink it in. She's beautiful and delicate, with the most unique honey-brown complexion and shining black curls and hazel-blue eyes that look like—

Butterfly's wings.

"Remi?"

The name is torn out of the very bottom of my soul. I haven't said it in *years.*

Now, as it rolls off my tongue, it feels like some secret hope I didn't know I had. Could it really be her? Here? Now?

Where is "here"? I don't know. I can't remember where I am or how I got here.

All I know is *her.*

That skin. Those *eyes.*

And *this is her scent*???

The lush aroma of fresh honey cake swirls off her. A complex, deeply sweet fragrance; almost caramelized, but with the distinct edge of something delicate and floral. I hear myself grunt, but I don't have enough blood left in my brain to parse why.

Because my cock and knot are *throbbing.*

The need to rut prowls under my skin, pushing its way to my blood, stripping my sanity away beat by beat.

For one manic moment, it seems like I might not be the only

one on edge. The omega scrambles to her feet. She makes a strangled sound, confirming that she's the girl I used to know when she breathes my name.

"Cassian?"

Before I can find the ability to *think*, fresh sweetness soaks into the air. Thick and warm and hot—each lungful is straight from an oven full of my favorite things. I feel the scent roll into my entire body. Every nerve crackles, a wash of hot sensation blazing over my skin.

Fuck. *Fuck.*

The moan that pours of out her is new. Very fucking different from the little giggles and sighs she used to make when we were teenagers.

No, this is the sound of a full-grown woman who's just scented something that's making her wet and weak.

How is this—

Am I—

Is she *real*?

A mirage, maybe. She always looked like one, even back then. If I feel her face, will she shimmer and disappear?

One of my hands floats up, fingertips grazing the smooth skin of her rounded cheek.

It—

She *feels* real.

Warm. Soft. Shaking like a leaf.

So much is the same. Her colors. Her fine-boned hands wringing together. Those *blue fucking eyes.*

And the clip in her hair.

She starts to speak but winds up pressing her mouth closed. Those lips... I remember those, too. So plush and pink. And I remember thinking they couldn't possibly be as soft as they looked.

They move, now. Forming the only word that could convince me any of this is actually happening.

"Bear? Is it really you?"

She gave me that nickname as a joke after I told her all of the guys on the team called me Beastly, and confessed I wasn't really sure how I felt about it.

"You're not a beast!" she'd huffed, adorably indignant. "You're a... bear."

I remember blinking at her. "...excuse me?"

She had flashed a smile, the small, impish one I liked best. "Yeah, you're a big, snarly, furry guy," she'd said, gesturing at my long hair. "But then, when we're on the roof and I get cold, you keep me warm. Big bear."

My eyes trace over the clip holding her black curls away from her face. Breaths heave in and out of me, but the rest of my body is frozen in place. Numb lips move without my permission, speaking the nickname I only had the balls to call her a handful of times back then.

"Butterfly."

chapter **thirteen**

DARK, *melted chocolate. Aromatic hazelnuts. Luxurious smoothness and flaky salt and nutty buttery—*

My life flashes before my eyes while I perfume, instantly dousing my panties in slick, and thoroughly embarrassing myself to the brink of death.

Oh. My. Lord.

I've had this dream before, too. A full-grown alpha-male Cassian who *wants* me in a way my half-grown almost-alpha friend Cassian never did. Forest green eyes that stare me down with *intent*, instead of pity.

The dream is familiar, but it's not usually so *vivid*.

Besides, Cassian wasn't designated when I knew him. I never got to find out what his scent was.

So why can I *taste* chocolate on my tongue?

And breathe the rich scent of hazelnuts?

Am I in heat? Is this some sort of episode? Am I going to wake up with padded cuffs on my wrists? Or Meg shaking my shoulders?

What other explanation could there be?

Aside from the obvious. Which becomes more and more likely the longer I look at him.

It's really Cassian. And he's... here?

He's here. In this room. One of the scent cards in the file Celine gave me.

He's here. And he smells like everything I ever imagined my perfect mate would.

Dazed hope sails through my mind, but it can't sink in. I've spent too many years denying it. Banishing it. Bashing it into pieces tiny enough to bury.

A manly version of the boy I once knew gazes back at me. Tension and ten lost years have turned his familiar features into something just new enough to thrill me, yet still so like the almost-alpha who appointed himself my unofficial protector.

His brows are thicker and more pronounced, but I recognize the scar slicing through the left one. The rest of his features are broader now: a slightly wider nose, a larger mouth, his cheekbones sharper and thicker.

Shining brunet lashes surround his dark green gaze, highlighting the whites of his eyes and the dusky half-moons under them. He also has a few creases on his forehead and a fair bit of dark stubble along his firm, flexing jaw.

But his hair is still too long—thick and deep brown, the color matching his dark chocolate scent. And the cleft in his chin still makes me want to smile.

He growls, low and pained, saying my name again. "*Remi*."

The air shifts, pressing his thick, aroused alpha-maleness into my skin. My body reacts instantly. Every nerve sings, hitting a high note. My vision tunnels, the edges blurring while my heart pounds harder and harder, sending fresh waves of prickles over my skin and shivers down into my core.

Another whine slips up my throat when I feel myself perfume —the tingly, wet release that always sends a skitter up my spine. It's hard for me to feel appropriately horrified about it when my body *aches* like this, though.

A sudden desire to nest overwhelms me. I want a dark, quiet place, surrounded by fuzzy blankets and cushions and smelling exactly like these alphas. Just the thought of going home to my closet-nest makes me want to burst into tears.

Cassian reaches for me, his hands curling under my forearms to offer support. "Remi?" he repeats, then steps closer, murmuring the other nickname he had for me. He only called me *butterfly* in private, as a joke. But, usually, around the others, I was: "Rems?"

"I—I—"

Should I run? Hide? I've never been so mortified or overwhelmed. He hasn't done anything to deserve being abandoned, but that isn't what stops my feet.

It's the sound of him trying to strangle a purr in his chest… and sort of failing.

Usually, purrs are reserved for intimate partners. The fact that he's working overtime not to make the sound for me finally spills the tears pooled in my eyes.

Is he trying not to scare me? Or is he rejecting me?

A rough, dry palm cups my cheek, lifting my face. I look up to find solemn green eyes, staring just inches away from mine.

"Sorry," he grumbles, voice vibrating with the rumbly edge of a growl. "I'm not going to hurt you. I'll give you back to Damon—"

Another whine flies out of me, even sharper than the last. Cassian heaves out a gust of relief, instantly snapping me closer, cradling me tightly against his enormous chest, and the crisp white button-down stretched over it.

"Fuck," he pants, speaking into my exposed shoulder. "When they told me you had to move out, I didn't know what the fuck to do. I was—" He swallows thickly, his voice dropping lower. "I worried."

That sounds a little more believable, at least. Cassian was always over-protective.

He hated that I had to climb up on the roof to meet him for our pre-dawn picnics of pilfered baked goods and library books. He never liked it when any of the other guys teased me or followed me around the common areas. And he especially loathed letting me walk anywhere alone in the dark.

Part of me always knew he'd be worried when he found out I'd been moved to the omega home. I felt bad for not saying goodbye... but once my perfume started, I was absolutely horrified by the thought of accidentally perfuming around him and revealing how he affected me.

I already lived under the mantle of constant rejection. I really didn't think I could handle the look on his face when he scented my arousal and balked.

Only... that's not happening, now.

The whole room is practically soaked in my honey-like scent, and he's still here, holding me and... *hard as steel*?

I squirm back, horrified by the way my body is forcing a reaction out of his. "Sorry!"

Behind me, Damon groans, dropping his head back to the couch and palming the front of his joggers. "Holy *fuck*, that is so good. *Jesus*, sweetness. Why would you apologize for making me feel like I just saw *God*?"

Cassian seems less certain about how he feels. Something pinches the space between his eyebrows. He grunts, shifting away from me.

Embarrassed because I felt him? Or mortified by having me as their omega?

I smell Damon's pumpkin spice just before I feel his hand on the back of my head, petting my hair softly. When I turn my head, he's smiling. "You two have met before?"

It takes a second for me to register his question as a joke. It must be obvious Cassian and I have met before. I mean, my thighs were almost clamped around his hips.

Cassian doesn't turn his head as he replies, "This is Remi, from the group home. The one I've told you about."

chapter fourteen

DAMON

I'M A DICK.

After spending ten years telling my packmate he was either crazy, pathetic, or some morbid combination of the two…

Shit.

I'd wait ten years for her, too.

This fact obviously stuns Remi. She blinks at Cassian in complete shock. The scent of honey-cakes gets richer, the lavender even more of a tease.

Good sweet *God*.

"You—I—"

She shakes her head, her dark curls bouncing. "I don't understand," she whispers. "We were just friends. I... I thought I irritated you. You were always annoyed with me, telling me I wasn't being safe."

I watch Cassian's gears grind in his skull. His lips part, but the only sound that escapes is an unintelligible huff.

I laugh. "Classic Cass. Let me guess, he snarled and grunted at you all the time?"

"Yes," she giggles. "It's not his fault, though. I was... annoying. I followed him everywhere when he was at the home. And I woke him up most mornings before the sun even came up."

Oh my God, she is so cute. I want to rip her out of Cass's arms and cuddle her forever. Instead, I lift my hand to touch her cheek.

"I can't imagine you ever annoying any of us, sweetness."

Her perfume is *perfect.* And knowing that burst of sweet sin came from something *I* said? My knot swells, ready to fill her until neither of us can move.

Drawn by forces beyond my control, I shift closer, not stopping until my shoulder is pressed against Cass's. Our quietest packmate snarls softly, his face pulling into a pained look.

"Can't let her go right now," he mutters to me. "Sorry."

Then to her, "Sorry, butterfly. I know you must want Damon, too. But it's taking all I've got not to claim you *right now.*"

She looks startled again, but her scent stays purely sweet. "I'm so confused," she whispers, looking back at him. "You... want me?"

Cassian is fierce when he wants to be. Fire snaps in his eyes as he stares back at her, scowling. "Not just that. I want to *take you home.* The same way I wanted to take you home every single day when neither of us had one."

Part of me wants to pout. *Leave it to Cassian to be a grumpy asshole, and yet somehow kick my ass in the romance department.*

I don't think I even care. Because Remi's beautiful face

softens in awe. And the tears shimmering in her blue-gold eyes make me *weak*.

Her lip trembles while she blinks at Cassian. "Y-you did?"

He did. I can vouch for him.

Getting our pack a real home always meant more to Cass than it did to me, or even Smith. I never connected the dots, but it makes sense.

He didn't want a home for himself.

His Alpha wanted one for *her*.

My heart cramps, aching as I watch the two of them relearn each other's faces. After a beat, I cup my hand around Remi's, turning her attention to me. "What do you say, pretty girl? Come home with us?"

Remi looks between the two of us. She shrinks down a bit, uncertainty filling her face. "That's what you want?" she asks. "You want— but your alpha has to say yes first, right?"

Oh. Fuck.

Right.

As if Remi somehow summoned him, I hear a clipped voice in the hallway, along with some shuffling. Leave it to Smith to delay getting his uppity ass in here so he can review paperwork with Balls Of Steel Celine out there.

I don't know how our sweet omega can sense that the leader of our pack is about to come in, but she straightens, turning to the door and quickly smoothing her pretty pink skirt. I'm not sure I like the apprehension and anxiety on her face.

Why is she so nervous?

Smith is going to eat her up.

chapter **fifteen**

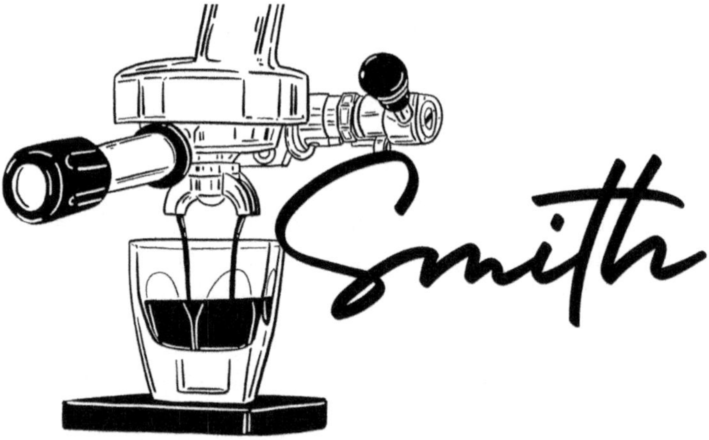

I LIKE LISTS.

Plans. Proof. Projections. Logic and preparedness have served me well throughout my life, even when it was painful.

I was raised to believe there's a correct way to do things. A right way to *be*.

It's the reason I decided to pay out the ass for a scent-matching service; so I could *know*, beyond a shadow of a doubt, that I'd made the right choice for my pack.

I figured it's science, right? How could they be wrong?

I still don't know.

All I know is, the second I walk into the room, I *feel* her scent in the air. My body goes numb, a high-pitched sort of whistle reverberating in my ear drums like a gunshot.

The air in my lungs contracts into two leaden balls. They drop down into my stomach while I pant, inhaling harder, trying to just *breathe*.

But I can't.

Can't breathe. Can't think. Can't make a decision or a plan.

My chest heaves.

Mine.

Honey.

Mine.

Lavender.

Mine.

All mixed into something lusciously smooth, delicious, and nostalgic. Cake batter, maybe.

Fucking hell. What *is* that?

Our omega.

The force of my will must send a pulse through the air that only she can feel, because the second the thought rips through my mind, she stands up straighter, visibly quivering as a burst of perfume fills the space between us.

Jesus, *fuck*.

That *scent*.

My dick throbs while hot blood pulses to my knot and saliva pools in my mouth, begging me to bite.

And whatever bolt of dominance she felt from me did *that*? Is it possible she'll like giving me control as much as I enjoy taking it?

I smother a growl in my throat, pressing my heels into the floor, so I don't leap across the room and take her pretty, unmarked throat.

She's honey and heaven, wrapped in pink silk. I don't know whether it's her pheromones or mine, but I would swear there's an ethereal sort of glow around her. Like she absorbs sunlight. Or slicks it over her skin before she leaves the house.

I expected to feel fuzzy, but my mind is sharper than it's ever been. My eyes trace over her, taking in every detail. Her carefully painted nails, the delicate bows holding her dress up. The unique patterns in her blue eyes.

"Pretty girl," Damon croons, his voice unnaturally soft. "This is Smith. Smith, this is Remi."

Remi.

She's beautiful.

Impossible to look away from.

Familiar.

How do I know her? How could we meet without me scenting how fucking perfect she is?

I'm not sure, but I do know that the instant stab of horror in my gut feels foreboding.

Despite that feeling, she's so clearly lovely. Scent and every other sense agrees. The only thing I don't understand is the sick roll in my stomach, telling me something is wrong.

Is it instinct? Does my Alpha want me to know there's something wrong with this omega?

No. That's not it. My Alpha is *begging* me to get closer. More like demanding, actually.

She doesn't feel the same way. It's obvious when she steps back, eyes widening. The warm cake-sweet scent filling the room singes. One word falls from her mouth, filled with trembling dismay.

"You."

Me? She knows me, too?

I look closer, searching for any small hint as to how. Her eyes flash to mine, the motion quick and fearful. With that one scared glance, recognition hits me square in the gut.

"You're the barista," I say, dread washing through me. "From Proper Coffee."

Her sweet scent burns. "And you're my boss."

chapter sixteen

Remi

I STARE at the alpha in front of me, blinking in disbelief.

It's—

Him.

The perfectly tailored navy suit. The terrifying scowl. The monogrammed cuffs.

The same ones that flashed under my face as he splattered steamed milk all over me a few days ago. Three letters, embroidered in no-nonsense-navy: *SCP.*

Now I know the "S" stands for Smith. The "P" stands for Pierson.

The "C" must stand for that one rude word I don't even like to think to myself.

It all makes sense. Their file said that the alpha owns a property development company. Smith must develop the properties and then invest in businesses. He's one of the alphas who's been stomping around, throwing orders at me.

In fact, this alpha is *the worst one*. He fired Nan. And he's the only alpha who feels entitled to bark at me.

"Faster."

"If you can't do your job, I'll find someone who can."

"We don't have all day to deal with your incompetence!"

"I don't give a fuck what your excuse for being pathetic is."

The longer I stare, the worse it gets.

I recognize his watch, too. Its flat, gold face caught the light as he tossed his scalding drink in my face. His cufflinks, too—each one a simple gold bar with smaller bookends on either side.

I know all of these tiny details by heart, because he's shoved so much dominance and intimidation at me, I've spent the last two months unable to look up at his face when he speaks.

Fear seizes inside of me while my mind races, trying to rationalize. Attempting to make sense of how he could treat me so callously while smelling so utterly *perfect*.

His scent. Why didn't I smell it in the coffee shop? As soon as I got close enough—I assumed the coffee grinder was the source of the earthy, overpowering aroma of fresh coffee.

But maybe it wasn't.

Maybe it was him.

Now that he's here in person, I sense that bitter richness underscoring Damon and Cassian's sweeter scents.

It's him.

His smell.

The same one I, ironically, fantasized about for years.

Because he's part of this pack. The pack I'm supposed to be scent-sensitive to.

Weeks of him yelling at me, calling me names, barking

orders… that must be what sent my Omega over the edge. *He's* the reason I've felt so erratic and uncomfortable lately. Even when I didn't recognize him, she did. And his actions were a heck of a lot worse than any average rejection.

It could also be the reason I've felt so frazzled and hormonal at work. My body reacted instinctively to his proximity, even when scent-neutralizers inhibited my mind's ability to comprehend why.

Frustration creases his features while he stares back at me, scowling. If I weren't so devastated, I might be annoyed that the expression does nothing to diminish how handsome he is. Between his square jaw, straight nose, and thick blond hair, it's undeniable.

He's shocked. That makes sense, too, assuming he never really looked at me too closely. I wear tons of de-scenter to work, and the other smells in there are so strong, he'd never scent me inside the shop. Between that and my oversized clothes, I'm sure I didn't seem too interesting.

No. To Smith, I was just another servant. Someone weaker and smaller.

Meaningless.

Certainly not good enough for him. Or his pack.

My scent burns, along with any hope in my heart.

No matter how much I denied it to myself, for a few minutes, I really did think Damon and Cassian wanted to take me home. I believed it was finally happening.

Am I really this naive after all these years? Haven't I learned better yet?

The queasy sensation in my stomach is so familiar, my eyes prick with tears. I know this feeling—it's a warning. My body is ramping up, filling with adrenaline, preparing for the pain. If I don't leave first, this pack alpha will ask me to.

And the last thing I want to do is burst into sobs when this gloriously handsome, horribly cruel man rejects me.

I move toward the door, darting around Damon and Cassian as I whisper, "I need to go."

Cassian starts to protest, "What's going on?"

I swallow a whine, unable to even look at him. If I do, I won't be able to move. And I *need* to.

The ever-darker scent of smoking coffee grounds underscores my anxiety. Smith is furious.

I chance another glance at his face and instantly regret it. Lord, why does he have to look like this? It's a good thing I didn't have the nerve to glance up at him all this time. If I had seen just how gorgeous he is when he's angry, I might have just dropped to the floor of Proper Coffee and presented.

Oh my God. *What is* wrong *with me?*

"Rems," Cassian says again, his voice edged with alpha insistence. "What happened?"

I shift on my bare feet, trying to ignore the slippery slick gathered at the top of my thighs. "I just need to go," I blurt, humming with the desire to flee and hide.

Cassian lumbers over to me, reaching out to touch my cheek again. His face drops into a fearsome scowl, but pure pain streaks through his eyes while he mutters one word that absolutely breaks my heart.

"Already?"

He doesn't seem angry. He seems like a man who's been having the best dream and was just told it's time to wake up. Resigned but not ready. Wistful for something he's still in but knows he's going to miss immensely.

Like he had feared this moment since he saw me again.

Like, maybe, he actually does want me to stay.

Damon chimes in, his voice closer than before. "Of course you can leave, sweetness. I'll drive you home right now. But I think we all want to know why you're in such a rush all of a sudden." He appears at Cassian's shoulder, pinning me with those light blue eyes, so full of hope and worry. "Please?"

I stare up into their faces—Cass's craggy with heart-wrenching longing, and Damon's full of hopeful eagerness. The twin scents of hazelnut and autumn spice wash over me, banishing a bit of my panic.

They steady me while I wipe at my face, sniffing and gesturing at Smith. "He's my boss," I say again. "And he's—"

Horrible, abusive, scary...

I hear approaching footsteps, but Smith stops a few feet from the others. Fire snaps in his dark eyes while he barks, low, "*Enough, omega.*"

If I weren't so totally overwhelmed, I might have the energy to be properly insulted. Some heat flares in my own eyes when I find the nerve to stare back at him, my spine straighter.

"Yes, *Sir.*"

Before any of them can give me another command, I do what my instincts are clamoring for and make my escape.

chapter
seventeen

DAMON

DAMN.

Celine has some balls.

Just before all three of us burst out of the room to chase Remi down, the female alpha's sharp features appear on the threshold. "Gentlemen! *Don't even* think *about it*," she snaps, low and even.

All three of us open our mouths to protest, but Celine belts out a no-nonsense bark that whips me upside the head. *"This is not up for debate. Remi has chosen to leave. You will let her go."* She pulls at her suit jacket and gives a solid nod. "Take a moment to collect yourselves, and we'll discuss your options."

As soon as the slab falls shut, the three of us have to take a full minute to shake off Celine's dominance. Then we need another two minutes for our brains to reset.

Because *holy shit*, this place smells like heaven. And hell.

Remi's stress raises my hackles on a visceral level. But the wet arousal woven into the caramelized honey and singed lavender is *ev-er-y-thing*.

Fuck.

Think, Damon.

Deep breath.

No. Wait. Don't breathe. Do not brea—

Annnnnd I have a boner.

I'm not alone, though. A quick glance around tells me that my pack brothers are all in the same, woody boat.

Apart from the poke-your-eye-out bulge in his two-thousand-dollar pants, Smith looks like he's ready to murder someone. Which is weird because that's usually Cassian's job. Instead, he just seems... frozen.

I shift on my feet. Clearly, there's some shit we need to talk about. This is unfamiliar territory for our pack. We don't usually have *discussions*. Or, you know, share about our feelings. Or talk, actually.

Cassian and I used to be different. He's withdrawn more and more over the years. And maybe, now that I've met Remi, that makes sense... but, at the time? I hated it.

Over the years, Smith has been gone more and more, too. He stopped showing up for every game. Then he stopped showing up for *most* games. Now we have a box with our pack name on it, sitting empty, week after week.

If I ever let myself slow down enough to think about it... yeah. That shit would hurt.

I found a new normal with them because I didn't have a choice. Silent workouts. Passing each other for three minutes in the unfinished kitchen sometimes. Sharing UberEats for holiday meals. Occasionally catching a game or a movie on TV.

It got to the point where random puck bunnies were the best companionship I had. Going home with a random girl wasn't really what I wanted—but, hell, at least it was *someone's* home. A few hours to trick myself into feeling less alone.

Because facing the truth was too hard. But no matter how much I tried to deny it, the fact remains: we are not the pack we used to be. And we have never been a pack that *talked*.

This room is making me itchy for about eight different reasons. But mostly because I don't have Remi on top of me. And the whole place is just *full* of her.

Shock echoes through all three of us while we stare at the door. Beastly shakes his off first, slowly turning to glare right at his brother. "What *the fuck* have you done?"

Smith doesn't answer. His scent is past super-dark-roast and edging more into smoking-cinders-after-a-nuclear-explosion.

Right.

Time to diffuse this clusterfuck of a situation.

"So, she's really the one?" I ask Cassian. "The girl from the group home? The hot one who used to bake you cookies?"

I remember being jealous that he got to leave school and head "home" to a cute girl who made him treats, while I had to shuffle back to whatever couch I had crashed out on that month.

Cassian laces his fingers behind his neck, muttering in a snarl, "I never said she was *hot*. She was sixteen, for fuck's sake."

Yeah, and we were seventeen. And shitheads.

Okay, okay. He might not have said "hot." He probably didn't even imply it. He always *was* weirdly protective of her. Chivalrous and shit.

At the time, I didn't understand why he gut-punched the guy in our weight-lifting class who asked him to bring in one of "his girl's" bras. Now, I get it. Anyone who talks about our omega's boobs is getting *wrecked*.

Which is definitely hypocritical, considering the number of mental jpegs I snapped when her sweet little nipples popped up today.

C'mon, Big D. Focus.

Smith's hands slacken, releasing the white-knuckle fists dangling at his sides. "She probably had to leave the home when her designation came in," he mutters. "I doubt it was safe for her to stay near so many emerging alphas with perfume like *that*."

He's practically growling by the end of the sentence. Which makes sense. As our pack alpha, his instincts must be riding him even harder than mine are. And right now, I'm like half a deep breath away from ripping that stupid door off its hinges.

"Do we even need to talk about this?" I ask, vibrating in place. "We're *obviously* going after her, hugging the stuffing out of her, and keeping her forever, right?"

"No," Smith says, his voice heavy. "I... it can't be her. I've seen her every day for two months. I would have recognized if she was ours."

He lets those words soak in before sighing and sitting down slowly—probably because of the monster trouser snake he's contending with.

Cassian flashes his teeth in a menacing gnash. "Can't you *feel* this? This is the first time in *ten goddamn years* that I've felt *anything good*. She's *mine*. Which means, if she isn't your omega, then I must not belong in your pack."

Oh. Fuck.

We're going there? So soon?

I shove air out of my nose, trying to think around Remi's perfume and distress. The fact that I literally can't tells me everything I need to know.

"Me neither, Big Hoss," I say, wincing. "I mean... this is *it*. Maybe the scent-neutralizers at the shop or whatever de-scenter both of you wear to work fucked with things, but now, you have to know she's the one. You wanted it to be scientific—well, here we are. She picked us. Before she saw you, she wanted to go home with us and try to be a part of this pack. There's gotta be some way for you to fix this."

Usually, Cassian's face is a mask of anger or a perfect poker face. I've never seen it look so... twisted. His mouth is frozen in a grimace, and his big brows are folded down, pulling at the scar over his left eye. I clap him on his shoulder, shaking him slightly.

"C'mon, Cass. We'll figure this out. It'll be fine. Better than fine. We found our *mate*, guys. This is a good fucking day."

Smith seems to snap into action. He checks his watch and sits forward, gesturing to the seats opposite him. "*Sit*," he barks quietly. "We need a plan."

A bit of Cassian's long-lost fire ignites in his eyes. "She's a *person*, Smith, not a hostile takeover. A checklist won't help us. She needs *nurturing*. And you still haven't even told us what you did to her."

Our alpha is stone-still. To an observer, he might even look calm. But his voice is gravel when he replies, "She works slowly, and she's often distracted. The other investors wanted to fire her. I tried to get her to pick up her pace."

Oh God. As someone who knows Smith, I can tell you that "pick up her pace" is code for yelling. If not barking.

It sounds like anyone's worst nightmare. Let alone an omega's. I don't know much about their designation, but I know an angry alpha can be terrifying for them.

And they like cuddly shit. I think.

Maybe I should have Googled.

Right now, I need to get these two off each other's backs.

"We can handle this," I butt in. "Smith will stop being a dick-head CEO—"

"Damon," he growls.

"—Cassian will apologize to Remi for having absolutely no game in high school—"

"Fuck off," he cuts in, back to his grumbling self.

"—and I'll lick her pussy until she never wants to leave us. Good plan? Good plan. Let's go find Balls Of Steel Celine."

"She won't help us," Smith snaps. "It's against their policy. Any information shared between alphas and omegas has to be done directly by them."

Cass cracks his knuckles, all feeling dropping off his face, leaving solid determination behind. “She’s mine. And no one is going to stop me from finding her and *making* her mine.”

Well, that sounds healthy.

Doesn’t some fairy tale start out like this?

A horror movie?

Close enough.

chapter **eighteen**

"REMI…" Meg's voice sighs through the phone. "Are you calling me from the floor of your closet right now?"

I hiccup. "No."

"You're a terrible liar," she points out, but there's no heat to it. "Tell me what happened? Are you safe?"

I burrow further into Cass's old sweatshirt, whining when it doesn't smell like him at all. When I try to tell her the whole story, I find I can't get past the Cassian part without her freaking out.

She interrupts, her voice is low. "The guy from the group home is *your alpha*?"

"Well, he's not—"

"And he's been waiting for you *this entire time*?"

"Well, it depends on what you *mean* by 'waiting,' but ye—"

"HOLY FUCK! Did you take pictures? Oh, wait! Names! Give me the pack name. I'm already typing."

Her enthusiasm makes me dizzy. I hear her thumbs against her phone's screen. A second after I manage to get the name out, she *shrieks*.

An alarmed male voice snaps over the line. "What? What's wrong? Peaches?"

Theo is clearly distressed that his omega sounds like a hamster that's about to be dropped into a blender. I don't blame him, but I'm running out of time to process what just happened.

"Meg?!"

My best friend stammers, and I hear her hand her alpha the phone, then yank it back. Theo makes a loud whooping sound and bursts into laughter.

"Oh my God, Remi. Cassian is *Cassian King*?"

"BEASTLY," Theo roars. "Oh fuck yeah, this is going to be *awesome*! I'm gonna go buy season tickets. Dibs on groomsman."

Meg's excitement quickly turns to accusation. "You *bitch*!" she squeals. "You get *Damon Mathers*, too?"

I want to cringe into nothing. *Not after the way I just ran out of there.* "Um, I mean..."

"Are they coming to get you?" she blabbers, so excited that it hurts my heart. "Are you packing? *Please* take the panties that don't come with a chastity belt attached. And make sure you have them help you move any big stuff."

The image of the Pierson pack in my hovel of an apartment is almost darkly comical. Or, actually, just... *dark*. My heart palpates from thinking about it, and not in a good way.

Lord.

Maybe it's for the best that I'll officially be alone forever. If they ever came here, I would be mortified. Cassian would *see* his ratty old hoodie in my bed. If we actually courted, he would see *everything*. My pitiful little apartment. My even-more-pitiful bank account.

And Smith, with his perfect clothing and his expensive haircut... I already know he thinks I'm trash because of the way he talks to me at work. If he sees that I'm using books to prop up my futon? He'd probably sneer so hard, he'd break his own nose.

Damon seems the most laid-back of the three, but he's so *gorgeous*. If he didn't mind the apartment, he would probably change his mind once he saw how I really look under all my makeup.

Who am I kidding? I'm sure they've all *already changed their minds. They're probably talking to Celine about being re-matched as we speak.*

Try as I might not to let it, the thought of being left behind sinks its claws into my stomach, slicing deep.

No one has ever wanted to keep me.

Cassian *knows* that. He *saw* it happen. I was always the reject; returned like a defective purchase.

Why would he want someone like *that*?

Meg is still shrieking. "Remi! Why aren't you jumping up and down?!"

I sniff, swiping at the corners of my eyes so my makeup doesn't run, feeling so overwhelmed I can barely think. "Yeah," I lie. "Y-you're right. It's great! I, um, I should go, though. I need to be ready when..."

The sun still rises tomorrow.

And the next day? I have to go back to work. With Smith.

If I even have a job anymore.

Which is unlikely, actually.

"...they come to get me."

Theo's booming voice cuts in. "Congratulations, Remi! I can't believe I'm going to get to meet Beastly! That guy is a *monster*. Best goalie in the NHL."

I've always hated those nicknames. *Monster. Beastly.* They don't suit Cassian at all. Even now that he's enormous.

It's surreal to even think about him as a fully grown adult. When I was still a teenager, I used to curl onto the floor of whatever makeshift nest I had, picturing him in there with me. Knowing he'd grumble and frown, but find some way to squeeze himself in without verbalizing a single complaint.

Bear.

He was always like that. Big, burly, with that thick, long hair he refused to cut. He acted gruff and prickly, but his heart was soft; and he always made room for me, no matter where we were.

Maybe he actually wasn't so irritated by me after all.

He probably is now.

The urge to return to him is so strong, I feel dizzy and nauseous from resisting. A whimper rattles my throat and I apologize. "Sorry."

Meg guffaws. "Sorry?! It's normal to feel this way, Rems! It just means they're really your mates!"

My mates.

I feel the words, deep down, tugging at me. And I know they're true. It's real.

But it's also impossible.

chapter nineteen

DAMON

SO, here's the thing.

I've never been *great* with rules.

Someone with some fancy-ass degrees on their wall could probably psycho-analyze me and figure out what, exactly, made me like this. Was it watching my parents break the law all the time? Was it the seething sense of injustice whenever they forgot to buy food, but somehow had the nerve to try to set rules for me?

Or maybe it was all that cheating I did in school. Copying answers from whoever sat closest to me, knowing I'd never be able to read the questions.

Hockey didn't help. I mean, there are rules and shit, but we also have a literal penalty box. On the ice. And the fans sort of love it when you end up in there. The bunnies always did, too...

So, it wasn't really a deterrent.

The point is: I am not a rule-follower. I'm a rule-*breaker*.

Is anyone really surprised that while Celine was arguing with Smith, I took a picture of the info on the front of Remi's Forever Matched file?

Exactly.

She left the damn thing on the coffee table, like two inches away from my phone, so. It really isn't even my fault that I'm here, turning onto Remi's street.

Which sucks, by the way. Holy shit. There are so many potholes that it looks like there's a meteor shower happening instead of a spring rain.

I haphazardly parallel park my Audi, frowning at the rain pelting my windshield. My hair is going to look ridiculous.

But every time I close my eyes, I see Remi's lower lip trembling. And every breath I take still tastes like her fear.

Fuck my hair.

It's cool and damp tonight. The kind of weather that keeps people inside. Years ago, Cass, Smith, and I would have squashed into the living room of the loft we used to share, arguing over the TV and whether Thai food is better or worse than Chinese.

Now, I'm sure our living room is as empty as it always is. Sealed up like a tomb, shrouds and all.

Jesus.

Having an omega is making me morbid.

I cup my hand over my brow and run across the back street. My footsteps pound along with the rain, slapping the uneven pavement. When I finally drop my arm and look around, squinting through the downpour, my spine snaps straight.

There's a hooded figure hanging around the building's stoop. Back hunched, hands in his pockets, pacing like an angry bull. A growl vibrates in the back of my throat, protective instincts rising.

I grew up surrounded by junkies. I've seen first-hand how much damage they can do when they get too agitated or impatient for their next fix.

When I snarl, though, the guy in the hoodie answers with a roar of his own.

A familiar one.

"Beastly?" I balk. "The fuck are you doing here?"

Cassian stands up and shoves his hood back, revealing unstyled, wet hair and a ferocious scowl. He throws his hand at Remi's building. "I've been here for hours! I came as soon as we left the match place! You think I'd let her be in this building alone? In this neighborhood? I'll fucking sleep on this stoop if I have to."

Wow. Okay.

Beastly is in A Mood.

I glance at the apartment building's foggy glass door and the small foyer beyond, all cramped with rusted mailboxes. It doesn't exactly seem like Fort Knox.

"Did you consider just, like, going in?"

He glowers, chest heaving in angry pants. "Yes, I considered it. But this is her safe place." He eyes the building dubiously, lingering on the rusted-out locks. "Well, she *thinks* it's safe. I don't want to just— She was *scared*, Damon. Of us."

Of Smith.

The bitter voice in my head is enough to twist my gut. I hate it when we aren't getting along, but I can't deny this is all our pack alpha's fault. Before he walked in, Remi didn't seem scared at all. He really must have treated her like shit.

My teeth clench on an angry sound. "She wasn't afraid of us," I argue. "It was Smith. And he's not here. I say we try to go up."

He isn't sure, but I can tell he's on the ropes. Little does his grumpy ass know, I'm going up there either way.

"She might be upset," I point out, trying a different approach. "She's probably all alone, crying..."

Cassian grinds his jaw, glaring at the building. "The sign says no alphas after eight p.m."

You remember what I said about rules, though, right?

FOR THE LAST FIVE MINUTES, I've basically bounced in place. Doing my best not to let the charred honey wafting into this dingy hallway send me into a protective frenzy. There's also a sharper edge to the lavender note that I'm not sure I love.

What could *that* mean?

Fuck me, I should've Googled.

Cassian looms behind me, still silently raging. "How did you know which apartment was hers?" I mutter.

"I read the address on her file and memorized it."

Fucking Cass. Always pointing out *exactly how much* of a dumbass I am.

I reach up to knock, tossing him a pointed look. "Let me talk, okay? You're all... Beastly. And our girl is a runner."

He puts his glower back on, rolling his eyes. But I don't hear a word of argument, either.

It takes a couple of minutes for Remi's quiet voice to come through the door crack. "Wh-who's there?"

Fuck, she sounds so sad. Scared and miserable and just... small.

I find myself crowding closer, my eyes falling closed while I press my forehead against the door. "It's me, pretty girl," I murmur. My tone drops lower, into the softer one I didn't know I was capable of until this afternoon. "I couldn't stay away. Can I come in?"

I hear her hand hit the handle before she stops herself. "C-come in?"

Smiling to myself, I glance over at my packmate. "Yeah, I

brought you a surprise. He's kind of pissed off, though. And, uh, wet."

The door suddenly falls away, revealing a petite omega in a thin, floral robe. The light in the hall is dim, but it's easy to see she's been crying. Her face is swollen, and her eyes look red and squinty. A cascade of mussed black silk spills over one shoulder in a clump of curls.

Shit. Was she in bed?

Omega, you idiot, my brain jeers. *She was probably in her nest thingy.*

More shit to Google.

A wave of her sharp, burnt stress floods out of the tiny apartment. Cassian snaps forward instantly, the harsh lines of his face fading into concern.

He isn't the only one. Remi makes a distressed sound in her throat and tugs us both in by our shirts.

"You guys!" she scolds. "It's pouring out there! You're going to get sick!"

She fusses with both of us, delicate fingers plucking at my soggy T-shirt and Cassian's drenched hoodie. I can't move—I'm too busy obsessively watching the way her face furrows into a pout.

She huffs, exasperated, and throws her hands up. "Honestly, what were you two thinking?"

That you are so fucking cute, I could die.

"It's Cassian's fault," I tell her, literally pointing my finger. "He went all moody-broody Batman on your front stoop."

Remi's fists fall to her slight hips, and she sniffs, tossing her hair back while she looks up at Cass. "I take it that means you saw the sign on the front door?"

Is Cassian *cringing*? Oh my God, he is. Why don't we have a *camera*?

"Yeah," he admits. "I, ah, saw that."

She tosses a palm at me but keeps giving him a piece of her

mind. "Damon might not care about rules like those, but I expect better from you, Bear."

I guffaw, pretending to act offended. "How do you know I don't care?"

Remi sways to a narrow closet, pulling towels off a high shelf. It's hard to decide where to look—her knowing little scowl or the way the back of her robe rides up.

"It's pretty easy to tell," she informs me. "I looked up your penalty stats. But you also seem like the kind of guy who used to cut class and end up in detention."

And you look like the cute little teacher's pet who would meet me in the parking lot afterward.

I smirk, trying for a charming quirk of my eyebrow. "You looked me up?"

Her stern expression wobbles while she *thwack*s a pink towel into my chest. "I... looked up the team. And you were a bit unavoidable since your face is all over everything. I learned a lot, actually. I didn't even know there was a hockey team in Orlando."

"Yeah," Cassian grunts, already drying his hair. "We hear that a lot."

An awkward silence falls between us. I see the exact moment it occurs to Remi that she just let two alphas into her apartment. Her eyes dart around frantically, finally falling on her own clothes—or lack thereof.

"I didn't expect anyone," she whispers, pulling the flowered fabric tighter around her body. "I'm sorry I didn't clean up or cook anything..."

Cassian shrugs out of his sweatshirt and places it in Remi's kitchen sink—which is alarming, since we're still next to the front door. He ignores how tight the space is and how wet the button-down clinging to his chest must be and steps forward. Lifting his hand to touch under her chin, he raises her eyes to his.

"Hey. We never expect you to clean or cook for us, Rems. We came because we want to take care of you. Have *you* eaten anything since you left Forever Matched? I didn't see any delivery guys, and I don't see any dishes."

She swallows. The motion looks thick. "I—No. I was in my... nest."

Definitely should have Googled that shit.

All I want is to pull her into my arms and kiss that big-eyed, uncertain look right off her face. The way she's biting on her lower lip and trembling, is *killing* me. My purr, ineffectual as it may be from over here, kicks up automatically.

"Let's get you food, sweetness," I try, hoping for a smile when I send her one of my own. "Anything sound good?"

She chews her lip harder, her eyes darting behind me to the closed door, a question lurking in the golden blue. I roll my eyes and attempt a joke, "Are you worried about *Smith*? Don't be. We sent him to time out. Let's just focus on getting you settled, huh?"

The smallest flicker of amusement flutters over her face. But then it's gone, and she looks even sadder than before.

Fuuuuuuuck.

Of the three of us, it's no secret I'm the most charming. And persuasive. *Usually.*

But what if I can't do this?

What if none of us can?

Scared shitless by that *impossibility*, I drift closer, turning her face to mine. My eyes bounce between hers, absorbing the incredible color and her tear-spiked eyelashes.

I skim my fingers up to her cheek and tuck some of her hair behind her ear, whispering, "Why do you look so sad, pretty girl?"

She swallows again, the sound sticky and painful. "I..." With a big breath, she tries to force herself to stand up straight, but only halfway manages it. Her whole body shakes.

"How did all of this get so messed up?" she whispers. "If he's my mate, why is he so..." She shudders, no doubt remembering what a dick Smith can be. "I don't know if I can please him. I've been trying for months, but he hates me."

Fucking. Smith.

"It isn't your job to please him," I half-growl. "It's his job to please you."

"And he doesn't hate you, Rems," Cassian murmurs, quiet but seething.

Remi only shakes harder. "You didn't see how angry I made him. I'm sure he won't want me in your house. You guys should just say goodbye to me now."

Um, excuse me? *Goodbye*?

My face furrows. "We just got here, sweetness. And I had to talk your *bear* out of sleeping on the front porch, so good luck getting rid of either of us."

Cassian steps closer, his big body pressing into her side. "We can do whatever you want, butterfly," he vows. "Order food, go out. If you wanted to leave this place right now and never come back, we would take you home with us."

Remi's scent is the first giveaway. It turns dark again—somehow sweeter and more stressed than before. I realize it's confusion when I see the way her mouth opens and closes, grasping at words. Tears fill her wide eyes and spill down her face.

Fuck, the sight of her crying is like having a cracked rib. My other hand immediately flies up so I can cup her head between my palms and press my forehead into hers. "Shh, don't cry, pretty girl."

My purr gets louder. "Talk to me. Tell me what's wrong, and I'll fix it for you. Or we can make Cassian fix it. Either way, please let us take you home."

"Smith would never want me there," she warbles. "And he—he scares me. I'm telling you; he *hates* me."

He doesn't. I know he doesn't, because he spent over an hour arguing with Celine, begging her to pull Remi's application out of Forever Matched's circulation. When Steel-Balls refused, he nearly shattered the door slamming it on our way out.

But I don't think this is really about how much Smith wants Remi. I think it's more about how much she *doesn't* want Smith.

She's right; he scared her. It's understandable and totally valid, which only means there's no way for any of us to undo it.

Except for him. Getting his head out of his own ass.

Which, based on past performance? Means we probably don't have a shot.

chapter twenty

CASSIAN

"HOW COULD ANYONE EVER HATE YOU?" Damon asks, his smile flirtatious. "Impossible. You should definitely come home with us so we can prove how much we all want you there."

Her wobbly lips try to flick into a smile, but she doesn't quite manage it. God. That's somehow worse than no smile at all.

I know what she's doing. Remi is trying her best to play with him, even if she doesn't want to. Trying to *please* him, even if it means her own feelings have to go by the wayside.

He doesn't understand. And I'm really fucking glad—because

the way Remi's feeling right now? I wouldn't wish it on my worst enemy, let alone my best friend.

Her butterfly blue eyes blink up at me, full of pain and doubt. I remember this exact look on a smaller version of her face.

The Remi in my memory is younger and more frail—but every bit as scared and heartbroken. She used to sit at the top of the stairs on Sunday afternoons, watching other kids go with their foster families or visit relatives while she was left alone.

Smith would come get me. I spent all week waiting for those three-hour visits. And every time, as I got to the door and looked back at her, I suddenly didn't want to go anymore.

Seeing the same look on her face now is enough to rip my beating heart from my chest.

I feel sick. Shattered. And so insanely *protective*.

My eyes lock onto hers, pouring my emotion into her. The ferocity coiling inside of me gives my murmur a slight growly edge. "Remi, I couldn't say this before, but I can say it now; come home with me."

Her breath catches, hitching as her fill. "I want to," she tells me. "More than anything. But I can't Cassian. Not if—not if he's there."

Damon weaves his fingers into her hair and rubs his temple over hers to scent-mark her. She sniffs. A dainty little sound that would usually make me smile, but right now it's another arrow to the gut.

"What did he do, sweetness?" D asks, his voice smooth and coaxing.

I wish I had his finesse, but I just... don't. Especially not now, when I'm torn between wanting to knot Remi so I can purr for her from the inside and hunting my stepbrother down to murder him.

Remi looks up at Damon for a long second, biting her lip, until she suddenly drops her eyes to the floor. "It's nothing like that. He was just... demanding."

I can't keep a hold of my growl that time. It slips out, the sound low and menacing. "*Remi.*"

She trembles, and I instantly regret my temper. With an apologetic face, I reach over and smooth her hair over her shoulder. The wide, fearful set of her eyes abates slightly, but her voice is still breathless.

"I don't want you guys to fight over me," she murmurs. "It makes me feel... wrong. Like I'm a failure as an omega. I should be bringing you all together, and instead I—I—"

"You," Damon says, more firm than I've ever heard him, "Did *nothing*, sweetness. Nothing wrong at all."

Some shuffling sound in the hallway distracts Remi for a moment. She chews her lip, eyes widening. "You guys aren't supposed to be here. There's a rule. If someone reports me, I could be evicted."

Damon sends me a look—a cock of his brow that suggests getting her evicted is one surefire way to get to take her home with us. I glower back, and he shrugs, rolling his eyes in a look that says, *You come up with a better plan, then.*

I fold my hands around Remi's head. "We'll go if you need us to, butterfly. But we'll be back."

Damon nods, stepping up to cage her between our chests. "Do you want us to bring Smith next time?"

She tries to smile. "If you want to, sure!"

She always was a terrible liar.

chapter twenty-one

PIERSON PACK GROUP CHAT

CASSIAN

Smith, I stg, if you don't get your ass down here.

DAMON

Bear will eat you

SMITH

Who the fuck is Bear?

CASSIAN

Long story

Just fix this

DAMON

no barking, Big Hoss

SMITH

I'm not an idiot.

CASSIAN

since when?

Remi

YOU DUMB, *bitch-ass motherfucking cunt.*

My Omega has a lot of feelings about me sending the Pierson pack away.

Those were our mates! Are you insane?!

I've tried to reason with her so many times; explaining that the pack alpha wants nothing to do with us and, therefore, I can't exactly move into their pack house.

An hour passes, and she's still no closer to accepting my rationale. I'm huddled into the corner of my closet-nest, trying to figure out some way to get calm enough to sleep, when another round of thumps rounds at my door.

Oh, sugar.

Someone told on me?!

If this is our landlord, coming to beat my door down at this hour, I'm almost certain he's going to kick me out. My apartment complex has an omegas-only policy after eight p.m. I had to tell Damon and Cassian they couldn't stay. If someone caught me letting them in or kicking them out, I'm toast.

Scurrying to the front door, I take a deep breath before throwing it open, already formulating an apology. And a plea for mercy.

But every word dies on my tongue.

Because Smith Pierson is on my doorstep.

There's no time to parse how I feel. I have to hide him before someone sees him.

Reminding myself not to let him intimidate me in my own home, I clasp my robe closed over my nightgown and fling the door open, hissing, "How do you guys keep getting in here? It's omegas-only after eight! I told the guys they couldn't stay!"

Smith steps over my threshold, radiating tension while he snaps the door shut behind him.

The overwhelmingly perfect scent of fresh-brewed coffee instantly fills the tiny apartment. My breasts peak under my nightgown and goosebumps break over my skin. I feel slick slip down my thighs, unhindered by any sort of panties.

Smith's face is murderous. His blond brows dip low over angry eyes, and his chest heaves. His nostrils flare, scenting the fear and arousal I can't control.

His body reacts in kind, the thick aroma of coffee pressing around me. He shifts from one foot to the other, and I notice a wide bulge running down the inseam of his trousers.

I drop my eyes to the floor, not wanting to let myself picture what's under his pants. My fingers tighten around the thin fabric hiding my half-naked state as I whisper, "What are you doing here?"

For a silent second, he sweeps his gaze around my tiny apartment. When he finishes his assessment, he straightens to his full six-foot-something and scowls at me. "You can't live here."

The force of his will pummels me. And I hate it.

Normally, I love being an omega. Even when it's hard, my instincts are the very deepest part of me. Now, though, the way he makes me feel is almost enough for me to question why I can't be stronger.

It takes a beat for me to realize this is *his* problem, though, *not* mine. There's nothing wrong with me or my Omega. He scared us. He's not supposed to be here. Now, he's throwing around directives like I should be grateful to follow them.

And that Omega voice inside of me? She is not impressed.

Before he answers, I raise my chin. "You should go," I decide. "I've had a really long day, and I need to get in my nest, now."

Smith's scent deepens, but so does his frown. "Didn't you hear me? It's not safe here," he insists. "Those cracks in the walls? They're vertical—indicative of structural damage. I wouldn't be surprised to find the foundation is compromised. Or non-existent."

My brain can't even process what he's saying. All I know is that I need him to get out of here before I perfume for real and we have a serious problem. "I'll take that under advisement," I return, as polite as can be. "Thank you for your concern."

When I move to open the door, Smith steps smoothly in front of me. "Listen, petal" he intones, leaning down to catch my eye. "You're not listening to me."

I step back and loose a huffing noise I would usually never dare to make. But my Omega is so pissed at this alpha, neither of us can really care much about angering him at the moment.

"*Petal?*"

He flicks a dismissive look at my flower robe before correcting himself. "Fine. You aren't listening, *Miss Skyes*."

"No, I'm not," I return calmly, crossing my arms. "You have no right to show up here and make demands. I don't even know you, other than the fact that you're horribly rude and spoiled and somehow feel entitled to be in my space after I've asked you to leave."

Smith's jaw ticks. "We can discuss my personal shortcomings at a later date. For now, I need you to tell me what it would take to convince you to come with me."

I wish I had the nerve to roll my eyes. Instead, I smile sweetly. "A miracle."

If I didn't know better, I'd say he might be enjoying himself. On my next breath, the thick, rich aroma of coffee is so strong and smooth that I almost feel dizzy.

After staring me down for several moments, he sighs, shoving his hands into his pockets. "Everyone has a price."

My mouth actually falls open. This alpha—who pays me peanuts at work and uses his superiority as an excuse to berate me constantly—is now trying to bribe me to get his way? And for what? So I can be homeless?

I look around the room as if there's something I might be missing. "In case this escaped your grasp," I tell him, "I don't exactly have a lot of options, here. I can stay in my apartment, or I can go sleep at my friend's house. She's about to have a heat, so I doubt that her four alphas would—"

He growls, "*Not* an option."

I resist the unladylike urge to snort at him. "Excuse me? They're happily bonded! I go over there all the time."

Smith takes two slow steps forward, each rippling with deadly intent. "Not. Anymore."

His alpha energy lodges a lump in my throat. My stomach squirms, trying to tell me to run and hide. Or whine and present.

chapter twenty-two

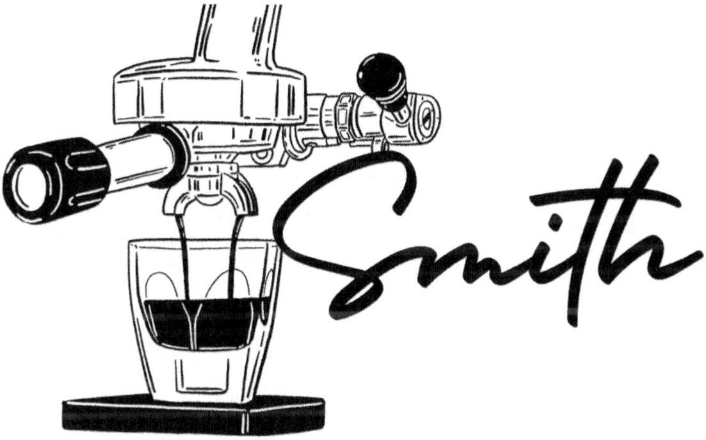

REMI SKYES' apartment building slants to the left.

There are several reasons why I find that disturbing, both as a consumer and a property developer.

But, mostly, I'm just disturbed by myself.

For one, I am an irredeemable asshole for the way I've acted. I already know that. I knew it as it was happening. I've even considered slipping extra cash into the tip jar on several occasions, knowing she would get the majority of it if I did.

Which is also appalling.

Money? That was my solution? Throw some cash at the person I treated like trash?

Growing up, Cassian and I never had money. Our parents were lower middle class. We were lucky to have *any* cash to put into a tip jar. Let alone hundreds of dollars of hush money.

When I look back on why I've done what I have to get to this point, it all makes sense. It was logical, methodical.

Necessary? I told myself it was, at the time.

I've done what I was raised to do—be a good alpha. Provide, protect, secure our future, change it for the better. I didn't realize *it* was changing *me*. I never expected to look up one day and realize I don't recognize myself anymore.

For example, did I seriously park outside an omega's apartment building for three hours?

Too proud to go ring her doorbell?

Too obsessed to leave?

I know the guys were here earlier. Cassian sent me a bare-bones text telling me they had tried to order her dinner, but she asked them to leave because of her building's rules. The end of the conversation was succinct, but the words weighed heavy on my mind.

You have to fix this for the pack, or there won't be one anymore.

I don't even know that I blame him. The hours of reflection have given me plenty of time to remember my teenaged brother, clearly head-over-heels for the girl who used to meet him in the mornings to read with him. He barely described her at all—hell, he barely spoke in sentences, back then. But, often, his stories about her were the only glimpse of the real Cassian that I got to see, week in and week out.

I remember the relief and gratitude I felt whenever I listened to him talk about her—this angel who somehow made his time in that shitty group home bearable.

And now I've hurt her. Scared her.

So. Many. Times.

I keep seeing the look on Remi's face when she recognized me. The utter devastation and… disappointment.

Fucking hell. That might be the worst part, after her fear. She thought today would be the day she met her soulmates, and I ruined it for her.

I'm not the pack alpha she wants or needs. She saw me at my worst. And now she probably can't trust me.

I failed her.

I failed my pack.

I still am. Because this omega is no closer to coming home with us now than she was when I arrived. And what's worse? She actually *needs* to. This place is a death trap.

The faint scent of mildew lingers, which means the air quality in here is poor. There are cracks in the plaster—vertical ones. Unacceptable. And I'm about 99 percent sure that if I opened a wall, I'd find lead pipes.

It isn't safe here.

It's built so poorly, I'm shocked it hasn't just fallen over.

The thought has me half-crazed while I stare her down. I'm so incensed, I can't even remember what we're arguing about from one second to the next.

Oh, right. She wants to sleep in a house full of other alphas. *Four* of them.

Dear *God*.

Is this what a heart attack feels like? Should I be calling an ambulance before I fucking *die* from whatever this ache in my chest is?

Control, I remind myself. *Maintain control.*

It's hard. Especially given the state of this tiny room.

She has the ceiling cracks, too. And a sloping pocket where her roof is distended, either from past or present water damage. I can't smell the mildew as strongly in here, but that's likely just because *she's* currently all I can sense.

Delicious honeyed cake batter soaks into my lungs with every breath. My cock jerks, brushing the fist in my left pocket. I exhale slowly, willing myself not to chase the throb pounding down my length and into my knot.

I know the basics of scent-sensitivity, but I never expected this *instantaneous need*. I feel like my heart might stop if I try to turn and walk away right now.

Remi trembles, sensing the aggressive pheromones I'm pumping into the small space. When a shiver skips down her spine, she straightens, thrusting her chest out and lifting her chin to expose her throat.

God, that graceful arc will look beautiful with my bite.

The thought startles me. I hate not being in control and, right now, I can't even see my own reins anymore. How am I supposed to pull back from this tug in my middle? It's yanking me toward her, tauter and tauter with every scrape of sweet-soaked breath.

She grasps her robe tighter. "P-please don't look at me like that."

Like what?

When I cock my head at her and raise my eyebrows, she blows out a hard breath. She has the softest voice, even when it takes on sharp edges. "What you're saying—all of these demands—aren't rational. You have no control over me, and you want to force me out of my own apartment? I know this isn't *much*, but I've done the best I can with what I have!"

I can see that's true. The fake flowers in empty jars. Her light pink paint. Old, well-worn books arranged in artful stacks, and pretty, hand-decorated picture frames.

She has nothing, but she's still a lady. Standing before me, this omega is the epitome of grace.

What if she couldn't go to school or get a higher-paying job because she didn't have any guardians or any resources? What if she needed us? Me. And I wasn't there?

Well, I'm here now.

I may not have much to offer in the relationship department, but Pierson Properties and our personal investments are thriving. As far as money goes, I can give her *everything*. All the things I never had. All the stuff I couldn't give the guys when we were young.

We have more than enough, now. And I can spoil this omega to the point of excess if she'll let me.

I can already tell she enjoys fine clothing as much as I do. The dress she had on today wasn't designer, but it was a nice fabric, and she clearly took good care of it. In fact, all her things appear perfectly clean and well-preserved.

Is she so careful with her things because she's a careful person? Or is she over-protective of her possessions because she's not used to having much?

It could be both, the way it is for me.

The longer silence swells between us, the more uncertain she seems. Eventually, her nature gives in to mine, lowering her lashes over those blue-gold eyes in a demur gesture of submission that makes my blood roar.

God. This is so much *more* than I imagined it would be.

An omega was the final thing on my list for the pack. We have our successful careers, our pack house. A central bond is the only thing left for me to get for the guys.

But this isn't some checked box on a list.

This is... *her*.

Our mate.

I feel it in a way I've never felt anything else.

And it's terrifying.

I'm not prepared. I don't know how to take care of her or what she'll need. I don't even know how to tell her how I feel. Or *what* I feel, for that matter.

I have absolutely no idea what to do. But I know I absolutely cannot mess this up.

"Remi," I start, but then she shifts from one foot to the other, and I see through the door looming behind her, into what appears to be a bedroom. My eyes snag on the opposite corner, and I freeze, every nerve in my body prickling.

"*What* is *that*?"

Her head swivels, face falling when she discovers that I'm staring into her closet.

Into the small nest—*on the floor of her closet.*

"Answer me," I warn, barely holding back a bark. "Is that what I think it is? Is that your nest?"

She tugs her robe closed tighter, her scent darkening with shame. "I—It's—It's dark and quiet in there," she squeaks. "These units don't have built-in nests, so it was either the closet or the bath—"

I hold up my hands, unable to even hear her suggest that she could ever use a fucking *bathtub* as her safe space.

Jesus Christ. I'm the worst alpha ever. My omega has been nesting in a closet half the size of a refrigerator.

"*That's* where you've had your heats?" I shout, a vein pulsing in my neck. "Alone? In a closet? For a week?"

Remi shivers at my rising voice. Instinct snaps her into "calm the alpha mode," and she tries for a sunny tone. "It's really not that bad," she rushes. "My heats only last five days, and I only sleep in there a few nights a—"

She *sleeps* in her *closet*?

Absolutely fucking not.

Absolutely. Fucking. Not.

"*Enough,*" I snap out. Aggression and dominance pour unwavering command into every word. "*Pack a bag, petal. You're coming with me.*"

chapter twenty-three

DAMON

I MIGHT NOT BE able to read, but I can count.

And everything Remi has fits into eight boxes.

They're big and sturdy, but still.

Leave it to Smith to essentially take an omega prisoner while also providing the best moving boxes money can buy.

When he told us Remi had "agreed" to move in with us after his visit last night, he left out the whole "against her will" part. When Cass texted her to ask her for a grocery list and found out she had basically been barked into submission, he gut-punched

Smith so hard that I'm surprised our alpha didn't barf up his own diaphragm.

Another epic shouting match ensued. That ended pretty quickly when Smith pointed out that his approach had, in fact, *worked*. And we had a lot more important things to do than argue if we wanted to get the house ready for Remi.

Which didn't go so great.

But we *tried*.

And when my alarm went off at quarter-to-the-ass-crack-of-dawn? I bounced my happy ass out of bed and zoomed right out the door.

After the way last night went, Cassian insisted on being there to pick Remi up. Since we have morning skate at nine, that meant a hell of a wake-up call for all of us.

You'd never know it from looking at Remi, though. She's buried any hint that all of this isn't peachy-keen by the time we pull up to the curb outside her place.

She looks cute as hell, decked out in another sundress with those same silver sandals. When I jump out first, bounding over to her, I can't resist taking her hand and twirling her, watching the way the skirt flutters around her legs.

My pretty girl.

I'm being a flirt, but when she laughs, the quiet lilt of it touches a secret place in the deepest part of me. The feeling echoes around in there, scraping all the air out of my lungs. Leaving me with the overwhelming feeling of complete awe.

"Damon?" Her cool fingers trace over my fading bruise and carefully touch my cheek. "Are you okay?"

I nod. I want to speak, but my tongue tangles in the back of my mouth.

Oh fuck. I literally can't even talk.

You've got to be *kidding me*.

Game is the only advantage I have over these knot-heads. If I can't charm her, what will she want with me?

While I choke on my own tongue, Cassian stomps over and snaps Remi right into his arms.

A *bear* hug, I guess you'd call it.

No, I won't ever let him live that down.

"Rems," he whispers, folding our omega up into his wide chest. "You okay? You sure you want to do this?"

I want to elbow him in the back and tell him not to blow this, but Remi smiles into his shoulder, nestling her cheek there. "I'm sure about you," she says, flashing her blue, blue eyes up to mine, pinning the breath in my lungs when she includes me. "Both of you."

There's no prayer of me keeping the huge grin off my face. I crowd in, dropping my forehead down to hers. "Me, too, pretty girl?"

Her little smile takes on a mischievous gleam. Holy fuck, *this girl.*

"You, too, *Trouble.*"

Is that my new nickname?

Done.

Stamp it, ship it. I am now officially Trouble. I'll have them announce it in this weekend's game.

And, actually? It works. When I fly down the ice? "Here comes Trouble."

This omega is brilliant.

Cassian looks marginally better when he sets Remi back down. "You need me to carry anything down the stairs?"

She shakes her head. "The furniture isn't mine. It stays in the apartment. I'll just go up and double-check that I didn't forget something, grab my purse, and we can go."

I offer to walk her up, doing my best to deflect from the ready-to-rip-each-other's-arms-off vibe between Smith and Cass. They're still scowling at each other when I open the building's front door, shooting them both a frantic *get your shit straight* look over her curly head as she floats past.

There's another edge to her scent today. Thankfully, I spent most of the night Googling. So, now, I know that the bit of slice edging her sweetness either means she's in *need*, or she's stressed.

And, unless she has a cardboard fetish...

This must all be very stressful for her. She's lived here for years. Days ago, she didn't even know we existed. There must have been a better way for Bulldozer Smith to go about this.

It's too late for that now, but her stress has my Alpha nudging me harder and harder with every step up the stairs.

Or maybe that's the sight of her hips swaying. Difficult to say.

Outside her door, she pats my arm softly and offers her small smile. "I'll be right out."

I want to go with her, but she must already feel suffocated enough by all of us. Deciding to leave it, I cast her my easiest smile as I agree, "Okay, sweetness."

Minutes pass. My foot starts to bounce. Then my fingers start tapping against my thigh.

Is she okay? Should I go in?

When it's been more than five minutes, I tap on the door. "Remi? You ready, pretty girl?"

There's some scuffling behind the door and then an ear-splitting whine cracks the air.

I've been a pro-athlete for most of my adulthood. But when I tell you I have *never* moved so fast in my *life*.

In a blur, I race into the tiny, empty apartment.

It looks so different than it did yesterday. Without Remi's special touch, I see what Smith is bitching about. This place is *rough*.

And I grew up in a trailer that didn't even have a toilet. So.

Remi is in her tiny kitchen. She leans against the cracked countertop, her eyes closed, and both arms wrapped over her body.

It looks like she's in *pain*. I lunge in her direction, sucking in a gasp that stops me dead in my tracks.

Oh holy *shit*.

This room smells like sweet-soaked *sex*.

Honey-drenched, horny *heaven*.

Fuuuuuuck. I want to drop to my knees. Bury my face between her thighs and stay under her twirly skirt for hours.

The razor-edge of her sweetness cuts right through my control, carving out any tiny bit of reason I may have had. I groan, gripping my rock-hard cock through my sweats in an attempt to strangle it into submission.

Remi jumps, her eyes big and round as they fly to mine. The pretty blues flutter, unfocused. "Alph—*Damon*. I don't feel so well. I—I think—"

She cuts herself off, wincing in pain. Her hand floats up to cover her lower abdomen as if she has a cramp there.

Fuck.

Google mentioned that, too.

Omegas are in pain when they need relief from an alpha and they don't get it. It usually happens during heats, but some of the articles mentioned that heat spikes happen more often in scent-sensitive packs. Especially ones that aren't bonded.

Is that what this is? What do I do?

You heard her. She almost called me Alpha. Which means it's my job to take care of her when she feels like this.

Somehow.

I could take her down to the guys? But then someone else might scent her, and this incredible perfume will be all over the building. Not to mention, I doubt she wants Smith around her when she's feeling like this. Things are still so fucked up between them.

Pulling my phone out, I send a quick text to tell them we're taking a minute, then I carefully move closer to Remi. She whimpers again, hurtling into my arms the second I open them.

Thick sweetness wafts into the air while I cuddle her, turning to put her body between mine and the countertop. My knot throbs, demanding I press closer and gently rub my hardness against her hip. It's just a little (well, big) tease, but she moans like I've just stroked over her clit.

Mmm. Fuck, but she's so sweet when she perfumes. I want to lick her slick up right fucking now. In this dingy kitchen. Next to the world's oldest dishwasher.

Remi trembles against me, shivering while her lips fall slack and her hands clutch at my T-shirt. I run my hardness over that sweet spot between her hip and her pussy again. Her knees buckle.

Before she can fall, I bend my leg to shove it between her soft little thighs. When my flexed quad muscles meet her core, she gasps.

Her file said she'd done some heats in clinics, which means she can't be a virgin. But this feels like the sort of reaction someone who has never been properly touched might have.

Either way, I'm here for it. She can be as turned on as she damn well wants. You won't hear one single complaint from me.

I stroke her face, brushing all of her hair back so I can kiss her cheeks and her eyelids. "You like the way that feels, pretty girl? Mm. God. I wish I could give you my knot right now."

A breath quivers out of her, ghosting over my cheek. "I—I want you to."

Only... she doesn't. There's fear in her eyes, along with embarrassment. She isn't ready for me to knot her at all. And, why would she be? We barely know each other.

I know she's *mine*. Ours. But the rest of it?

We need time. I don't want this to be like every other woman I've charmed, burning fast and furious and based entirely on one thing. I want everything with Remi to be different. Right.

The person I've been won't be enough. She deserves someone selfless and smart and just... better.

And I'm going to be that guy.

No matter how delicious she smells.

Holy fucking—

Her scent is so thick in the air, I can *almost taste* her. It's torture, until I realize that there's no reason that I can't get her off. Just because I'm not going to let things spin out of control, doesn't mean she can't take me for a test drive.

In fact, the only thing stopping me from ripping those wet panties right off her cute little ass is—

Nothing.

Nothing is stopping me.

"Can't knot you here," I mumble, juggling her as I shift to make room to slide my hands under her skirt. "But there are other things I can do." *Stuff that wouldn't make it impossible for us to leave after. Or get any more perfume in this place.*

Remi makes a small, pained sound. From the way her pupils blow, I wonder if she's even the one driving right now. I might be dealing with her Omega, which would mean I'm not facing my brilliant, logical pretty girl at the moment. Her Omega will only understand a yes or a no.

I hold her gaze so she can see the way mine burns. "I *never* want another alpha to scent you while I'm making you come. Unless it's Smith or Cassian. I *guess* they can watch."

Oh, my sweetness loves that idea. Her pupils expand along with the cloud of her perfume. She whines again, her hips softly bucking toward mine. "Yes, Alpha."

Fuck. Me.

I might come in my pants.

My chest rumbles, molars grinding as she nestles her face into my throat and starts kissing me. Licking, nipping, and *moaning* into my neck. Fuck, it's so hot. My hands skim up the outside of her thighs and dig into her hips, feeling the ruffled edges of her panties.

"What's gotten into you, pretty girl?" I murmur, giving in to the urge to scrape my teeth over her shoulder. "You feeling needy today?"

"I—I'm sorry," she starts. "I don't know what's wrong with me."

Tender protectiveness washes through me. I drop my temple to hers, scent-marking her. "There's nothing wrong with you, baby. I like you exactly like this. And when you were polished and pretty yesterday. And last night, when you were all rumpled in that cute-as-fuck nightgown. I'll take option D, all of the above."

She whimpers, and the sound goes straight through my cock, forcing a burst of pre-cum. Her body responds to my thicker scent, perfuming furiously.

For a second, I almost lose my grip. The urge to *rut* pounds at my pulse points. I swallow it down, exhaling as calmly as I can. My voice still sounds like gravel when I turn my face into hers. "Tell me what this cunt needs from me."

Just when I think I won't make it—*my instincts are too strong, her perfume is too good*—she somehow says the perfect thing.

"I hate"—she pants, squirming against my leg—"that word."

A laugh sloughs out of me. *Cunt?* She's rubbing herself all over my leg, but she objects to me saying *cunt*?

Oh my GOD. Could she be any more *adorable*?

Smiling, I nuzzle another mark against her throat. "Sorry, sweetness." My hands find the small of her back, massaging as I amend my request to exclude the word she hates. "Tell me what you need."

She whines again, the sound so urgent, it breaks my brain. And immediately banishes any sort of amusement.

"Alpha—" she squeaks. "It *hurts*."

It has to be a heat spike. She isn't warm enough to be in a real heat, but she's clearly in pain. The only way to give her relief is easing.

Which is a polite way of saying she needs an alpha to make her pretty little pussy feel good.

Put me in, coach.

I only hesitate because I honest-to-God cannot decide where to start. It feels like waking up on Christmas morning to a mountain of presents and feeling the giddy overwhelm of not knowing which one to open first.

Do I untie these bows holding her sundress up? Or tease her through those soaked panties? Should I take my cock out or make her beg to see it?

I won't fuck her here—as much as I'm dying to. For one, I want to take this slow. And the guys would likely murder me when we finally get back downstairs.

But, more importantly, omegas in spikes aren't in their right minds. I would never assume she's down to fuck when I haven't *asked* her. And, right now, she can't really answer.

So sign me up for a throbbing knot, I guess. Totally worth it.

When she senses my pause, Remi's scent singes slightly. Her voice shakes. "Alpha, do you not—"

Fuck. That.

I press my lips right over hers, kissing her long enough to halt any sentiment that would end with me not wanting her.

And maybe a tiny bit longer, just to get the smallest taste of her honeyed sweetness.

But, God, that one little drop is like an electric charge to my cock.

I grunt, the sound vibrating between our lips. She breaks off with a gasp, eyes big and round, the blue down to a thin band.

Is she blushing? Oh, I'm going to corrupt this sweet girl. And she's going to love it.

chapter twenty-four

WHERE AM I?

Why am I here?

And why is the alpha not naked?

I've forgotten just about everything. But as the gorgeous, muscle-bound alpha in front of me presses closer and reaches under my skirt, I don't care.

He bends his neck, putting his face level with mine. I search it, trying to think. Failing, but feeling safe anyway.

I know him. He's here for me. He's... *mine*.

When I rub my cheek over his, his blue eyes snap with electric heat. The rest of his snarling expression softens. "God," he rumbles. "You are the sweetest fucking thing, pretty girl. I want to make you feel good."

His thumb skirts along the edge of my panties, brushing lightly, just a smidgen away from the bundle of nerves throbbing for his attention. I whine and squirm, trying to get him to touch me properly.

The alpha's chuckle is a dark, sensual sound. "Needy girl. I love it. Want me to pet this pretty pussy, sweetness?"

My hair bounces around my shoulders while I nod, frantic. "Please, Alpha. I'll be good, I promise."

He grins, and it's the single most beautiful face I've ever seen. "Damn, baby, Smith is going to *eat you*," he says, laughing low.

Who?

What?

Do I even care?

Before I can figure out what he means, his smile takes on a feral edge. "You think you're a good girl? I'm going to show you just how naughty you are, baby. By the time we fuck, you'll be begging for my cum and my knot. And I'll always give you everything you ask for."

There must be something seriously wrong with me—because his cum and his knot sound like nirvana right now. I picture him pumping me full and knotting me deep, keeping everything he gave me right where he left it. Another high-pitched keen flies out of me.

He curses roughly. His thumb breeches the edge of my underwear, dipping into the squelching wetness at my opening. "Fuck *me*, Remi."

He strokes through the slickness, groaning. The sound pierces me right where the unbearable pressure builds. I *need* him. His cock and his knot. I can feel both, and he isn't giving them to me.

When my next whine sounds distressed, he hums. "Shhh, pretty girl. I've got you."

His teeth clamp at the base of my throat at the same second he glides his thumb up to my swollen bud. It's so wet, he has to press down to get any sort of friction. When he does, sensation pours through me, tightening the coil of tension pulling taut between my hips.

The tease of his bite and the rough circles of his thumb have me chasing his touch, pumping against him. He snarls under his breath, scraping his canines over my throat as he releases me. "That's my dirty girl," he coaxes.

He slips his touch off my pulsing clit, dipping back to tease me inside. I buck harder, crying out for his knot. The emptiness has my body clenching around nothing, and he feels it.

A roar rips out of his chest. He hitches me up higher, using the weight of his body to hold me half-propped on the countertop. His other hand fumbles with his sweats.

"I'm sorry, baby," he pants. "If I don't touch my knot right now, it's gonna explode."

My eager moan is enough to encourage him. I try to look down and see the way he's gripping himself, but my bunched-up skirt and our torsos block my view.

He hooks both arms under my thighs and reaches toward our centers. One hand grabs the hot, thick length brushing my thigh while the other returns to my dripping pussy. He strokes over both of us at the same time, and we both pant.

"That's it," he roughs out, hoarse. "Ride my hand, sweetness."

My body obeys, rolling into his touch until I feel the edges of my vision fade out. A rush of sensation floods my body, pulsing from my pussy as it bears down on his fingers. Damon feels me coming and growls, twisting his wrist to knead his knot.

Before I've slid down from euphoria, he has my panties fisted at the crotch. With one sharp snap, he rips them right off my body and uses them to catch his own release, flattening me into the cabinets while he jets thick white ropes into the frilly blue thong.

Pleasure softens the fierce lines of his expression, turning him from the determined alpha back into Damon.

My Damon.

While my consciousness returns, I feel a swoop of fear. Did I just humiliate myself by letting him do that? My Omega seems thoroughly convinced that this alpha is hers... but is *Damon* mine?

Probably not.

He's a famous pro-athlete, and we only just met. There's no way he feels that kind of loyalty to me, yet. I'm supposed to be proving myself worthwhile, and instead, I'm having omega meltdowns and begging him to get me off?

I'm surprised he hasn't already bolted.

Though, as he sweetly adjusts the skirt of my dress and brushes my hair back, it doesn't seem like he's desperate to escape. He doesn't seem to be looking for the right moment to leave me or tell me I've failed some sort of test.

Maybe I need to give our connection more credit. They *all* came to get me today. That has to be a good sign, right?

I'll just have to work harder at pleasing them. Keep my focus. Make note of everything they like and don't like, individually.

Damon clearly likes the idea of corrupting me.

Cassian will probably have his own set of needs.

And Smith—

Smith will never love me or want me, but surely I can prove myself useful to him in other ways. I'll be able to impress him eventually, even if it's just with the cleanest house or the best meals he's ever seen.

I can do this. I can make them want to keep me.

Damon waits for my body to stop trembling before he gently places me on my feet and pulls his sweats back up. I'm disappointed not to get a better look at him, and his lopsided grin tells me he knows it.

My ruined panties wind up in one of his pockets. He whips his phone out of the other one and frowns at it for a long second before finally breaking into another smirk.

"Sweetness, I think we might be in trouble."

My stomach drops, reality sinking in. I've just basically had sex. With Damon. With the door open...

Did anyone hear? Were we loud? I was so out of my mind I didn't even—

Damon cuts off my anxious spiral by holding his phone up, displaying about twelve unread text messages from Smith and Cassian. Or, as his phone says, "Big Hoss" and "Beastly."

It makes no sense. I fret while we both slip out of the apartment.

Why would Smith blow up his phone? How would he know what we were doing? It's not like he's—

Here.

Standing in the hallway, arms crossed, glaring furiously. And, somehow, the flagrant bulge at the front of his graphite suit pants doesn't diminish his intimidation. It only adds to the effect.

The pack alpha holds out his hand. A demand, not a request. "We're leaving."

chapter
twenty-five

PIERSON PACK GROUP TEXT

DAMON

Remi's upset.

Be down in 10 minutes.

CASSIAN

Is she ok?

Does she need me?

Goddamn it, Damon.

SMITH

Damon, answer us.

I'm coming up there.

DAMON

Sorry. Couldn't really talk. Didn't have a free hand.

CASSIAN

Are you kidding me?

SMITH

Damon, is there something you need to tell us?

DAMON

Other than me making your good girl come all over my fingers?

No, not really.

Remi

IT'S hard for me to be too anxious with Damon radiating excitement behind us.

He's all too happy to follow behind, making small talk like nothing just happened. When we step up to their loaded-down truck, Cassian gives him a withering look and silently stuffs a set of keys into Damon's hand before turning to lift me into the back of the cab and scoot in after me.

Unbothered, Damon flashes his mischievous grin while he gets in the driver's seat. "This is Cass's truck; and he never lets anyone else drive it, so he must really be dying to sit with you, pretty girl."

The pack leader mutters something while he gets into the passenger seat and slams his door. He clearly isn't in a joking mood. His heavy brows fold over his dark eyes as he swivels in his seat, reaching into the back to buckle me in. I watch in disbelief while he adjusts the straps and even tugs on them to make sure they're secure.

As soon as he faces forward, Damon throws the truck into gear, and we roll away from the curb. Cassian seems to relax when he sees that his packmate doesn't plan to run his pick-up off the road. He turns, facing me with his whole body and running his eyes over me.

Oh no. Did Cassian somehow find out what Damon and I just did? It's bad enough that Smith knows but now Cass, too?

Will he be mad? Will he want me to leave? Will Damon stop him?

Cassian feels me shrink down and grunts, curling one arm behind my head and reaching his free hand over to tuck a strand of hair behind my ear. He shoots Damon an annoyed look. But when he turns his face from his packmate to me, his expression instantly morphs into soft concern.

"You okay?" he asks. "He behaved?"

My heart melts. Big, grumbly bear. Always protecting me first and foremost.

I nod, my voice shaking. "Yes. He was..." I remember the way he held himself in check while still saying the filthiest, sexiest things I'd ever heard, "perfect."

One of Cass's dark brows lifts. "Perfect?" he repeats. "Is that a challenge, butterfly?"

He's...

Flirting. With me? Him?! *Cassian?*

My lips fall open. "Y-you're not mad?"

The corner of his mouth quirks up. "Damn right, I'm mad. He got to you first. I'm going to have to punch him later."

Cassian's version of flirting is so different from Damon's. It's dry. Almost matter-of-fact. Which somehow makes it even hotter.

He drops his forehead to mine, nuzzling gently, holding my gaze while he covers Damon's scent-mark with his own. Inhaling, he makes a low growling sound in his throat.

Heat flashes in his green gaze. He grinds his teeth together before he tries to distract both of us. "Did you eat breakfast?"

Smith cuts in. "I'll get her fed once we're home. You two have practice in an hour and a half."

I probably shouldn't like the way they clearly discuss me among themselves—otherwise, how would Cassian have known what happened upstairs?—but it feels good, somehow. Like they must really, truly care. Plus, I like being something they have in common.

Cassian frowns at his stepbrother but presses in closer, essentially letting me snuggle into his body without having to unbuckle my seatbelt. When I rest my face against the soft part of his shoulder, he gently winds his fingers into my hair, pausing to touch the embarrassing butterfly clip that I wore just for him.

His touch is reassuring. Damon has a more direct approach.

"You'll have to excuse Smith, sweetness," he says, still upbeat. "He took the morning off to come here and that's, like, an earth-shattering event for him. He'll probably have a bunch of calls and stuff to catch up on this afternoon. Plus, he's just an asshole in general. But you know that."

Well. Yeah.

But I can't really agree, can I?

I'm saved when Smith's phone buzzes in his pocket, proving Damon's point. The pack alpha rolls his eyes while he answers, but Damon catches my gaze in the rearview mirror and winks, waving his hand at their leader as if to say, *You see what I put up with?*

Everyone stays quiet while Smith goes through his work call. I get the feeling that silence might be normal for Cassian; but the slumped set of Damon's shoulders and the slight edge to his scent make me think he's struggling.

While Smith argues with someone about a zoning restriction, Damon steers us out of the city center, heading toward a very familiar residential area. Through the car's enormous moonroof, the copse of ancient oak trees and Spanish moss overhead catch afternoon sunbeams, forming kaleidoscopes of leaves and light. Wind whispers through the canopy, overlapping with cheerful bird chirps and the sound of our tires bouncing over brick roads.

The historic neighborhood is one of the most sought-after in Central Florida. The combination of posh and homey make it perfect for well-to-do packs who also want a quiet hollow to raise a family.

Under ordinary circumstances, I'd be giddy. This is my dream neighborhood—and when we turn off one of the main streets, onto a quiet loop, I realize we're only a few minutes away from Meg's pack mansion.

From here, I could safely walk to her house. She could come to mine.

Well, not *mine*.

Theirs.

But, still.

I *should* be excited. Instead, I feel the buzz of panic, humming under my skin.

A pack like this? In a *place* like this? With an alpha who already thinks I'm incompetent? My margin for error just went from minuscule to nonexistent.

You practiced for this, I tell myself, bracing as Damon flicks his blinker on and begins to turn off the side street. *Just remember your graces*.

Because I may not have had those when Cassian knew me, before, but I do now. I made sure I would never disappoint any pack that might take me home, and it's time to put my money where my mouth is.

The SUV rocks slightly as we exit the brick road and roll up the base of a long, curved driveway. From my vantage point behind the driver's seat, I see that the piece of property must be quite large. There's a big open lawn, shaded by towering oaks. The outline of the house sits way back from the road, mostly obscured by the twisty, low-hanging tree limbs.

Whoever is responsible for their landscaping needs... help. The lawn is shaggy, longer in some places than others, and full of dandelion weeds. There are some dead palm fronds off to the side, piled haphazardly next to the ten-foot-tall hedge wall that seems to surround the entire lawn.

Even with those hints of disrepair, the property feels stately. With a little polish, it could be beautiful.

We roll up the drive slowly, prolonging the moment when we finally pass the cluster of trees and the house emerges.

Oh. My. Lord.

It's—*big.*

And it's a *mess.*

The structure itself is as charming and gorgeous as I ever could have dreamed. A large French-style farmhouse. With its worn stone facade, wooden shutters, and neat rows of windows, it looks like someone plucked it right out of the *Provence* countryside and dropped it on the Pierson pack's lawn.

Aside from the fact that it's falling apart.

Half of the shutters hang at awkward angles, highlighting the fact that many of their mates are simply missing altogether. The windows are covered in sawdust and pollen, a yellow film coating the crystal glass. The stone front steps and front door landing are scuffed. And there are six different patches of paint and whitewash splashed around the exterior—presumably because no one ever got around to actually choosing from the options.

I open my mouth to ask what on earth happened here, but, thankfully, I remember my manners at the last minute.

"It's lovely," I murmur. "So much... character."

Damon snorts. "Is that code for 'needs a ton of pain-in-the-ass work,' pretty girl? Because, in that case, Cassian and Smith have a lot of *character*, too."

Cassian snorts. "And you're so low maintenance?"

Even when he frowns, Damon is too beautiful. The way his lips pout just isn't even fair. "I am!" he protests.

Cassian makes a rough sound that sends tingles through my belly. When he notices me squirm, he raises one eyebrow. "You think I'm exaggerating?" he says, glancing at Damon. "Just wait until you see his bathroom."

I MUST HAVE SUBCONSCIOUSLY convinced myself that the inside of the house would be better than the outside.

Because once I'm in? I'm appalled.

Do these fine, successful men really live like this? Construction dust all over the floors, scratched hardwoods, furniture under tarps, and paint cans that look like they haven't been touched in months.

I note holes in the walls where sconces were ripped out but never replaced; a stack of broken shutters from the outside in the corner of the dining room; and one whole room that's just furniture no one ever moved all the way in.

There's also a roach on the floor.

I'm pleasantly surprised to find that it's dead.

So at least someone planned pest control, at the very least.

But the rest of this place? It's a runaway steam engine with no brakes. Who started all of these projects? And why didn't anyone finish anything?

As he watches me delicately step over the roach carcass on the threshold, Smith has the grace to look mildly chagrinned. Was all of this *his* doing? How could someone so polished have a house that looks like *this*?

My Omega huffs. *And he had the nerve to call* us *incompetent?*

Internally, I frown at her, doing my best to keep our conflicted feelings off my face.

Hush, you.

"We, uh, got a bit ahead of ourselves here," Damon pipes. "We bought the place knowing it needed renovations, but then there was a debate about whether we should choose everything ourselves or wait for our omega..."

When Smith turns to me, he waves at the wide, arched opening at the back of the dining room. His tone is all clipped formality. "The kitchen is just through here. It's the most finished space in the house."

Damon bounds ahead, leading me out of the formal foyer—with its sanded-down staircase—through the dark, empty dining room, and under the cased opening. What little air I have managed to inhale instantly flies out of me on a gasp.

The rest of the house, the pack, and this day may not be anything like the fairy tale I expected—but *this*?

This is my kind of heaven.

The kitchen takes up the entire back half of the house, stretching from an informal living area off to the left through a charming dining nook with bench seating and curved wall of French doors, and all the way to the large collection of white-trimmed windows forming a tall arch along the back wall.

I ignore the ripped-up backyard beyond the glass, turning instead to the cooking area that occupies the center of the big wall across from the kitchen table and the windows. With the natural light beaming in, the white marble counters and polished oak floors gleam, underscoring just how bare the unpainted cabinets look.

I let my eyes roam over them, hunting for appliances. When my gaze trips over a white enamel stove with gold knobs, I swear my heart flips.

Cassian's hand squeezes around mine before finally releasing me. When I send him an anxious glance, he nods at the beautiful kitchen and murmurs, "Go on. I know you want to."

It's so strange how well he knows me. And, really, when I think about it, I know him too. I'd bet all two hundred and eighty dollars in my bank account he has a stash of books around here somewhere. And they'll be perfectly organized, even though I'd go double-or-nothing that all of his clothes are lying around in rumpled piles.

I suddenly want to hug him and hold on forever.

The rich scent of hazelnuts dipped in dark chocolate sends sparkles fluttering through my blood. Fresh wetness gathers between my thighs, slipping out of me along with a burst of honey-cake perfume. And, thanks to Damon, I don't have any panties to hide it.

Oh, Lord. I don't have the first clue how to handle this

awkward sexual tension between us. We never had that kind of relationship before. Will he really want one now?

His nostrils flare, his wide jaw flexing. The way his eyes soften while mine fill makes it seem like he already has his answer. "Later," he murmurs, hushed. "We'll talk, butterfly."

I nod. The second I float forward, Damon swoops in, spinning me into his side and giving me a tender squeeze while he guides me deeper into the kitchen.

His smile is contagious while he gestures at the beautiful room. "You said you like to bake, right, sweetness?"

I did. Before Smith eliminated my job.

Stuffing down my grievances, I'm relieved at how easy it is to smile back at Damon. "In here, I bet I could make some serious treats."

His eyes light up. "Treats? For me?"

I have to laugh. He's just so enthusiastic, even when he has an attitude. "If you'd like," I agree. "Just tell me what your favorites are."

"Damon," Smith sighs, pinching the bridge of his nose and rubbing his eyes. "*We're* meant to be courting *her*, not the other way around."

My mind stutters to another halt, trying to process the thought of Smith attempting to court me. I can't even form an image of that. Every time I picture us alone together, I shudder at the thought of him barking orders at me.

At work.

Last night.

He can't seem to stop himself.

Which means, technically, it isn't safe for me to be alone with him.

Which... is going to be an issue, apparently.

Cassian glances at his phone and curses quietly. "D and I have to go, Rems. Morning skate starts at nine every day, but we're usually back from conditioning by one or two. I'll text you about lunch, okay?"

I open my mouth, my automatic people-pleasing instinct to agree kicks in. But then I realize what he's saying.

They're leaving.

And I'm going to be here alone. With Smith.

chapter twenty-six

WITHIN TEN MINUTES, both of my hockey-playing alphas have enormous duffle bags of equipment slung over their shoulders as they head out the kitchen's back door. They both pause, Damon kissing me in a way that should be illegal, and Cassian sweetly nuzzling my cheek.

But then they're gone.

And I'm on the chopping block.

The door falls shut, and I startle, my features creasing as my eyes dart around the room. Smith misreads my terrified expression as judgment and shoots me a cool look. His shoulders tense and he jams his hands into his suit pants. "It's fully functional," he snaps, almost defensive.

The kitchen?

He thinks I don't approve of *the kitchen*?

As if the rest of the house isn't ten times worse.

It doesn't make sense, based on what I've seen from him so far. Yes, he's aloof; even a bit callous—but he appears extremely put-together and into appearances. Living in a half-finished house like this must be killing him.

So why hasn't he done anything about it?

I bite my lip, considering the pack alpha and his snarling expression. The scent of coffee is thick in the room—in the whole house, really—but, at the moment, it's less smooth-freshly-brewed and more pungent-over-roasted.

Stress. Which means, no matter how unaffected and detached he seems, this really is hard for him.

Maybe he's embarrassed? I can't say I'd blame him. This place is his responsibility, and he obviously isn't managing it in the same obsessive way he manages his businesses.

Clearly, he has the money to do anything he wants. I suspect this doesn't really have anything to do with funding. After all, I'm no millionaire, but I didn't have roach remains on my floor. Or sawdust. Or—are those Cocoa Puffs?

Oh dear.

Somehow, while the others were here, I managed to block out the reality of just how bad this place is. It's such a *shame*. Underneath all of this grime and indecision, the house's bones are *beautiful*.

Maybe the alpha is the same way, my Omega whispers.

She's been so sassy lately, especially about Smith. This softer tone gives me enough pause to gather my nerve. Eyes scanning over the room, I search for anything I could say to put him at ease. When my focus falls on the pristine, unpainted cabinets, I get an idea.

"Light blue."

His jaw muscle ticks, as if speaking to me in a level tone is strenuous. "Excuse me?"

"For the cabinets," I murmur, moving to hold the skirt of my soft blue sundress off to the side, giving him a visual of what the cabinets would look like if they were the same color. "With this white quartz? And maybe gold handles."

Smith just... stares.

Geez. Why is he so rude?

Is it possible the scent tests and my Omega are wrong? He *feels* relatively safe—when he isn't barking or drowning me in alpha dominance. But how could I have a mate who's so cold and demanding? And how can I make him like me?

Besides, didn't Damon say they were all waiting for *me*? And that's why this place is in shambles?

Instead of backing down, I wait politely. He eventually narrows his eyes and walks over, staring down at the portion of my dress that's pinched between my fingers and then over at the Calcutta Gold counter.

"Approved."

My Omega instantly seethes. *I know this asshole did not just—*

HUSH, YOU.

I swallow the unladylike urge to guffaw, returning his earlier words to him. "Excuse me?"

"I approve," he clips, sliding his hand into his suit jacket. He extracts a flat billfold and pulls a credit card out of it. Instead of handing it to me—and, you know, having to *touch* me—he sets it on the quartz counter and steps back with a curt nod.

For a long moment, I'm baffled. Then, I see that the carbon-fiber card isn't emblazoned with his name. It's the pack's.

Pierson Pack.

"I'll call and add your name to the account this morning. The card has no limit." He clears his throat, pulling at his sleeve cuffs. "Use it for whatever you need."

I look down at it, trying to understand. Does he mean...

different clothes? Because I'm holding my skirt up? Surely he can't mean...

Do they even make credit cards that could pay for all the work this house needs? Should we be taking out a loan against our mortgage or—

Oh.

They probably own it. And have enough money to pay for everything outright.

Smith must sense how foreign that concept is to me because he produces another card. *Mallory Taylor.*

"Miss Taylor does all of our property renovations at Pierson. She coordinates the contractors. Call her, and she'll send over crews for anything you think the house needs. Give her the credit card info to pay for the materials, and the company will take care of labor costs."

My head spins as I half-turn, taking in the enormity of the property and all the things it will need. A rude word climbs halfway up my throat before I stab it and swallow it down in a wad of dismay.

You have to prove yourself to this alpha somehow. Guess now's your chance.

TO CALL SMITH'S TOUR "PERFUNCTORY" would be generous. He keeps his irritatingly handsome features set in a snarl the entire time, sloughing out one-word descriptions for each room we pass.

"Den."

"Parlor."

"Foyer."

By the time we reach the second floor, I've tallied thirty-two things I need to attend to on the first level and ten are safety hazards. My sandals are pinching my toes, I'm slightly out of breath, and I almost tumbled right down the stairs when I slipped on one of the sanded, unfinished steps.

Turning on the landing, Smith casts me a scowl and opens his mouth before closing it again. He clears his throat—a gesture I'm learning to associate with him forcing himself not to bark at me.

I wonder whether he realizes that stopping himself doesn't really help much. His waves of dominant force still wash over me, even when he makes himself choke down the command itself.

All he's accomplishing is keeping me on edge. My Omega *wants* to *obey* as much as my pitiful heart wants to *please*, but neither of us have any clue what the order is.

"My room is at that end of the hall," he says, shoving his hands into his pockets. "Cassian's is the next door on the right, and Damon's is here, at the top of the stairs."

I follow his nods and then keep going, turning to the right stretch of the hallway and the double doors at the end that mirror the portal to his room. "What's over here?"

He lets out a hard sigh. "The Omega Suite is at the end. The rest are guest rooms and a guest bathroom."

The Omega Suite.

He moves in that direction and my heart somersaults. Will it have a nest? A bed big enough for Cassian or Damon to fit in it with me? Heck, I'd be thrilled with one that's big enough for *me*, after sleeping on an extra-thin twin mattress for as long as I can remember.

But Smith stops in front of the last door on the left and knocks it open.

Inside, there's an unfinished guest room, covered in a thin layer of dust. A new mattress, still in plastic, sits on a metal skeleton. There's a dresser of some sort, though I can't see it because of the tarp over it. Aside from the two square windows on either side, the room is utterly empty. Not a blanket or a pillow in sight.

"You'll stay in here," he says, looking around the room as if it's the first time he's really inspected it. "I have to get to the office now, but I'll have the guys bring your things up as soon as they get home."

My mouth drops open in shock. He isn't even going to carry my boxes in for me? He's leaving them outside?

Seeing my face, Smith frowns. "Of course, you're welcome to unpack them yourself. Cassian left his keys for you. They're on the kitchen island. I'll have a set of house keys made for you at some point."

At some point?

And he's sticking me in here? A spare room that's literally inches away from the suite he reserved for their *chosen omega*?

Everything inside of me sinks. I've been in this position before. Going home with a new family, hoping they'll really invite me in... only to be given a cot in a corner or a sofa bed.

It isn't so much the accommodations as what they say.

And this is the Pierson pack's equivalent to a basement futon. It says, in a tone as clipped and cool as the alpha's, *"Don't get comfortable."*

He must really hate me.

How long will he let me stay here? Can I possibly convince him to keep me?

Smith points at the one closed door in the room. My heart lifts, thinking that maybe I'll at least get a temporary nest.

But he tilts his chin at it before turning to stride away. "Towels are in there."

chapter
twenty-seven

CASSIAN

I THOUGHT I LIKED SILENCE.

But the fact that not one single sound has come from upstairs in *three hours* is making me crazy.

I've tried working out. Reading. I've even cleaned. And Damon *helped*.

Things around here are fucking grim.

I've read the same two pages eight times, and I can't remember one single word. Damon left for a workout with his trainer an hour ago, and I've been sitting here ever since, pretending I'm not glancing up at the ceiling—and the omega suite—above me every ten seconds.

It doesn't help that, for the first time in my adult life, I'm horny as hell.

I spent years trying to muster any sort of enthusiasm for sex with the random puck bunnies who threw themselves at me, and my Alpha never so much as glanced up. But now? Just knowing that Remi is here, inside the house, has me adjusting my sweats every three minutes.

Smith sighs from his place at the kitchen table, tapping at a spreadsheet on his iPad. "*Cass*," he growls, pausing me. "Leave it."

I curse him out under my breath, muttering my disagreement. He lowers the paper clutched in his left hand and pins me with a severe look.

"It's her first night here. We asked her if she wanted dinner, and she said no. We asked her if she wanted *anything*, and she said no. You offered to stay with her, but she turned you down. Leave. It."

But here's the thing: these specific desires may be unprecedented, but the *urgency* isn't new for me. I've felt this way before. Ten years ago. When I woke up to the patter of footsteps.

Something is *pulling* at me, tugging me toward the stairs. And I'm about 60 percent sure it's more than some pathetic desire to see her face. Or the ache in my knot.

"Because you're such an expert," I snap back at him, ditching my book and rolling to my feet. "Fuck this. I'm going to check on her. You want to come?"

He starts to get up before he forces himself back down. "No," he grinds out, almost like he's scolding himself. "She's fine, and you're being ridiculous."

I shrug. He might be right.

Except not really, because when I get upstairs, Remi's suite is sealed up, and there's no light under her door. It's only eight—is she really asleep already?

She told me she hasn't been sleeping well recently, so I doubt she could pass out this early in a new place. Still, I try to move silently while I close in on her door and try the handle. It's locked.

My first thought is that she's gone. Climbed down a tree like the flighty little ninja she's always been. But my alpha instincts tell me she's still close by.

Where would she go, if she's not in her room?

I stomp down the hallway, even more agitated than I was moments before. Turning for the stairs, I almost miss the faint sound coming from the other end of the long upstairs landing.

It's quiet, but the second I hone in on it, my instincts fly at me. My feet move without permission, bringing me to—

My own room?

That's where the noise is coming from. A soft, feminine voice. Singing.

Is that... ABBA?

A painful pang sinks through my chest. I remember her humming the same tune a lot back in the group home. She used to tell me that one of the best ways to feel happy was to act happy. I would catch her singing stereotypically upbeat pop music whenever she felt scared or stressed or sad.

I shoulder into my bedroom, moving slowly and carefully so I don't scare her. Only, she isn't anywhere I can see. My bed—*God, don't look at it too long while she's in here, or you'll rut her into next year* —is empty. So is the leather club chair shoved against the bookshelves.

The balcony doors are shut. My bathroom looks just like I left it.

Which means my butterfly must be in my closet.

"Rems?" I rasp, tapping on the door with two knuckles before I pry it open. "You in here?"

Her singing stutters to a stop just before I see her, curled into a ball and sandwiched between my shoe rack and a few spare pillows. The walk-in is the smallest one in the house, but it's still big enough for me to step inside and turn around. Even so, she's picked the most cramped corner to hunker down in.

I can't really see her face without the light on, but when I move to flick the switch, she whines. My hand falls back to my side.

She begins to apologize, her voice tight. "Cass! I—I'm sorry. I —I was—"

When I sink down to my knees, I can finally lean close enough to see her face. Without her usual makeup, her eyes look tired and her skin seems too thin. Almost translucent.

But, God, is she beautiful.

I reach over and smooth a thumb across her cheekbone, feeling her trembles. "It's okay, butterfly," I murmur, moving closer. "Did you need a dark, cozy spot? Is something wrong with your nest?"

She hesitates, biting her lip before she finally nods. "I'm sorry. I tried to use the bathtub in my room, but there's only a shower stall in there and—"

A cold sort of fury grips my lungs. "Your bathtub? Why? The omega suite has a full nest in it."

Her teeth sink down harder, leaving her pink lip nearly white. "Smith didn't want me in there. He gave me a guest room, which is great! But, um, I think you guys must have been using it for storage because the closet is full of filing cabinets and storage bins. I couldn't fit in it."

What. The. Fuck?

Am I going to have to kill my own brother?

My teeth grind together. "He locked you out of the Omega Suite?"

Remi's shoulders bounce on a shrug, shifting the fit of her enormously oversized hoodie. "I didn't check the lock."

But I did.

That *motherfucking asshole.*

Remi senses my rising aggression and makes herself smaller, swallowing a whine that I barely catch the end of. Forcing myself to focus on her, I shake my head and drop down beside her, somehow wedging myself between her side and the wall. "My closet is the smallest one, huh?"

She nods again, gazing up at me without one speck of guile. "And it smells like you," she whispers, "I... Your scent makes me feel the safest."

Jesus.

Fucking stab me in the heart. It'll be quicker.

The next thing I know, I'm stripping off my shirt and pulling her into my naked skin. "Come here."

She instantly scrambles closer, whining some more while she rubs her cheek into my pecs, my throat, the underside of my chin. I groan, relishing the way her scent sends electricity through my veins.

My hands clench fistfuls of her sweatshirt. It's black, just like the one I gave her back in the group home. Actually, it's about the same size, too. And it has the same bleach stain on the shoulder.

"Rems," I mumble into her hair. "Did you keep my hoodie all this time?"

She whimpers as her scent darkens in shame. "Yes."

I hug her harder, concentrating on not crushing her. It's hard to focus when I feel breathless. "Why?"

She cringes in my arms. "The day you gave it to me was the day I... had to leave."

Because her designation came through. I recall the other girls whispering and giggling about it that night in the mess hall. It was the only time in my young life I'd ever considered fighting a group of chicks.

Remi stares, willing me to understand some unspoken confession. It takes me a moment, but I finally snap the pieces together. "It was—You reacted to the sweatshirt? To... me?"

Her entire body sags with relief and dejection. She drops her gaze down to my chest. "Yes. And I felt so guilty and embarrassed about it, I just wanted to leave before I saw you and it happened in front of you. It all feels so stupid, now, but at the time, I honestly couldn't think of anything more humiliating or violating than perfuming for you and forcing you to have to acknowledge it."

She leans back and bites her lip, apprehension all over her pretty face. *Hell.* Does she want me and worries I don't feel the same way? Is she scared I'll reject her for some reason?

I see the way she holds herself around Smith—all prim and proper, every expression pleasing or passive. I hate the thought of her putting on some sort of act for me.

Fuck that shit. We didn't need it back when we were friends, and we're not going to do it now.

I cup my hands around hers, holding them between our chests. "Rems, I just want you to be yourself. And, in case I haven't made myself clear—I *want* you. I'm hard because of *you*—not just your scent or any of the alpha-omega stuff. It's *you*.

"If I'm being honest, I always had feelings for you that were... *more*. I was just an idiot. And we were young. But the way I feel about you has never had anything to do with you being an omega or me being an alpha. Pretty sure I knew you were it for me the second I saw that pink, sparkly butterfly clip in your hair."

Crystal tears spill over her cheeks, splashing down onto my pecs. I let the purr strangling my lungs come out, unleashing the full force of the deep rattle for the first time in my life.

It feels... good. *Really* fucking good when she whimpers and scrambles into my lap.

Nothing has ever felt like this, for me. Is this what people are going on about? Why Damon always hit it with as many puck bunnies as he could get his hands on?

I thought there was something wrong with me. A missing piece.

Maybe it's her.

The way I feel about her. This aching smolder in my middle every time our eyes meet. It warms my blood and fires my nerves until every place her skin brushes mine leaves simmering pleasure behind.

And, God, I *want* her. My body craves hers in a primal, carnal way I'm unfamiliar with. I can't explain it—all I know is the thoughts running through my head are new and all-consuming.

How tight and slippery would she feel around my cock? If I made her come, would I be able to feel it, squeezing me? Bringing us even *closer*?

She tucks her chin into her chest, hiding her face while she whispers, "Can I tell you a secret?"

It's only fair, since I have a feeling I'll be confessing a few of my own before the night ends. "Of course."

"I've thought about you," she whispers. "Every time I have a heat, I—imagining you there with me was the only way I could get through the fear. I always felt safe with you and the pain—"

She breaks off on a squeak that slices my heart. "—you were the one thing that made me feel better. And then, after it had been years, I thought about what you probably looked like, now... and it always turned me on."

Her whispered words hit the hollow at the base of my throat and sink down. The feeling—this soaring, bursting, *bleeding* feeling—in my chest almost overwhelms me.

It's too much, too soon. To go from years of empty nothing to *this*...

I breathe hard, bracing myself to tell her what needs to be said. "Remi..."

Jesus.

I never expected I'd ever have to tell *anyone* this. Never expected anyone would *care*. But I know Remi does. This will mean something to her, and that's what matters.

"I never wanted anyone else," I murmur. "After you left, my alpha and I didn't even notice other girls. Or guys. And I couldn't seem to force it, so I just—let it be."

I look at her, and she stares back. A thousand words fill the silence between us, all of them unspoken but, somehow, understood.

She only says four, but they're perfect. "You waited for me."

And, yeah. I really did.

Because I was always meant to be *hers*.

All this time. All these wasted years. I grind my teeth, swallowing the hoarse lump in my throat.

Remi's tears glisten in the low light. An ache reverberates through my depths, down into my fucking soul. It turns my purr into a pained, serrated rumble.

"I'm yours, now," I tell her. "But I don't think that's a new thing, butterfly. I was always yours. I always will be."

chapter twenty-eight

CASSIAN'S EYES BURN, the dark green smoldering. My heart beats in my breast, pounding shivery adrenaline and thick arousal through my veins—the hot and cold twining.

In this small space, Cassian's rich scent presses all around me. It's the reason I came in here. I wanted this exact feeling—my alpha, all around me.

He's inside me, too. Not physically, yet. But when he made his confession, I felt him reach in and touch a part of me no one else ever has.

He understands me. Still, after all this time. The parts of me that don't even make sense to myself are crystal clear to Cassian.

He knows me so well, but he's still here. He's still... mine.

I was always yours.

I always will be.

Straddling his lap, my forehead only reaches his cheek. I nuzzle there, whispering against his jaw, "Tell me what you want to do. We can go slow or wait—"

Very deliberately, he wraps his huge hands around my hips and brings my body flush with his, seating my wet panties directly over the firm girth tucked into his waistband.

Our eyes lock—his roiling with a seething sort of certainty. "I did wait. For you. For *this*. And now I want you so badly, I can't even fucking *think*, butterfly. *Please*."

His gruff sincerity is almost as sexy as his big, hard body. My perfume floods the closet, slick squelching through my pajama bottoms to coat the outline of his cock.

Shudders roll through him as a rough sound scrapes out of his throat. I ride a burst of insane bravery all the way to Cassian, falling forward and pressing my mouth over his.

Our lips brush and part, clinging for one sweet second before his tongue slips into my mouth. He grunts, catching me with both hands wrapped around my arms before clutching me closer. One brawny hand slips up to grasp the messy bun at the back of my head, while the other slides to my waist and tugs me against his erection. Grinding.

His length strains under his pants, pressing into my molten center. When I take over and set a rhythm, his eyes turn wild. Shaking breaths punch out of him.

The wet fabric between us sticks and chafes. Biting my lip, I stretch up and touch the drawstring of my shorts, a question clear on my face.

Cassian answers by setting his fingers over mine, pushing the damp cotton down, baring me to him. While I balance on my knees to get them all the way off, he shoves his own pants down.

His erection springs free, instantly jerking up to the thick lace of his abs.

Oh my Lord. *He's huge.*

I mean, I guess I expected that? It makes sense, since the rest of him is large. But Damon is only a bit leaner...

Are *all* alphas this big?

Apart from the silicone penises stashed at the very bottom of one of my boxes, I don't have much to compare him to. The alphas at the heat clinic were all anonymous. They walked up to my little cage, saw my presented hindquarters, and went to town without so much as glimpsing my face.

This is my first time ever *looking* at a man's... manhood.

I definitely shouldn't squeal.

That would be so dorky.

When he sees the way I've frozen, half-naked and halfway over his erection, Cass flashes his rare, beautiful grin, his green eyes crinkling. He smooths both hands down my face. The tender motion matches the low purr under his voice.

"You can touch it."

"Are you—are you sure?" I ask, and instantly feel like an idiot.

Cassian's chocolate-hazelnut goodness gets deeper. His thumb caresses my lower lip before he offers another of this short-lived-but-beatific smiles. "Very sure."

I wrap all of my fingers around him, stretching to fit his girth. A rumbling growl layers over his purr while he watches me glide light touches up the length. I feel him pulse against my palm, the wide crown already weeping.

Curiosity gets the better of me. I bend forward, dipping to kiss it and coming away with his essence on my lips. Cassian's deep, shredded groan shudders through me the same second his taste hits my tongue. A desperate whine slips out as I stroke him harder, hoping to lure out more of his salty, dark chocolate pre-cum.

His hand closes over mine, slowing me. In a blink, he has our bodies repositioned, my slick, empty center clenching just inches above the hard throb of his cock.

He spreads his legs, hooking my knees around them to spread me wide, too. His thighs feel as thick as tree trunks and every bit as solid as the steely length I just tasted.

My hands go to his wide, muscled shoulders. He's solid, covered in warm, perfectly tan skin. The tendons in his neck strain under my touch, his strength unyielding while he stares back at me and clenches his jaw.

"I want to feel you," he rasps, pupils blowing wide. "You'll take it. And use it however you want. Get yourself off on my knot. Rub your sweet little pussy all over me."

He may not be experienced, but Cassian is a true alpha. He already has me in his thrall—pumping out solid, soothing certainty as he continues to hold my gaze.

"Relax, omega," he says. "Don't think about it. Just do what feels good. Can you do that for me?"

Right now, I feel like I could do anything for him. Happily.

"Yes, Alpha."

He lets his head fall back on a groan. "My perfect fucking girl," he rasps. "Always my girl."

His bare cock pulses when I press down onto it. The feel of our bodies colliding, the slick friction between us, is delicious. His biceps flex as he manhandles my thighs, easily picking up my rhythm and holding my entire weight.

My clawed hands go to his shoulders, blunt, pink nails tearing into his skin. He looses another growl, flexing a wave of alpha power that hits me square in the chest. When the rolling motion of my body stutters, he cups one hand around my nape and looks right into my eyes.

"*Mine,*" he growls. "And you're going to come on this dick."

He's right, I am.

When he puts a hand on my waist and guides me all the way down, along the underside of his soaked cock, and rubs my clit against the thick swell of his knot, everything flashes white. A shriek sails out of me while my core pulses, pleasure coursing through every nerve.

Cassian starts purring before my cheek even lands on his chest. Beneath me, his entire body is as hard as a rock, the muscles tense and trembling. But he holds me so carefully, tucking his face into my hair and breathing hard.

"Remi... do that again."

I giggle softly. "I don't know if I can."

His huffed laugh quivers. "You want to stop?"

We're still on the floor of his closet, but he doesn't seem to mind. I do my best not to shift around on top of him too much as I lean back, finding his heated gaze. "What do you want to do?" I coax, reaching over to smooth my palm over his stubbled cheek.

His ferocious features melt slightly. "I was going to suggest we—"

He doesn't say it. Instead, his eyes drop to my lips. Two green lasers trace the over-bitten curves.

And I realize: he wants to kiss me. He wants to *keep going.* This big, grumpy mountain of muscles and menace wants me, but he doesn't know how to ask.

My heart cramps as a true grin stretches over my face for the first time all day. "Alpha," I whisper, shuffling closer, pressing my hips to his. "Did you want something?"

I should have known better than to poke the bear.

He makes a deep sound that shoots straight to my core, strumming at the throb between my legs and turning my nipples to stiff points. Fire flares in his irises as he snaps his arms closed and growls, "I want *everything.*"

If I thought I'd get away with teasing him just because he hesitated, I was wrong. One hand grips the curve of my hip to grind me down into his lap, while the other covers the nape of my neck, holding me still for ravaging.

The kiss isn't gentle, the way it might have been ten years ago. And it isn't anything like Damon's teasing, flirtatious dance. No,

Cassian kisses with *ferocity*. Some mind-bending, panty-melting blend of unbridled passion and raw strength.

I gasp as his tongue slips into my mouth, rubbing along mine in a forceful glide that liquefies my insides. Fresh slick gathers at the tops of my thighs. When Cassian snarls into my mouth, I know he can feel it.

We kiss until my lips are tingling and his rich hazelnut scent has turned my thoughts into a thick, dizzy soup. Until my legs are shaking, and I can't help but whine for him, the sound betraying how desperate I am to feel him deeper inside me.

With a roar, Cassian rips me upright, positioning his throbbing cock right against my soaked slit. The touch of his hot, solid length is enough to have me gushing more, mewling just from the heat of his body and mine.

Cass stares at me, his eyes somehow wild and tender at the same time. "Do you want it?" he rumbles, fingers biting into my thighs. When I keen, digging my nails back into the firm flesh of his shoulders, he lifts me straight up, pausing when I'm hovering over his crown. "Do you want me? Like this?"

YES.

I nod, frantic. "Yes, Cass, *please—*"

"Knot or no knot?" he asks, wild, green eyes bouncing between both of mine. I start to tell him to knot me as deeply as he can, but my core cinches tight, remembering the pain I experienced in that heat clinic. Cassian reads my answer before I've even had time to process it.

"We'll wait," he decides, projecting that same smooth certainty that soothes every insecurity.

Gratitude and affection fill my eyes as my forehead falls to his. "Yes, Alpha," I say again, whispering.

He loves that. Heat shimmers in his irises, his pupils edging the green into a thin band. With the same gruff gentleness he reserves just for me, Cassian kisses me hard and tilts his chin to our laps. "Take it."

He holds himself still while I lower myself onto his length and moan at the slick, delicious stretch, my inner muscles instantly clamping around his thickness. His chest heaves, vibrating with growls he has no prayer of swallowing.

"Fuck, you feel like heaven. *Jesus.* Your pussy was made for my cock, wasn't it, butterfly?"

"Yes, Alpha," I say again, unable to resist bouncing on him. When he bottoms out deeper than I ever thought possible, I scream, and he goes wild, pumping his hips in the smooth, powerful bursts of a true athlete. Somehow doing all of the work despite my position on top of him.

I can tell he's close when his pants turn to ragged half-breaths. He grabs my nape, pulling my face to his. "Come here."

The new position presses his pulsing knot right against the bottom of my buzzing clit. He makes a circular motion one way and then the other, capturing my high-pitched whine with his lips. His tongue slides against mine the same moment my second climax hits, locking my muscles around his girth.

He answers with a deep moan of his own, spurting hotly while he groans into my mouth.

And, you know what?

I take it back.

I should definitely poke this bear way more often.

chapter twenty-nine

DAMON

DID you know that being incurably horny makes cardio a hell of a lot easier?

Just something I learned during my home workout this morning, after waking up to an upstairs hallway that was absolutely *soaked* in the scent of honey-drenched *sex*.

Tossing a set of thirty-pound free weights onto the rubber mat on the floor of our converted garage, I remind myself that I have a plan here. I want Remi to know how much she means to me—*I* want to know how much she means to me—before we go there.

I tell myself this is normal. Google even said so. Packs and bonds develop at different speeds.

And Cassian got a ten-year head start. The bastard.

I'm considering another twenty minutes on the treadmill when he comes shuffling into the gym. For the first time in a long-ass time, there isn't a scowl on his face. In fact, one *might* even call that a smile. Sort of.

It strikes me that this is an opportunity. It's been years since we talked as much as we have in the last twenty-four hours. Maybe I can keep the momentum going.

"I've never been prouder than I am in this moment," I joke, gesturing at the nail marks visible under his gray tank top. "So our girl's a scratcher, huh?"

I'm expecting some version of "fuck all the way off, Damon," but instead Cassian *winces*.

Uh oh.

Considering I can't remember the last time he even *talked* to a girl, there's a chance he might have had some stamina issues.

"What?" I ask, pausing at the look on his face. "Were you rusty?"

His cringe stretches into a grimace. I wipe a towel over my forehead and drop onto the weight bench, giving him my undivided attention, along with a shrug I hope looks casual. "You can tell me. I won't be a dick. Just this once."

He lets out a deep breath, hanging his head back to mutter at the ceiling. "I cannot believe I'm doing this shit." He rolls his head forward and his shoulders back. "I'll make you a deal."

Oh, fuck yeah. "I'm listening."

His face falls into his familiar frown, but he lays out his offer anyway, snapping in his no-nonsense way. "I'll teach you all about Remi if you teach me all about sex."

I blink. Then blink again. "Oh-kay..."

"We can trade information," he goes on. "Since you don't know anything about her yet, and I don't know anything about fucking or knotting omegas. Or... anyone."

My eyes bug out. "You don't—You didn't—"

"Not until last night," he grits. "And she's happy. Very happy. But she's also the sweetest fucking thing, and I know she wouldn't necessarily tell me if she *wasn't* happy, so I need to learn... everything."

My mouth drops open. "So. Wait. *Wait.* This whole time, you were—"

"Yes," he grinds out, losing his patience. "Jesus. Do you want to trade or not?"

I picture us trading tips. A smile stretches over my face. I reach behind myself and hand him one of the weights I was using. I know from experience—sometimes, when you have to humiliate yourself by admitting you need help, it's easier when you have something else to pretend to do.

It works. He sits opposite me and starts doing curls. I watch the way he takes a deep breath and holds it for a second, feeling a pang of sympathy for him.

All this time, my random hook-ups and the bits of connection they provided were the only way I stayed sane. But Cass has been *totally alone*. More alone than I realized.

After a second, he blows out a sigh and nods at me, determination stealing his gaze.

Because he's tough as fuck. The kind of guy I've always appreciated having on my team.

So I do my best not to let my shit-eating grin show as I settle in. "Okay, lesson one—wait. How long is your tongue?"

"SO, THESE PEOPLE JUST... BAKE?"

Remi sits next to me on the couch, nodding with big golden-blue eyes that reflect late afternoon sunshine back at me. "In the tent."

"They bake in a tent," I repeat, trying to get a handle on her favorite Netflix binge. "They bake in a tent, and they're all British?"

"No," she corrects, "They all live in the UK. They can be from all over."

I squint at the white tent on the screen, the rows of pastel mini-kitchens set up inside of it. "And they... try to eat all of the desserts?"

Her giggle has become my favorite sound in the world. Whether I'm kissing her neck, twirling her around in her skirts, or tackling her into the couch every evening. That one little laugh sets my world right-side up.

"They are judged on how well they bake things," she explains. A thought crosses over her face, a crease forming between her brows. She picks up the AppleTV remote and hands it to me.

I hate the phony smile she pastes onto her face. "Let's watch what you want to watch," she suggests, just a bit too bright to be believable. "I've...been here all day."

She does that. The small white lies. Always trying to please us instead of telling us what she wants or likes.

I swear, I almost had to get an interrogation lamp out to get her to admit she doesn't eat pepperoni. And the way she refused to give me her size so I could buy her a new jersey for our game this weekend was nothing short of exasperating.

But then, I just keep thinking: how scared must she be to feel like she has to put up this front all the time? And how do I prove she never has anything to be afraid of, as long as I'm around?

Reaching over, I grab her waist and lift her right on top of me. "Um, I don't think so, sweetness. I was promised British tent baking"—I hit play—"Let's fucking do this."

I'm rewarded with another giggle as she snuggles into my bare chest. At Cassian's very growly—very *bear-like*—insistence, I've been wearing sweats around the house. For now. But I draw the line at shirts.

I don't know what kind of weird chivalrous shit he's playing at, anyway. As if I don't hear the two of them going at it every night. As if I don't use the sounds of her gorgeous moans and mind-shattering whines to stroke my cock next door.

So far, Remi and I have taken things slow. That's new for me. Which is why I think it's important.

This is my omega. I want her to know how I feel about her before we take things further than they've gone.

Of course, I'd never let that stop me from giving her whatever she needs.

Cassian and I have been taking turns sleeping in that stupid guest room with her. The bed really isn't big enough for one alpha, let alone two. I barely fit on the thing with Remi wrapped into my side, so I have no idea how Beastly is doing that shit. Unless he just has her sleep directly on top of him, which might not be such a bad idea...

Remi shifts, crossing her forearms over my chest and propping her pointed chin on one to cast me a curious look. "What are you thinking about, Trouble?"

Oh. My scent is thicker, and she can tell. Her honey-cake lusciousness winds into the autumn spices and makes my mouth water as I toss her a wicked grin. "Your bed, baby."

She starts to smile back, but a dark thought streaks through her light eyes. She tucks her face behind the barrier of her folded arms, hiding the lower half of it from me.

Fucking Smith.

I thought Cassian would rip his arms off when we found out our pack alpha hadn't put our omega in her suite. And, worse, he *locked her out of it.*

It took almost an hour and every ounce of his pack leader power to subdue both us long enough to explain. Some bullshit about the room needing new floor varnish and fumes or whatever. He promised it would be ready soon, and then we made his insufferable ass clear out space in the adjacent guest room to give Remi some semblance of a nest.

The extra room is too big to be a proper one. And it doesn't even have a mattress. Cass and I have already decided that if the suite isn't ready by this weekend, we'll just turn one of our bedrooms into her room and convert a walk-in closet.

Not having a permanent space of her own is clearly stressing her out. Almost as much as having a pack alpha who hasn't even touched her yet.

This isn't good for her. I may not be an omega expert, but I've downloaded four audiobooks about caring for our girl in the last week. And all of them stress the importance of alphas offering affection, reassurance, and connection.

So sign me up for British tent baking.

For a few moments, she watches the show while I watch her. She looks tired; the shadows under her eyes cleverly concealed with makeup.

She's an expert at looking perfectly put-together, but I want her to feel like she can be herself here. What will it take to get her to stop wearing foundation and heels around the house? That bun doesn't look comfortable either, pulling her hair back so tightly.

Remi's phone vibrates. She holds it under my chin and reads the message, humming lightly. "Meg."

I haven't met her best friend, but I feel like I have. She talks about her so often that I wonder if she even knows she's doing it.

Smoothing my hand over her head, I loosen the hair pins there and start to work my fingers through her curls, purring for her. "Did you want to bring her with you this weekend? Our box has a ton of room, and no one ever uses it. She could bring her alphas."

Remi gives a delicate shiver. "Smith would have a fit," she mutters.

"He won't be there." I say the words to reassure her, but they come out much more bitter than I intended.

Our omega's eyes flicker, processing what I just said. For a second, some steely look passes through them. It's gone in a blink, and when she bites her lip and glances down at her phone, I know she really wants to take my offer.

"I'll talk to Big Hoss and text Meg for you," I decide, petting her silky black hair. "Right now, you only have two jobs."

She arches one thin brow and half-smiles. "And what are those?"

I snuggle her securely, nuzzling my cheek into her forehead to scent-mark her. "To relax," I whisper. "And tell me what the hell a crumpet is."

chapter thirty

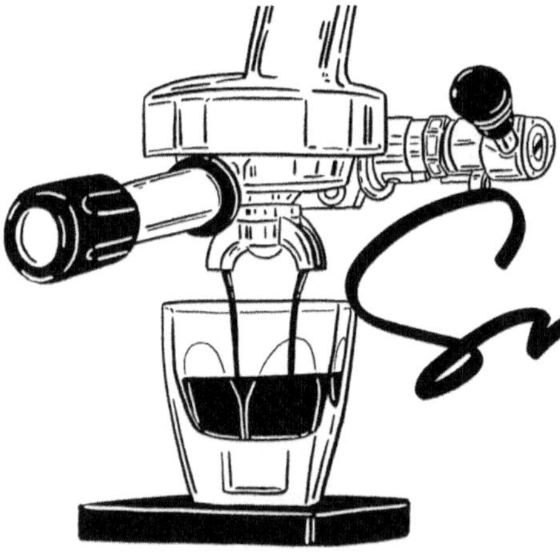

Smith

I STAND OUTSIDE the back door of the house, bracing myself.

Knowing that the second I step inside, my shit will get rocked. Because this is my new routine—avoid the house as much as humanly possible, only to come home and have it all topple on my head the second I walk in.

Tonight feels different. My Alpha is prowling just under the surface this time. Waiting. Knowing this is his moment.

Because she's only been here for four days... but she's fucking *everywhere.*

And I'm just about out of control.

I can't stand outside forever. Eventually, I'll have to walk into the kitchen. The second I do, her scent hits me, and my hands curl into claws.

Motherf—

It's too delicious. My entire *body* pounds as the taste of her honey-soaked essence coats my tongue. Sinks into my soul. Shreds my heart.

My cock has been hard all damn day. But now? It's stone. My knot pulses at the base, the throb as insistent as the lust swarming my blood.

I have to have her.

Now.

Now.

The edges of my vision blur into oblivion. It's a warning. A rut is coming on. And I have about three minutes to get out of here before—

Her moan is quiet. Muffled by something. But every nerve in my body alights. Focus reels out of my grasp, replaced by the pounding pulse in my head.

My feet move, carrying me through the house faster than they normally would. Pursuing the distinctly feminine sound of pleasure echoing from the second floor.

I've heard stories about rut-blockers being no match for a scent-sensitive mate, but I didn't understand until now. This feeling—where I'm here, but also not in control—is new to me. I'm still in my head, which *would* be helpful, but my brain seems oddly detached from my body.

I take the stairs two at a time, ripping my clothing off. My skin feels hot, the fabric of my favorite suit chafing in a way that infuriates me. My tie and shirt hit the floor of the landing as I turn toward the source of the noise, following it to Damon's open door.

From the shadows, I can see everything perfectly. They're just inside his room, Remi's small body flattened between his and the wall.

Control, control, control.

My Alpha snarls, lunging toward her. I reach behind myself to grip the stair-rail, holding back so I can watch. Knowing I can't touch her.

Especially not right now. Damon would likely take it as a threat, and we would end up traumatizing her with whatever brawl ensues.

Instead, I let myself stare, roving my hungry eyes over the scene playing out in full view of the hallway.

They look damn good together. Their black hair and blue eyes. Their contrasting skin tones. His hard, bigger body, and her soft, delicate curves.

Remi's dress is still on, though there's a pretty pink bra and matching panties discarded in the hallway. Leave it to Damon to get both off without removing her outfit. He's still in his shirt, but—*shocking*—no pants. I assume he's already gotten off because his briefs are balled up in a wet clump on the floor, and his dick is hard, but his knot isn't.

There's no way he could possibly be experiencing the same earth-shattering perfume I am without his knot blowing up. Unless he already came.

Which would also explain why he's on his knees, with Remi's thighs spread for his mouth.

"You like that, sweetness?" he pants, groaning. "Has no one else ever licked this sweet pussy before?"

She keens, her head falling back. "N-no. Cass said you would want to be the first one to do it."

Damon growls, "Damn fucking straight."

She perfumes again, her slick catching the low light of his bedside lamp as it drips down his chin and onto his shirt.

"Alpha, please!"

Fuck me. I'm going to end up jacking off right here, aren't I?

My hands fly to my belt at the same second Damon reaches for his own cock, snarling as his tongue curves up, into her opening.

"See what you do to me, pretty girl?" he breathes, stroking himself. "You already got me off, and I'm still gonna come all over the floor because you taste so good."

Remi fucking loves that thought. She whines as I clamp my hand around my own knot, squeezing the pulse and kneading it.

While I watch, she threads her fingers into Damon's hair, gently touching it as her hips snap against his face. "Damon," she moans, soft and sweet. "This feels—this is—"

Remi gazes down at him, her face slack and helpless, her eyes loving and full of wonder.

The expression hits me like a bag of bricks.

Fuck. *No.*

I can't do this. I can't watch her like this. She's vulnerable, and she wouldn't want me to see that.

I haven't earned that.

Before the rut bearing down on me can take over, I do the only thing I can to appease my Alpha, without splattering the omega in our scent, and bend to pick up her panties. The perfume on them has my teeth aching to bite. I turn away without allowing myself a second breath.

But the motion catches Remi's attention, and our eyes lock through the shadows.

chapter thirty-one

DAMON'S SNORES sound almost exactly like his purr.

After he finished shaking the foundation of my universe with his mouth, we cleaned up, and he bundled me into his arms and carried me to the guest room before promptly passing out.

I can't really blame him. He caught me in the hallway after three hours of conditioning and then gave each of us multiple orgasms. For some reason, though, my Omega is still on edge.

Okay, that was a lie.

Of course I know the reason.

Smith saw us.

He saw *everything*. And, if I'm not mistaken, I believe he had my missing panties wedged in his fist when he stalked off.

I'm not sure if that makes me want to preen or scream. My insane Omega loves that he wants us so badly that he can't resist taking a token. But the rest of me is hurt by the fact that he disapproves of me enough to even try to resist his Alpha in the first place.

Tiptoeing out of the bedroom, I pretend I'm just venturing out to look for those underwear. Surely, he didn't really *take* them.

Right?

I know what I saw, but somehow I can't believe it until I'm standing in the dark, silent hallway, staring at the blank floor.

They really are gone.

Damon's snores are still audible out here, along with low music coming from Cassian's room. He probably put that on earlier to give Damon and I some semblance of privacy. When I creep down that side of the hallway and peer into Cass's room, I find him asleep, sprawled on his too-small double bed with a book on the pillow next to his face.

With a small smile, I turn off his lights, pull his door shut, and start to turn back toward my half of the upstairs.

But a deep, feral snarl stops me cold.

What—

Unless some other alpha or a wild animal got in the house, it has to be Smith. Neither of the other scenarios seem likely, especially since I personally oversaw the installation of a new security system two days ago.

"S-Smith?" I squeak.

Another roar replies. A full-body shiver moves over me, peaking my nipples and sending a wet trickle down my thighs.

Seriously?! I think at my Omega. *What is* wrong *with you?*

She gives me a hard shove toward Smith's bedroom—the double doors opposite the locked-up Omega Suite. *Bitch, get in there!*

I stumble forward, drawing closer just in time to catch a low, pained moan. The sound is softer than his usual voice; and something about that instantly makes me wetter.

Honeyed perfume swirls off of me while I press my ear against the door—and it opens.

I never curse. Not even in my own head.

But...

Fuck.

I AM GOING to be homeless before the sun comes up, aren't I?

Judging by the way Smith's furious, dark eyes burn into my face? I should really go pack.

"Omega."

He speaks, but the voice isn't his. There's no clipped formality or dry edge of disapproval. Instead, it's quiet, layered with something rougher. Wild.

He's also *entirely* naked.

Just... *so* naked.

Sprawled in an armchair off to the side of the cavernous room, the pack alpha is barely visible, save for some moonbeams and a slice of light coming from what must be his ensuite bathroom.

The glow of it is enough for me to see the way his brows furrow. His wide, white chest, heaving. And the unhinged look in his eye.

There are other things to see, of course. But I don't let myself look, spinning around with an *eek* and throwing my hand over my eyes.

"I'm so sorry," I babble, reverting to habits from work. "Sir. I'm sorry, Sir. I heard a noise and I—"

His growl is low and long. The sort of sound a tiger would make from the shadows as it stalks its prey. "Say that again."

Every hair on my body stands on end. I try to breathe, but the air is absolutely *saturated* with his rich bitterness. It spirals down into my lungs, but only leaves my chest tighter. My answer comes as another squeak.

"I heard—"

"No." His cool command is back, the rougher tone an undercurrent that makes my toes curl into his plush cream carpet. "The first part. What you call me."

I realize what he means, nearly gasping. "...Sir?"

He shifts. Another low, tortured moan slips out of him. Then he bites out a hiss. "You need to leave. I can't stay in control if you're *in* here."

The subtle emphasis implies that he was already fighting some urge back before I interrupted. But what could it be? And why? He doesn't like me.

But his Alpha does, my Omega sing-songs.

This fluffing *slut*. She's going to get both of us kicked to the curb! Or, you know, *mauled*.

Should I run? Or will that make it worse?

My mind races, trying my best to recall everything I've ever studied about alphas and ruts.

Running would definitely be stupid. Alphas are programmed to chase. If I act like a scared rabbit, he'll turn into a rabid wolf.

The smartest thing to do, of course, is to give in. Smith is on rut-blockers. If I let him think he's getting what he wants, he may be able to settle his Alpha down long enough to override him.

His baser urges won't let up until he has my supplication. My knees shake, a tremor of answering desire from my Omega weakening them.

I decide to go with it. After all, she knows this alpha better than I know this man. She was the one who recognized him when I didn't.

The second my knees hit the ground, another snarl rips out of him. I watch him grit his teeth and try to hold in his bark. He fails. The command hits me like a dart.

"*Crawl to me.*"

My belly flips. Slick bathes the apex of my thighs. With nothing to soak into, it slips down my legs and smears as I follow the alpha's order, crawling from the double doors to his throne.

Because, at the moment, that's exactly what it is—a throne for a hedonistic king.

Dominance *pours* off him. Savage energy that somehow melds perfectly with his coiffed hair and flawless body, making for a regal sort of rawness.

The Smith I know is cool and unyielding—like steel—I know he's there, holding everything up, weighty enough to crush me, but he doesn't fascinate me.

Like this, though? He's *captivating*.

Bold and wild and dark, with just a razor-thin edge of polish.

Black eyes glint as I sway to a stop. Panting, I sit back on my heels and keep my head bent, avoiding eye contact. His Alpha likely wouldn't see me as a challenge, but I don't want to rile him any more than I already have.

His hot, heavy hand lands on my curls, slowly sifting through them in a gesture that almost feels absent. "Mmm," he rumbles in the layered voice, cool over rough. "Is the rest of you this soft?"

I know what he's really asking. And what he wants to hear. Every instinct preens as I tilt my head to the side, letting the moonlight from the windows behind him illuminate my blank throat as I sweep my lashes over my gaze.

"Yes, Sir."

His fingers flex, snapping up a handful of my hair and pulling tightly. I'm afraid to provoke him, but thrilled that I can. The combination of pride and lust primes my body in a way I've never experienced before.

And I... like it.

More wetness seeps out of me. I whine, restlessly rising onto my knees to scoot closer to him. The new angle changes the way the light hits him, allowing me to see everything the shadows hid before.

Like his long, thick cock. The huge knot swollen at its base.

And my missing panties, wrapped around it.

I expect some sort of embarrassment when I finally tear my gaze up to his. Instead, I find him watching intently, eyes ablaze.

"Did you lose something, little petal?"

A quiet gasp sinks into my lungs and evaporates, leaving his warmth behind. "Yes, Sir."

Smith bites his bottom lip as he groans, bringing his free hand to his knot and stroking the silky fabric down his length. All traces of teasing leave his expression as his Alpha briefly edges over his control.

Smith gnashes his teeth, his sculpted lips pulling into a snarl. He fights back another bark. Barely keeping the sting out of his tone, he orders, "Give me your slick."

I don't know what he means until his fist tightens in my hair pulling me closer. And I obey because...

I want to.

Despite everything, I really *want* to.

Shaking, I reach between my thighs to gather the wetness there and bring my hand between his legs. He spreads his powerful quads, the muscles flexing as I wrap my palm over his flushed cock and leave my essence behind.

Smith gives another soft sound that goes straight to my stupid, battered heart. My chest cramps while my stomach squirms, wanting *more*.

Scenting my perfume, some of the tension leaves his posture. The fingers in my hair relax slightly. When I look back up at him, he's someone I recognize again. Dark eyes drop to my lips.

"Fuck, I want your mouth."

No, he doesn't. Because he doesn't like me, and he'll remember that as soon as he's done. Plus, I've never gone down on anyone before. I'm sure I'll be terrible my first time.

If it were Cassian—or even Damon—I might be brave enough to go for it. But this is the pack alpha. I'm deathly afraid of being anything less than perfect around him.

My scent darkens with shame. Smith's thick brows press low again. Before he can ask, I admit, "I don't know how, Sir."

For one breathless moment, he's entirely still. When I dare to glance up at his face ,there's conflict in his eyes. The calm dark and flashes of wild light, flickering back and forth in his irises.

When he speaks, it's the double voice that gives me delicious chills. "Would you like to learn?"

The offer is surprisingly kind. And the way his fingertips begin massaging at the roots of my hair reminds me—he may not be close to me, but his Alpha is my Omega's mate. He means her no harm, even when he's out of control.

Smith won't hurt me. Not on purpose.

And he's giving me a choice.

I nod at them—the man and the beast he's grappling with—giving myself over to both.

chapter thirty-two

SMITH'S EYES match his scent.

Dark and mysterious. Overpowering to someone else, maybe.

But there must be some part of me that even I didn't know about. Because when he lets go of his length, leaving it to bob with my panties still wrapped around it, and buries both hands in my hair with dominant force, a moan slips out of me.

"Open your mouth," the rough, cool voice directs.

I bend forward on my knees, resting my palms against the insides of his thighs for balance. Muscle ticks under my fingertips. My lips part.

He strokes my panties down his length again before slipping them off and tucking them into some side pocket on the over-stuffed chair.

"Wider."

His wildness is defeating his composure, but I'm not afraid. The more his Alpha snaps forward, the more my Omega comes to the surface to soothe him.

I move my hands without thought, caressing the sensitive skin under my fingers with tenderness. Hoping that, maybe, this man isn't as cruel and cold as he seems. Maybe he's just never had anyone to give him this.

It isn't love, because I don't love him... but it's soft and gentle. Giving.

When another pained moan scrapes out of his throat, I know I'm right.

No one ever gives him anything.

It's a strange, dangerous game we're playing. He's in control, but not. I'm feeling deeply for him, but at least half of those feelings aren't *good*.

There's a moment of stillness where our eyes meet. His voice sounds softer as he murmurs, "Do you know how beautiful you are?" Heat and hurt flash through his dark irises. "It tortures me."

His muscles swell under my touch, his body snapping forward. "*You* torture me," he goes on, losing any semblance of gentleness. "Even before I knew you were ours, having you around made me fucking crazy. So now you're going to make it up to me with your mouth, petal."

Smith uses his grip on my hair to arrange me where he wants me, tilting his hips to get the tip of his cock to my open mouth. Instead of shoving it directly inside, he rubs the smooth, firm flesh of it over my tongue. Teasing me with his flavor until a whine builds in my chest.

He hisses. "Have to go slow. Can't fuck your throat the first ti—"

I move too quickly for him to stop me, sliding my lips down,

down, down, as far as I can manage. He snarls, both hands yanking my curls painfully until I bounce back up to his cockhead and swirl my tongue around him.

A strangled groan leaves his mouth while mine works. The hands on my head lose their viciousness, allowing me to attempt to pull him deeper.

I see what he meant when he hits the back of my throat, and I have to work not to gag. I expected it, but I didn't expect to feel him petting my hair.

"Shh," he reassures, half-growling, "What you're doing is perfect. I can teach you more next time. When I'm not—"

My fingers find his knot, ending his attempt at chivalry. I knead the hot, swollen skin the same way I saw him touch it through my panties, giving rhythmic squeezes and sliding back to touch the balls hanging underneath.

Every time I alternate between the two, his cock jerks between my lips, rewarding me with rich, delicious pre-cum. It reminds me of Cassian's taste. And imagining the two of them at the same time nearly makes me perfume hard enough to pass out.

Moaning, slick soaking my thighs, I take him deeper, sucking harder. Until angling to let him slip into my throat feels natural.

The second I do, everything changes again. His fingers twist into my scalp, tugging without finesse. A rabid roar sloughs out of him, and he begins pumping his hips up into my face. Basically... *fucking* my mouth.

It's a thought that might have horrified me, weeks ago, but right now? My nipples are so tight that I have to use one of my hands to touch them while the other clamps over his knot, stroking it harder.

"My omega," he growls, all gravel and sin. "*Mine.*"

He's fully in rut, I realize. Lost to a haze of lust and need.

He doesn't mean what he's saying.

I repeat that to myself, but it doesn't stop my body from responding; my clit from throbbing for his attention. Every muscle in my core clenches, aching for the feel of his knot expanding inside of me.

I can't speak, so I just moan again. Letting my neck go limp so he can use me the way he wants. I swallow my thick saliva and his delicious taste, the muscles of my throat constricting around his girth.

Smith looses a snarl that could shatter glass, thrusting mindlessly, unable to stop. He comes in a torrent, emptying down my throat. When he finally begins to pull out, he's still coming, dribbling delicious bitterness over my tongue while he falls back into the armchair.

His eyes fall shut as his body goes eerily still. From all of my research, I know it's a good thing. It means that what I did broke the rut's grasp. Now he'll sleep for a while and wake up back to being himself.

I know all of that, but it doesn't stop the pang that hits my heart, sending hurt reverberating through my body. With him passed out, I'm just alone.

Mussed and dirty, with a tender scalp and a body wound tight for release that isn't coming, I turn and crawl back out the way I came in.

chapter
thirty-three

CASSIAN

I WAKE up to that tug in my middle.

Remi.

I know she's close by—but I never imagined she'd be *this* close.

When I blink and roll over, I find her huddled under my sheets, curled into a ball at the foot of my bed.

What the—

It was Damon's night to share her room with her. So how did she end up in here? And why didn't she wake me? Or at least try to share my pillow?

I guess the bed sort of screams, *No Room For You*. This mattress is only big enough for one. A very deliberate decision I made when I bought it. But, for her, I would have made room. Or slept on the floor.

Instead, she's in the fetal position, wadded up between the tops of my feet and the wall I have the bed pushed up against.

"Butterfly," I mutter in my sleep-drenched rasp, bending to lift her up into my chest. "What are you doing in here, baby?"

She stirs, burying her face against my naked chest. The sheet wrapped around her shifts, showing me that, underneath it, she's bare, too.

I rearrange us as best I can with little room, flattening her body between mine and the wall. When she hums something incoherent, I nuzzle my face into her hair.

"Was Damon snoring again?"

She sighs. "No. It wasn't his fault." Blue-gold eyes blink open to peer at me in the gray pre-dawn. I remember thinking, just a few weeks ago, that everything around me felt gray. And now she's here, in my dreary bedroom. And all I see are her colors.

Remi's front teeth sink into her pink, puffy lip. "I'm sorry if I woke you up."

"'S okay, Rems," I mumble, lost in the way she smells and feels and—*God*, wake me up like this every morning.

Her body is so warm and soft against mine. I rub my nose along her temple, inhaling the honey cake sweetness. And freeze.

Is that *Smith*?

Why is his scent on her? And so strong, too.

When I lean back to lift my brow at her, she bites her lip harder, blanching it. "I'm okay," she blurts. "He didn't mean to do anything, but he was in a rut, and I went in his room, and—"

My entire body stiffens. "He *what*?"

"No, Bear," she pleads, trying to grab me before I can jump up from the bed and stalk off to kill my asshole brother. Her fingers slip over my arm, scratching me accidentally when her grasp proves no match for my rage.

I'm on my feet and halfway to the door before a distressed whine stops me cold. When I whip around, she's curled into a ball, hugging her knees. Her eyes are wide, beseeching.

"Please," she whispers. "He already hates me. I'm scared. After last night... I don't want him to make me leave. Please, Cassian. Just drop it."

My fingers flex into fists. "He can't just—just—*have* you like that, Remi. He can't have you if isn't going to take care of you the way you deserve. I'll kill him."

She stands on shaky legs, wobbling slightly while she weaves around my rumpled piles of clothes and tries not to trip on the sheet clutched over her breasts. "I know," she murmurs. "We didn't go that far. He didn't do anything I didn't consent to. It was just a little rough. But I'm okay, see?"

Like she's showing off a new outfit or doing one of her spins for Damon, she twirls in a graceful circle. Some of my fury cools, seeing the small smile on her lips. Even if it looks forced.

God, I want to see her smile for real.

Enough of these half-smirks and shy almost-grins. Even the smiles she gives Damon seem put-on sometimes. Like she thinks she has to flirt with him to make her happiness worth his while.

I look past her, to the balcony and the world beyond. The sky is gray-blue, lightening by the second.

"Come on."

She takes the hand I stretch out to her, following just behind me while I clear a path to the double doors. They stick, but I muscle one open and step halfway outside, sizing up the situation.

Not too bad. Only about four feet up to the rooftop.

I take my sheet from her clutched hand, snapping it open and bringing the tails together to tie them between her pert little tits. "Cass," she huffs. "What are you—*ah!*"

Lifting her with both hands, I stretch up until her arms are level with the edge of the roof. She catches on instantly, scrambling up with an extra boost from my hand on her ass.

Getting myself up beside her takes a little more effort, but years of chin-ups come in handy. I scrabble up beside her, landing on my boxer-covered ass just as I realize I probably should have dressed us both first.

Looking around, though, I see it's not a problem. Our house is the tallest one on the street by at least half a dozen feet. And the copse of old oak trees surrounding us provides enough coverage to make the neighbors a non-issue anyway.

Even if everyone in the neighborhood saw my boxers, I wouldn't care. Because when I turn to look at Remi, she's *beaming.*

A full, true grin. Just as beautiful and bubbly as I remember it being.

Years fall off her face as she smiles at me. Warmth blooms in my chest. Creeping vines of joy and wonder wrap around my throat, leaving it hoarse as I say, "I knew I picked this room for a good reason."

Somehow, her grin gets bigger. "Do you know which direction is east?"

I get my bearings and point to the right. She spots a dip between two sections of the roof, and we both crawl over to it, settling down in a secure spot where we can both lie on our backs and face the sunrise.

Keeping her sheet tucked around her, protecting her delicate skin from the rough shingles under us, I pull her into my side and hold her there.

Color climbs into the sky. First, the weakest lavender, followed by thin pink and hazy gold clouds. It's fucking beautiful. Breathtaking, just like it was the first morning I met her.

Just like all those secret morning meetings, Remi watches the sunrise, and I watch Remi. And slowly, with every breeze that ruffles her hair and every pensive gaze at the pink clouds, something inside of me that's been broken for a long time feels like it's finally knitting back together.

When the sun starts to make its appearance on the horizon, she turns to me with a question in her eyes. "Bear?"

It's just one word. I have no idea how I know exactly what it means, but I do. And I instantly know my answer.

Normally, I kiss her like I literally cannot wait another second. This time, it's slower. I draw her body into mine, molding my lips over hers gently.

I want to erase whatever happened last night. Show her she can trust me. That I'll always be here for her, as her friend and her lover and every other goddamn thing she needs.

That I'll be her alpha in every way, if she'll have me.

Remi opens her arms and legs, leaving the sheet flat underneath her as I position myself on top. She shucks my boxer briefs, glowing blue eyes snagging on mine when she reaches up to touch my jaw. "Please, Bear," she whispers. "Are you—are you ready?"

Her arousal is a thick, heavenly burst of honey, hanging in the morning mist around us. But I know that isn't what she means.

Whatever part of her held back before; she's ready to let it go now.

Up here, with me. In our secret spot. With a sun rising overhead.

She wants all of me.

I drop my forehead to her shoulder, feathering kisses along her collarbone as I push my cock into her soaked center. She arches her neck, moaning softly as she takes me down to the root, knot and all.

I haven't swelled all the way yet. While I still can, I work myself in and out of her wet, perfect heat, pausing to grind against her clit on every plunge.

It doesn't take long before we're both panting. Her hands slide over my back, feeling the way my muscles move while I pulse in and out of her pussy. I kiss her throat, scraping my teeth over it as my knot begins expanding, tugging at all of the nerves inside of her every time I work it in and out.

She feels fucking exquisite, gripping everything I give her with silky, slippery heat. The final time I bottom out inside of her, she squeals, bucking her hips up into mine as her orgasm moves through her.

Remi's inner muscles lock my knot into place. Pleasure erupts in my core, sending molten bliss through my veins.

For a moment, I feel like my insides are the same color as the golden mist surrounding us. Even after my climax fades, that feeling lingers in my chest, sinking into the purr that rolls out.

Just for her.

Always for her.

chapter thirty-four

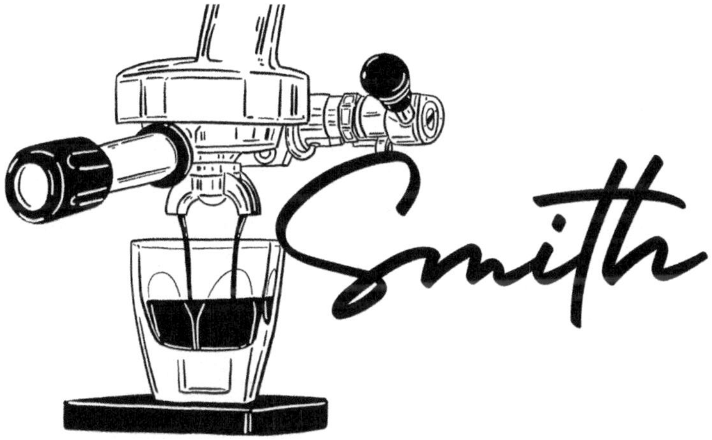

THIS IS SICK.

I should leave.

I know I should leave. I don't even want to be here…

My feet stay rooted to the floor. In fact, they may even press into the sticky linoleum a bit more. Like my body is staging a sit-in to protest my brain.

You caused this, asshole. Now you get to sit here and watch.

It's been a week since Remi moved into the pack house, and my life has turned into a living hell.

A living hell with homemade muffins, lemon-scented candles, and fresh flowers on every table.

So, really, it's heaven.

But hell, nonetheless, because our omega hates me.

And I don't blame her. Especially after the other night.

While I remain paralyzed, the line at Proper Coffee slogs forward, bringing new customers up to the register. I should at least pretend to be doing something, but I can't.

The fact is, I've fucked this whole thing to hell and back. Treating an employee like a servant. Scaring an innocent omega. Barking her out of her home. Putting her in our guest room. Rutting her mouth like an animal.

The worst part may be: I don't regret making her leave that mold-infested hovel any more than I regret making her suite perfect before I let her see it.

She deserves a perfect room and a beautiful nest. Especially since she has to put up with the likes of me in order to live in our house.

The same house that Remi's whipped into shape. Doing what I couldn't accomplish over two years in a matter of *days*.

It started with the kitchen, of course.

I've continued my irregular working hours, doing my best to avoid run-ins with her. Not wanting to scare her or be a looming presence she can't avoid. Not wanting to smell her perfect perfume and end up rutting her into a wall the way I almost rutted her into my bedroom floor.

One day, after leaving well before anyone was awake and coming home after ten, I walked in the back door and found the cabinets painted a light, powdery blue. They looked fantastic. I was so impressed that I opened one to see if she had the insides done as well.

Only to find food.

In *our* kitchen.

Not Cocoa Puffs, either. But actual *ingredients*.

The next night, I discovered that weren't just for show. Sometime after eight, I slipped in the back door, intending to go up to the desk in my room to keep working. But a cheerful yellow note on the island stopped me cold.

Alpha,

Your dinner is in the oven. Please turn off the warm setting when you retrieve it.

-Remi

I stared at that fucking dash for way longer than I'd like to admit, feeling nauseous about it. Wondering what she'd use to sign a note to Cassian or Damon. If their three scents—twined and soaked into the couch, the kitchen, the upstairs bedrooms—were any indication, I bet they'd at least get a smiley face.

Yet, no matter how much our omega clearly loathes me, I find a plate of food in the oven every single night. All of it has been delicious, nutritionally balanced, and heaped with extra protein. As if she took a special class on cooking for alphas.

Hell. Maybe she did. That wouldn't even surprise me.

And the one night my meal was clearly something the three of them had ordered in? She left me an *apology*, explaining that Damon requested Chinese food and promising she would go back to her meal plan the following night.

Which, she did.

While I did everything I could to avoid going home, I also did everything I could to avoid setting foot in Proper Coffee. For one, I hadn't replaced her when I forced her out of her old life and into ours. That meant I had no idea what sort of chaos would confront me when I walked in.

But, more importantly? I honest-to-God could not face being in the room where I made her *hate* me.

Eventually, I didn't have a choice. I had to come in and deal with the place—whether that means selling it to another investor, ripping it down to rubble, or something else entirely.

Despite all of my mistakes, all of the shit I buried myself under... I somehow managed to keep it all together.

Until I walked in here this morning.

And found Remi behind the counter. *Working*.

In a surreal moment of horror, I realized—I haven't been sneaking out of the house before she wakes up. *She* has been sneaking out of the house before *I* wake up.

The reason the manager never called me to bitch about being short-handed?

We weren't.

Because Remi found some way to haul herself down here without a car every morning.

And after working her shift? She went back to my pack house and spent hours doing *more work*. Cleaning, renovations, gardening, cooking and grocery shopping and decorating. And catering to three alphas intent on having their way with her.

How on earth has she managed all of that?

The guys likely have no idea. If she made some excuse for why she isn't there when they wake up, they probably think she's out shopping or exercising most of the day. They have morning skate, anyway, followed by conditioning. I bet they arrive home right after she does, thinking she's been there relaxing all morning.

Fucking hell.

This is the first time I've *seen* her in days. She looks as lovely as ever, her light brown skin flawless, and her curls styled into an elegant bun. She has on one of her sundresses, I note. It's very different from the way she used to dress for work, and I wonder why until I catch her glance over at me and tug the neckline of her dress up.

It's for me.

She's dressed up *for me*. In case I came in here and saw her.

Does she do this *every day*? At home, too?

Holy fucking shit. I didn't know I could hate myself any more than I already did.

While I watch, a middle-aged beta woman with two kids orders. The manager—who I suddenly have the violent urge to strangle—lazily types the drinks in...

...and the little omega I can't stop staring at scrambles into motion.

For all her poise, she's jumpy. *Rushing.*

After weeks of standing over every latte, drawing cutesy shit in the foam, *now* she's decided to be efficient?

Or was I just not paying attention before? Maybe I saw what I wanted to see. All of the moments she allowed herself to slow down... I tallied those against her because I couldn't figure out the insistent, insane urgency pulsing in my blood.

Now I know why she made me feel so agitated. It was my Alpha, trying to help me recognize our mate. But I've been using my instincts to conduct business for years. When they tried to direct me for more personal reasons, I couldn't understand them.

If I'm honest with myself, I've spent months dreading this stop on my daily schedule, hating the way something about the shop twisted my stomach into knots. There didn't seem to be any reason *why*, but every time I came in the door, every aggressive, impatient urge inside of me would lunge forward, trying to rip the reins away.

It made me more agitated than usual. Ruder, I'm sure. And I'm not a particularly forgiving person on a good day. Now, I flinch every time a new memory comes to me.

Fucking hell. Did I really call her *incompetent*?

And pathetic.

Guilt. That must be the reason I can't get up and leave. Why I can't look away.

I watch Remi work, remembering all of the things Cassian ever told me about her when he was in the group home. It wasn't much.

The impressions he shared were just flickers—a rooftop,

books, cookies, a butterfly clip. I recall thinking that she sounded like an imaginary friend. Then, as the months went on and he started to show up with a vaguely smile-like expression on his face, I remember thinking that maybe she was an angel. Some ethereal creature, sent to save him from drowning in his own apathy.

Really, she was just a girl. A sweet, giving sort of girl who had nothing but still shared her books and her desserts with a lonely boy.

And I made her *cry*. Every. Day.

I am a fucking asshole.

A fucking asshole who can't stop staring.

Remi sets the latest round of drinks on the service counter and stretches her neck out, tilting her head one direction and then the other. I watch the way the sunlight reflects off her blank throat and feel a prick of arousal. Along with a heavy truth, sinking on top of my lungs.

I want her.

But I don't deserve her.

chapter
thirty-five

COOL KIDS ONLY

DAMON

kiss emoji Hat trick for you tonight, pretty girl.

CASSIAN

I cannot believe you named this chat Cool Kids Only.

I hate myself for even texting in here.

REMI

I tried to tell him!

Besides, we should really add Smith.

He'll be mad.

CASSIAN

You let me worry about Smith, butterfly.

DAMON

We are* the cool kids, I don't make the rules.

Sweetness, if I get a hat trick, will you give me a kiss?

REMI

I gave you one literally ten minutes ago, Trouble.

But I will give you a different treat *wink emoji*

DAMON

Gotta go.

Gonna take me ten extra minutes to get into my gear with this boner *attached image*

CASSIAN HAS LEFT THIS CONVERSATION

THIS HAS to be the worst decision I've ever made.

Though, to be fair, *I* really didn't make it.

That would be Damon, who quite literally took care of everything—planning the evening, inviting my best friend, and securing our box seats, and sourcing the shirt on my back.

Some responsibility could also go to my Omega, who squeed like a schoolgirl with hearts in her eyes when Damon purred for me and told me to let him handle everything.

He did exactly what he said he would, organizing everything seamlessly. He figured he and Cass would leave the house around six, but Meg and her alphas would be there to get me at seven. He also told me that he'd cleared the whole thing with Smith and had left a jersey for me upstairs on the bed.

Which is how I ended up here.

In a special section of the hockey arena's club level.

With Meg and *all four* of her alphas.

"Ronan," Theo, her biggest, burliest man grunts, his mouth full of nachos. "The food here makes our stadium food look like ass."

Their billionaire pack-leader and intimidation master cuts Theo a severe look. "I'll take that under advisement."

The truth is, the Osprey's stadium is a paradise compared to this arena. Cassian explained that the Timberwolves have been considered up-and-comers for a long time—they've never won a title, and therefore they don't have the funds for the lavish renovations this place would obviously benefit from. But, still, it's clean. Well-lit. There are plenty of seats, and our box is at least semi-private, with tinted partitions between us and the next booth.

Meg runs her hand over Ronan's salt-and-pepper hair. "We have better cocktails, at least."

Considering the hockey arena only sells domestic beer on tap, I would have to agree. I've been sipping the foamy liquid in my cup for twenty minutes, but I haven't really made a dent. I'm too nervous.

Hours of watching hockey videos online while I cook has somewhat prepared me. I also watched some game tape from their last match with Cass one night, both us piled on top of one another in my little bed.

I thought I felt okay about witnessing the whole thing in real life. Now that we're here, though, I'm beginning to feel like this was a huge mistake. And not just because there's a beta couple in the open-air box next to ours who won't stop whispering while they shoot glances at me. I hear the words, "Pierson pack," "never," and "puck bunny" before I decide I don't need to know any more.

Sheesh.

I suppose I might wonder why I'm such an object of fascination... if I hadn't found one of Cassian's Timberwolves sweatshirts folded on my chair, waiting for me.

Which may or may not have made me perfume.

Thank the Lord I'm wearing *two* pairs of scent-blocking panties.

What have I gotten myself into?

Meg says nothing as I slip Cassian's sweatshirt on, swallowing a whine at his perfect hazelnut scent. When I notice her sharing a smug, knowing look with Declan, I narrow my eyes.

"I didn't say anything," she laughs, holding up her hands. "Just tell me: What is a hat trick, and is it as dirty as it sounds?"

Declan chuffs into her hair, hiding a smile against her temple.

"What?" Meg cries, throwing her hand toward the ice. "*Look* at them!"

I turn my head and peer down at the ice. Half of the Timberwolves skate lazy circles around the right side of the rink while the other half—

Well.

I'm not actually sure what they're doing.

But it looks like... humping?

It's hard to tell which one is Damon from high up, but it's easy to spot Cassian. For one thing, he will not stop looking up at me. After I privately told Meg about what happened before I snuck out for work a few mornings ago, she assured me that it's normal for an alpha to be a little extra over-protective after their first knotting.

Well, Bear had already taken over-protective to a whole new level before. Now? He's practically my unofficial bodyguard.

Even if he didn't glance over at me every minute or so, I would still recognize him right away. His goalie pads give him excess bulk. Not that they seem to be any hindrance to him.

While I watch, he absently sinks into a lunge, pulsing his hips forward before switching legs. When he drops to his knees to thrust into the open air, my mouth falls open.

"Actually," Dr. Archer chimes, "Those stretches are essential, especially for goalies. They have to drop to their knees and strike as quickly as possible, so their muscles need to be warm at all times."

As if he can hear Archer, Cass spreads his thighs wider and jerks his hips forward even more insistently. Meg follows my open-mouthed stare and then turns to Declan, frowning. "Why don't you stretch like that for me?"

Declan shrugs and smirks. "I do. Just not on the field."

They both snicker, Theo joining in, but I still haven't gotten my jaw off the floor.

Finding Damon in the sea of teal jerseys doesn't help. I finally get a flash of his jersey, the block letters clearly proclaiming, MATHERS.

A second after I see him, he glides to a stop and does a few of the pulsing lunges before sinking into his own hip thrusts. And I swear I catch the flash of his grin as he lays his lower body flat on the ice, hips down, and goes to town.

"Oh c'mon," Meg cries. "Now they're just milking it."

HOCKEY, as it turns out, is insane.

Enormous grown men, on ice skates? Speeding around a slippery surface? Throwing elbows and fighting with sticks?

My anxiety is next-level.

Even before Theo drops down into the chair beside Meg's and speaks over a munching mouthful of popcorn. "Hey, Remi, where is your other alpha? Aren't there supposed to be three?"

I huddle lower in my seat, playing off my shudder of dread as a reaction to the cold arena. "He's working."

That might be a lie. I actually have no idea where he goes or what he does during the day, only that he usually isn't back at the pack house until after I fall asleep. By design, most likely.

Though, he did show up at Proper Coffee this morning. After dressing up and making the two-mile walk out of his fancy neighborhood to the city bus every morning for over a week, I was grateful he'd finally seen my efforts at least once.

He's obviously avoiding me. It's the only logical explanation for why he would come to the shop every single day for months and then abruptly stop the same day we were matched.

Still, would it kill him to give me even the faintest glimmer of approval? He just sat in the corner for three hours and stared, never indicating whether he noticed my nicer clothes or faster work pace.

I, on the other hand, noticed that he had on a new tie. This one was brighter than his usual drab colors—a light pink that matched the frilled pocket square in his breast pocket.

I still didn't know what to make of that. Is he changing his attire to impress me? Or some other woman?

Make it make sense, Alpha, my Omega pouted, fed up with him and his mute staring. *And while you're at it, you could, you know, talk to us.*

That would be nice. Especially since our Cold War has left me constantly wondering what he thinks about the changes I've made to the house. Thanks to Mallory and his teams of contractors, I've gotten the stairs sealed, repaved the front walk, and finished the kitchen cabinets. Next week, there's a group starting work on the swimming pool, and a troupe of painters scheduled to finish the interior and exterior walls.

Asshole.

For once, I agree with my Omega's attitude. Smith could at least say *thank you* for the dinner plates I leave him.

I'd take a text. Or a Post-It.

Instead, I find his plate clean, washed, and drying beside the sink every morning. I put it away before I leave the house, and we start all over again the next night.

I'm trying not to let it devastate me. But it does.

When I was young, I used to watch sitcoms where families sat down to dinner together every night. It looked so cozy and idyllic—everyone at the same table, passing bowls of food around, trading stories or hashing out family decisions.

It was everything I wanted.

And now the pack alpha—my supposed *mate*—won't even show his face for a meal.

The Jumbotron lights up, flashing neon as the word GOAL scrolls across it, along with Damon's number. I look down at the ice just in time to watch him lift his stick and point it right at me. The enormous screen hanging over the ice gives me a close-up view as he holds up three fingers, flashes his gorgeous grin, and mouths, "That's three, sweetness."

Three goals in three periods. A hat trick. Just like he said.

And I almost missed it because I was so distracted by Smith's nonsense.

Meg leans over, whisper-shouting in my ear. "I think I'm jealous!"

My stomach sinks. I force a laugh. "Don't be."

chapter thirty-six

DAMON

BY THE TIME Beastly fights his way out of his mountain of padding, I'm already darting past him, dripping wet from the world's fastest shower.

His mouth twitches. "Remi texted."

Um, *yeah*. "She's meeting us in the tunnel. Can you *move your ass*? I want my treat."

For the first time in ages, Cassian laughs. *Out loud*. He's shaking his head while he does it, but it still totally counts.

"Yeah, sure." When he sees how stunned I am by his nongrumbly attitude, he shrugs. "I get it. I need to talk to Smith, anyway. But if you get dibs on tonight, I'm taking tomorrow morning."

Greedy bastard. He already had *this* morning, even though it wasn't his turn.

Which meant I had to go to morning skate grumpy and horny. It's a miracle I didn't end up punching someone. Again.

I trip into my jeans, not even bothering with briefs, de-scenter, or my whole hair routine. Fuck it. When I get my pretty girl home, she and I are going straight into the huge tub in my bathroom.

Cassian finally gets all of his bullshit off and throws a towel around his hips. Whatever good humor he had before is gone. He seems edgy now.

"I think I can scent her in the hallway," he mutters, rushing by me to shower quickly. "You better go."

My bag is over my shoulder the next second. I stuff my feet into shoes while my left hand finishes the buttons on my black shirt. Within seconds, I'm at the locker room tunnel.

Cass is right. She's out here, waiting. I can sense her stress the second I take a deep breath.

At first, I think it's because she's as anxious to see me as I am to see her. Then, I hear a deep, taunting tone.

"—little thing like you doing out here?"

My girl's timid voice answers. "I'm waiting for my alphas. Can you not—I'm sorry, can you not touch me?"

Fucking *what*?

I break into a run, turning out of the tunnels that empty into the hall outside the lockers. When I round the final corner, I find a guy in a cheap suit looming over Remi.

Her back is against the cinder blocks as she shrinks down into Cassian's Timberwolves hoodie. The stranger practically lays himself on top of her, his arm stretching over her head, face hanging near hers. "I saw you in the Pierson pack's box tonight.

Do you have a comment about Damon Mather's contract expiring this season?"

Remi shakes her head, nearly tripping as she tries to slip away. "No. I don't have a comment."

He lifts his hand, fingering one of her loose curls. And I lose my shit.

The fact that this guy is clearly press should probably give me pause. My Alpha doesn't give a damn, though. I grab his shoulder and rip him away, flattening his ass into the wall while I fist his jacket. "I *know* I did not just see you *touch* my omega."

This guy has a mangy face. Lean with wild eyes and unkempt facial hair. I guess some people might call him good-looking, but they probably won't anymore, once I fuck up his nose and knock all of his teeth out.

He sneers at me, cutting a quick glance back at Remi. "That's a hot little piece, Mathers. *Delicious*. She was about to let me take a bite."

Maybe facial reconstruction is too good for this guy. Maybe he just needs to... I don't know. Die.

Remi's voice sounds panicked. "Damon, I swear, I—"

"I know, baby," I tell her. My Alpha unleashes a wave of dominance unlike any I've ever manifested. The reporter bares his teeth, but it immediately calms my omega. She steps up behind me, her hand landing on my shoulder as the muscles under my button-down tick.

"D," she whispers, "I just want to go home."

Fuck. It's the first time she's ever called our house her home. And that has to be more important than breaking this asshole's face. Because *she's* more important.

With one last shove, I release the smaller alpha and nod toward the tunnel. "If I were you, I'd get out of here. Because if Cassian King gets out of the showers and scents our omega on you, you're dead."

This guy may be slimy, but he isn't stupid. And whatever he

sees on my face seems to convince him I'm not exaggerating even a little bit. No one wants to see what Cassian would do if he finally snapped. Not even me.

He stomps off, muttering and brushing at his suit like I've wrinkled it. My hackles don't lower until he's out of sight and Remi's honey-cake warmth goes from burned to slightly over-baked.

"I'm sorry," she starts, murmuring into my back, hiding her face. "I probably should have waited for you guys in the box, but I was excited to see you."

I spin and open my arms, lifting her for a deep, claiming kiss. "You never apologize for that," I say against her mouth. "Never, sweetness. Promise me."

She melts into my embrace, resting her forehead on mine. "I promise."

Her thin brows spring up, excitement gilding the gold in her eyes. "Do you still want your treat?"

I choke out a laugh. "Here?!"

She nods, utterly serious, and starts to struggle out of my arms. For a moment, I'm confused and a little bit worried. I mean, if my girl wants me, I don't ever want to say no, but I'm not sure if my Alpha can handle having her perfume here—knowing strangers like that reporter are hanging around. Not to mention the rest of my younger, unbonded teammates.

My apprehension fades as she turns and bends to pick up a small plastic container with a mint-green handle. It's just about the size of my palm, perfectly portioned to contain exactly one cupcake.

Glowing with pride, she presents the treat to me. "It's your favorite," she tells me. "Chocolate with cream cheese frosting."

And I swear to God—somehow, this single cupcake is even better than a blowjob.

Because it's *her*. This is how she shows she cares about people. She *made* this for me.

Her smile is everything. I feel it reverberate through my chest, down into my soul. Knowing, in that moment, that I have fallen so *impossibly* in love with her.

"It's perfect, pretty girl," I murmur, taking my treat and offering her my free hand. "Let's go home."

chapter
thirty-seven

CASSIAN

THIS HAS BEEN a long time coming.

Honestly, when Smith finds me sitting at the kitchen island in the middle of the night, waiting for him to walk in, I'm shocked he seems even marginally surprised.

Of fucking course I'm here to call his ass out.

Who does he think he is? As if we didn't sleep in the same house growing up. As if we didn't claw our way up from the gutter to build this one together.

The back door falls shut behind him. His brows arch. "Cass. What are you doing down here?"

I crack my knuckles, staring at him over the spotless expanse of the kitchen island. This place really is immaculate. Remi must be working herself to the fucking bone. The thought puts a growl into my voice as I pin him with a glare.

"Waiting."

Smith scowls, sighing. "Cassian, it's after midnight, and I haven't even eaten—"

"But you will," I cut in. "Because Remi left you a plate. Made you a special meal, actually, since D and I ate with the team and she had dinner with her friends."

I turn, pointing at the stove. "So, she stood there and prepared a whole-ass meal for *you*. The ungrateful asshole who won't even *talk* to her."

He opens his mouth, but I cut him off. "You forced her to move in here!" I shout. "You barked her out of her home and put her in a dusty spare bedroom with no nest. Last week, I found her in my *closet*, Smith. Hiding. Because of *you*."

He swallows but doesn't move to speak again. Instead, he drops his briefcase and slips his hands into his pockets, nodding at me to continue. My next statement hits him like a bullet.

"She was harassed tonight. By a reporter. It happened in the tunnels, after the game. She was waiting there for us. Alone. Because *you* weren't there."

Charred coffee swells to fill the room. He speaks through his teeth, barely moving his lips. "Is she all right?"

I checked her over myself, twice. Even after seeing that the guy didn't leave so much as trace of his scent on her, I still had to talk my Alpha down in order to leave her upstairs.

"She's fine," I mutter, trying to convince myself as much as him. "Damon drew her a bath."

His glower deepens. "Are you sure you shouldn't be up there? Is Damon capable of controlling himself?"

The question infuriates me, because anyone who had observed Remi with Damon would find it ludicrous. But he actually seems concerned. Which shows just how out of touch he is.

"Have you even *seen* her with Damon?" I ask, spewing all of the vitriol I've been storing up over the last week. "He's been taking care of her every damn day. Cuddling with her, watching her shows, listening to audiobooks so he can follow along with whatever she's reading. He's a good fucking alpha to her. It's bullshit that you don't know that. You should be here, watching and finding a way to be a part of this, too."

He ducks his head like he's dodging a physical blow. I see it, then—the tension in every line of his entire body. His jaw, clenched so hard I can hear his teeth grit.

"She's *perfect*, Smith. So goddamn beautiful and sweet and just—*fuck*, what is wrong with you? Don't you want her? How are you avoiding her like this?" I demand. "It's Damon's turn to sleep in that shitty-ass bed you threw her in, and I'm climbing the walls because I can't be with her. Don't you feel it?"

He's going to mutter something about his rut blockers, and I'm going to have to kick his ass into next year. Or he'll make excuses.

The room isn't ready. He has too much going on at work to come home for dinner. She isn't complaining, so why am I?

Because she *never will*. She's too scared that he'll reject her. Send her away. Take yet another home away from her.

Because he's *hurting* her. And I am her protector.

He opens his mouth. And, I swear to God, I'm ready. Ready to pummel him. Or challenge his leadership.

But then he says the two words I never thought he would.

"You're right."

My entire face crumples. "What?"

"You're right," he repeats. "I've been out all day, thinking about this. *Her*." He raises his dark eyes to mine, pained. "Did you know she's been sneaking out of here every morning to work at the coffee shop?"

She's been doing *what*?

"She goes for walks," I correct, repeating what she told me.

His smirk is humorless. "Smart girl," he mutters. "She is technically walking. To the bus stop. Then she works an eight hour shift and comes back here in time to make it seem like she's been home all day."

Oh. Holy. Shit.

How did I not notice that?

He's right. She's smart. She told us she likes to go for early-morning walks. Which isn't even really a lie... it just isn't the truth either.

I collapse onto a barstool, jamming both hands through my hair. "Fuck."

Smith edges closer, until he's standing at the opposite end of the island. Pressing both palms into the squeaky-clean, polished stone, he stares sightlessly down at the note she leaves for him each evening.

"Yeah... I know," he croaks, pausing. He clears his throat. "The thing I can't figure out is why she feels like she needs to do all of this. She knows you adore her. And Damon, obviously. We moved her in here, took on all of her expenses. Why is she trying to do everything on her own? Why keep showing up at the shop?"

I glare at him, refusing to believe he's this clueless. Then, it occurs to me that he might actually have no idea what she went through.

Did I ever mention it? Probably not. I wouldn't have broken her confidence that way, back then. And once she was gone? It would have felt like talking shit about someone I used to care about.

Still cared about. Will always care about.

Will always... *love*.

So goddamn much.

My chest tightens, aching as I rub my palm over my sternum and stare my brother down. "Smith, think about it. Think about where she lived."

His brows fold over his dark eyes. "I know she has no money. I've already given her the pack's card, and she knows we'll pay for anything she—"

I shake my head. "No. Smith. *Think.* She was an orphan. A true one—not like us. Compared to her, we were just... unlucky. Our parents died—but at least we *had* parents. A home. A family. And then we had each other. She was just alone, Smith. No one wanted her *ever.* Not even her own mother."

Saying all of this shit—it hurts. Every word feels like a thorn, torn from a tender spot at the base of my throat. They scrape out of me in rusty rasps.

"I used to watch her," I whisper. "When other kids had visitors on the weekends. She sat at the top of the steps and saw them all go. No one ever came for her."

Smith's features crease in a wince. "So she's doing all of this... to show that she's appreciative?"

The whole ripping-his-arms-off thing Damon suggested is sounding more and more appealing.

"No," I grind out. "She's *scared.* She went to foster homes. They all returned her. No one wanted to keep her. I imagine she worries you'll do the same thing."

Smith snaps upright. "I would never, *ever* send her away," he growls.

I arch a brow at him. "I would never, *ever* let you. But I'm not the one who feels insecure, here. You need to figure out how to make her feel like she has a real place in this pack. Especially if you ever expect to bond with her. Jesus, Smith, you won't even *talk* to her—you think she's going to want you inside her mind?"

He scowls. "I'm trying not to scare her! She's afraid of me!"

I wave at hand him, the way he's glaring and bellowing and pumping out waves of aggression that would bowl over a weaker alpha. And swamp an omega like a tsunami.

"Yeah, no shit."

For a long moment, Smith just stares at me. His dominance pummels my resolve, telling me to back down.

But for Remi?

I never will.

chapter thirty-eight

SOMETIMES, the only way to live without the things you want the most is to convince yourself that you didn't really want them that much in the first place.

I'm an expert at it.

For years, I lied to myself about my little apartment. My tinier bedroom. The closet floor nest.

Because I didn't want to let myself imagine *this*.

It's a dream.

Wrapped in the surreal dread of a nightmare.

Because it is *perfect*. But I don't know where I am or how I got here.

Moving in a slow daze, I sit up on the huge, fluffy bed underneath me. Didn't I go to sleep in the guest room? Crammed up against Damon?

Where is he? And why didn't my alarm go off at five?

I don't know how, but there's sunlight streaming into this huge, rounded room. Too strong to be pre-dawn light.

The first thing I notice are the windows. There are eight—tall, narrow, and intricately arched, like something out of a cathedral. They fill the curved wall at my back, offering views of the front yard, backyard, and the horizon.

I'm still in the pack house, my brain peeps. That's the new front walk I just had installed. And the pool repair supplies are piled out back.

Whichever room I'm now in must be at the very end of the house, because the view is beautiful. Treetops and golden light glowing through them. It filters into the bedroom, highlighting plush ivory linens surrounding me and the soft pink paint adorning the walls.

The rug on the floor provides color. It's enormous, a pastel image of dozens of different blooms. I see that there's a coordinating duvet folded into a neat rectangle at the end of the bed I apparently slept in.

It's hard to say if it's truly as large as it feels. With so much natural light reflecting off the crisp sheets, my eyes just catalog a sea of softness.

There's also, I note, a canopy. Or the top part of one, anyway, flowing from the metal frame overhead and back down behind the white iron headboard.

Even without touching anything, I can tell whoever chose all of it selected the very best of the best. Silk thin enough for sunlight to slant through it. The thick, even pile of the rug. Hardwood floors that have been polished to a perfect shine. Someone even sourced molding for the doors and the ceiling to match the pretty windows.

It's feminine and luxurious in a way I've only ever imagined. The more I look, the more I love it. Antique furniture that coordinates without matching. The engraved, scrolly mirror over the vanity. And —when I turn almost all the way around so I'm facing the doors again—a curved corner with three floor-to-ceiling bookshelves.

I think I'm hyperventilating. Did Cassian and Damon do this? If they did, will Smith be angry? And where are they?

This bed doesn't have either of their scents and—after sleeping with both on my pillow each night—my Omega doesn't like it. A whine spills out of my throat, echoing through the big room.

"Remi?"

I jump, squawking as my hands fly out to gather sheets over my nightgown.

Smith stands off to my left, leaning against the curved wall with both of his hands in the pockets of his pants. With all the natural light in here, his blond hair and neutral suit look especially polished and handsome.

Oh my God.

I missed work. I somehow ended up in a new room and my phone didn't go off, and now I missed work, and Smith is here to fire me or ream me out, or tell me to pack my eight boxes and get out of his—

"I made this for you," he says, turning to the desk beside him and picking up... a silver breakfast tray.

My jaw drops.

With clipped footsteps, he brings it over to the bed and sets it on a nightstand within my reach. When I look down at, my jaw *unhinges.*

There's a latte. And a flower.

Is it my birthday?

Do they even *know* my birthday?

No, to both, probably. Especially not *this* alpha.

I shrink back, overwhelmed by all of the things I don't understand. Afraid this is some sort of trap. Or a test.

My voice wobbles. "Y-you didn't have to do that. I can make your coffee before I leave in the mornings. And this room is—it's too big for just me. I can go back to the guest room. D-did I sleepwalk in here or...?"

Smith frowns, the expression intimidating. "I carried you in here last night. This is the Omega Suite."

He turns to scowl at the entire room. "It still isn't finished," he mutters. "I wanted it to be done before I gave it to you."

I'm... shocked. Even though it makes perfect sense. Of course, this was all Smith. Cassian knows how much I love to read, but I can't fathom him choosing luxury linens. And Damon may have style and taste, but he would never think of tiny details like crown molding or antique doorknobs to match the dresser's hardware.

Smith raises his chin slightly, the muscles in his cut jaw flexing while he nods to the side. "Your bathroom is right in there. And the door beside it is your nest, little petal."

I'm not sure if I like that nickname. On one hand, any term of endearment from this cold, distant alpha feels like a triumph. On the other, no matter what he calls me, I can't stop hearing all of the things he once snarled at me instead.

"Some of us have shit we need to do. We don't have all day to deal with your fucking incompetence."

It's hard to reconcile that cruel alpha with the cool, composed man in front of me.

Until I look a bit closer.

And see that the muscles in his jaw are ticking. The pulse in his throat throbs. And he appears to be gripping the insides of his suit pants.

He's tightly-wound. It doesn't surprise me, now that I see the level of perfectionism he's capable of. No wonder he didn't have it in him to do the whole house, if this is the sort of standard he sets for himself.

I'm not sure I like how much I understand that.

I'm not sure I want to admit that I'm exactly the same way.

Instead, I lean forward far enough to peer into the bathroom, past its open door. Just like the others, the portal is tall and broad enough for the alphas, made of solid wood, and carved to match the windows.

On the other side, I see an ensuite bathroom that looks more like a mini spa. Or perhaps something on one of my Pinterest boards.

For one, it's pink. Blush quartz countertops and a trough sink with three brushed brass faucets. Pale pink paint with one feature wall covered in modern floral wallpaper. It takes a moment for me to realize it matches the rug in the bedroom exactly.

I do a double-take when I see that the chandeliers also match —both gold with glass bubbles. The bathroom version is a perfectly proportionate miniature of the big one.

Smith's voice sounds quieter when he speaks again. "Your ensuite contains a walk-in closet, a separate room for a toilet." His voice drops lower. "And a special nest entrance."

My eyebrows jump. Meg's nest has its own bathroom, which honestly sounds a bit overwhelming, in my opinion. It never occurred to me that I could have a traditionally-sized nest with its own special entrance to my bedroom's ensuite.

Huh. I bite back a rueful smile. *Not only is the alpha-hole a successful developer, he's a* good *developer.*

Smart, creative. Clearly too good at his job for his own good. Yet, somehow, he got over whatever hurdle prevented him from finishing the rest of the pack house in order to make this room perfect.

For *me*?

It might still be a test, I remind myself. He could be watching my reaction to see how I behave. If I'm grateful enough. Or worth all of this extravagance.

The problem is, I cannot currently access the instincts I need to please him. Because my Omega is irrationally angry about this scentless bed and my other two missing alphas.

When I blink up at Smith, the grooves around his mouth carve deeper. "What?" he demands. "What's wrong?"

Great. Now I've made him angry. No matter what I do, I just can't seem to make him *happy*.

Everything inside of me coils low, hiding from the frustration on his face. The tightness pulling at his features gradually goes slack. He sighs, stepping closer.

"Remi, I—" He drops his chin, adjusting the monogrammed cuffs of his shirt before he clears his throat and raises his head. Our eyes lock, but there's no command in his. For the first time ever, I can look at him without my insides going brittle.

"I would like to—I would like *an opportunity* to fix this. Starting with understanding you better."

Is my mouth hanging wide open again?

Yep, my Omega chirps. *It sure is.*

"So, tell me," he says, taking another step toward the bed. "What's upsetting you? I want to fix it for you."

My lips snap together as I try to swallow the hoarse lump rising in my throat. But he's looking at me so intently, wanting to take care of me. Or at least, take care of *this*.

I force myself to speak. "The bed is so nice, but it doesn't, um, smell right."

If I weren't ten seconds away from crying, I might think his face is sort of funny. His brows crouch low as he runs his eyes over the rumpled sheets behind me. And I can tell he hasn't got the first clue what I'm talking about.

"It doesn't smell right," he repeats. "As in, you want new sheets? Different detergent?"

Lord help me, but this level of alpha cluelessness is actually sort of adorable. My lips twitch as I shake my head. "No. I mean, it doesn't smell like you."

He blinks. "*Me?*"

His incredulity steals my nerve. I bite my lower lip and sink back a bit. "Or Damon. Or Cassian."

It's supposed to be all three of you, knot-head.

You know, I tell my Omega. *You really need to get this entitled attitude in check.*

Bite me, she sniffs. *Since, apparently, no one else around here is going to.*

I watch as Smith processes this information, and his frown recedes. "Oh. Of course. Right." Another uncomfortable half-cough. "How do we, ah, fix that?"

Part of me wants to groan, because this is *painful*. Another part just wants to grab him by his tie and yank him onto the mattress. Instead, a startled, disbelieving laugh trips out of me.

The second it happens, I start to panic. He'll think I'm laughing at him. He'll get angry. Will he take this room back?

But instead, his mouth curves up in the most handsome, wry half-smile I've ever seen. One of his thick blond brows arches.

"Am I funny to you, petal?"

I shake my head, trying my best to straighten out my face. "Nooooo, I just... Well, to answer your question, usually alphas sleep in an omega's bed with them. Or they give the omega items that have their scent on them."

Bless his heart, he actually looks around as if he's going to magically find a basket of worn alpha clothing to hand me. "Right," he mumbles, "That makes sense. All right."

He turns back to me, frowning but also distinctly... not angry. Which is new. "What else?"

My mind spins, trying to decide where to begin and what he's even asking for. Does he want some sort of list? Or a lesson on my designation? For some reason, both ideas make that coil in my center curl tighter, pulsing with hurt.

Smith watches me carefully and speaks before I have to. "No," he says, quiet. "This isn't right either. It shouldn't be your responsibility to teach me. I'll figure it out."

The knot inside of me loosens a little. "Are you sure? I can—"

He shakes his head. "No. You're already doing too much. Which is something I need to talk to you about." His dark eyes pierce mine. "Do you *want* to work?"

Do I...?

Who *wants* to work?

Then again, I guess some people do. Meg loves going into the office with Ronan. And I didn't mind my job when it was just baking all day long.

Now that I'm here, though, with their amazing kitchen... It seems silly to ask him to reinstate my former position at Proper Coffee just to give me access to a decent oven.

Smith reads my expression, his own softening slightly. He lifts his hand and then pauses, halting himself for a long second before he reaches over and slowly smooths his palm over my loose curls, brushing some off of my face.

"You don't have to go back there, Remi. Stay here. Keep making the house just the way you want it. Use that card I gave you to buy anything you want. And I mean that—*anything*."

My brain conjures absurd images of dozens of things—outlandish stuff like yachts; and small things I've never had the heart to purchase for myself, like fancy headbands. He surely can't mean *anything*.

Besides, there's only one thing I really *want*. Or, need, rather.

Smith watches my eyes skirt toward the only closed door in the large, round room. "*Especially* that," he growls, low. "Anything you need for your nest, you buy it. End of story."

I try to ignore the stab of disappointment that hits me. We're supposed to furnish our nest together, but he doesn't know that. Or maybe he doesn't want to.

That would make sense. I can't get him to come home for dinner; what are the odds he's going to want to take a whole day to shop with me?

I'm guessing not great.

I nod, swallowing hard. "Yes, Sir."

The hand resting in my hair flexes. I hear his sharp intake of breath, his scent spiking. Rich warmth fills the air, and my shoulders unwind, content to have one of their scents in my space.

His hand slowly slides off of me, bringing my attention to the pop of color tucked into his neutral suit's breast pocket. Like his tie, it's blush. But unlike the solid piece knotted at his throat, the pocket square looks like the one I noticed on him yesterday.

Patterned. Gingham, actually. Delicate white and pink checks, silky fabric. Much more cheerful than his typical, masculine accessories.

The fold is off, too. Instead of a simple square with crisp creases, this pocket square—

—isn't a pocket square.

Because it's *my missing panties.*

And he's wearing them as an accessory. Tucked into the front of his suit jacket where everyone will see them. Showing me off to the world, even though no one else will ever know what they are.

But *I know.*

And when I chance a glance up at him? I know that *he knows* that *I know.*

But what does it *mean*?

Smith gives nothing away. His eyes swirl, two whirlpools of dark heat. "Have a nice day, little petal," he clips, walking toward the door. "Thanks for the pocket square."

chapter
thirty-nine

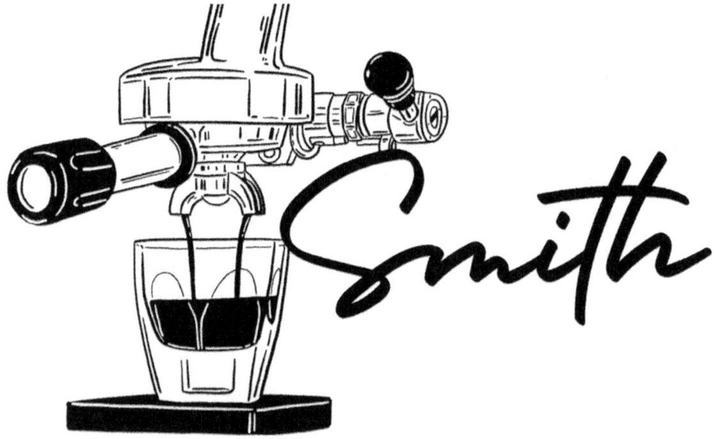

REMI IS PERFECT.

It's a nightmare.

She floats around our kitchen like she was born to be there—an angel flitting between clouds, pulling heavenly baked goods out of thin air. So far, this week, she's made bread, brownies, scones, and cupcakes. They all look and smell incredible; although, nothing smells quite as delicious as her.

It isn't just her kitchen prowess. It's the way she moves. The sway of her perfectly pleated skirts, a ladylike turn of her heel. She's polished and pretty.

Perfection.

And I can't touch her.

There's one exception. Every morning, I bring her a latte in bed, and she lets me brush her hair back. I ask her what she's planning to do that day and tell her to behave. She says, "Yes, Sir." And I walk out of there with a throbbing knot and her pilfered panties in my pocket.

Because—yes, this omega is so perfect, she now *leaves me her panties.*

Without making a fuss or saying a single word to embarrass me, she simply began leaving a different pair of folded, silk panties out with my dinner note each night.

She must know what I do with them. She *saw* me do it. Yet, every day, I find a new offering.

I've been trying to make my own in return. Starting with making more of an effort to work from home when I can. Now, the kitchen table is covered in a layer of paperwork while I sit in one of the newly-acquired chairs, watching her.

She's in a light purple sundress today—one with a proper pleated skirt and a thin belt at her waist. Her hair hangs loose, the black curls swinging down her back while she dips into the oven and produces a tray of muffins.

An expert, she angles the pan just so to check the edges, gliding a toothpick into the center of the least-browned pastry. She hums to herself while she works, the quiet strains of some pop song. It seems oddly upbeat, given the burned-honey aroma in here.

Remi only smells stressed when she has to be alone in a room with me. As soon as Damon swoops into the kitchen, wearing a red pair of his silky briefs and nothing else, she smiles and turns sweeter.

He still frowns at her, sensing the distress lingering in the air. Before he can open his mouth, though, the cunning little omega stretches up onto her tiptoes and presses her plump, pink mouth over his.

Damon groans, instantly putting his hands all over her. One grabs a fistful of her skirt, wrinkling it. I feel a vein throb in my forehead.

"You look so pretty, sweetness," he tells her, all soft. He rubs his cheek against hers until she beams. "Prettiest girl in the world."

Yes. She really is.

And she hates me.

Cassian comes in next, carrying a book in one hand and his phone in the other. Now that Remi's here, he's shirtless all the time, too. Much more than he ever was before. Though, maybe she likes it that way.

I wouldn't know. Because of that whole hating-me situation.

Remi leans around Damon's bicep to smile at my brother, her blue eyes alight. "Hi, Bear!"

I've never seen Cass grin so much. His face stretches into a wide smile while he bends to drop a kiss on her forehead. "Butterfly. I brought you something."

He hands her the book in his hand. I see he has tabs in it, marking places he wanted to share with her. That notion might make me happy for him if I weren't currently dying of envy.

Remi's expression glows while she smirks. "So, funny story..." She trails off, leaning over the island to pick up a different book. She hands it to him. "I got this for you."

Cassian blinks at the gift before lunging for our omega; sweeping her up onto the counter and stepping between her legs. She giggles and squeals, the sound muffled when he mashes his mouth over hers.

When he's done mauling her, he presses his face into her neck. She pets his hair like it's the most natural thing in the world and holds her other hand out for Damon.

"I have a treat for you, too," she tells him.

D instantly perks up, sliding in beside them. "A treat?"

She nods, gesturing to the pan of fresh muffins. "They're your favorite."

Damon pounces on the pan, popping two of the perfectly formed banana-walnut muffins out of the silicone baking sheet.

Did she bring that thing here with her? She had no nesting supplies, but packed a muffin pan? I almost smile at the thought, until I remember that I still haven't been invited into her nest.

Have the others?

What will happen during her heat?

Omegas need their pack alphas there above all else during heats. That's a well-known fact; but I've never looked into what happens when the omega has rejected that alpha. I, stupidly, never thought I would need to know that.

I assumed our scent-sensitivity would work all of this out. But that isn't happening, is it?

We can't help our attraction, but there's no *connection*. Most days, she doesn't even meet my eyes. I don't think I've even seen her wearing a T-shirt, yet. It's like she knows when I'll be around and goes out of her way to make herself into a version of herself she thinks I'll find the most palatable.

Could that be a pack leader thing? Do I intimidate her?

A depraved part of me wants to. Her shy sweetness radiates natural submission—and my baser urges shove at me, telling me to find out how deep that deference goes.

But, in the moments when I have enough blood in my brain for it to fucking work, I know none of this is good. She isn't being herself. She's still frightened of me. No matter how submissive that makes her, it isn't *right*.

Besides, *true* submission is earned through *trust*. And the way her scent turns bitter and her fingers flinch at my proximity screams her discomfort.

She doesn't trust me—with her body or her heart.

I don't blame her.

But I think it may be time to do something drastic.

chapter **forty**

EVERY MORNING, I wake up between two hard walls of muscle.

Two *bickering* walls of muscle.

"Your toes are touching me," Cassian grumbles, tightening the forearm around my waist to bring my back flush with his chest.

"Yeah, and your arm is under my pillow," Damon smirks. "Did you have a point? Other than being a pain in the ass?"

"*Shh*. You're going to wake her up."

"No, *you're* going to—"

I blink, finding Damon's stunning blue eyes inches away from mine. In the soft morning light, his black hair is glossy and disheveled. He winces. "Sorry, sweetness. I tried to tell Cass to pipe down."

My bear reaches around me to punch his packmate in the bicep. "Dick."

I giggle, and Damon grins, leaning close to kiss me and murmur against my lips, "Best sound in the world, pretty girl."

Cassian's face nuzzles at the back of my neck, scent-marking me. "Huh," he grunts, grumpy as ever. "You finally got me and D to agree on something."

I laugh again, snuggling back into Cassian's thick, solid embrace. His lips graze my shoulder lightly, followed by his teeth, eliciting a burst of perfume that has me hiding my face in my hands.

Damon isn't having that, though. He plucks my fingers to the side so he can see my eyes. Still grinning crookedly, he adds his hands to the mix, sliding one down to trace my nightgown-covered curves.

"Mmm..." He glances over my head at his packmate. "I think we owe our omega for waking her up."

Their omega. My stomach flutters with excited tingles.

Cass grinds his hardening cock across my backside, teasing me, and concurs, "It's only fair."

Heat flashes through Damon's aqua irises. "I have an idea."

I squeal as he grips my hips and rolls, yanking me on top of his big, beautiful body. Sunlight slants through the arched windows over us, pooling between his abs, highlighting the grooves carved into his pelvis.

By the time I realize he has no boxers on, he's spreading my slick core over his perfectly-waxed pubic bone, softly gliding the hard ridge over my slit. I moan, and he answers with a strangled sound.

Beside us, Cassian huffs. "Is this for her or you?"

Damon casts him an annoyed look, sighing. "The man has a

point, sweetness. Putting my cock in your pretty pussy isn't exactly penance." A spark ignites in his eyes. "Besides, I told you: I have an idea."

In one fluid ripple of movement, he lies back and pulls my body up to his face. He almost has me over his shoulders when I freeze up, protesting.

"What?!" I burst, my face heating. "No. I can't—I can't—"

"Sit on my face? Gush slick all over my chin? Drown me in your sweetness?" Damon blinks up at me, all false innocence. "Why not, baby?"

I cringe, shifting on my knees to hide the effect of his words. It's useless, though, when twin trails of slick roll down my parted thighs.

Cassian's big hand lands on my back in a soothing caress. "If you don't want to, you don't have to, Rems. But, trust me, D would love it." He raises one thick brow. "Hell, *I* would love it."

He glances at Damon. "I bet I can get her off faster than you can."

Damon laughs, the huff of air hitting a sensitive patch just above my knee. "Like this? Good luck, Beastly."

I gape at them both, shocked and turned on by the steady, no-nonsense eagerness on both of their faces. "You... you both want to—do that? But what if I—I don't know—crush you?"

They look at each other and stifle laughter, but Cassian's eyes are kind when he gazes up at me. "You're light, butterfly. I think both of us are capable of holding you up."

Silly. Of course they are. But I still bite my lip, looking from Cass's face to Damon's, which is just inches away from my center.

"What if I suffocate you?" I blurt.

His grin spreads slowly. "Then, on my tombstone, I want it to say, 'Here lies the luckiest fucker on Earth.'"

A nervous titter escapes me. "Okay, okay. We can try it, I guess. But what about Cass?"

My bear's green eyes glow. "Don't worry about me."

He and Damon share a look that can only spell trouble, but I don't have much time to contemplate it. Because ten seconds later, Damon shifts under me, scooting down to put his face right between my legs.

I shake as I gaze down at him while he stares up at the juncture of my thighs in absolute rapture. "Goddamn," he mutters to himself. "Prettiest pussy on the planet. And you smell like heaven, sweetness. Can I have it? Please?"

Panties in bed have been outlawed. It was, in Damon's words, his "one and only alpha power trip." I suppose that's paying off now, as he guides my hips down and finds my bare skin with his lips.

Cassian's chest vibrates with a suppressed growl. "Tell me how her cunt tastes."

When I tense up, Damon chuckles. I feel his smile against my inner thighs while he mumbles, "She hates that word."

Cass looks to me for confirmation. Seeing my pout, flashes his rare grin. "Sorry, butterfly."

His eyes are light and teasing, but the squeeze he gives my thigh is sweet. I expect him to maybe get on his knees and touch me while Damon licks me; but, instead, Cass reclines with his arm folded behind his head, entranced.

I'm about to balk when D's fingers tighten on my naked hips, fisting my nightgown out of his way and tugging me straight down in one powerful motion. I gasp, his full lips and the prickle of morning stubble vibrating against my mound.

"Fucking perfect," he mutters, low and pained. "Gotta have it, pretty girl."

His tongue sweeps out at that same moment, lapping a smooth semi-circle over the top of my clit. I whimper, swaying forward automatically. He hums his approval, pulling me down harder.

The slick heat of his tongue tracing up and down, his thick lower lip teasing my slit while the upper lip rubs at my clit. It feels incredible, but I can't shake the feeling that it must be uncomfortable to him.

When he feels my thighs shake, he groans and pushes my hips down harder. The next lash of his tongue slips into my pussy, and I whine. The sensation is so much better than I ever imagined—and being able to ride it instead of lying back makes it feel even dirtier.

Cass purrs, though it sounds ragged. "That's my girl," he praises, reaching down and pulling his thick cock from his boxer briefs. "Ride his tongue. I bet you taste like heaven."

Lapping up a fresh burst of slick, Damon growls his agreement. The sound sends a vibration over my sensitized skin. My body clenches, trying to tighten around the tease of his tongue.

And then—

I'm in the air.

There's no time for me to panic before Cassian grabs my waist in his left hand and rips Damon's right hand away with his own. With a tug and a lift, I go from straddling Damon's face to mounting Cassian's.

"What—" I start to gasp, but there's no time. Cassian latches his lips to my clit and sucking hard.

Every nerve in my body sparkles, while the tension in my core coils tighter. A wail rips out of me, the sound fading into a high-pitched shriek when he begins circling his tongue around the bud he's still pulling into his mouth.

Beside me, Damon pants quietly, grabbing his knot with both hands. In some distant part of my mind, it occurs to me that he isn't angry, or even annoyed. Which means they must have coordinated this, somehow.

I can't find the brain space to care how, or why, or what that means—as long they *don't stop*.

Cass purrs louder while his hands grip my bare buttocks, the thick fingers long enough to curl over each cheek. Damon watches with burning blue eyes and licks his shining lips. "Tease that tight little asshole, Cass."

Oh my—

Ah!

Cassian's smallest finger strokes along the puckered entrance, making me buck forward. Damon casts me a wicked grin that tightens my nipples, watching while his packmate collects my wetness and rubs over my back hole lightly, pushing just the tip of his finger in.

Everything inside of me cinches as I whine in pleasured dismay. Cassian groans deeply, releasing my clit to pull each of my pussy lips into his mouth, teeth grazing gently.

With that teasing bit of fullness in my backside, everything he does feels incredible. Especially when he pushes in just a bit deeper and rubs at the wall between my ass and my pussy.

I perfume so hard, I feel dizzy. It has to be too much. What if he can't breathe—

He hums, the sound reassuring. Then, he issues the only bark he's ever given me.

"*Drown me, omega.*"

My body obeys, pouring more slick over his lips. Beside us, Damon twists two fists over his cock faster and harder. His eyes are wild as he bites back a snarl.

"Give her to me."

Cassian huffs out deep breaths as he passes me back to his packmate. This time, Damon rotates me so I can watch them both stroke their cocks and fondle their knots.

Damon uses two hands, one always gripping his knot or his balls while he strokes with the other. Cassian prefers one hand, but he grips harder.

I wish I could pay closer attention and learn what they each like up close. But D's teasing licks and deep plunges into my pussy put me right on the edge.

Before long, I truly am riding both of their faces. And each time I think I'm about to tip over the edge for one of them? They pass me back to the other.

When I'm covered in slick and sweat, begging Cassian to finish me off, he finally has mercy and crams two thick fingers into my pussy while the other plays with my ass.

A few firm circles on my clit have me seeing stars, screaming both of their names, while the tight bundle of need in my middle releases in a hot burst of liquid pleasure. They both roar, their scents thickening while they each get themselves off.

I collapse between them, panting and shaking. Right back where I started, with two muscled chests surrounding me, each immediately breaking into a purr.

"WHERE ARE WE GOING?"

Cassian keeps his big, rough palms over my eyes, leading me from behind. "Just a little bit further."

I giggle, trying not to trip while I reach back to smooth a hand down his thigh. "Can't I have a hint?"

His voice is grumbly and very bear-like. "No hints."

We turn to the right, going from the hallway to his bedroom, I think. I'm still not sure, exactly, since he carried me up the stairs after dinner and spun me around before turning me toward our destination.

"Okay," he husks, pressing his whole body into my back and sliding his hands from my face. "You can look."

It is his room. Only... It isn't, really, anymore. There are no more piles. And the corner where he used to have his double bed is now just as full of bookshelves as every other wall.

A new oriental rug covers the tired wood floor. A lacquered wooden ladder is propped up against the shelves. And a cozy egg chair takes up the space where his mattress used to be.

My lips fall open in shock. "It's..."

"Our library," he finishes matter-of-factly. "I ordered all the books we used to read and trade, plus a few dozen other ones and the stuff you had on your Amazon Wishlist. My leather chair can stay over there, but I this, uh, egg one is for you. I figured, since it has a lot of pads and pillows and *mmphf—*"

My mouth crashes onto his, smashing the rest of his explanation. Cassian catches me around the waist and lifts me up, deepening our kiss with a low groan.

When I pull back, grinning, his green eyes bounce between mine. "You like it?"

"I love it," I whisper. "But won't you miss having your own room to sleep in? When you get sick of me and Damon and—"

This time, he cuts me off, brushing our lips together much more tenderly than I did. "I will never get sick of you," he murmurs. "I wanted to give you the library we always wanted. But I also wanted to show you; I don't need a backup plan. Your bed is my bed, now. I never want to sleep anywhere else. Because I love you, Rems. Always have, always will."

He's always been a man of action, not words. But he knows me—he knows how many times I've been turned away. So, he did the grand gesture *and* made sure to say the words out loud, too.

Cassian waits, our gazes locked, even when mine clouds with happy tears. "I love you, too, Bear."

His lips quirk up, the smile soft. "I want you right here," he tells me. "In our house. In our bed. My girl. Okay?"

I nod, springing up to hug his neck again. "Okay."

chapter forty-one

DAMON

"*WHAT* ARE YOU *DOING*?"

Um. Fuckin' *rude*.

I know I'm not the hardest worker in the pack, but damn. Cass could at least *act* like the sight of me asleep on a pile of books isn't some apocalyptic omen.

Half of them are from Remi's friend's doctor alpha. He dropped them off for me, along with "some helpful research." Dude is *intense* with his research shit. There are tabs and neon streaks and notes in margins.

Which I'm sure would be excellent, if they didn't all look like hieroglyphics to me.

The AirPods in my ears died a long-ass time ago. Can't say I blame them. I listened to eight straight hours of audiobooks.

On the plus side, I think I might have learned something. *Maybe*? At some point...?

I look around at all the titles, blinking—as if that will help to clear the way the words run together. My stomach seethes. Remi really *does* love books. What if I can't relate to this part of her? Will she eventually connect with the others more because I'm an idiot and she's brilliant?

I can't give up this easily. She's my fucking soulmate. I'll listen to every audiobook on the planet if I have to. Even the super nasally ones.

For her? My ears can bleed. I don't give a fuck.

Besides, if the book thing doesn't work out, that Bake Off show actually *slaps*, so.

Smith comes downstairs, frowning and muttering something about Remi being up in her nest. Then he breezes out the door, promising he'll *try* to be home for dinner.

It hasn't actually happened yet, but maybe today's the day. He seems like he has a fire under his ass and a twitch in his left eye. Plus, he didn't even try to mock me for all the books he found me passed out on.

Cass leaves next, grunting about me being a "lucky asshole" because he and the other defenders all have to be fitted for new gear today while I have the morning off.

The house is too quiet. I decide it's probably a sign I should be doing my conditioning in our home gym, but some weird instinct stops me.

It starts as a prickle at the base of my scalp, tiptoeing up my nape. Difficult to describe, other than the indistinct sense that I'm *needed* somehow. A minute later, the faint whine of insistence becomes a scream of urgency.

Leaping to my feet, I streak right upstairs. *I'm coming, pretty girl.*

Turns out my Alpha is maybe a bit dramatic.

When I burst into Remi's suite, I find her struggling with... a bra?

I stop on the threshold, gobbling up the sight of her topless body while she twists and huffs, fed up with the straps on her shoulders. As soon as she hears me chuckle, she freezes.

"Damon! I'm changing!"

Shy, sweet thing. Like she wasn't riding my face into oblivion the other day.

"Sorry, sweetness," I tell her, strolling over to help. "What's the problem with this bastard? He giving you trouble?"

She flashes her blue-gold eyes over her shoulder, smirking. "*You're* giving me trouble, Trouble. But, yes, the strap is too tight."

I agree, nodding. "You should definitely just burn it and never wear one again."

A bit of color touches her cheeks. "But then everyone would see how small my boobs actually are."

I click my tongue at her and she narrows her eyes, challenging me. "Oh come on. You have to admit; they're small."

She's right. Everything about her is dainty, even her curves. As far as I'm concerned, she's exactly perfect.

I tilt my head at her. "Okay, sure, but that's like saying ice cream is cold while neglecting to mention how fucking delicious it is." I bend my head and nuzzle between her tits, groaning quietly. "So fucking delicious. It's a crime to cover these beauties with bras."

Remi giggles. "If I burned all my bras, everyone would see my nipples," she whispers, eyes dancing. "And you and I would have to bury the bodies of all Cassian's victims."

Good point. Because he would *definitely* murder anyone who stared at her tits too long.

I help her get her strap to work and watch while she pulls a light blue blouse over her head. When she's covered, I pull her into my arms and hug her securely, mumbling a confession.

"I thought something was wrong. I had a weird feeling."

She goes still, peering up at me. "I was—I actually was upset before you walked in."

It doesn't take a genius for me to see why. She has all sorts of packages strewn around her room, half-opened. There are even a few propped in front of her nest. I feel a giddy wave of anxiety just looking at them, so God only knows how she feels.

A solution comes to me, so simple that I know it must be brilliant. "Put some jeans on, sweetness. I have an idea."

chapter forty-two

DAMON LOOKS EXACTLY the way you would imagine a pro-athlete to look driving his convertible.

Cool and stupidly gorgeous.

Or maybe I'm the stupid one, because it's all I can do not to openly gape at him.

After telling me to change into jeans, he ran off and returned in a pair of his own, along with the softest gray sweater. It's late March, not nearly cold enough for sweaters in Florida, but he made me grab one before he escorted me down to his Audi.

While my curls fly everywhere, his thick black hair remains

slicked into his usual carelessly coiffed style. Equally dark aviators shield his eyes as he laces our fingers together and steers one-handed through the curving roads that lead to town.

Maybe he wants to go shopping, I fret. That would be ill-advised since I finally broke down a couple days ago and went on a late-night online-ordering binge. With Cassian and Damon at an away game on the other side of the state, and Smith doing his usual work-late routine, it was my first night in the pack house alone.

Normally, I would have hidden in my nest until one of them came home… but the nest is still an entirely empty round room with a bare mattress built into the floor.

Hence the panicked shopping.

While I chew on my lip, Damon whips us into a parking lot at the back of what looks like an old warehouse. It's huge, made of white metal.

When I raise a brow at him, he cocks a crooked grin and squeezes my palm. "Come on, pretty girl. I want you to play with me."

I REALLY SHOULD HAVE KNOWN.

"Size seven?"

Damon's still grinning as he dangles a pair of skates in front of me. I nod, doing my best not to openly pout.

Apparently, I fail because he chuffs a laugh as he drops to his knees and starts to remove my sandals for me.

"Cassian told me you had a bratty side, but I didn't believe him," Damon snorts. "I approve, for the record."

It's my turn to giggle. "That's because *you're* a brat!"

His megawatt smile somehow gets even more dazzling. "Only all the time."

I'm not sure how he does it, but this alpha always knows exactly what to do to stop my anxiety dead in its tracks. I often find myself laughing with him, unable to remember what I was even worrying about minutes before.

But, this time, the thing I'm worried about is sort of strapped to my ankles.

"I don't know how to skate," I whisper. It's something I haven't told any of them because I assumed they would be disappointed.

But Damon keeps smiling as he stands, dusting his hands off and moving to tug off his own shoes. "I figured you needed a tutor, sweetness. This is me volunteering. Insisting, actually. Because once we start popping out babies, I'm signing them alllllll up for hockey."

Babies?!

Um.

UMMMM.

When I blink in dismay, his grin takes on a wry edge. "Too soon?"

I nod.

He shrugs his stacked shoulders, unbothered. "Inevitable, right?"

If he wasn't currently blowing my mind in a whole different manner, I might be mind-blown at the way he can somehow put skates on while standing up. In forty seconds flat.

"I mean," he continues, bending down to flatten his hands on either side of my thighs. Until his perfect face is looming right in front of mine, aqua eyes snapping with electricity. "I'm your alpha, right?"

A dizzy thrill streaks through me. "Y-yes?"

"Mm," he says, smirking. His hands find mine, pulling me up to my feet as he straightens himself out. "And you want a family, right?"

We're moving. Walking toward the empty ice rink. Or, rather, he's walking, backward, and I'm sort of gracelessly stumbling while he holds most of my weight on his forearms.

"Right," I squeak, my eyes darting to the ice that's only a few feet away now. "Damon, are we allowed to be here? What if —what—"

He stops on a dime, letting my body tumble right into his. Even balanced on skates, he catches me easily and pulls me right up into his arms. My legs cling to his waist, the skates accidentally knocking his backside.

He doesn't mind. Not even when I wind my arms around his neck and cling to him like a child having their first swimming lesson.

I glare down at the ice. He laughs and kisses my nose. "God-damn, you're cute. Though, I do feel like I should be insulted. Don't you have any faith in me at all?"

As if to prove his point, he glides onto the ice while balancing my weight. Effortless. Smooth as that grin of his.

He skates backward lazily. Almost... indolent. Teasing me, I realize. Showing me just how silly it is to be afraid of skating with the likes of him around.

"And to answer your question," he murmurs, ducking to put us face-to-face again. "This is the rink the local minor league team uses. They're on the road this week, so I knew it would be empty. I pay the maintenance crew to let me use it sometimes. When we're done, I'll text them and someone will come smooth things over. No one will ever know we were here."

I turn my head, looking around. The rink really isn't small. It's a huge warehouse-type room. Almost a miniature of the arena the Timberwolves use, without all the fancy bells and whistles like the enormous Jumbotron or the panels of screens along the walls.

This place is simple. Almost cozy, despite the size and the endless rows of empty bleachers.

"It reminds me of what I thought high school would be like," I breathe. "This is how it always looked on TV."

Damon nuzzles his face into mine. The gesture is comforting.

He must know that omegas without guardians don't get to go to school. "I would have had the biggest crush on you, pretty girl."

I bite my lip, imagining him back then. He must have been uber-popular. Fun and athletic and gorgeous, with that scoundrel's grin to boot. "Somehow, I highly doubt that."

Damon gives me side-eye, his aqua-blue irises contrasting those shiny black lashes and his pale skin. "*Psht.* Trust me. I would have sat behind you in class and watched your pretty hair bounce around your shoulders. And your cute little fingers arranging all your notes. I bet you would have had a special color highlighter for every class."

My cheeks glow because he's right. Before my designation came in, that's exactly how I was. Damon chuckles, kissing my blush. "Adorable."

I want to cringe. "I was a bit of a—" *total dork* "—nerd. You wouldn't have thought I was lame?"

He frowns. "What? No way. It's fucking sexy how smart you are, sweetness. And I like the buttoned-up prim-teacher's-pet vibe. Makes corrupting you even more fun. Plus, you have to know by now that Cass has been *in love* with you *forever*."

My heart pounds. Cassian has only said those words to me a few times, but every night when he gathers me into his arms and hugs me, I swear I can *feel* them. The same way I used to when he was just my friend, huddling into my side for warmth on those cold rooftop mornings.

He isn't a wordy person, but he always makes me feel cared for. So does Damon, with the way he actively engages in all of my hobbies and constantly checks in with me.

Smith, on the other hand...

Sometimes, I think Damon may be the smartest of them all. He seems to be to read all of our minds, staring at me just a second too long before he sighs. The warm gust tingles over my chilly cheek. "Do you think you'll ever forgive him?"

His question confuses me, for a moment. All this time, I've felt like I had to please the pack alpha. Convince him of my worth. But ever since the first morning that he brought me coffee, Smith has seemed...

Sorry.

Like maybe I'm the one rejecting him, instead of the other way around. And, you know what? Maybe I should be. Maybe I *am*. Because if the way Damon and Cassian treat me is the right way for an alpha to treat their omega, then I think I have every right to be furious at Smith. Not to mention all of the things he did before we knew we were supposed to be mates.

I try for a joke, pasting on a smile I don't quite feel and replying with a question of my own. "Do you think he'll ever apologize?"

Heaving out a deep breath, Damon turns us in an easy circle. "I'm not sure he knows how to. Not out loud anyway. He'll just work himself to death to make up for everything— it's the only way he thinks he can."

With money.

It's another astute observation. One I've caught onto myself. Every time we've ever been alone together, Smith tries to ply me with material wealth. Offering me anything and everything. Without really *giving* me anything.

"What do you think I should do?" I ask quietly.

Damon spreads his feet and arches us in a wide curve, spinning to a smooth stop. His face leaps in surprise. "Me?"

"Yeah," I whisper, stroking his cheek with my cold fingers. "You're so much better at relationship stuff than the rest of us, D. What do you think?"

The question seems to shock him. I've noticed that the others don't ask his opinion very often. Which is silly because he has the highest emotional intelligence in the pack by a mile. Then again, he diffuses conflicts and solves problems so smoothly; I doubt they even notice he's doing it.

He drops his forehead to mine and nuzzles there. Scent-marking me, the way he does every time I seem even the least bit uncertain. He's *sweet*. In a way I never expected. Between his crooked grin and bedroom eyes, I thought he'd only want to give me one thing.

But Damon gives me everything he has.

And I might be more than a little bit in love with him.

"I think," he starts, speaking slowly, as if testing the words. "I think that only you can decide what feels safe to you. And that's all that matters to me."

He kisses my cheek softly, adding, "But I hope he figures his shit out so you can forgive him one day. Because all of us, together? Shit, sweetness, that's everything I ever wanted and never had."

My heart pinches as I nestle my fingers into the hair at the nape of his neck. "What do you mean?"

He sighs, moving his feet again. The ice beneath us gets carved to ribbons before he finally answers.

"My parents were assholes," he finally says. "I, uh, left. Left them, I mean. When I was fifteen."

My fingers freeze. "But where did you go?"

His sad smile is a weak approximation of his usual grin. "Here and there. I had a lot of friends. Slept on a bunch of couches. Ate a lot of free cafeteria food."

Likely because he was just as charming back then as he is now. That's fortunate, I guess, but I hate that he felt he had to take care of himself like that.

"Did they—" I can only imagine one reason why I would ever leave a home—*with parents*—but I know I come from a very different perspective on this sort of thing. "Did they hurt you?"

Damon's shoulder lifts in a shrug, but his features harden. "Sometimes. Not a lot. Usually not on purpose. They were both drug addicts. Or *are*. I don't really know. I haven't spoken to them in more than ten years. When I left, they didn't exactly come running after me."

My arms tighten immediately, hugging him around the neck. "D... I'm so sorry."

Damon cuddles me, securing his muscled arms around my

back and nestling his face into my hair. When he closes his eyes and rests there, everything inside me melts. "Thank you," he says into my skin. "It was a long-ass time ago. I'm mostly better about it now."

I get what he means when he says "mostly." I've "mostly" gotten over being abandoned at birth. I'm an adult now, and I can understand, rationally, why people give children up.

But that doesn't make Christmas alone hurt any less. Or other occasions.

I try to paste on a bright smile, ignoring the pang echoing behind my breastbone. Damon's ice-blue eyes trace over my expression. After a long beat, he narrows them slightly.

"Tell me something," he requests.

"Tell you... something?"

A spark lights his gaze. "Yeah. Something you don't think I want to hear."

My lashes flutter, confusion quirking my brow. "Why would I do that?"

Damon spins us quickly, flashing his crooked grin. "Because... I think you keep a lot of things to yourself so you don't upset us. I want you to tell me something real and true, that you think I won't like. So I can prove to you that you're *my* omega. All the time, no matter what."

My heart rips in two; fear and longing tugging it in opposite directions. And below all of that, there's awe. Damon's emotional intelligence is way beyond anything I ever would have imagined.

He's nothing like I originally thought he was. He's so much *more.*

Maybe, if I show him some of my true colors, he'll feel the same way about me.

Thinking this, I whisper the first confession that comes to me. "I hate my birthday."

He practically pouts. "What?! Why?"

I feel like the most pitiful person on earth, but it's too late to turn back now. Sighing, I hide my face against the hot, autumn-spiced skin of his throat.

"It's the same day they gave me away."

Damon stops breathing, and I squeeze my eyes closed.

He's going to hear how pathetic I am and run for the hills. He won't want me anymore, and he'll tell the others I'm defective, and then they'll finally figure out whatever it is that made all the others return me, too.

But he asked to hear this. I have to follow through and give him what he wants, so I scrape out the rest of this dark thing I've never told anyone else.

"The day I was born is the same day they gave me away; and every year, even if I'm doing something fun with Meg... I have to remember that, however many years ago, someone looked at me and decided they didn't want me."

For the longest moment, everything is still and silent. All I hear is my own breathing, too quick and muffled by the collar of his sweater. Finally, Damon moves, slowly skating us to the edge of the rink and setting me on the low wall surrounding the ice.

When he leans back, just far enough for me to see his face, he cups both palms around my head. "Remi," he says, staring right into me, "*I* want you."

My eyes sting while he crowds closer.

"Okay? I want you, sweetness. I want all your muffins. And I want to hear about your pirate romance books, even if I still don't actually believe that's a thing. I want to watch Bake Off with you and score for you at every game and hold you all night, every night. *I want you*."

chapter
forty-three

DAMON

THE PRETTIEST GIRL in the world is looking up at me with tears half-frozen on her dark eyelashes.

I wipe my thumbs under them, glad that holding her has kept my hands warm. She gazes into me and blows out a slow breath.

"Damon, I love you."

For maybe the first time ever, everything inside of me goes still. And the only thing echoing back at me through all the silence is... *fear.*

Not for me, for her. Because I'm not good enough for this

woman, and I never will be. She's too brilliant for me. Too innocent and selfless.

What could I ever give her? *Myself*?

What a great deal. An alpha who can't even read. Who can't really *work*.

What will happen when I have to retire from hockey? The oldest guy on our team is only thirty-one, and he's nearing retirement. That gives me maybe five years? If I'm lucky.

But I've always been lucky.

And I've always figured shit out when my back is up against the wall.

I don't give up. And I'm not giving up on this. Never on this.

Her lips quirk up slightly, but her eyes fill. Waiting. She's waiting for me to grow some balls and tell her how I feel back.

I nudge my nose against hers. "You're too smart not to know that I love you, too, right? You know that?"

Her breath quivers. "You do?"

"Sweetness," I whisper, brushing my lips over hers. "I didn't even know I *could* love someone like this. I—" My voice drops lower. "You smile at me, and I'm *all in*, Remi. You and me, no matter what. I'm all in for you."

Tears stream down her cheeks, but her pink, perfect lips spread into the exact smile that lights my soul up. "All in," she whispers, still grinning. "I like that."

I grab her, spinning us both as I skate in a circle. Her laugh floats up into the eaves, reverberating off the empty arena. Reminding me that we're here all alone.

And, fuck, do I want her. She's never smelled quite this sweet—quite this *happy*—before.

It isn't her perfume or anything sensual, but it's *joyful*. And her joy makes me want to be close to her in a whole new way.

When she clamps her cold little hands on either side of my face and pulls me into a kiss, I'm glad we've never been here before. Because we may be in the middle of a hockey rink during the middle of the day, but when her tongue timidly strokes into my mouth, I know she wants the same thing I do.

And it's so much *more* than fucking.

She pulls back, her eyes wide and full of feeling. "Are you sure?" I murmur, then flash a crooked smile. "*Here*?!"

Remi giggles, the sound rewiring my brain. "As if you wouldn't be up for it, Trouble."

I skate her cute, bratty little ass toward the exit before thinking better of it. When I turn abruptly, a shrieking laugh peals out of her.

"Where are we going?"

"Well, I have it on good authority that you like to *act* like a good omega, but you're actually a very naughty girl. So I'm going to have to put you in the penalty box."

We skate right up to it, gliding to a halt at the entrance. The box is tight, with just barely enough room for what I have in mind. And so what if I bruise my shoulders and my knees?

For her? Bring on the bruises.

She lets me set her on the narrow bench seat, her eyes flashing mischief at me as she tilts her head in a coy challenge. "What's my penalty?"

See?

Cassian can treat her like glass, and Smith can buy her as many frilly dresses as he wants, but I've always known better. This omega has a naughty side. And I'm going to be the man to bring it out of her.

"Five minutes," I return, dropping to my knees at the edge of the box and waving a hand at my erection. "For high-sticking."

When she laughs again, I know she's probably looked up what high-sticking actually means. Which, of course she did. Perfect girl.

I pull my sweater off, leaving the T-shirt underneath it askew while I urge her to lift up long enough for me to slide the thicker material under her ass. Then, while she's arched, I take advantage and unbutton her jeans, shimmying them down to her ankles.

Honey-soaked sex hits my senses, filling my mouth with saliva. My canines pulse, begging me to bite the flawless brown skin of her upper thigh. Leave my claim on her.

Instead, I squeeze my knot through my jeans and growl. "My perfect, dirty girl. Have you been wet for me this whole time?"

She bites her lip and nods slowly, eyes rounding. "Yes, Alpha."

Fuck. Me.

I dig my hands under her ass and tilt her forward, angling her the way I need to. My lower lip touches her first, slipping over the bud peeking out from the top of her pussy lips.

Remi gasps, her hips already bucking. "Shh, baby," I murmur, kissing her clit softly. "I've got you."

"What if someone comes in and sees?" she whines, still trying to press closer.

I chuckle in my throat. "They won't be able to see. The box hides everything I'm doing. Just relax for me. Remember, you only have five minutes in here."

Her body rolls against my mouth as I swipe my tongue out, tasting the sweet warmth dripping from her pussy. It's heaven and nirvana and three wishes from a genie's lamp all rolled into one incredible burst of satisfaction. The feeling rolls through me as I groan, huddling closer and gliding my tongue between her folds.

Fuuuuuck.

I follow her cues. Listening while she pants and whimpers. The underside of her clit is her favorite spot. I rub at the sensitive patch there before sliding down to slip into her. After a handful of circuits, she lets out a gorgeous cry and floods my face with honey-sweet slick.

Fuck, fuck, fuck.

Before I can even remember how to breathe, she claws at my shoulders and the back of my head. "Damon," she whines. "Alpha. Please. I want you."

I shove to my skates, reaching down to pluck her into my arms. As I drop to the bench, she spreads her thighs as far as they'll go.

My hands frame her face, capturing her attention before she can sink down on me. "I can't knot you here, okay? I want us to be somewhere safe the first time."

Her eyes glow, shining as she leans into my cheek and scent-marks me. "Yes, Alpha."

She's a secret fucking tease. And *I love it*. I love her. The words pour out of me again as I adjust the spread of my knees and yank her body down, impaling her on my throbbing cock.

"Love you, pretty girl. *Goddamn*, do I love you."

In this freezing box, she's a scorching squelch of pure heaven. My vision goes white from the heat of her.

Fuck. Shit.

Her pussy is *tight*, gripping me hard enough to rip the breath from my lungs every time she uses my shoulders to push herself up.

I didn't think about this before, in my desperation to be connected to her. It didn't occur to me that she would be the one directing the pace for our first time, doing most of the work.

And you know what? My dirty girl can *fuck*.

Good *God*.

Am I going to die in this penalty box?

Is this omega about to fuck me to death?

Well, I did say I was all in, so. Goodbye, cruel world.

Death by Penalty Box Pussy. Told you I was lucky.

My knot pounds, filling more with every slide of her luscious body over mine. My balls draw tight, tingling from the cold air and the warm slick dribbling down them. I clutch my hands onto her hips, my head falling back on rough pants.

"Fuck, sweetness. *Yes*. You ride my cock so good. Dirty, beautiful girl. Fuck me harder. Show me who I belong to."

Remi moans, picking up speed until I can't process anything other than the pleasure building at the base of my dick. It spreads up into my abdomen, cinching every muscle as her wet heat strokes my dick harder and faster.

When she bends forward, rubbing her clit all over my knot, I almost lose my shit right then and there. "*Fuck*. Naughty omega. I told Cass about that. Did he show you? Is that why you've been letting him take care of this sweet pussy every night?"

To my delight, she actually answers me. "Yes," she cries. "Damon, I'm going to—"

She makes herself come, grinding us together as she clamps around my length until stars burst behind my eyelids. I snarl, snatching her body against mine and holding her down as I fill her with thick washes of cum.

Remi takes it all, snuggling as close as she can while I shudder over the edge. When I finally float back into my body, she's pressing soft kisses into my jaw.

"I think my legs are too shaky to skate," she huffs, giggling.

Shit. Mine too.

I smooth her hair back with both of my hands, considering our options. "Guess we're stuck in the penalty box for a few more minutes, pretty girl."

She scoots closer, tucking our hips together and letting me stay inside of her. It's the exact intimacy I was after, and I drop my forehead to her shoulder, absorbing it.

"Hey, Damon," she whispers a second later.

"Yeah, sweetness?"

She bounces slightly on top of me. "You're *all in*."

The stupid pun makes me laugh way harder than I have any right to. I clutch her to my chest while I snort, shaking my head. "Damn right, I am."

chapter forty-four

PIERSON PACK GROUP CHAT

CASSIAN

What am I picking up for dinner?

DAMON

Can't think.

Remi looks so hot right now, I could legitimately die.

REMI

They're just muffins, Trouble.

DAMON

She's leaving out the part where she ran downstairs in a thong to get them out of the oven.

Aaaaand she just put an apron on over it.

I'm officially dead.

SMITH

Remi, I won't be home for dinner, unfortunately.

But I think you know what I want as a side for whatever you leave out.

CASSIAN

Can we focus?

DAMON

On how amazing our omega is? Absolutely.

CASSIAN

On dinner. Chinese or Thai?

REMI

Smith doesn't like Thai. And I already ordered Chinese.

It's on its way :)

DAMON

Marry me.

...

Did I make it weird?

I made it weird.

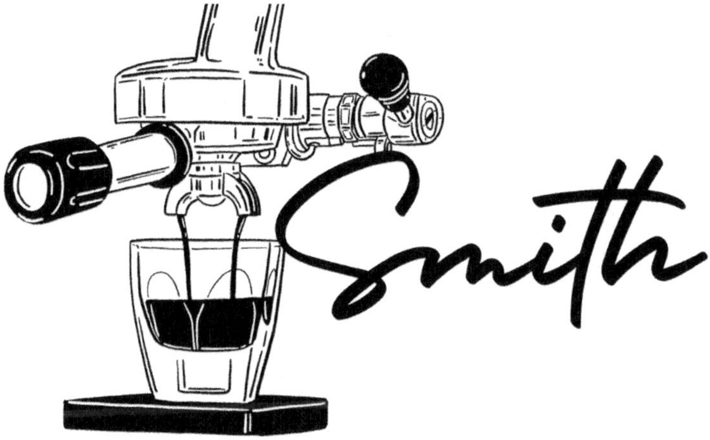

"HARDER!"

I've never been in a room where every single person is simultaneously having the most humiliating experience of their life.

Until now.

"Is that all you've got, alpha?"

I suppose, technically, it isn't *every* person. The two omegas at the front of the room certainly don't seem fazed in the least.

In her crimson kaftan and matching turban, it's impossible to tell how old Irene Underwood is. She moves like a cloud of perfume. Wafting from one side of the conference room's platform to the other, filling the air with a powdery sort of scent each time she sweeps past my end of the front row.

Her male counterpart is every bit as attractive and age-ambiguous as she is. But Julian Channing stands to the back of the stage, his arms crossed loosely and a small smirk on his goateed face.

For twenty-some years, alphas, betas, and omegas have whispered about this rumored alpha-training.

Is it true some alphas really didn't know how to care for their mates?

Do two omegas honestly run a whole class for it? Together?

And whose alphas are the ones that stand around the room, watching the other, much younger alphas' every move?

I can't tell. But every time any of us so much as flick an annoyed look at either of the elder omegas, threatening alpha auras creep from the corners of the room.

At first, I wondered what the older gentlemen were doing here. It would be monumentally stupid for any of us to disrespect Irene or Julian—they're practically famous for what they do, and we all had to sign a mountain of paperwork just to *apply* for this exorbitant class.

But I quickly deduce we're not dealing with the best and brightest alphas in the world here.

The one standing up on the platform with them is clearly having the worst two minutes of his life. When Irene arrived and immediately asked everyone gathered to close their eyes for a visualization exercise, he had the gall to laugh.

Which, as it turns out, was quite the mistake.

Now, he clutches a limp piece of fabric in his left hand and clears his throat. "I—well, uh—"

Julian chuckles. "Show us again." He cocks his head, coy. "*Deeper* this time, *alpha*."

Christ.

I should have brought a flask.

I can already tell the alphas in this room fall into two categories. The ones like me, who know they fucked up and are here of their own begrudging will... and the ones who are here because someone is making them.

I have a feeling Stage Guy is in the second column.

The rest of the alphas in the front row cast each other furtive glances, sizing one another up and, at the same time, checking that no one is looking right at us.

I accidentally make eye contact with a guy three chairs down from mine. We both immediately fling our gazes away, but it's too late.

Dear *God*.

Didn't I run high school track with that guy?

Isn't he a big-time broker, now? And he's here?

Well, so am I, I guess.

A fresh round of shame worms its way into my guts as I shift, crossing my ankle over my knee, doing everything I can not to let my leg bounce with anxiety.

It's a lot harder than it should be; then again, I'm in a room full of similarly aggravated alphas. My instincts tell me not to turn my back for even a moment.

What am I *doing* here?

I picture Remi, laughing, as Damon twirls her in their daily dance around the kitchen. Cassian stepping between her thighs and putting his forehead right on her shoulder—his supplication and trust, the effortless way she accepts him.

You're here because your omega hates you. And you can't take it anymore.

I really can't. The last few days have been torturous, ever since she started sleeping with Cass *and* Damon. It was bad enough hearing her with my little brother every night. But now it's both of them, and I had forgotten that Damon has absolutely no shame.

He's fucked her in every hallway, on every surface of the kitchen, and seven different ways on the couch.

Yes. I know it was seven. Because I watched.

And, no, they didn't know I was standing on the other side of the back door, peering through the window the entire time.

That's the other fucking problem: in addition to being a panty thief, I'm becoming a bit of a voyeur. Always pausing for several beats too long outside her door before I bring in her coffee. Or standing around corners, listening to the way she gasps and sighs while the guys have their way with her.

Between her cold shoulder, my stockpile of panty-pocket-squares, and the vigorous way I've been masturbating, I'm surprised my dick hasn't fallen off.

The alpha on stage looks like his has shriveled up altogether.

His eyes dart over the rest of us while we shift uncomfortably —all of us grateful we aren't him and scared that we might be next. He lifts the article of clothing to his face, using it to channel his half-assed purr again.

Come on. I might not be an omega expert, but even I can purr better than *that*.

Irene doesn't care much. She snaps at him, rolling her eyes while she waves him off. "That's quite enough, I think. The rest of you? Take out your omegas' clothing items."

My joints feel stiff as I take the folded nightgown out of my inner jacket pocket. It's one of the few items she brought with her from her old apartment. I convinced myself it was fine to *borrow* it from her room since it clearly needs to be replaced.

The thing is pretty flimsy. Thin and small—just a slip, really. But the worn, heart-patterned fabric sends a pang through my chest every time I look at it.

It acts like a trip-wire of sorts. The second I focus on it, a rumbling begins behind my sternum. I strangle the would-be purr, but not before Julian's knowing gray eyes snap to me.

They flicker away almost as quickly, but I don't fucking like it.

Remi is the only omega I want looking at me.

That thought feels stupidly dramatic, but my Alpha grunts in agreement before settling back down, content we're finally on the same page.

As if he's given me any choice.

As if you would want any other choice, he huffs.

Such a dick. I wonder if anyone else argues with their instincts like this.

While the rest of the alphas awkwardly fumble their various pieces of omega clothes, the two on the stage watch us all, muttering to themselves.

Julian speaks, and Irene nods. Even before she looks up, my scalp prickles. And I know, in my bones, she's about to look up, point right at me, and say—

"You."

THANKFULLY, I'm not the only one selected. There are six of us out of the twenty-odd alphas in the room. Two are male alphas in suits similar to mine. One is covered in tattoos. And two are female alphas—a businesswoman in a wrap dress, and a tired-looking woman in athleisure.

Fuck. Why are we here? Did they already pick the worst of us out of the crowd? Are these the hopeless cases?

The other fifteen stay behind with Irene, while Julian leads our smaller group to a quiet corner.

My eyes snag on the alpha wearing leggings. We exchange a grim look, as if confirming for one another that we're both pieces of shit.

Julian touches a stack of chairs pushed into the far corner, and one of his alphas appears in a blink, unstacking enough seats for seven. Before he steps back to his position along the wall, he tenderly scent-marks our instructor, meeting his gaze for a beat before stepping away.

That same painful stab strikes my heart again. *Shit.* I don't know if it's guilt or jealousy. Some unholy combination of the two probably.

Because I don't want Remi to be afraid of me. She should be able to *count on me.* I want to anticipate her needs so she can trust me to fill them.

Behind us, Irene peppers the others with questions. Rapid-fire—she barely gives the alphas time to respond before moving on.

How many hours of sleep should omegas get each night? Do they have any special nutrition requirements? What sorts of food should they eat during their heats?

Those feel like things we should all know. Julian listens to her for a few seconds before turning his laughing eyes on our smaller group. They take on a note of pity as they jump from face-to-face. Preparing, I'm sure, to give us the bad news.

We're the worst of the worst.

"You six are here because you're different from the rest of the group," he starts. My stomach sinks lower. "Most alphas who come here are here on someone else's orders. But you..."

He looks at each of us in turn, finally resting his focus on my face. "You six are obviously here because you feel like you're terrible alphas. And it's killing you."

The second he says it, the tension in the circle shifts. We're all relieved not to be pegged as the lowest of the low, but we're also... ashamed.

That's what this feeling is. What I've carried in and out of our house every single day since Forever Matched. The reason I can't show my face for meals or bring myself to do anything more than deliver her morning coffee.

Shame.

I don't recognize it until I see it on five other faces, but there it is. Gut-clenching, soul-crushing, and completely my own fucking fault. It smolders in the pit of my stomach, forcing me to drop my eyes to my loafers and grip Remi's pilfered nightgown with clenched fists.

"The thing is," Julian goes on, almost soft. "If you feel like you're failing your omegas, you likely are."

I already knew that. But hearing a stranger say it out loud? *Fuck.*

My throat works over a swallow while I stare down at the slip. There's a tiny tear, just beside one of the thin straps. One Remi has repaired with the tiniest pink-thread heart.

She isn't a person who throws things away when they break.

And I'm not a person who gives up.

chapter
forty-five

THE PIERSON PACK'S box is way too big without Meg and her alphas crammed into it.

They're at home this week, prepping for her next heat. I talked to her this morning, and she seemed excited more than anything. I listened to her babble happily and wondered whether I would ever feel the same way.

Right now, the thought of my next heat makes me feel... well, hot. Burning with embarrassment and buzzing with apprehension. But also distinctly warm between my thighs.

It's odd, living in a house with three alphas—men who are

supposed to be *mine*—but still not knowing what my heat will look like. Will they all want to be a part of it? What if it happens while they have games scheduled? What if I end up alone with Smith?

Why does that make me feel *warmer*?

Nope.

Not going there. Especially while I'm alone, about to watch two of my alphas play the most violent sport I've ever seen.

I'm already on edge as it is. Cassian was taciturn all day. Much grumpier than usual. Although, he didn't really treat me any differently. He just seemed to be seething about something.

I see that same intensity out on the ice already. Once his stretches are done, he skates impatient half-circles around the goal. It's like pacing on ice. Every few minutes, he turns his head to look up at my box, and I try for a reassuring smile while I wave.

Could he really just be worried about me up here alone?

I don't have much time to contemplate it before the lights go down, plunging the arena into darkness. The Jumbotron lights up, announcing the players. Flashing their faces beside their names and jersey numbers.

If Meg were here, she'd probably suggest we play Smash or Pass.

Tittering to myself, I open Snapchat and send her a clip of the introductions, along with a note suggesting she make this into some sort of game for the Osprey's followers next season. She writes back right away, sending a screenshot of one particular player from the video, along with one word: *Smash*.

It's Gunnar Sinclair, the guy the press keeps insisting will replace Damon. And, yes, he is, objectively smashable. All dark hair and mysterious eyes that make Damon's look docile.

Not surprisingly, my Omega practically foams at the mouth as Damon is announced, his unfairly handsome face lighting up the screen as hundreds of fans scream for him. It doesn't escape me that half of those screams sound more like moans.

I might be bothered if my alpha didn't skate onto the ice and immediately spin to find me, pointing his stick up to our box with a wide, luminous grin.

Cassian is always the last name announced, as is customary with goalies. He lumbers out in all of his pads, cutting a no-nonsense path right to the goal.

Damon must notice he's off, too, because I catch him whipping his head over to watch Cass get settled. They shout something to each other over the bass pounding through the stadium's speakers. D's shoulders bounce up in a shrug, and I take that to mean he isn't too worried.

Now if only my Omega would get the memo. I feel like there's a hamster wheel in my chest, spinning faster and faster.

My anxiety seems unfounded. The lights come up, the puck hits the ice, and they're off. I watch as the opposing team works Damon into the boards again and again. He still manages to score, which is good because Cassian is definitely not himself.

By the middle of the second period, I am distinctly *stressed.* Damon is fighting for his life out there, dodging several players at once. With the defenders spread thin, trying to assist the offense and guard the goal, Cassian is on high alert.

He's blocked upward of twenty shots, but three have snuck through. Damon scored once and Gunnar has another goal, bringing the score to 2-3.

I'm on the edge of my seat, biting my lip hard enough to blanch it, when the door to the box flies open. I jump, whirling around to find—

Smith.

The pack alpha stalks into the room, chest heaving slightly. "I'm late," he says, scowling at me. "I meant to be here an hour ago."

I blink at him, processing. By the time I realize that was a Smith Apology, he's dropped his briefcase against the box's low front wall and folded himself into the seat beside mine.

Shock slackens my features while he settles in, bending

forward to rest his elbows on his knees and narrow his dark eyes at the play unfolding below us.

He's here. With me. But he smells... like another omega?

The hairs on the back of my neck stand up. When Smith senses me stiffen, he turns and runs his eyes over my posture, lingering on my Timberwolf-teal dress and Damon's borrowed team jacket.

"Where were you?" I ask, whispering.

He meets my eyes, his softening. "Just in a meeting, little petal. It ran longer than I expected."

I open my mouth to ask him if there was another omega there, but he stuns me into silence by bridging the distance between us, bending close enough to rub his cheek against mine in a deliberate scent-marking gesture.

"I missed you," he says. "How was your day?"

Resembling a fish choking on air, I blub multiple times before finally swallowing hard.

This might be your only chance. Remember your graces, my anxiety hisses. *Show him you're worth talking to.*

"It was good," I say, sitting up straighter. "I ordered groceries and prepped some meals for the guys to take on the road next week. Damon asked for more muffins, and Cassian wanted a thermos of soup since they're heading into colder weather. The pool crew started repaving. They asked if we wanted a waterfall feature, but I'm leaning more toward a fountain, if that's all right—"

Smith's hand finds mine. Warmer and larger than I expect it to be. He squeezes and sends me a pulse of steadying energy. "A fountain is great. Whatever you want is fine. But how are *you*, Remi?"

Flabbergasted.

A small smile touches my lips as he continues to stare at me intently, waiting for a real answer. "I'm okay," I reply. "Worried about Cassian, a little bit. He was edgy today."

Smith's brow furrows. "Hm. He does have moods, but I'm guessing this was beyond that?"

I nod, still stunned that he's listening to me. Talking to me. We're... like a team.

"I'm not sure what could be making him so anxious," I continue, chewing the corner of my lip. "I—We *spent time together* this morning. He had practice with Damon. I made them both an early dinner. So, I'm just not sure..."

Smith's mouth actually quirks slightly at my innuendo. "Sounds like he's a spoiled bastard." His focus flickers to the place where my teeth are nipping my skin, and his voice grows warmer. "I'll speak to him and take care of it, all right? I don't want you to worry."

He flexes his dominance, but not in a way that's aimed at me. Instead of a bulldozer, it's more like... a weighted blanket. Soothing my nerves. "I'll take care of everything," he assures again, looking right into my eyes. "You just relax for me."

He's saying everything I've wished he would say for weeks. But why now? Is this *guilt*? Does it have something to do with that other scent on him?

I guess that isn't fair. It isn't *on* him. More like *near* him.

You're being crazy, I tell my Omega. *He probably just rode an elevator with someone, and you're going all Fatal Attraction over it.*

Don't be a dumb bitch, she argues back. *Look at him. Do you feel this alpha energy? What omega wouldn't want to juice themselves on that knot?*

Good Lord. *Juice?*

She may be borderline feral for these alphas, but my Omega has a point. I *do* feel the BKE, as Meg calls it. And I'm trying to ignore the way it makes my core clench.

Too late. Once I think about it for half a second, perfume spins off of me while slick wets my panties.

Smith's chest rumbles, but the sound is less of a growl and more... almost...

Is he *purring*?

Or trying to?

Resisting the urge to pinch myself—because, honestly, if I *am* dreaming? Let me sleep—I scoot a bit closer. He lifts his arm and drapes it over the back of my chair. "Are you cold?"

No, I'm trying to hear your chest, seems like a weird answer. So I nod and let him gather me into his side. The rich bitterness of his coffee scent twines with his crisply laundered dress shirt and some sort of mild de-scenting cologne. The effect is a spicy, clean, dark smell that makes my insides tingle.

Smith glances sidelong at me. His expression seems conflicted, like he's trying to decide what to say. Or if he should speak at all.

In the end, he lowers his voice a bit. "Want to know a secret?"

I *want* to open up my phone and record this for later. Because I know I will start gaslighting myself about whether this actually happened the second we snap back to our typical, polite-but-separate reality.

He leans closer and confesses, "I hate coming here. Watching the coach bark orders at Damon and Cass makes me crazy. And this entire place needs to be dehumidified. Whoever installed their air conditioner did a shoddy job."

I remember the way he reacted when he saw my old apartment. Maybe this is a particular hang-up of his, but it feels like there must be more to it. After all, he lived in a half-finished house before I showed up.

"What else?" I ask, still looking up at him.

A bit of tension leaves his shoulders. "I'm not sure. Every time I'm here, I leave feeling angry. Even when we win."

Well, it isn't much. But it is *something*, isn't it? Effort—however clumsy.

Below, a buzzer sounds. We both glance over to find the red light behind Cassian's goal flashing, meaning the other team has scored again.

2-4.

Smith curses under his breath, the sound vicious despite the gentle way his arm wraps around my back. "He never misses shots from the left," he mutters. "What the hell is going on?"

I unpack his words and turn to him, my face lifting. "You watch their games?"

Smith frowns, his eyes still following the play action on the ice. "Of course I do. I watch every game on live-stream. I'm at the office, most of the time, but—"

He cuts himself off, looking at me with wider eyes. "They think I don't watch their games? Because I'm not here?"

I nod, resisting the urge to laugh at his indignant expression. "Well... yeah. Did you ever *tell* them you were watching at work? Or tell them they played a good game?"

Smith holds my gaze for a long moment, thinking, and then sighs. "I guess I didn't."

"You should tell them," I suggest, wincing and cringing as Damon gets shoved into the boards again. "Especially after tonight."

The words are barely out of my mouth when it happens. Smith goes rigid. Below, Damon's head snaps up. And Cassian?

Cassian *roars,* loud enough for me to hear him dozens of rows up.

And then he lunges right out of the goal.

chapter **forty-six**

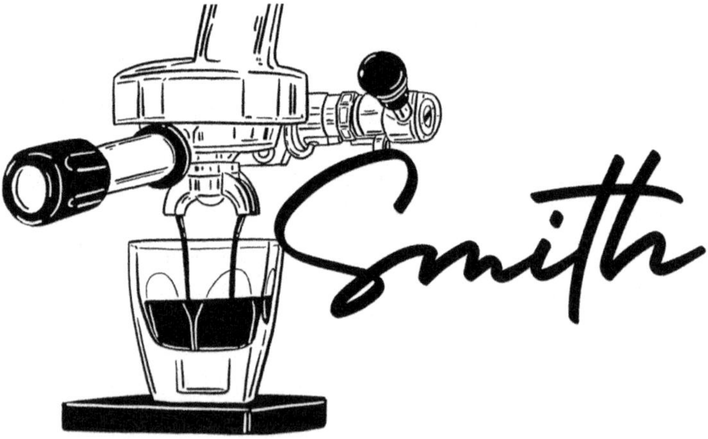

BY THE TIME Damon and I haul Cassian into the house, I'm ready to call for a tranquilizer.

He fights us hard, ripping his strength into our hands and arms while we struggle to drag him out of the truck that smells like Remi.

I sent her home in my car, and Damon drove Cass's while I wrestled with him in the backseat. Now that we're here, I'm not sure how to protect her.

"We could hide her," Damon grits, shoving Cassian back from the stairs. "Or knock him out."

It takes a moment for me to realize the whole house is dark. Usually, when she comes home, Remi turns on certain lamps. She likes pretty lighting, and has every room staged to absolute perfection. It's odd to find everything so dim when I know she's upstairs.

Cassian can sense her. His focus shifts from fending us off to removing what's left of his uniform. The roar he lets out rattled the windows in their panes. I grind my teeth, waiting for Remi's answering whine.

But, instead, her voice is clear and soft. It floats down the steps. "I'm up here, Alpha."

She appears at the top of the stairs, naked under a silky pink robe. She has her hair down, her makeup removed. And her scent. Holy God. She must have showered her de-scenter off quickly because her perfume is pure, perfect honey.

I inhale it, feeling my canines pulse with the urge to bite. Which is when I realize—she isn't afraid. There's no burned undercurrent to her. Maybe a tiny bit of nervousness, judging by the slight rounding of her blue-gold gaze. But, otherwise, she seems steady.

I still hold Cassian back. My mind races, trying to decide what's best for both of them.

One of the suited alphas in my small group earlier had a story like this. He went into a rut and scared his omega half to death. Ever since, she hasn't been able to be alone with him. Remembering the tortured regret in that guy's eyes is enough for me to summon a ferocious bark.

"*You will wait.*"

Damon instantly freezes at my back. Cassian's body jerks, trying to shake off the command. When he can't quite slip free, I use his collar to jerk him upright.

"You don't have to do anything you don't want to do," I say, turning to gaze up at Remi. "We'll wrestle him all night if we have to."

It's true. I'll bark until I'm hoarse if it's the only way to protect her. Although, Damon's "knock him out" idea has some merit.

But Remi squares her shoulders, lightly tossing her hair back. "It's all right," she says. "This is what he needs. Let him go. He can chase me."

I'm not proud of the way my cock jerks. Hearing the snarl I smother in my chest, Cassian lunges forward. I barely manage not to lose my grip on him, speaking through a ticking jaw. "Excuse me?"

A small smile touches her mouth. "He can chase me, catch me, then knot me," she says, clear and calm. "You can both watch if you like. I'm going to lead him into the nest as soon as you let him go."

Fucking hell.

She has a whole *plan* for this? Somehow, that strikes me as very "Remi." She's a good girl—so fucking good—but she clearly has a secret naughty side to her. I saw it the night she came sneaking into my room. And she leaves me panties to use as pocket squares, as if that isn't entirely deviant.

She's also organized and poised. She doesn't seem scared or irritated. She almost seems... excited.

Perfect omega.

My own Alpha growls his approval, vehement. For half a second, my pack leader instincts war with mate inclinations. I want her for myself, but I need to keep my whole pack safe.

What did Julian tell that tattooed alpha tonight?

Leadership is sacrifice.

Mastering my body takes a moment. When I'm firmly in control, I give Cassian a shake. "*You're going to chase our omega down,*" I bark, low and even. "*And when you find her, you'll take her in front of us. We're going to watch.*"

I cast Damon a quelling look. "*Just* watch."

He mutters something that sounds like, "Lucky son of a bitch," but starts pulling his gear off. I shuck my jacket and start to unbutton my own sleeves, releasing my stranglehold on Cassian, along with one final bark. "*Go get her.*"

Cass takes off, crashing up the stairs. Remi gives a squeal that makes me want to hunt her down myself. Then, she's scurrying away.

For a long moment, Damon and I stand shoulder-to-shoulder, staring in awe. His eyes flicker to the rumpled pile of clothing on the floor, brows quirking. "Are those Remi's panties?"

chapter forty-seven

A POUND BEATS at the base of my throat while I watch Smith hold Cassian back.

My rutting alpha is beyond all reason—teeth gnashed menacingly while he rips his uniform off. Torn fabric flutters to the floor as Smith fights to restrain him.

But I...

I want him. I want to be chased. My instincts are wired for this.

Run.

Not because I don't want to be caught. But because I *do*.

It's heady to know I can do *this* to someone so powerful. Watching the way his muscle-bound body strains against the bonds of Smith's commands, all I want is to feel all of that strength aimed at me. Dedicated to *filling* me.

If I had time to think about it, I might ask myself why. Some omegas like throwing their alphas into rut because they enjoy being tossed around. Others enjoy the ego boost of turning the tables on the designation that so often has control over us.

For me, I guess ... it's a form of devotion.

This alpha isn't in his own mind anymore.

But I'm still the only thing he wants.

There's a purity to that. It's honest. Real and raw in a way that so many interactions *can't* be.

His eyes are blank, aside from burning intent. Focused entirely on *me*. My stomach flips as I step away from the stair rail and tell Smith to let his brother go.

There isn't a moment of hesitation. Cassian takes off immediately, his distant eyes locked on me.

My instincts snap forward, taking control of my body. A burst of perfume swells in my wake while I sprint down the hallway. Bone-rattling roars echo behind me, along with the sound of crashing footsteps.

I weave toward my bedroom doors, feeling the hairs at the back of my neck wave as adrenaline prickles through me. Thick fingers close around the sash of my robe at the small of my back. I twist, squeal, and slip free of the whole garment.

Cassian grunts, surging after me as I skid through the entrance of the Omega Suite and make a sharp turn for the nest.

In the distance, I hear the others approaching. It makes Cass slow down long enough to send them a snarl, his Alpha warning the competition that I'm *his*.

Arousal tingles through me again, a rush of slick running between my thighs. "Alpha," I call breathlessly, backing toward the nest door. "Aren't you going to catch me?"

His head snaps to face me, the movement too quick to look natural. His nostrils flare. A low rumble builds in his chest.

One footstep.

Two.

He approaches slowly, now that there's nowhere left for me to run.

Waves of dominance and pulsing, punishing lust roll off of Cassian. I whine automatically. The small sound physically collides with him, his muscles clenching as it hits.

"Omega," he roughs out. "Mine."

"Yours," I allow, carefully leading him to the nest door. Inside, it's dark. The strips of skylight built into the ceiling only let a few stray moonbeams in. They glow weakly in the round, dome-shaped space. Blue and milky white paint the true colors of the linens and walls in shades of silver and pale.

In the dark, with his body bared and his cock curved up between his legs, Cassian looks like the beast he always claims to be. He's huge—tall and hard and so *strong* it makes my core ache. The tight lace of his muscles expands while he sucks in a deep breath, tasting my scent.

With a serrated sound, he launches his full weight at me. This time, I'm too slow for him.

And he catches me.

With rough hands, he snatches my waist and my hair, lifting me right into his body while he charges into the nest. I cry out, twisting to try to give him a better chase, but he has me in an iron grip.

It's one thing to run, knowing he'll catch me. It's another actually *being* caught. But now that he has me and I can't move, a bolt of panic streaks through me. My scent singes slightly.

"*Cassian. Gently.*"

I used to hate Smith's barks. Every single one made me feel sick with dread and half-crazy from anxiety. But right now? The weight of his dominance seems more like slipping into a cool pool after lying in blistering sunshine.

It isn't crushing. It's soothing.

I see a flicker of relief on Cassian's face, too. Our alpha is here. He's going to protect all of us.

Smith steps into the nest first, still wearing his button-down shirt and slacks. My Omega doesn't like that, but she's thoroughly distracted. At least he's taken his shoes off, leaving him in socks that match the blue pair of my panties he's had in his jacket pocket today.

While Smith remains firmly focused on Cassian's face, flexing his power to keep him in check, Damon comes in behind him. Naked, of course. Stripped down completely, with an erection bobbing between his cut hips.

Our gazes meet for a second. His flickers around the nest and comes back to me, a small, utterly sincere smile on his lips.

He likes it, I think with relief.

None of them have ever been in here before. And for a second, I'm disappointed they aren't seeing it in the daylight. But then I consider how Cassian would feel being left out of that—if only mentally—and decide this may be for the best.

Still, it's *very* Damon to notice. He knows this is important to me and saw how much work I put into to picking things.

Not for the first time, I wish we were bonded so I could send him a beat of gratitude. I've had those thoughts more and more, lately, and it's getting harder to suppress them.

Especially in here.

All of their scents are full-force, saturating the air and my nest linens with the perfect combination. Bitter and earthy, brown-sugar spice, and the rich smoothness of chocolate. It all swirls together and settles in my lungs.

Hearing the soft whine in my throat, Cassian's dark eyes snap from the encroaching alphas back to me. "Omega," he husks out, fingers flexing into my flesh. "Need you."

And, God, he does. I see it burning in his eyes. He needs *me*. I'm the only one who can give him back to himself.

"I'm yours," I tell him, reaching up to touch his cheek. "You can have me, Alpha."

Cassian snaps me into his chest, locking his arms around me and lowering us to the mattress. It would possibly pass for a hug if I didn't feel like a kitten being strangled by a gorilla.

"*Gently,*" Smith orders again. He moves with caution, kneeling slowly at the nest's edge. But even that is enough to trigger a vicious snarl from Cassian.

It reverberates against my ear, sending a skitter of nerves through me. When his Alpha senses the shift in my perfume, he makes that growly purring sound again, dropping his forehead to roughly nuzzle at my neck.

Bear.

Even in a rut, he's still grumpy and cuddly. Still the man I know, somewhere in there. I smile into his messy, overly long hair, feeling more at ease.

When I relax, he does, too. The bruising pressure of his fingertips eases. He inhales at my throat, groaning. "*My omega.*"

"Yes, *yours,*" I whisper, shivering from the bark. I brush all of his loose hair back and wiggle against him. "I want your knot, Alpha. Can I have it?"

Instead of replying, he tips me back until I land on the creamy silk underneath us. His face is fierce as he leverages his body over mine and shoves in deep.

The first punch of his cock into my body knocks all the air out of my lungs. There's not a single moment to get it back, because Cassian starts to *rut,* his hips snapping like a piston, grinding our pelvises together.

I try not to struggle, not wanting to alarm the others or aggravate him, knowing he doesn't even know what he's doing at the moment. When he suddenly rears back and opens his mouth, there's barely time for me to whimper before he strikes.

But Smith is there.

"*No,*" he barks, covering my entire neck with his large hand. "*You will not bite her.*"

Cassian grunts his displeasure, but keeps right on pumping, dropping his face to my breasts instead. A wash of relief rushes over me, followed by a swift kick to the gut.

Did Smith stop him because he doesn't want me in their pack? If Cassian claimed me, that would be it. Smith would have to commit to letting me stay.

He must really not want that if he was willing to interrupt a rutting alpha just to—

The fingers at my throat flex subtly. My gaze flies to where Smith crouches just beside my head.

His deep eyes trace my face as he adds, "Not *yet*."

chapter forty-eight

CASSIAN

REMI WAKES me up just before dawn.

She likes to do that, doesn't she?

I can feel how early it is before I even open my eyes. That might have pissed me off, two months ago, but, now, I just lower my face into the sweet-scented curls grazing my chin and smile to myself.

My girl.

I move to hold her more securely, feeling unfamiliar aches in my lower back and abdominals. My half-awake mind stumbles over yesterday's conditioning routine, our practice, our game—

Oh holy fuck.

The night comes rushing back to me in a blur. The fight, the fog that came over me like a red mist. The *rut*.

God, no. I rutted her all night. In every position. If I'm sore, how battered is she?

My eyes fly open. I jerk upright, almost knocking her flat onto her back as I shift to put us chest-to-chest. She's naked but covered in a fuzzy blanket I've never seen before. The fact that it's soaked in her scent keeps me somewhat calm while I scan over her body, looking for injuries.

There are bruises. Around her arms and at her hips mostly. But still, they're bruises. And *I* put them there.

A pained sound sticks in my throat while I bend to brush my lips over a patch of marks clustered at the top of her thigh. She shifts, blinking awake.

"Mmm," she hums. "Bear?"

She doesn't sound angry. Her voice is sweet and dreamy, full of relief and a little hint of teasing. "Or is it still my alpha down there?"

Her alpha.

I guess I really am, now. I've rutted her. Taken her. And judging by the way she's acting right now? She... *liked* it?

My arms constrict, a shaky breath sloughing out of my lungs while I tug her closer. "*Butterfly.* Jesus, I'm so sorry. How long was I gone?"

Remi hums, stretching lightly within the cage of my biceps. "All night," she murmurs, tilting her head back to peer over at the gray light just barely touching the window strips above us.

That's when I realize—we aren't in our bed. We're inside her nest.

And it's fucking beautiful.

"Look," she whispers. "It's sunrise."

Yeah, it is. Outside—and in here, too.

Because my girl made our nest to resemble the early-morning view we've always shared.

The domed ceiling is a perfect meld of soft pastels. Blended ombre paint creates a smooth effect, blurring the colors from pale pastels to brilliant bright pink, tangerine, and yellow. Her nest cushions match, the colors ranging from the very lightest on one side to the dark, more vibrant hues on the other. Gold accents glint in the weak sunshine coming through the strips of skylight arranged in a sunburst over our heads.

"Rems," I whisper, looking around. "Baby, did you make us a sunrise nest?"

Her smile is the genuine, guileless one I love so much. She nods, bouncing excitedly while she sits up. "I did the paint! And I picked all these cushions to match. Do you like it?"

Do I *like* it?

Even after finding Remi and remedying my Alpha Apathy, I couldn't picture myself getting truly excited about a nest. I'm not a person who "gets" decor or aesthetics the way Smith and Damon do.

I should have known this woman would find a way to make this feel like mine, though. Ours.

"Butterfly," I husk, rolling on top of her and burrowing my face into her neck. "I love it. I love *you*."

She giggles, squirming under my weight. "I've never been in here this early," she says. "Look, you can see the colors through the skylight. They match the ceiling."

But I can't look. I can't see anything but her.

It doesn't matter anyway. Nothing could possibly be as beautiful as she looks right now, sleep-mussed and starry-eyed, grinning goofily up at me.

And I'm the beast who rutted her all night long.

My scent smolders, and she shifts around again, the humor falling off her face. She traces her fingertips over the crease in my brow. Our eyes meet. I fall into butterfly-blue, lost in the pretty patterns and my own chagrin.

She blinks, her voice softening. "Bear, I'm okay. Everyone is all right. It wasn't your fault."

God, she's too fucking perfect. For any of us. And maybe I ought to feel guilty about that, but I can't. Because, really? No one could ever deserve her.

But I know I'm damn well going to try.

Palming her soft ass in my hand, I bring her flush with my lower half and wrap her thigh over mine. When I drop my forehead to hers, she sees the intent in my eyes and smiles softly, nodding.

We make love slowly. She lets me hold her the whole time, keeping our faces together and our eyes locked. I touch every part of her, finding all of the secret spots that make moans fly from her lips to feather over my mouth.

Remi lets me make her come twice before I finally push my cock back into her, sliding down to my knot. She kneads her fingers there, every motion soft. After last night, it feels fucking perfect.

When the sun finally rises, it's a whole new day.

And I'm new, too.

chapter forty-nine

CLICKING INTO THE CALENDAR APP, I eye the date and bite my bottom lip hard enough to sting.

I'm having major planner anxiety for two reasons. One is that I don't have the nerve to mark my upcoming heat down in the iCal. It's supposed to hit the first week of the playoffs, which is *impossible* timing for all of the guys.

The chicken part of me wonders if asking them to be there with me during such an inconvenient time will be the deal-breaker I've been dreading.

Because... seriously? How can this really be my life?

It can't be. This has to fall apart—and soon. If the timing of the heat doesn't scare them off, my crazy Omega probably will once her haze takes over.

All that anxiety is plenty to keep me busy, but there's a second reason for the way my stomach seethes. And it's happening tomorrow.

This week has been marked since I created the pack calendar weeks ago. Now, the clear blue bar I strenuously avoided thinking about has finally arrived.

Timberwolves Away Games.

There are four in ten days.

For ten days, the guys will be away from the house. From me. And Smith.

Who will still be here. With me. *Alone.*

As if on cue, Damon swoops into the kitchen. The tight, silky briefs he prefers would honestly look ridiculous on anyone else, but he pulls them off. Even when he's frowning in consternation.

"Sweetness? What's wrong?"

We spent the better part of last night in my bed, doing everything but knotting. He insists he wants the first time to be extra-special, even though, by now, his Alpha must be as desperate for it as my Omega is.

Cass has been visibly calmer since his rut. When he walks into the kitchen, I note with pride that his posture is loose and his face is calm. Our eyes meet, and his spark—half heat and half worry.

"Butterfly. You're stressed. Is D being annoying?"

Damon sputters before shooting Cassian a middle finger. "Fuck off, I was just checking on our girl!"

With a sad half-smile, I point to the line on our calendar. Damon leans over my shoulder, his brow creasing and his lips moving while he stares at the words.

I've begun to suspect he has trouble reading. When I first noticed the way he tenses up whenever Cassian and I discuss books, I thought he just really hated them. Then, one afternoon, he showed me his overflowing Audible library and mentioned two audiobooks he burned through during conditioning that week.

Now, as he visibly sounds out the three words I've typed in, my heart gives a pang. If he struggles, I wonder why he's never told me.

Do the others know?

Cassian doesn't seem to notice. He flicks a glance at the screen before scowling and dropping onto the stool next to me, all grumbly. "Stupid fucking away games. Hate this shit."

When he senses Damon and I both smirking at him, he rolls his shoulders back and meets my eyes, muttering, "I don't like leaving you."

I reach over and touch his stubbled cheek. "I'll be okay, Bear. Smith will..."

Sit at the kitchen table, watching my every move. Bring me coffee and pat my head every morning. Disappear to a five-to-eight appointment mysteriously labeled, "Smith—Meeting" every night and come back smelling ever-so-slightly like another omega...

"...look after me."

Damon and Cassian exchange a look. They've clearly talked about this. D opens his mouth, hesitating slightly. "Pretty girl, if you don't want to be home alone with him, we can make another plan."

Cassian nods. "Maybe you could"—He grits his teeth— "go and stay with Meg."

It means a lot that they're willing to even suggest that. I know the thought of me, alone, in a house with other alphas—even happily bonded ones—makes them both crazy. They're only offering it as an option to make sure I'm comfortable while they're on the road.

"Her heat ended two days ago," I say, laughing lightly to hide my anxiety at the thought. "They're probably all still asleep."

Yesterday, she sent me twelve "sword-cross" emoji followed by the "mind-blown" one and twenty-eight water droplets.

Which, I suspect, were not meant to indicate actual *water*.

So that will be a fun phone call.

I replied with a string of question marks, but they're still unread. I would bet money on her being crashed out for the rest of the weekend.

Damon's hot, bare chest slides against my back. He drops his lips to the place beside the strap of my dress, skimming his mouth there with a rumbly growl.

"I can't wait for your heat, sweetness. I bet we can go waaaaaaay longer than Meg's alphas. Football players are pussies. They're not even allowed to fight with their fists."

Cassian grunts his agreement, the corner of his mouth flinching up. "Pussies," he agrees. "They probably take breaks, too. So many fucking breaks in football."

Oh Lord. I have a feeling that, when the Pierson pack and the Ash pack actually *meet*, Meg and I might be in for some serious...

Well...

Dick measuring.

Even so, a pang of longing echoes through me. I would really love for all of us to get together. Normally, in these circumstances, it's up to the leader of the newer, less-established pack to reach out to the more established pack's alpha. That means Smith would have to call Ronan.

But that's just tradition. I can do it myself, I suppose. No one would really *care*, aside from me.

Cass glances down at the calendar on the iPad in front of me and raises his brow. "Looks like we'll find out next month."

I follow his thick, pointed finger to a Sunday. The event marked there isn't one I added. We all have our own colors, and this block is red, indicating that Smith added it.

Dinner with Ash Pack.

Smith comes strolling into the kitchen, dressed immaculately in a gray suit, with one of my pale pink panty sets neatly folded into his breast pocket. When he notices the way all three of us stare at him, he pauses, lifting his brow at us.

"Yes?"

Words fall out of me without permission. "You called Ronan."

His nod is clipped, but his voice oozes self-assurance. "It's customary for the alpha of the newer pack to contact the more established pack leader to arrange the first dinner party."

It sounds like he's reciting from an etiquette book. The sort of thing I enjoy that no one else seems to care about anymore. When his dark eyes land on mine, I can read them easily.

I care, too.

This has happened more and more, recently. I'm not sure how I feel about it, but Smith appears intent on making it clear just how much we have in common.

A lot of it is obvious, I suppose. We both like to dress up. Keep a nice house. Organize our agendas.

We're both old-fashioned.

Maybe that's why he hasn't even tried to kiss me yet. Despite, you know, that whole rutting-my-throat thing.

He can probably sense that I don't know what to make of him. I spent months shaking every time he walked into Proper Coffee. Rewiring that fear hasn't been easy, but I don't quiver every time he comes into a room anymore.

We share space more and more easily, it seems. He's been much better about acknowledging me, pointing out every little change around the house, and thanking me sincerely for every single meal I make.

He still doesn't mention the panties. Or come home at dinner time. But I suspect that has more to do with whatever "meeting" he goes to daily than it does avoiding me.

As if to prove my point, Smith approaches. The others naturally clear a path for their alpha, allowing him room to stand beside me and drop a gentlemanly kiss to my cheek.

"You may want to check Thursday night," he murmurs, stepping back.

I blink down at the calendar, my eyes roaming over the upcoming weeks. Sure enough, there's another line on there that I didn't see before, written in red under the guys' away game schedule.

Date Night—Remi and Smith.

chapter fifty

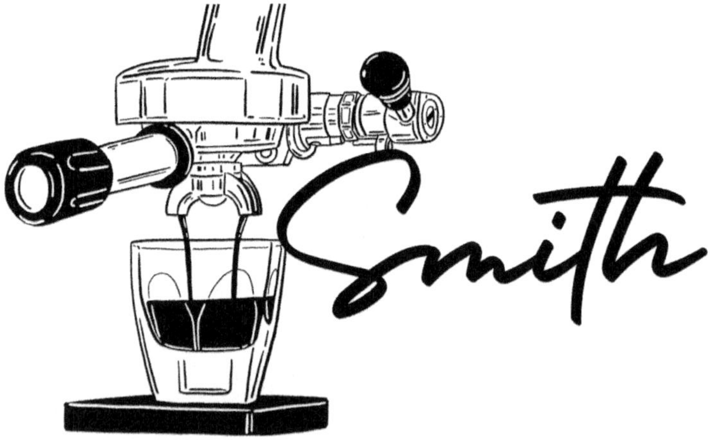

ACCORDING TO IRENE, there's only one reason for an alpha to miss one of her illustrious classes.

Date night.

An idea so obvious, the fact that I missed it and had to be reminded that dates *exist* was almost as mortifying as having her question me about my plans in front of every other alpha in the room.

When I told her I wanted to take Remi to the most upscale, famous restaurant in town, Irene tutted, reaching up to adjust my tie the way a grandmother might mess with her grandson's hair.

"Now, now," she said. "Where's the fun in that? Where's the personality? She's courting you, is she not? So show her *you*, Mr. Pierson."

Well. Easier said than done.

I changed the plans half a dozen times before they felt right. Or, rather, felt like "*me.*"

A concept I am much less familiar with than I'd like to admit.

This morning, when I brought Remi her coffee, I also included a gift bag and instructions to open it when it was time for her to get ready. As soon as I get home from the office and finish changing, I find she's followed my instructions.

My good fucking girl.

"Smith?" she calls through the half-open doors of her room. "Is this… right?"

I look down at my own outfit, suddenly questioning the whole plan. Especially the part where I wear shorts.

I'm surprised I even *had* shorts, let alone the kind you wear for swimming or leisure. This pair is black and shorter than I would normally select. They're probably Damon's, actually, but at this point, I have to act like I did all of this on purpose. Even in my own head.

Striding to her door, I linger at the edge and all the air seeps out of my lungs.

Fucking hell.

Mistake.

This was a mistake. Clearly. How on earth did I imagine I could be any sort of gentleman while she's wearing *that*?

I picked the bikini out myself, ducking into an upscale women's boutique between site visits earlier this week. On the model, the ice-blue fabric seemed like a safe choice. I've seen her wear the pastel color before.

I've forgotten how lovely it looks against her honey-brown skin, though. And I definitely didn't consider how tempting I would find the long, curling straps tied into bows at her hips and across her bare back.

God, but she's beautiful. The blue sets off her eyes. Her gold flecks stand out, the cornflower color pops brighter. Silky black hair cascades down her back in loose coils, brushing the feminine slope just above the small of her back. There are two dimples there, teasing, as she turns to frown at me.

One elegant black brow arches. "We're going swimming?"

I can't help but smile at her confusion, trying for a shrug. "If we want."

Her hands go to her hips. "Well, is there a dress code where we're going?"

We really are alike. Everything about her—the posture, the pout, the question itself—feels relatable to me. Because if someone told me we were going out and then handed me a swimsuit, I would also question their sanity.

"Just throw on one of your more casual dresses," I tell her. "Sandals are fine, too. Bring a spare change of clothes."

She nods, instantly snapping into gear. It's an interesting combination, the way she's too smart not to ask questions or need to know the plan, but also submissive enough to accept that I have it figured out.

While Remi disappears into her bathroom and the attached closet, I turn to find the door to her nest open for the first time since Cassian's rut. It was very dark, then, and I was too focused on keeping myself—*and the others*—in check to properly look around.

What I see now draws me across the room, until I'm standing at the threshold, staring in.

I was supposed to do this with her. I didn't know it, at the time. When Julian gave our small group a lesson nesting and nest etiquette, I felt sick. Part of me had hoped she wasn't finished with it yet, so I could help her at least a little bit. I should have known better, though.

"Omega."

Remi comes rushing out, her hands at the nape of her neck,

securing a necklace that matches her new suit and the white sundress over it. Her eyes look wide and nervous as they dash between me and the nest. "Is... something wrong?"

Control.

I'm barely keeping myself together.

Control, control, control.

"Come here," I say, then remember myself. "Please."

She swallows visibly, her hands falling to her sides while she floats toward me. Stopping at my side, she peers into the nest and scans the room, searching for the source of my dismay. When she, apparently, finds everything the way she left it, she turns to me.

"Did I do something—"

"Perfect," I interject, taking her delicate hands in mine. "Remi, this nest is beautiful."

And so are you.

Especially when she beams up at me, her eyes lighting with happiness from my compliment. "Y-you like it? I've had the idea for ages, but I wasn't sure..."

We would take care of her in a rusty shed if we needed to. And I doubt any of us would care, once her heat perfume kicked in.

But this is beyond comfortable or sufficient.

This is every bit as perfect as *she* is.

The theme is clear—sunrise on one side and sunset on the other. She even lined them up from east-to-west—a weak, buttery flare on the eastern wall of the round room, and a bright, orange disk sinking into the western wall's "horizon."

I touch one of her cheeks, bending to scent-mark the other. "It's lovely. Did you hire an artist to do the painting?"

I hate the thought of anyone outside our pack inside this sacred room, but she needs to have everything exactly the way she wants it. She shakes her head, though, and I feel relieved.

Until she says, "I did the paint myself. For Cassian."

Because sunrise was their thing. She planned the theme of her dream nest based on those mornings they spent together.

If I wasn't already painfully in love with her, I would be right this moment. With this woman who loved Cass when I couldn't; and kept him alive for me while I was trying to get our life back on track.

"You really are an angel," I rasp.

And then I kiss her.

chapter fifty-one

I CAN STILL TASTE Smith an hour later.

Our kiss didn't last more than one brief second. A soft brush of his lips. One sure, leisurely glide of his tongue along mine.

While I was still in shock, he led me down to his Range Rover and told me to get comfortable. I found out why when he pulled onto the interstate, heading east.

On our way, he asks me questions.

Not inquiries—things about the house, my plans, the pack. But actual, personal questions that only seem aimed at getting to know me better.

Ignoring the way my lips still tingle, I tell him about meeting Cassian, becoming friends with Meg, and what my job used to look like—before his investment group purchased Proper Coffee.

He asks thoughtful follow-up questions and some that just feel silly—cats or dogs? (Cats are obviously smarter and cleaner). Chocolate or vanilla? (The correct answer is *why choose*?) Favorite color? (Seasonal.) Food? (He says croissants don't count and demands I name "an actual meal," to which I begrudgingly admit I'm a sucker for really good pasta.) Place?

That last one stumps me a bit. I haven't really had the opportunity to travel much. The only excursions I ever went on were state-funded field trips to various Florida locales.

While I explain, blushing from embarrassment at sounding so uncultured, Smith's warm palm finds my thigh, squeezing gently. "You would love Paris," he muses. "All the pastries and flower markets. *Versailles*. The art. Great shopping, too." He smiles wryly. "Although Cassian would moan in every store, and Damon would bitch at every museum."

I look down at his hand, the long fingers slowly stroking my skin. That one touch—this whole *evening*—feels like a gesture.

I'm not sure when or why it started, but I've noticed things like this more and more. Sweetly nuzzling my face before he leaves in the morning, the way he's tempered his intensity to make his stares less intimidating and more steadying.

He's really *trying*.

And I want to try, too.

Swallowing nerves, I try for an even tone. "Maybe... that could be a good trip for just the two of us?"

Smith turns his head, casting me a stunned look that quickly melts into the first true grin I've ever witnessed on his handsome face. It's a beautiful smile—warm and masculine—made even more genuine by the way his eyes crinkle.

"That's an excellent idea," he praises. "I'd love to take you shopping there."

I try for a completely innocent look. "Buy yourself some new pocket squares?"

Smith's laughter might be the best sound I've ever heard. Every bit as alluring as his smile, but layered with joy; and a note of surprise that makes me want to laugh, too.

His phone is plugged into the Range Rover's center console, pumping out some horribly whiny alternative rock. When he sees me glance at the display, wincing, he chuckles again. "Here, little petal. Pick whatever you like."

The Smith Pierson is handing me his phone?! It doesn't seem real. He's practically married to this thing. I don't think I've ever seen him without it on his person.

Except maybe that one night... in his room...

I take the iPhone, swiping it open and scrolling his Spotify. Unlike Cassian and Damon, who always shared their account and recently added me, too—Smith has his own. Of course.

The playlists feel like a whole lot of nothing. Smooth jazz, vague alternative, and something called Mellow Oldies. The sort of music someone puts on because they're trying not to listen too hard. Pulling a face, I abandon all of his saved songs and go hunting for new material.

While I'm scrolling a text alert pops up at the top of the screen. *Irene*, the contact name says. Along with one sentence, *Missing you tonight!*

I blink at the phone as the alert tucks itself into the top of the screen. As if nothing ever happened.

chapter
fifty-two

"REMI?"

I barely hear my name. My mind spins through the last few weeks, clicking pieces together. He's unavailable from five until eight most nights—at some sort of daily meeting he doesn't volunteer any information about. And when he turns up? I can sense that he's been around another omega.

What if my instincts weren't being psycho? Has he really been spending his evening with another omega? Is that why he's never tried to get anything more than a kiss on the cheek from me before tonight? Is he getting everything he needs from someone else?

"Remi?" I can't deny the alarm in his voice. "Are you all right?"

My face feels like it's made of dry clay while I set the phone back in the center console. "I'm..."

What? Surprised? Stupid? *Heartbroken*? He won't like any of those reactions.

Am I supposed to just be okay with this? That's how a more sophisticated, worldly woman might react. It's not like he and I are sleeping together. Or having any sort of relationship among ourselves. This is our first date, technically. Maybe, if I try really hard, I can sway him away from whoever Irene is—

"*Remi.*" Smith's gruff, irritated voice matches the way he yanks his hand off my leg and scoops up his phone. Keeping one eye on the road, he glances at the stack of unopened alerts that cascade from the top of his screen when he pulls the tab down.

I can see his gears churning, trying to figure out what I saw. The moment he realizes his mistake, his expression hardens. The hand gripping the wheel goes white-knuckled as he sets his phone back in between us. His posture tightens.

"Remi..." he grunts. "I—it isn't what you think."

I must still be in shock because even that lame line doesn't hit me the way it should. I blink at the side of his face, feeling my insides go cold. He flinches, cringing slightly.

Oh right. My scent. It must be horribly burned by now.

I'm shocked and a little offended that his isn't. Nothing like the first time we met as mates, at Forever Matched, anyway. This is more...tingly. In a bad way. It makes my nose itch.

Embarrassment, I realize. Not stress or anger or shame. He's just...embarrassed? By having a *mistress*?

Is she even a mistress? I'm not really this alpha's omega. Maybe I'm *the mistress—*

Smith guides the SUV off the road, slowing to a stop on the

side of the highway and turning to face me completely. His low, even voice interrupts my spiral.

"Petal. Try not to panic. It...Irene isn't a woman I'm seeing. She's my teacher."

I swear, you could hear a pin drop inside my head right now. Empty silence echoes back at me while that word swirls around.

Teacher? For *what*?

He clears his throat, which is his tell. He's telling the truth, but he doesn't like it. "After you moved in, I realized how little I knew about being the sort of alpha you deserved," he says, quiet and gruff. "I decided I needed help."

Oh. My. God.

Images of the high-and-mighty Smith Pierson—in his perfectly pressed suits, scowling over lessons on slick and nesting—leave me gaping. "That's where you've been every night?"

I sound small and wobbly. Smith's scent deepens, growing darker. He instantly leans closer, gathering my hands in his, and sloughs out a deep breath. "Yes. The classes are... intensive. The course only lasts a month, so Irene and Julian—the omega instructors—insist on perfect attendance."

And here I thought he had avoided all of the family dinners I tried to make because he couldn't stand me. When, really...

I squeeze his hands. "Smith—"

He purrs, leaning closer, his smooth, sexy voice dropping into a murmur. "Don't. I don't want you to thank me or think this means you owe me anything. You deserve alphas who know how to take care of you; who make you feel as cherished as you are. You owe me nothing for doing what I need to do to become that for you. But I owe you an apology for not being that alpha when we met."

I'm torn between smiling and tears. My eyes water while I smirk. "Are you ever going to actually *say* you're sorry."

A spark moves through his dark eyes. His sculpted mouth quirks in wry amusement. "Have I never said that out loud?"

A giggle bubbles out of me. "No!"

He grins—a quick, pure expression of delight. It fades as he looks down at our entwined fingers. With utter sincerity, he bends his face to my hands and kisses both of them. When he speaks, I can still feel the brush of his lips, his words a rumbling skitter across the thin skin of my wrists.

"I'm sorry, angel. I'm so sorry that I ever scared you or hurt you. I'll regret the way I treated you for as long as I live."

He means it, with every tiny piece of himself. I can feel it. And as I sit there, in his luxurious leather car, watching him literally bow to me....

This isn't what I want.

"Smith." I cup my palms over his stubbled jaw, lifting his face back to mine. "I don't want you to live with that sort of regret. I want—"

I want you to be happy.

That's all it really is, isn't it? All my perfectionism and my constant desire to please him. I want him to be happy.

With me.

When I finally get the words out, he listens, more intent on what I'm saying than anyone ever has been. I watch his deep, brown eyes bounce between mine, absorbing the words. When they crease in pain, I realize it's the good kind. The sort that makes your heart ache.

He leans his forehead into mine for a long moment, letting the tension slip off his features. "There's something I need to show you."

TURNS OUT THAT, even after discovering his Deep Dark Secret, Smith Pierson is still a mystery.

When he turns off the interstate and begins driving us toward the ocean, I naturally assume we're going to the beach. Instead of heading for one of the public access points, though, the Range Rover cuts a sharp right onto a sandy residential street.

With the sun nearly setting, tangerine light suffuses the coastal area. Slants of orangey gold slice through the narrow street's foliage. All the beachy sorts of plants make me smile—sea grapes, bougainvillea, hibiscus bushes.

It doesn't take long for me to see that the impressive landscaping along the street is hiding some pretty luxe houses, though. They all sit far from the lane, their backs to the ocean, fronts obscured by palm fronds and elephant ears.

A nervous niggle starts in my stomach. Is Smith about to pull into one of these million-dollar homes and show me a whole new estate I have to become the mistress of in order to impress him?

We do make one final turn, into a crowded, unevenly paved driveway. I lean forward, looking out the windshield at the house in front of us, blinking my shock.

...what?

It's the smallest house on the whole street. In fact, one could easily mistake it for the neighbor's pool house. Or even a quaintly designed storage shed.

It's neither, though.

It's a bungalow.

A tiny white bungalow, trimmed in garish turquoise paint and standing on sandalwood stilts. It has a worn roof and flaky window tint and the front yard is a veritable jungle...

But it's adorable. I'm instantly in love.

"What is this place?" I buzz, beaming at the flamingo mailbox hanging beside the front door.

Smith gives nothing away, coming around the car to open my door and help me step onto the white-sand-covered concrete.

While I drift toward the little place, he clears his throat and begins to ramble. "I thought we might... stay here tonight. If you'd be open to it, I can order dinner, and there's a hot tub in the back. No pool. But there is beach access."

He must be a damn good developer because he's a terrible

salesman. I bite down on a teasing grin and nod along, letting him give me all sorts of useless information.

Now that I don't think of him as the terrifying alpha who intimidates me anymore, it's easier to find him cute when he babbles about square footage.

Even when he's muttering on, he's still in command, leading me right up to the house using a keypad on the front door. My eyes trace over the sign hung above the doorframe, thinking that it's super ironic—for both Mr. Perfectionist and myself.

Don't make perfect the enemy of the good.

Damon would love that. And Cassian would say something akin to, "Duh."

Smiling to myself, I follow Smith inside, seeing that this isn't a typical vacation rental. Unlike a furnished pad, it's empty, aside from a table and two chairs.

The tiny home is one long living area, narrow but with a high A-frame and natural wood beams that stand out against the bright white beadboard covering the ceiling. There isn't much to it—a small living room area to the left of the entrance, a cased opening leading to a dining nook, and a tiny kitchen tucked off to the side.

But the whole back wall of the house is a hodgepodge of windows. Warped antique glass, seafoam-stained panes, and some that are crystal clear. It doesn't really matter because the view is incredible.

There's nothing fancy about it. Just a clear, straight shot at the ocean. Pale sand, gray-blue water, and a hazy pink sky. I stand and stare at it from just inside the front door.

Smith takes my hand, threading our fingers back together as he pulls me through the cased opening and into the small kitchen area. I see it has appliances— newer ones that don't match the worn, round table and chairs at all.

Ignoring the room, Smith guides us out one of the stained-glass French doors and onto a back porch that's as wide as the kitchen itself.

The house is totally out of balance. Clearly designed by someone who just loved this view and the ocean so much that they didn't mind sacrificing half of their home's footprint to make room for an outdoor living space. The more I look out at the water, the less I can blame them for it.

"Who owns this?" I ask, lifting my free hand to touch a set of shell wind chimes. "I like their style."

Smith waits for me to look back at him and his rueful half-smile. "It's mine."

My fingers twitch against his. "*Yours*?!"

The humor falls off his face. He turns to the ocean, sighing. "I bought it as an investment property two years ago. It's a prime piece of land. Great street. Every other house here goes for anything north of ten million dollars, but this one..."

His pensive expression draws me closer to him. "This one?" I prompt.

His blond brows furrow. "This one belonged to a very old man. An alpha who bought it back in the eighties. For his omega."

He swallows. "When she died, he lived here without her. Refused to sell it to anyone, even though he got offers for more than five million. He said *no*. Got a reputation for turning down any developer who darkened his doorway. And not being very polite about it, either."

A slight smile touches his mouth, but not his eyes. "I thought I was hot shit, back then. We'd just made our first—well, *a lot* of money. And I wanted a beach house. For the pack. Our future family. Whatever.

"So I came here, determined to tell the old bastard anything he wanted to hear. I told him we had an omega who loved the beach. I told him we wanted to have kids and bring them here to play. And I swore—up and down—that I wouldn't tear the place to the ground the first chance I got..."

He glances at me, a familiar darkness in his gaze. "Knowing that's exactly what I would actually do."

My heart squeezes, aching for the alpha who missed his lost love and couldn't stand the thought of letting her home be dismantled. I'm almost afraid to ask, "Did he sell to you?"

Smith nods slowly. "I was very convincing."

My stomach sinks, along with the bubble of hope that had risen in my chest. "So this house... you want to tear it down?"

He gives a hard, breathless laugh, the sound rueful. "I *can't* tear it down," he huffs. "I've hired the crew and called it off a dozen times. Every time I try I just—" He shakes his head, looking back out at the view and murmuring, "I can't do it."

There was a time when I would have told you I could never, ever love this alpha.

But right now? I think I really could.

Especially when he turns his dark eyes back on me, saying so many things without words.

This is personal, I realize.

A real, true piece of Smith. No polish or shine or pretense or power. This forlorn place, with its beautiful story of love that's been lost to the tides of time—this is the sort of thing he carries around with him. Hidden under all his expensive suits. Inside his heart.

"Why did you bring me here?" I whisper, needing to hear him say it. "What did you want me to see?"

He releases another breath, glancing fondly at the charming little house. "That alpha? I hated him. And it took me months to figure out that I was *jealous* of this lonely, angry, old widower. Because he had a real *partner*. Someone he made decisions with. Like another half. And the more I planned to tear down everything they built together, the more I realized what I really wanted.

"It wasn't the property or the money or any of that shit. It was his life. A pack. A partner. A *mate*."

I remember wondering why a man like Smith had ever submitted an application to Forever Matched in the first place. He seemed so solitary—what would *he* want with an omega?

This.

He wanted a connection. A *partner*.

"You wanted me to see you," I realize out loud, whispering.

He cups his hands around my face, strumming his thumb over my lower lip. "I wanted you to see me. And when I tried to think of a place that felt like me, this was it."

I glance over at the house, feeling its magic soak into my center with every pull of salty ocean air. When I look back up at Smith, for the very first time, it isn't hard to tell him the truth.

"I love it."

chapter fifty-three

DAMON

"DO you want to talk about it?"

Our Uber driver is a beta guy a little younger than us. He glances up in the rearview mirror when he hears Cassian's question and quickly looks away when he catches my packmate's scowl.

I stare out at the bleak gray evening in whatever godforsaken corner of Minnesota we're currently driving through. Or maybe it's Michigan. Hard for me to remember when we've been on the road for nine days and all the hotel rooms look the same.

This is ironic. A few months ago, any interest in my well-being from Cassian would have been a welcome change of pace. Now, though, I don't know if I want us to talk.

Nausea coils in my middle while I clutch a stack of unreadable paperwork in my left fist. Every time I try to look at it, the letters rearrange themselves into symbols I don't recognize.

I don't know what it says.

But I know what it means. And so does Cass. *He* read the damn thing—in ten seconds, of course—right over my shoulder, the same moment Coach sheepishly handed it to me.

I didn't get much from the fight that came after that. Except that Cass is upset, and Coach feels shitty about what's happening. Though not enough to stop it, apparently.

"Can't believe this," Cass mutters, letting his head bounce against the seat behind us before jamming his fingers into his hair.

It's still sweaty. Neither of us showered after this last game because Coach approached me with these stupid papers as soon as we came off the ice.

He didn't need to. When they pulled me out to put Gunnar in, sometime during the middle of the third period, I already knew what was happening.

The press has been on about it for months. I stupidly believed it was all clickbait bullshit. Maybe I should have paid closer attention. Or worked out harder. Or watched my penalties more.

Either way, the writing is on the wall here.

I'm being *replaced.*

This is important, I coach internally, glancing at the paperwork. *You can do this. Just read the first line so you know what it says.*

Narrowing my gaze, I focus on the jumble of characters I know must really be words. Some of them are clusters I've memorized.

I see my full name first. That feels like a bad sign.

This is a legal document.

There are some numbers, which probably form a date of some

sort. The rest are small words like "on" and "for." The stuff in between is gibberish to me.

Fuck. Fuck. Fuck. What do I do? Do I tell Cassian I literally can't read this?

I've avoided telling anyone for fifteen years. Ever since I told my father, and he started calling me *Dipshit* instead of Damon.

I wonder if Remi has put it together yet. She's so smart, it wouldn't surprise me. Although, I'm sure if she had, she would treat me differently. At least a little bit.

There have only been a handful of people who noticed my deficiency, but every single one of them definitely lost some respect for me after they knew. I wonder how bad it will be whenever Remi finally realizes...

I actually can't think about it too hard, or my lungs stop working.

We go over a pothole, jostling the car, and Cass cuts me a sideways look. "What does the rest of the paperwork say? I only looked at the first page."

Oh, God, this isn't working.

I snap my eyes closed and hunch over my lap, thrusting the papers over to my packmate. "Here. I can't—just tell me what they say."

There's a long beat of silence before he takes the document. And another one after he shuffles the papers around. "It's actually not as bad as I thought," he murmurs. "Nothing is decided. They've put your contract in review, pending the playoffs."

My mind spins and I realize it's because I'm not breathing. When I force myself to inhale, it all makes sense in the worst fucking way.

They have Gunnar. He can do what I do, *almost* as well, for a lot less money. If they sever my contract, I'll be on a different team, in another state. Or I'll be nothing at all.

I doubt Remi will want to be bonded to an alpha who can't be with her for any of her heats. Or any of the other shit. Good days, bad days, anniversaries, *birthdays*.

An image of her blue-gold eyes, shining with tears while she described years of hating her birthday looms in my head. I have a whole plan to make sure she never spends the day feeling alone again.

What if I won't even be there?

That can never happen. I *promised* her she wouldn't be alone anymore. I swore we would take care of her, *together*.

Frantic, the wheels in my head spin faster, trying to churn up some sort of solution.

I could quit. Stop playing hockey and stay home and—

What? Without this career, I'll have none at all. It's not like I can do anything else. I can't even read the damn paperwork telling me *I have to* do something else.

And I can't leave Remi. *I won't*.

So, basically, I have to *crush* the playoffs. Or walk away and show everyone what a disappointment I really am.

A low wave of fury rolls off Cass. "Some warning would have been nice. And giving you this shit on the road? Jesus."

He has a point. It was a dick move to wait until we finished our road series to tell me. Strategic, but shitty. I won most of these games, with a little help from Gunnar. That's not to say the rookie couldn't have pulled it off, but that's not the point.

They used me, knowing they were going to put me through this.

My throat is sticky as I force a swallow. "What can I do?"

Cassian flips through the pages, scanning them with his lightning-quick gaze. "Smith will have to call the lawyers. But we've all discussed this. We knew they had this option."

That's true. I knew there was a chance my contract might not get renewed. But I never let myself think about it much. I'm usually the lucky one, remember?

I told myself I would work it out when I had to, never expecting it to *actually* happen. Just like I never expected I'd be completely all-in in love with an omega who needs me to be worth a damn.

I scrub my hands over my eyes, but I can't feel them. Are they numb? Or is it my face?

Cassian takes a long look at me and hesitates before setting his hand on my shoulder. When I can't seem to make myself blink, he grumbles, "Listen. There's a chance, if you play well enough in the playoffs, they'll drop this whole thing. They haven't released you yet—this is just notice that you're in review. If you post enough points in the playoffs and we actually win, they'll have to renew your contract."

I finally raise my head, meeting his heavy stare. "And if they don't?"

A wince pulls at his features. "It will suck, but we can get past it. We can get you a job at Pierson Properties or—I mean, you wouldn't want to keep playing, right? If it meant moving away from—"

I watch him choose his next word carefully. When he finally settles on it, the pain in my chest pulses.

"*—us*?"

Because it isn't just Remi. She's the biggest part, now, but I'd also have to leave Cass, too. My brother, basically. And *his* brother, who's more like the only family I've ever had.

Could I walk away from all of them?

If I don't, I'll be a washed-up former athlete.

Hockey is all I've ever been.

If I leave it behind, what do I have left for Remi?

"I think..." I look back at the rumpled paperwork piled between us. "I think I need your help, Cass."

chapter fifty-four

I'D FORGOTTEN ALL about Smith being a contractor in his former life... until we had to figure out how to turn on the hot tub.

He seemed to snap into a version of himself I'd never seen before, stripping his shirt off and getting on his back to access a panel of controls tucked under the railing on the deck. Within thirty minutes, we had a perfect whirlpool and the most delicious Italian takeout I've ever eaten.

It's clearly from an upscale restaurant, but Smith takes the time to unload everything onto the only two plates in the whole house, arranging my pasta on a turquoise plate with seashells around the rim.

When I smile at the dinnerware, he smirks ruefully. "You'll need to put your skills to good use around here, angel. Aside from the table, there's just a nightstand and a bed."

My brows draw up. "One bed?"

He pulls the cork out of a bottle of champagne—the single item I found in the refrigerator—and meets my eyes steadily. "One bed."

Does that mean he finally feels like I'm ready for whatever he wants to do to me? Or maybe he's planning to take me home and tuck me into my own bed *alone*?

It seems unlikely we're going anywhere when he pulls a second bottle out of the to-go bags and places it in the fridge to chill for later.

The hot tub is a luxury I've never experienced before. While Smith wades right in, arranging our dinner on a wide wooden ledge built around the lip of the bubbling pool, I linger at the edge, dipping my toe in.

It *is* hot. *Whoa.*

When Smith notices my hesitation, he leaves our plates behind and comes over, holding out his hand. "It's okay," he murmurs, eyes soft and dark in the waning sunset. "It feels really good once you're in. Trust me?"

I do. So much more now than I did even a few hours ago. When I slip my fingers into his, something hot and bright flares in his gaze. He wraps his free arm around my waist and lifts me right in.

The water is sweltering... for a moment. But as soon as I'm in it, the heat melts my apprehension into a puddle.

Smith watches me relax, his approval clear. Even before he slides his hands over my back and murmurs, "Good girl. Always so brave for me. And so fucking beautiful."

He bends as he roughs out the last few words, scent-marking my forehead with his. When I can't quite strangle the whine that ekes out of me, he hums and pulls me closer, gliding backward through the water and landing on the bench seat with me in his lap.

"This okay?" he asks, reaching for my plate. "I want to feed you."

Every coherent thought flies out of my head. "Y-yes? If you want."

His smile is no less handsome up close. A sexy quirk of his lips that's somehow wry and genuine. And—oh Lord—is there a tiny dimple in his left cheek when he smirks like this?

I've never been close enough to notice before. Now, sitting across the spread of his muscled thighs, it's impossible to look away.

He angles us perfectly, bringing bites of tortellini right to my mouth. The creamy mushroom sauce he ordered is incredible. I hum happily, and he chuckles.

"Right? I love this place. We don't have one in town, though. You have to drive out here to get it."

I swallow and let myself cuddle a little bit closer to him. "Maybe we can bring the guys next time? All of us could have a family dinner there."

Easy affection curves his mouth. "You and your family dinners."

I try not to let tension creep into my posture, recalling all the times I made a big meal only to leave his plate untouched. But Smith is watching me now. He sees the way I freeze up and makes a low noise of apology, nuzzling my cheek again.

"I'm sorry, petal."

No qualifiers or explanations, just honest remorse. "So sorry," he repeats. "Let's choose a night every week, and I swear I'll be there. In fact, I'll come home early and help you cook."

My belly quivers with nerves. I know he's trying to show me that what I want matters to him, but part of me still feels like I should explain why I'm like this.

I accept the next bite of food from his fork, chewing before I sigh and whisper, "I've never had a family dinner before."

He goes still, leaving the utensil on my plate and staring at me for an eternity. The gears in his mind grind as he processes my mortifying confession. When he finally understands, his arms lock around me in a hug to rival his brother's crushing embraces.

"Fucking hell," he breathes. "I'm such an asshole. Remi. Angel. Jesus, I'm so sorry. I didn't think—*never*? Not one time?"

I go back through all the foster homes I went to. There were meals at family tables, usually served in an assembly-line fashion. Grease-stained bags of fast food. Lots of soggy french fries. But never a time when I felt like I was gathered at a table with my family.

"No," I confirm. "Not one time."

Smith exhales hard, ruffling my hair. His voice sounds hoarse. "I'll never miss another one. Petal, *I swear*. Please forgive me. I'm so sorry."

I do forgive him, as much as I can. The hurt is still there, aching like a bruise on my heart. But when he buries his face into my shoulder and scent-marks my throat, I feel the pain start to evaporate.

A rolling rumble revs in his chest. His purr is just as perfect as I remember—smooth and soothing, all the way down to my soul.

"Come here, angel," he husks, gently turning me so I'm sprawling on his lap, my back pressed to his chest, and my head resting on the broad ledge of his shoulder. His forearm hooks around my waist, comforting in the weightlessness of the water.

He keeps feeding me bites of delicious food, brushing his lips over my temple every few moments. The periwinkle sky fades to violet before he musters his will and speaks again.

"I've made a lot of mistakes. Sometimes, I wonder if you'd still want me for your alpha if you knew all of them."

It's another piece of him. One that hits me right in the gut. "You could tell me," I whisper. "And then you'll know."

His arm cinches tighter. "It's a long list, little petal."

Finished with my dinner, I turn and mark his neck with a kiss. "Okay, what's the worst thing?"

A shaking breath escapes him. He hangs his head forward, pressing our foreheads back together. "I failed Cassian. That has to be the worst thing."

I reel back, my face crumpling. "What? How? You've done incredibly well!"

His answering smile is hollow. "That's now. At first? Fuck, everything was a mess. I wasn't eighteen yet, so he had to go into the foster care system. When I turned eighteen, I tried to get him back.

"He was so—I know you didn't meet him until later, but at the time, he was only nine. And he was scared. I wanted to raise him myself, but I had no job. No degree. Shit grades because I spent all of my time fucking around, not knowing our parents wouldn't be around."

He shakes his head. "It took me way longer to get myself together than it should have. By then, he was practically a grown man."

I touch his cheek, feeling the prickle of his five o'clock shadow. "Why did it take you so long?"

"I was just"—He makes a half-groan sound—"Fuck, I don't know. I wanted us to have money and a nice place to live. So I just kept working more and more, trying to achieve enough to *feel ready*. But it never happened."

I remember the charming sign on the front porch and how ironic it seemed. "You made perfect the enemy of the good."

His expression flickers, pain creasing his brow. "I do that."

Just like he did with their house. And my suite.

Because he cares. So much. *Too much*. Like I do. And it paralyzes him, the same way it sends me into a tizzy.

"Me, too," I tell him, leaning closer. "Maybe... we could help each other stop?" I almost laugh. "Or maybe Cass could help us. He's good that way."

"Damon is too," Smith grumbles. "Except when it comes to his hair products."

Indignance surges through me. I slap the water, sending a splash at his chest. "Hey! That's my alpha! And he's actually a lot wiser about a lot of things than either of you give him credit for. He was the first one to actually *try* to get to know me and do the things I enjoy. And he's smart, Smith. Think about all the scrapes he's gotten himself out of. Think about where he started and where he is, now. *He* did that. All on his own."

Instead of blinking at me, Smith listens, brow furrowed in concentration. When I finish, he nods. "I agree, actually. I keep asking him if he wants to help me out with Pierson, but every time I mention it, he acts like I've asked him to feed his balls to a den of lions."

I didn't know about Pierson. That mollifies me, somewhat. Though, I wonder if it has something to do with the way he struggles to read basic household things like our calendar or the notes I leave for them.

"Sometimes," Smith mutters, reaching over to take the last bite of his steak. "I wonder if Damon is on to something, avoiding the business like he does."

I always assumed Smith loved what he did. Otherwise, what was the point of him being there so much? He has clearly made more money than we will ever need.

"If you don't like it, why do you do it?"

Smith spreads his arms out, snatching a glass of champagne for me in one hand and picking up his own in the other. After a couple of swallows, he sighs.

"I used to like it. Lately, though... I don't know. I'm always taking things apart. Leveling people's memories into dust and paving over them. And, yes, we build things... but do we really *make* anything *good*? I'm just not sure anymore."

I think about Proper Coffee. How it technically looks and does better now. But it lost all of its character and softness along the way.

"Have you ever thought about doing something else?" I wonder out loud.

He cocks his head to the side, regarding the dark horizon pensively. "I don't think I've let myself think about that in a long time. Maybe I should."

I'm about to agree, shifting to pick up the bottle of sparkling wine and refill his glass—but my body has other ideas.

As soon as I rise up onto my knees, one of the hot tub's jets strokes across my bare stomach, the pulse of the heated water making me gasp. Smith's lips quirk up; his eyes darkening for completely different reasons than they were a moment before.

"Stretch up a bit more."

He doesn't ask, but it isn't a command either. More a sensual suggestion. The knowing gleam in eyes makes me want to listen to him. This is clearly a man who knows what he's talking about. Much more than I do.

I bring my knees closer and lengthen my lower back. The pounding sensation goes from hitting just below my navel to vibrating at the apex of my thighs.

I gasp again, rearing back. Smith's hand is there, though, keeping me from falling into the water. His body presses into my side while his warm palm strokes a soothing line over my spine. "It's okay," he murmurs, kissing my shoulder. "Give yourself a moment to adjust."

A small beat of alpha power accompanies his words. Not enough to be forceful; just enough to make me feel like he's in control. It's reassuring—I don't want to be the one making these decisions. I love that he likes to take over and let me relax.

My muscles unwind as he steps up behind me. His hands find my hips, stroking soothing circles as he tilts them the way he wants them.

His voice sends shivers down my back. "Spread your legs."

Goosebumps skitter over my skin, leaving my nipples painfully hard under the triangles of wet, clingy fabric covering them. As if he can read my mind, one of Smith's hands presses flat to my stomach before sliding up. He pauses at the lower edge of my bikini top, his thumb stroking the straining tip.

A charge zips straight to my clit. For a second, his touch is all I can feel, all the more powerful for being the only stimulation. When he bends his knee and uses his thigh to push mine apart, the pulsing jet suddenly hits right where my body throbs the hardest. Hot sensation shoots through all of my limbs, the pleasure almost overwhelming.

"There you go," he murmurs, gentling me as I squirm and whine. His fingers pinch my nipple until my head falls back onto his shoulder.

He nuzzles my temple, his voice growing rougher while his words grow sweeter. "Beautiful angel. Seeing you like this is such a gift. Do you know that? How precious you are?"

The hand at my hip sketches lower, his blunt nails digging into my upper thigh while the jet pulses against my pussy. I buck backward. His hard length presses into my back. Smith hums, ghosting his lips over curve of my neck.

"So beautiful," he praises. "I can't tell you how many times I've thought about biting this pretty neck, petal. Too many fucking times."

The sensation of the water hitting me is so intense. More than anything else I've ever felt before. Smith's fingers slip closer, flexing as he grips the flesh of my thigh, his knuckles brushing the edge of my bikini bottoms.

"Do you want them off?" he asks. "I'll fill this sweet cunt with my fingers right now."

I gasp again, my backside grinding into his solid length. "That's a rude word," I pant. "I don't—" A whimper breaks into my scolding. "—like it."

Smith's chuckle is as warm as the hot water beating at my clit. "All right, angel. Noted. I think you'll like this, though."

The hand at my breast moves to tease my neglected nipple while he dips his fingers into the bottoms, slipping two right into me. It's clear, even with all this hot water swirling around, I am soaked with slick.

Smith groans roughly, the sound vibrating against the bare skin of my throat. "So tight and slick for me. Good girl, Remi. So good for me."

I was right before: This alpha knows exactly what he's doing. His long, thick fingers press forward and stroke deeper, finding the place made for his knot and massaging the clenching ring of muscle until my vision begins to blur.

"My knot's going to feel so good in this tight pussy, petal. I'll stretch you just right. Let you come all over me until you can't take anymore." His teeth graze the thin skin below my ear, his voice a gravelly rasp. "And then you'll give me one more anyway."

While his middle and forefinger work inside me, his thumb flicks the flimsy fabric covering me aside, he and spreads my lower lips, sending the jet of overheated water right onto my clit. The hot pulse instantly sets off my climax.

Keening, I bear down on his hand and let my body clamp around his touch, feeling so many different types of pleasure at once. His fingers rubbing the place that pounds for his knot. The stream of liquid heat caressing my clit. His hand roughly clasping my breast, still thumbing my nipple as his teeth close around my throat.

Bubbles erupt in my veins—as hot as the ones swirling through the tub, more sparkly than the effervescence in our champagne. Smith growls his approval, telling me how perfect I look and feel while I come for him.

And maybe—just *maybe*—I believe him.

chapter fifty-five

Smith

CARING for Remi is so much more than I ever expected it to be.

I know who I am. I know what I like.

And, to an extent, both of those things have always made me the more dominant, generous party in my past relationships.

But this feels entirely different. It isn't just about how much *control* I can exert, how many orgasms I can pull out of her. This is everything I've ever wanted but never found.

It's a *gift*.

Every time she lets me work her over, takes the pleasure I insist on, submits to my control. She *isn't* taking—she's *giving*.

Her trust, her body, her pleasure. It's all an incredible, indescribable gift that I surely don't deserve.

I'm taking it anyway.

I'm taking everything she'll give me and giving her everything I've got in return. That's how this is going to go from now on, I decide, bundling her into a towel.

She's dazed and languid, blinking up at me with soft blue-gold eyes. I lead her into the house, pausing beside the back door to shuck my wet swim trunks while pinning my own towel around my hips with my fist.

Remi follows my lead, removing the scraps of material she had on during the first four orgasms I gave her. Knowing she's entirely naked under her beach towel leaves my mouth watering as we step into the quiet, cozy house.

Even before tonight, I had a soft spot for this place. But now? I'm never going to be able to tear it down or sell it someone who will.

Now, it's *ours*.

Remi floats into the middle of the empty living space and turns back to me. Her head tilts in a coy gesture, but her eyes lower demurely.

It's a tease. She has a bit of brat in her. Topping from the bottom—but doing it so beautifully, she knows none of us will deny her.

That's especially true when she drops her towel.

Motherfucking hell.

She's so goddamn gorgeous. Her makeup has melted off, but I love that she's bare for me, exposed in every way. Flawless brown skin over petite curves and fine bones. Her pert tits, the dusky nipples pointing slightly upward. The sweep of her feminine hips. The sweet, pink folds peeking from between her luscious thighs.

She must be overstimulated, by now. I pulled every last bit of pleasure I could get out of her, absorbing the way she let me have everything each time she fell over the edge.

This was never about me, though. Tonight is meant to show

her how I want it to be between us. How she'll be the center of my entire world, mine in every way. *If* she'll have me.

I didn't expect anything more than that—so when she holds out her hand, it takes me a minute to understand what she's offering.

More.

She wants to give me more.

It feels impossible. But the longer I hesitate, the more her face seems torn between desire and doubt. The fear of rejection flashes through her features, so easy to read, now that I recognize it.

My towel hits the floor. I come right at her, my hands gripping her naked ass and the nape of her neck to lift her into my charge. I sweep her right up into me, finding her mouth with my own as I stalk to the bedroom.

I want her so badly, my cock has long gone numb from the constant throb pulsing through it. It bobs heavily, grazing the wet heat bathing her upper thighs, the feeling sending a tingle through the straining length.

A fresh burst of perfume flows from her body, hitting me in a dizzy rush. I couldn't scent her arousal in the hot tub; and it warms some deep, secret part of me to know how much I wanted her, even without that element in play.

Fuck science. This isn't just about being scent-matched anymore. It isn't about being mates. It's *us*—Remi and Smith. And she's so much more than some *thing* I can't resist.

She's an angel. A temptress. A brilliant little brat who gets away with everything because she knows exactly how to act like a perfect lady.

And I *love* her.

The feeling pours through me, stronger and truer than anything I've ever felt. So sharp and sweet, it almost *hurts*. I grunt into her mouth, our tongues twisting around the agonized sound.

She whines, reacting to all my emotion with her own. Giving. Still giving. More and more, as she throws her head back and lets me nestle into her throat, marking it with love-bites since I can't have the real thing.

Yet.

It's still possible she won't ever want me that way.

I don't care. She can have anything. If she wants me to suffer without her bond for the rest of my life to make up for the way I treated her, I will do it.

And if she wants to form bonds with Cassian and Damon and leave me out as a punishment? I have to accept that. As long as she lets me have *her*, I'll survive.

Our wet lips slip together in a filthy, fucking sort of kiss. When she nips at my mouth, I snarl, my dominance erupting in a wave I can't control.

"You want me to fuck you, omega?"

She nods, whimpering. "Yes, Sir."

Another pulse of power infuses my reply. "*Present.*"

Remi rolls out of my arms and onto the mattress, immediately situating herself on her hands and knees. The thin light from the room's single lamp glows off her shimmery honey skin, the globes of her ass are enough to have me gripping my knot, kneading it to relieve the pulsing ache there.

"Lower," I urge, wanting to see her entire slit. "On your forearms."

An unpleasant tremble racks her body. When I note the way she hesitates before moving to obey, I snap out, "Stop."

She freezes instantly. I smooth both palms over her ass, soothing her quivers. There's something about this that scares her.

"Tell me," I murmur.

Remi shakes slightly. "The h-heat clinic. They have omegas on their forearms for their whole heat, presenting through a—box."

She means a cage. They aren't "boxes"—they are metal cages. I've seen how those places are set up. After buying a few to dismantle them, I can easily imagine how uncomfortable that would be for her.

Picturing her bent in half for four days fills me with rage and a thick wash of self-loathing. Why wasn't I there for her? I'll never forgive myself for the fact that she had to resort to that or the dubious meds omegas have to take to suppress their heats.

The guys already assured Remi she could stop taking hers. This will be her first heat without them and her Omega will definitely want to present for us. There's no rush, though. Especially not tonight.

Before I can move her into another position, she decisively pushes her forearms flat to the bed, raising her ass higher. "I want to be able to do this," she murmurs, quiet but strong. "This is important to me. Can you—can we try?"

Sweet little petal.

"Of course we can try," I tell her. "Pick a safe word first."

She considers this for a second, turning to press her face into the sheets, hiding half of the impish smirk twisting her pink lips. "Latte."

Damn. Fair enough.

"Good choice," I chuckle, my voice rasping. "Say that if you need me to stop. Otherwise, we'll keep going."

Her lips twitch up again. "Yes, Sir."

"Good girl," I praise, running my hands over her body with more intent. "So fucking good. Are you going to take this knot? Make me your alpha?"

She nods, her damp curls bouncing against her nape. "Yes, Sir."

Fuck, she's so perfect. "You look exquisite," I tell her, kneeling up on the bed behind her. "Presenting for your alpha. You're doing so well, angel. I'm so proud of you."

Another wash of perfume fills the air with honeyed warmth. The taste of it is enough to make me half-feral. My voice turns to a growl as I rub my cock between her spread thighs, coating myself in her sweet slick.

Goddamn it. She already feels too good. Her heat bathes my dick as I slide myself back and forth, using my crown to tease her overworked clit slightly. She mewls, pushing her hips back, into my hands. Her eagerness makes me smile and I let it show, knowing she won't see.

"Impatient," I tut. "I'll have to work on that."

My perfect little petal sweeps her lashes over her eyes. Textbook submission; so flawless, my blood smolders in my veins. "Yes, Sir."

I take one last moment to admire her, stroking up her spine to nestle my fingers in her silky, kink-curled hair, wrapping it around my fist without pulling. She responds to the position exactly as I hoped—her back expands on faster breaths, a fresh dribble of her honey wetting my cock.

When I push the head of my dick into her, my vision momentarily dips. Her walls cinch around the wide crown. A rough curse sloughs out of me.

Remi's whine is soft but soaked in need. My body responds automatically, bucking to fill her slick, tender pussy with steel heat.

Fuck. Me.

My control is usually absolute, but once I'm inside her? I can't even see it anymore. Don't want to.

She's already submitted. She's here, laid out. *Mine.*

Now I'm going to make sure she fucking stays here.

With every thrust, I feel us growing closer to each other. She spreads wider for me, relaxing into her pose. I move with an undercurrent of tenderness, wanting to erase any traumatic memories she might have. Replacing them with how much I love her.

I roll my hips, creating a rhythm she can take without rousing. Showing her, with every pulse of my body moving into hers, that she can trust me. I won't ever let this hurt her again.

The hand in her hair pulls softly, turning her face so I can watch pleasure glaze her features. My free hand touches her everywhere, memorizing the way she feels under my fingertips. Warm, vibrant, and soft. My petal. An angel who fell into my bed.

I'll never deserve her.

But I can make her feel the way she deserves to feel.

The thought renews my determination. I drill into her, pressing down and forward so every thrust grinds my knot against her clit. Her pussy pulls me in deeper, the clenches of her core drawing us closer and closer.

I feel it coming half a second before it happens. Her body accepts mine all at once—the outer muscles relaxing while the ones deep inside tug me in, popping my knot into her.

Ecstasy explodes through my base, snapping up my spine. The way she feels is a fucking miracle. Smooth, slick, hot, tight—and *everywhere*. I look down, nearly coming the second I see the way I disappear completely into her perfect pussy.

Growling, I rut as smoothly as I can while we're partially locked down. "Fucking hell, angel. This pussy was made for my cock. My knot. You feel so good. I'm going to come so hard inside you, I'll never be able to leave."

She cries out, the sound strangled and almost... plaintive. I replay what I just said, barely coherent, but able to hear the part that might have hit her particularly hard.

Churning my hips against her ass, I bend over her body to murmur into her hair. "I'm never leaving," I pant. "I'm never leaving you, angel. Never. Never. *Never*."

Remi sobs as she comes, the deep, throbbing clench of her core milking my cock until I glaze her depths with cum. My knot expands, sealing us together, setting off another climax for both of us.

My little petal trembles as I gather her up and arrange us on the bed's only pillow, tucking her into me. I bury my face into her neck and stroke my hands over her skin, murmuring my promises to her, over and over, until she falls asleep.

chapter fifty-six

SAD SAUSAGE FEST CHAT

SMITH

If either of you are late, I'll have your balls.

CASSIAN

I'm on my way. Had to get some special wine Remi asked me to pick up.

DAMON

Coming home now. I have flowers for our pretty girl.

CASSIAN

Fuck. I got Rems flowers.

SMITH

I had some delivered this morning.

DAMON

If the card said, "petals for my petal," I'm never going to stop laughing.

Btw, did anyone buy a vase?

SMITH

Fuck.

CASSIAN

Fuck.

DAMON

On it.

But that's totally what the card said, didn't it?

CASSIAN

WATCHING my big brother with Remi is really fucking annoying.

And cute, I guess.

If you're into that sort of thing.

In a turn of events that's shocking to *no one*, they work perfectly together. Smith may not be a chef, but he's every bit as scrupulous as Remi is. When she gives him a direction, he follows it to the letter, moving around the kitchen like he's there with her every night.

I'm in his usual place at the kitchen table, feeling a weird sense of role-reversal when he steps up behind her and wraps an arm around her waist. She's entirely focused on some gravy bubbling in a saucepan, frowning at it while he drops his forehead to her throat and scent-marks her.

He's been all over her since we came home from our road stretch this morning. And, apparently, for the last three days, in general. I don't even think he's been to the office, unwilling to leave her for that long.

I remember that feeling, after the first time I knotted her. It's particularly bad for pack alphas, according to Damon's research. Which explains why Smith is hogging her right now even though we're the ones who have been away for almost two damn weeks.

I'm trying not to be a jealous dick.

I'm *really bad* at not being a jealous dick.

Absentmindedly, Remi reaches behind her and pats the side of Smith's hair. He smirks, though she can't see him, amused that she barely notices his advances at this point.

When he turns his face into her hair and whispers something, she suddenly whips her head around. They share a private look that leaves him grinning and her lowering her lashes in the most beautiful cock-tease of all time.

The scent of her perfume winds across the kitchen. I grit my teeth to keep from getting up and going over to her, wanting them to have their time together.

But my girl feels me struggling.

Butterfly-blue eyes flit to mine, her face warming in the special, unguarded smile she seems to reserve just for me. It's younger and more carefree, somehow, than the sassy smirks she gives Smith, or the flirty giggles she saves for D.

Not for the first time, I wish I could *feel* her. The looks she gives are everything, but I want to be able to reach for her without ever having to glance up.

That's a lot, for me. I've always liked silence. Being alone. The thought of having someone in my head is pretty much my worst nightmare.

But Remi?

She's already there. All the time.

A whisper. Sunshine. The color and lace and warmth I don't have.

Having her in my blood doesn't feel like an intrusion. It's more... completion. I wasn't *whole* before. Now I am.

We are.

I watch her read my face. The humor falls off hers, but the joy remains, shining in her gaze. "Bear, come help me?"

God, she's the sweetest fucking thing. How did we get so damn *lucky*?

I don't need the bonds to know Smith is thinking the same

thing when he meets my eye over her head and begrudgingly moves aside.

"I'll check the rolls," he says, nuzzling her cheek again. "I'll be right over there."

When he finally moves away, Remi lowers her voice into a stage whisper and shoots me a mischievous look. "He thinks I don't know where the oven is."

My mouth twitches into an involuntary grin. "Does he realize you've been leaving him food in there for a month?"

She shrugs her bare shoulder, shifting the strap of her pink dress. It's the same one she had on that first day—at Forever Matched—and I'm not much for clothes, but maybe we should hang this one article in a frame or something.

"I don't know," Remi replies, all put-on innocence. "Maybe his memory is going. You know, he *is* old."

She yelps, and I realize Smith smacked her ass. A week ago, she might have shrunk down if he even touched her. Now, she flashes him an indignant scowl and he walks toward the fridge with a shit-eating smile on his face.

Which is when I see that—

Smith is in *jeans*.

And he doesn't have shoes on.

Goddamn.

Remi literally fucked his brains out.

It's a shame he's in such a good mood on the one night Damon and I have to ruin it.

We've only been back at the pack house for a few hours, but he's clearly spinning out. After greeting our girl, instead of joining her and me in the nest, he said he had a headache and went back to his own room. Smith checked on him while Remi had me occupied and told me later that he found him listening to another of her audiobooks.

Now, as he comes slinking into the kitchen, I move to give him access to her.

"This smells amazing, pretty girl," he rasps, sidling into her other side. He nuzzles his forehead into her shoulder, scent-marking her before dropping a kiss to her cheek. "Thank you for making us dinner."

Remi giggles, oblivious to his somber expression. "I make you dinner all the time," she points out, bending to examine the bubbles in her gravy. "But this is my first time making Smith's favorite, so it might be a disaster."

She's too modest. The meal already looks incredible, and it's still on the stove. Rice pilaf, green beans in some sort of sticky, buttered glaze, a cast-iron full of perfectly rendered pork chops, and a pot of pepper gravy to smother them.

Damon hides his face in her hair, inhaling deeply. "What can I do to help?"

She juts her chin at a stack of white dinnerware. Which is new, just like the table she gestures to next. "Can you guys set the table? Everything will be ready in five minutes."

Smith comes back over as D and I jump to our task. He meets my eyes across the kitchen table, his look significant.

And I don't need a pack bond to see what he's thinking.

chapter fifty-seven

DAMON

REMI PICKED my flowers to go on the table.

I don't know why that puts a big-ass lump in my throat. But it does.

I can barely eat, staring at the light pink and violet blossoms, half-listening while Cass describes each game of our road series in grunts.

He's talked me down a dozen times, but I still feel like I'm about to fuck everything up.

Something I feel increasingly guilty about, after coming home and seeing how absolutely fucking perfect our pack house is now.

The last time we had a road series, we came home to shrouded furniture, dust bunnies, and a general air of depression.

But now?

The whole house is immaculate. Glossy wood floors, tasteful navy-and-light-blue furniture. Perfectly painted walls, accented with strategic patches of blue-and-white patterned wallpaper. Fake pink peonies on all the tables. Area rugs so soft that you sink into them when you walk.

Cass went off to hunt our omega down, but I couldn't move. One thought repeated in my head, again and again—*She gives us everything. And I'm about to have nothing.*

My thoughts race while my fork chases my food around my plate. When I hear my name, I startle.

"Damon?"

All three of them are looking at me. Remi's eyes drop to my dinner, her teeth nipping her lower lip. "Do you not like it? I think I put too much pepper in the gravy."

Smith sways close enough to kiss her head. "It's perfect, petal." His eyes land on mine, brow quirking. "Are you okay, Damon?"

I open my mouth, but nothing comes out. How the hell do I explain this? I'm being replaced? I'm washed up? Please still love me?

Fuck.

"Damon." Remi sets her utensils down and stands, coming around the table, right to me. My body reacts without my useless brain, opening my arms for her. She folds herself into my lap.

Fuuuuuck.

But she feels perfect. Everything locked up inside of me unclenches immediately, tension receding like a tide getting sucked into a wave.

Only... the wave doesn't come crashing over me. Instead, while she fits her face into my bare shoulder, the waters still.

Plush lips graze my collarbone. "Trouble," she whispers, "what's wrong? Do you feel sick?"

Not anymore. At this moment, I feel like I could eat ten pork chops. Shit, I'm hungry. When was the last time I was able to get a full meal down? Two days ago? Before that last game.

Remi watches my face closely before pivoting on my lap and scooping up a forkful of food. When she holds it up to my mouth, her eyes wide with hope and worry, I immediately wolf it down.

Damn, that's so good. She's so good. For me. *For all of us.*

My insides settle, their seething soothed as she feeds me another bite. This is supposed to be something alphas do for their omegas, not the other way around. But I don't care.

Smith does.

He picks up Remi's plate and starts carving her meat for her. Scooting his chair closer, he offers her a bite of her own for every one she gives me, pausing to pet her hair every few moments. When he stops to squeeze my shoulder, I'm so shocked, I could fall out of my chair.

His dark eyes meet mine over Remi's head, solid and sure. "Whatever's happening, we'll work it out," our pack alpha says.

I tilt my face into Remi's hair again. This is the part I've been dreading—the thing I can't figure out. I don't know what to say or how to explain.

But, then, suddenly, I don't have to. Remi peeks up at me. Our eyes lock, and I can just tell—she knows.

She's known this whole time.

And she's never treated me any differently because of it.

She listens anyway, letting me tell my whole story while Smith watches with a concerned frown. By the time I wind my way through every single humiliating detail, Remi has tear tracks over her cheeks. As soon as I finish, she stretches up in my lap and presses her damp lips to mine.

"I wish I could feel you," she whispers.

My heart seizes. She's talking about a pack bond. Because she wants to be able to sense what's going on inside of me.

A dark laugh huffs out. "Even right now?"

She cuddles closer. "*Especially* right now."

I lean back and look into her eyes, sparkling with tears and soaked in sincerity. She means it. She wants to be with me, in me, even when I'm a mess.

Maybe that's the whole fucking point.

We've been fragmented for so long. How will it ever get any better if we aren't willing to take this leap?

Smith's voice is even and completely devoid of judgment. "What do you think, Damon?"

I turn from him to Cassian. Just a few weeks ago, wasn't I thinking that no one ever cared about my input? They're both looking at me, now. Listening to *me*.

So I say what needs to be said.

"I think we should bond."

chapter fifty-eight

"NOW?!"

Oh my God. I am so not prepared for this! I haven't even asked Meg all of the questions I have. I haven't done a refresher on the procedure or looked up the benefits of doing it during my heat versus—

"Not now."

It's Cassian.

When we all whip around to look at him, we find him staring his stepbrother down. "She isn't ready," he adds, completely correct. The smallest half-smile pulls at his mouth. "But maybe we should practice."

Smith slides his gaze to me, running it over my face. "Hmm. Good point. We haven't even given her a preview."

The predatory intent slithering through his dark gaze makes me perfume. "Sorry," I whisper to D, shifting in his lap. "Guys, Damon is—"

"—in heaven," he groans, scraping his teeth over my bare shoulder. "Pretty girl, you know you never have to do anything you don't want to. But, right now, I can't imagine anything that would feel better than being inside you."

He hides his face against my neck, whispering his last confession, "I want to knot you."

I don't think the others know that he hasn't, yet. It's a special thing we've kept just between us, after he explained that he wanted the first time to be perfect. That fact that he wants to do this now, with the guys in on it, after telling us all these hard, vulnerable things, means the world to me.

Damon carries me over to the kitchen island and sets me on a barstool, while Smith and Cassian begin clearing the table, working in unison. I watch them move at a breakneck pace, stifling a laugh.

It's *amazing* how quickly three men can clean an entire kitchen when they're properly motivated.

Cassian comes for me first, flopping a soggy dishrag over the edge of the farm-style sink and barreling right over. He tosses me over his shoulder, secures an arm around the backs of my thighs, and motions for the others to follow him.

"Did you see her smirking at us while we cleaned up?" he grunts to Smith, jostling me lightly. "Brat."

Their pack alpha is alarmingly even. "Hmm. Brats get punished."

Damon snorts, throwing his own attitude into the mix. "Since when?"

From my place over Cass's shoulder, I barely catch Smith reaching for the hockey gear the guys left by the front door when they came home. He bends at the waist, snatching up one of Damon's sticks.

Oh. Dear. Lord.

I already know he likes putting me over his knee until he has me screaming, *"Yes, Sir."* When I raise my head to catch his eye, I hope my apprehension isn't too obvious. "Are you going to spank me with that?"

He smooths his palm over my cheek. "Never, petal. That would hurt you. What I have in mind will still be a challenge, though. For you—and the other brat."

He does hit Damon, though, landing a hard swat to the shoulder. D chuckles, raising his brow at me. "Hear that, sweetness? They want to challenge *us*. Guess it's their funeral."

Cassian grumbles, "I bet I can last longer than you."

Damon tilts his head. "No chance."

"What do I get when I win?" my bear wonders.

"When *I* win," Damon returns. "You're going to buy every pizza I order for all eternity."

I cast Smith an eye roll. "They like to compete about these things."

He raises a brow, the arch look unbearably handsome. "How gallant."

Damon's crooked grin turns my fluttering insides to jelly. He slaps his alpha's shoulder. "That's what we have you for, Big Hoss. Keep us all in line."

Oh, Smith definitely likes that idea. And judging by the gleam in Damon's ice-blue eyes? I'd say he's well aware of the effect of his words.

Can't he see how smart he is? He has all of us figured out so completely, I'm not sure anyone really grasps how well he knows us. That alone takes a special kind of intelligence that most people simply do not possess.

At the top of the stairs, Smith points to the left. Cassian hauls me in that direction, busting into the alpha's bedroom and stomping over to the low armchair I found Smith lounging in that one memorable night.

For a moment, I'm confused about why we're in here. Smith clips over to his dresser and opens the top drawer, selecting two pairs of my stolen panties from among his accessories.

Two?

And why would I need more *underwear in this situation?*

When he tosses Damon's stick onto the bed and drops the lacy scraps on top of it, I finally understand.

They're about to tie me to the hockey stick.

With my own panties.

"LET ME."

Smith's idea may be savage, but his voice is soft. Cassian sets me on my feet and steps back, letting his brother slide his hands along my hips, feeling the silky fabric of my dress.

"That day," he rumbles, bending to brush his lips along my ear. "At Forever Matched? I thought you looked like a present." He skims his fingers along the ribbons at my shoulders, the rich scent of coffee becoming bolder and smoother. "All pretty and pink, tied up with bows."

Slick begins to slip out of me as he unravels both straps. The top portion of the dress, along with its built-in bra, falls. When my tiny breasts bounce into view, Damon groans low.

Cassian appears at my back, his hands dropping to fist the blush fabric roughly. "*I* wanted to rip this damn thing off," he mutters, sharply tugging it over my hips. "Strip you bare. Get rid of all the frills. Until you were just wearing my fingerprints. My scent. *Mine.*"

Damon crowds into my side, grinning while he reaches

between me and Smith to thumb my lower lip. "It was this smile for me. The second I saw it, I was all in, baby."

I tilt my head toward him, meeting his mouth with own. He growls, immediately weaving his long, strong fingers into my hair, twisting our tongues together. Smith starts shucking his clothes, giving both of his packmates orders as he goes.

"Cass, take Damon's sweats off."

"D, slide off the rest of her dress. Now."

No one argues with him or the surge of lustful dominance roiling in the room. For a second, the sensation, combined with how thick his scent is in this room, throws me back to the memory of him in rut. My nipples stiffen while a whine builds in my chest.

When Smith steps into my front, he's naked, his solid length smearing pre-cum over my belly. "Perfect, petal," he purrs, cupping my breasts. "Look how fucking pretty you are."

Damon finally breaks our kiss, panting while he steps out of the sweats Cassian left around his ankles. "So pretty," he rasps, bending to suck a love-bite into the thin skin under my ear. "Smith, whatever you want to do to us, you better do it fast. I need to be inside our omega."

Cassian nuzzles the other side of my neck, scent-marking me before leaving a matching hickey of his own. "I want her ass," he grunts to the others. Then, to me, "You gonna relax and let me fill you up, butterfly? Is that okay?"

I feel around for his hand, guiding it between my thighs. When he feels how soaked I am, he growls louder. "Fuck, that's my girl."

"Sit down, Cass," Smith commands. "Angel, Cass and his cock will be your seat. Damon, bring me your stick."

Instinctually, we all *want* to obey. Even grumbly Cassian, who mutters to himself while he sprawls on the wide chair. He slouches back, propping his elbows on the arms and tilting his hips forward. His thick length bobs, smacking against the tight lace of his abs as he spreads his stacked quads and lifts his brow at me, teasing.

"See something you like, Rems?"

By now, I know poking him is exactly how to get what I want. I toss my hair back and smile wider. "Nothing I haven't seen befor —*eep*!"

Cassian rips me right off my feet, flipping me around and planting me right on top of his abs. I grip his powerful forearms, pink fingernails curling into the solid strength holding me upright while I spread my thighs over his hips for balance.

Like this, his cock is right in front of me, lined up perfectly with my clit. I start to rub myself over him, but Damon returns with his hockey stick, and Smith stops me.

"No," he murmurs, smooth and dark. "It's my turn, not his. So be my good girl and let my brother work his way into your ass while I taste this pussy."

For once, Cassian doesn't complain. He stretches back into his propped-up position, watching with heated green eyes as I lift myself onto my knees and scoot down his lap. Smith goes to his knees between Cassian's, reaching up to spread my slick over my backside.

"Fuck, you smell so good," he roughs out, working his fingers into my ass. "So sweet. Do you know how many times I've thought about bringing you in here? Letting you fuck my face the way I did to you that night?"

He sounds wild, but the passion in his dark eyes feels tender. This is him, making amends, *again*. My hands fall to his head, twining in his thick, light hair.

"Smith, it's okay."

"It's never okay," he says into my lower stomach. "Never okay to scare you, angel. I'll spend the rest of my life apologizing for ever doing that."

The way he stares at the apex of my thighs is almost... reverent. He slips the two fingers deeper into my backside and then bends forward, dropping a light kiss right over my clit.

"Fuck, yes," Damon hisses, coming to stand at the side of the chair with his stick in one hand my panties and his cock in the other. He strokes the silk along his length and lets his head fall back, groaning.

I whimper and squirm, lodging Smith's fingers deeper inside me. Feeling me clench over his knuckles has my alpha moaning, pressing soft kisses and quick nips over my spread pussy lips. When he adds his tongue to the mix, I cry out, grinding down onto his face, trying to chase the slick sensation teasing the edges of my clit.

Under normal circumstances, he might try to edge me longer. He loves controlling my pleasure, drawing it out. Showing me how much my body can take before it collapses. This time, though, he makes a low sound of encouragement, letting me use him the way he once used me.

When I find the perfect angle, everything inside of me pulls tighter. My eyes fly open, running over the sight of Smith, kneeling between my legs. Then Damon, kneading his knot. Pleasure erupts like a volcano of molten gold, shooting hot, shining bliss through my body.

Smith twists his hand and adds a third finger to my ass. My pussy gushes, soaking his chin and his wrist. He snarls, and I sway, dizzy from the rush of coming so hard. Damon releases himself to catch me, keeping me upright while he and Smith leverage me over Cassian's cock.

I feel it pulsing between my legs, thick veins throbbing up his shaft. When the flared head grazes my puckered opening, I whimper and he purrs, the sound soothing. My core muscles unclench, relaxing as he tilts his hips to slide the first few inches in.

We both moan. I don't know how *I* feel to him, but he's scorching hot. And the gentle pulse of his arousal makes my pussy even wetter.

"Butterfly," he husks, nipping at my ear. "More. *Please.*"

Smith stands, taking Damon's stick and the panties. He nods toward me, dark eyes wild. "Get in her pussy, or I will."

Damon doesn't hesitate. He stretches over my body, pressing his palms into the chair's arms, caging me between their chests while he lines himself up. Cassian grunts, sliding in deeper as my body instinctually shifts to accommodate both his angle and the one Damon needs.

"More," he grits out again, moaning while he gets his wish and pushes deeper. "Ah, *God.*"

For a second, as they both shove all the way in and release a serrated series of groans, I forget all about Smith and his plans for that stick. It isn't until I'm pinned between Cass and Damon, skewered on both of their cocks and feeling so full I swear I'll tear in two… that I feel that cool, metal stick touch the back of my ankle.

Oh my—is he going to—

I can't think for long. Damon's hips snap forward at the same second Cassian's drop down. I whine, throwing my arms around Damon's neck to keep me balanced. By the time I get a hold on their rhythm, Smith has both of my ankles secured.

He lifts the stick, sliding the panties tying me onto it wider and wider. Until the spread of my legs presses the stick into Damon's back. My knees automatically bend toward my sides, forcing D to sink deeper. But when he tries to pull back, he can't.

Smith's voice cuts between us, wicked and dark. "I told you, brats get punished. Now, Damon is going to have to get off by feeling Cass pound into your tight little ass, petal. He'll feel your pussy milking his cock, but there won't be a damn thing he can do about it."

He's right. Every time Damon tries to thrust, the stick digs into the small of his back and my feet slip further apart, which just brings him in tighter.

"Fuck," he moans, dropping his forehead to my hair. "Remi, sweetness. You feel so good and I. Can't. Move."

It doesn't matter, though, because Cassian is strong enough

to do the heavy lifting for all three of us. His abs cinch as he holds himself up, reaching down to grip my hips and bounce me on their cocks, pounding both of them into me.

Damon and I both moan, my fingernails digging into his shoulders. He snarls when I scratch him, clamping his teeth over my shoulder. "Dirty, sweet girl. Mark me up," he hisses. "Can't fucking wait to have your bite on me."

Cassian likes that idea, too. A deep rumble echoes in his broad chest, his cock vibrating inside of me like a tuning fork. When my inner muscles clamp from the sensation, both alphas grunt. A warm palm lands on my head, petting my hair back. When I look at Smith, I find him gazing down at me, fisting his straining cock. When I whine, his lips ghost up, and he steps forward. "Open, omega."

Panting to obey, I show him my tongue. He gently grips my hair, positioning me so he can slide into my mouth, his hips wedged between Damon's shoulders and Cassian's chest.

The bitter richness of his pre-cum is deliriously delicious. My brain goes fuzzy and numb while I suck his throbbing length, whimpering for more of his taste.

"Good fucking girl," he growls, his harsh, urgent tone so at odds with the sweet way his hands cup my head. "God, I love you so much. We all do."

"So. Goddamn. Much," Cassian grinds out, thrusting harder and faster.

Damon nods, his damp cheek grazing mine while Smith leaves another burst of his pre-cum on my tongue. He lifts one of his hands off my head and roughly grips Damon's hair instead. My blue-eyed alpha groans, leaning into the pain.

"Rub your knot against her clit," Smith tells him. "She'll pull you in when she's ready for it. Which will probably be in about ten seconds, when I fill this pretty mouth."

My answering whine is sharp. I hollow my cheeks, sucking him harder while Damon follows Smith's orders and grinds his hot, throbbing knot into the aching nub just inches from his cock. I scream, the sound muffled around Smith.

His head falls back. He drops Damon's hair and starts gripping his own knot instead, listening to me moan around his length as he cups his balls and strokes the swollen pulse at the base of his shaft.

Cassian's thrusts get sloppier with every drive, until I feel him erupt in hot washes. "Fuck. *Fuck. FUCK.*"

Tingles race up my back. Damon shouts as my body reacts to Cassian's climax and clenches deep, tugging D's knot right where I want it most.

"Holy shit. Remi. Jesus. *Yes.*"

His knot inflates, filling me and massaging every inner muscle to perfection. My nerves stretch and sing, sparkling with pleasure that snaps the tension balled in my core. I moan around Smith's cock, and he pulls back, spurting all over my tongue, letting me taste him exactly the way I need to.

When I swallow, he sweetly wipes the tears from my face and makes sure every drop of his rich flavor makes it into my mouth.

"Good girl, taking all your alphas' cum. You did so well," he soothes, making quick work of our hockey-stick spreader bar. It drops to the carpet, and Damon groans, flexing his back and hips as much as he can with our bodies locked together.

It takes some crafty maneuvering from all three of them, but I wind up straddling Damon's lap, propped against Smith's headboard, with all of my alphas touching me. D works his fingers through my hair, while Smith smooths his palm over my back. Cassian has my hand pressed into his face, where he turns to nuzzle it every few minutes.

All three of their purrs meld into the best sound I've ever heard. It leaves me blissful and boneless.

Some time later, I bolt upright. The guys instantly snap to as I scramble off Damon's rapidly deflating knot and run for the doors.

"Sorry! I left a pie in the oven!"

chapter fifty-nine

REMI'S BAG OF DICKS

CASSIAN CHANGED THE NAME OF THIS CHAT TO REMI'S BAG OF DICKS

SMITH

Explain yourself.

DAMON

Is this really you Cass?

What's the secret password?

CASSIAN

Shut the fuck up

DAMON

We need a new secret password.

CASSIAN

Theo made me do it.

DAMON

And you didn't deck him?

Aww did my big bear make a **real friend**?!

CASSIAN

You have to stop calling me that.

SMITH

Damon, enough.

DAMON

Or else what, Bear?

CASSIAN

Or I'll tell Remi.

DAMON

....

Fine.

Fucker.

SMITH

Seriously? Remi is more threatening than me, now?

CASSIAN

100%

DAMON

Oh yeah, for sure.

REMEMBER when I said that putting all of my alphas in a room with all of Meg's alphas seemed like a good way for someone to lose an eye? With all the dick-waving?

Um, yeah.

About that.

"Do you think one of them is going to drown?" I fret.

"Eh." Meg chomps into a tortilla chip that's full of queso. "I think it's more likely one of them will end up with a black eye."

I might smile, remembering Damon's shiner the day we first met. But, at the moment, I'm worried my trouble-maker alpha is going to crush Cassian.

Archer watches the mayhem unfolding in their pool and shakes his head. He removes his glasses to clean them with the hem of his white linen shirt, muttering, "You'd think they would pick something a little more dignified to humiliate themselves with. This just feels... obvious."

"We can—" Declan's head gets dunked under the pool water, interrupting his shout. He reemerges ten seconds later, snarling, "—hear you!"

"Good," Archer chips back. "This is embarrassing."

Theo whoops, his tree-trunk thighs flexing around Declan's head while his shorty-short pink swim trunks bunch at the other alpha's ears. Meg snorts quietly into her margarita, wincing. "Dec probably should have been on top."

That was my alphas' strategy. Which is how Damon ended up on Cassian's very broad, very bare shoulders, duking it out with Theo. To say the big tight-end is "balanced" on his quarterback packmate's shoulders would be a generous way of putting it.

I lean closer to Meg. "There's a good joke here, somewhere. They're playing chicken, but it's an *actual* cock fight?"

She grins. "Close enough. Still, you can't complain about a view like this, right?"

She has a point. Even if my preheat hormones weren't running rampant, I couldn't complain about a swimming pool full of gorgeous, half-naked, pro-athlete alphas. Wrestling. And *wet*.

Fanning my face, I sip my drink until the straw sucks on air. A solid palm lands on my shoulder, kneading the skin under the thin strap of my white sundress before skimming down my arm.

"Here, angel," Smith rumbles, stepping into my back. He wraps his arm at my waist, passes me a new drink, and bends to purr in my ear, "Are you feeling all right?" He nuzzles my neck. "You smell *very* all right."

My heat perfume started this morning. The old Remi wouldn't have even noticed, having no reason to get excited.

But now? I gave myself away before I even got out of bed.

Though, I refuse to believe that was *my* fault. Smith must have known how sexy he looked in that navy suit before he wore it to bring me my coffee. And the way Damon rubs his daily Good Morning Wood into my backside just isn't even fair. Not to mention all of Cassian's broad-chested yumminess being the first thing I see when I open my eyes.

Now that Smith sleeps in my bed, too, we've had to start up a rotation. But even when it isn't his turn to hold me or wrap around me from behind, he's always there. And he always wakes up before the rest of us to bring me coffee.

He told me, on one of our date nights, that he sees it as a way to make up for how he acted when I worked at Proper Coffee. When I asked him how long he plans to go on doing it, he told me he figures we'll be even sometime around our eighties. I laughed and told him *his* eighties would be a long time before *mine*. Which earned me a spanking when we got home.

Ronan comes up behind Meg, and Archer subtly moves away. My best friend rolls her eyes at them, casting me a look. I hide a giggle in my drink.

She has a point.

These alphas are *ridiculous*. Even happily bonded, with another pack in their house, the Ash pack alphas feel the need to keep one man at Meg's side at all times.

And my alphas are *worse*. I'm sure that has something to do with my heat perfume, and the fact that they can't "feel" me yet. But Smith hasn't left my shadow since the others got in the pool.

I wore my swimsuit, intending to go in with them, but the cramping in my lower abdomen has me feeling less-than athletic. The guys have asked me a thousand times if I'm in pain. And even though I've mostly broken my fibbing habit, I haven't been totally honest with them about this.

The playoffs start in two days. And I *refuse* to be in heat for the first week of games the Timberwolves have to win to continue to the next leg. Because I *refuse* to put Damon in that position with everything that's going on.

You hear me? I tell my Omega. *I REFUSE.*

All I get back is a snort of derision, along with a mental image of all three of my alphas, naked, in my nest, and attending to my every whim.

So that's going well.

Bitch.

Damon shoves Theo hard and finally sends him careening off Declan's shoulders. He hits the water with a mighty *thwack*! The pool sloshes around, while Cassian ducks down to get D off him. Damon whoops victoriously, coming right over to me.

Holyyyyyyy....

He's *way* too gorgeous, all shining muscles and bright blue eyes. Even the way his dark hair swoops over his forehead in wet waves is sexy. And when he braces his palms on the deck and flexes every muscle in his upper body to haul himself out?

Smith's teeth nip at the soft part of my neck. He growls, sensing my perfume and reacting as discreetly as he can.

Damon is way less concerned with propriety. His gaze snaps to mine, zeroing in. "I won, pretty girl," he flirts, then twirls me into a dip and goes right for my mouth, kissing me breathless.

Cool pool water seeps into my cover-up, but I don't mind. Especially when Cassian appears behind me a moment later, sliding his arms around my waist and holding me up while Damon slides his tongue along mine.

"*We* won, jackass. Now give me a turn."

They're both pumped up—probably some combination of the competition, my heat symptoms, and the fact that we're surrounded by other alphas. Through their wet trunks, I feel Cassian's erection rub into the small of my back as Damon's connects with my belly.

Smith looses an even warning bark. "*Easy.*"

Meg lets out a peal of delighted laughter, while Ronan chuckles. He thumps my pack's alpha on his shoulder and smiles fondly at Theo, who's shaking his beard and long hair out like a golden retriever. "I remember those days."

Smith smirks. "So you're saying it gets easier to manage the impulses?"

Ronan and Archer answer in unison. "*No.*"

As if to prove their point, Declan flops onto Meg's pool lounger, planting his face right over her thighs. "I lost," he pouts into her bikini bottoms. "I need something to revive me."

My best friend bends her leg, kneeing him in the stomach. He rolls off her with a groan, and Theo high-fives her, winking. "Saving it all for me, right, peaches?"

Good Lord. There are so *many* of them. All half-dressed and strong-smelling and *everywhere*.

Meg shoots me a wide-eyed look that I return. She waves her hands around her blonde messy bun, snapping, "That's it! Alpha pheromone overload! We need some girl time!"

Damon's face drops into an expression of outrage that makes me laugh. Hearing me titter, Cassian rolls his eyes, fighting off his own smile. Smith puts a hand on each of their shoulders. "You should both go and clean up before dinner, anyway."

Ronan nods. "Archer's about to put the burgers on. Declan? Can you show the guys where they can shower and change? I want to speak with Smith."

My brows curve in surprise, but Smith flashes his reassuring grin. "Pack alpha stuff," he mumbles, briefly kissing my lips. "We'll just be over by the grill. You relax, petal. That's an order."

I can't help the grin on my face any more than I can control the butterflies in my belly. "Yes, Sir."

With the size of Meg's pool deck, "over by the grill" is about twenty yards away. She waits until all the guys are out of earshot before she erupts into giggles.

"Holy shit," she gasps, swiping under her eyes. "I can't wait until you're bonded. Right now, Damon is talking shit to Declan, and Theo is trying to make Cassian be his friend. Once you're all bonded, we'll have both sides of the conversation. Like spies behind enemy lines."

I try to picture the two of us sitting together, relaying our alphas' every thought while they talk among themselves. It does sound entertaining... and overwhelming.

When she sees the look on my face, Meg's softens. "It's not as... *much* as you're probably imagining," she tells me. "In order for you to hear what they're thinking, they have to specifically 'knock on your door,' so to speak. And you can always put up your Do Not Disturb sign if you need a break. They'll all understand that. Especially once you've all been in each other's heads for a couple of weeks."

She glances over at the grill area with an unbothered shrug. "Ronan has his up right now."

I wonder what "pack alpha stuff" he's discussing with Smith. Looking like salt and pepper—Ronan's dark hair and Smith's light—they both lean over one of their phones, brows furrowed. Behind them, Archer nods along with whatever Smith just said, listening while he places enough burgers on their double-wide grill to feed an entire hockey team.

"Is it nice?" I ask, dropping my voice into a whisper. "Being bonded?"

Meg grins. "It's...incredible. You never have to miss them because they're always right here." She taps the center of her chest. "And the way they love me... and each other... it's just an amazing thing to be at the center of. You'll see."

More nervous jitters squirm in my middle. "I think I'm scared. Which is crazy. This is all I've ever wanted. Being chosen, being in a pack... but it's so *permanent*. What if they change their minds?"

Meg's mouth pulls down in a soft frown. "Remi, babe, that would never happen. They all love you." She half-smiles, nodding subtly. "Look for yourself."

Smith is staring at me, his expression intense. When he sees that I've caught him, he quirks an eyebrow, scolding. I can't actually hear his thoughts, but I might as well be able to.

You're supposed to be relaxing.

I toss him a flirty flip of my hair. *Yes, Sir.*

Back to grinning, Meg waves a dismissive hand. "You guys are going to be great." She bends to the side and grabs a small box. "Here, I got you something."

"Meg!" I cry. "You know you don't need to do this sort of thing anymore."

"I know, I know. But I couldn't help myself."

I pluck the ribbon off and remove the lid. A laugh and a sob tangle in my throat when I see the Timberwolf-blue heart-shaped sunglasses inside.

My best friend smiles, so genuinely happy for me that I can *feel* it. She waves at the matching orange pair nestled into her hair. "Now we both have eye protection," she says, grinning. "For all this dick measuring."

chapter **sixty**

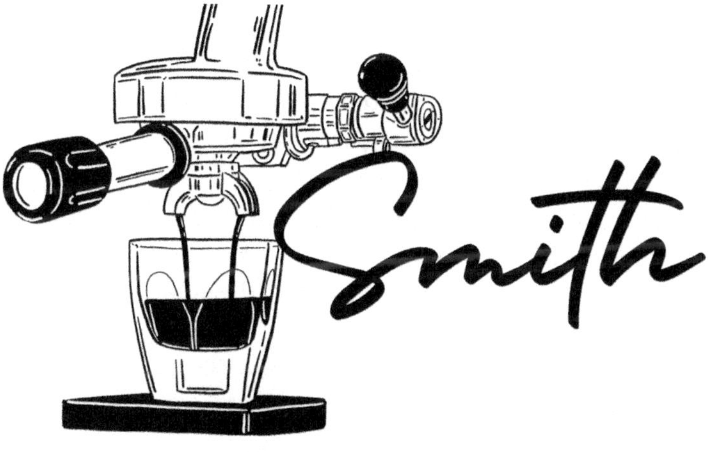

THE PANTIES TUCKED into my suit jacket are red.

They barely have enough material to make a single fold, but this is the pair I took off my omega this morning after coffee, and I've gotten oddly sentimental about wearing whatever she provides. Even if they still smell faintly of her pre-heat perfume.

My Alpha isn't sure whether we love having it on us or hate that any other person in the entire universe might notice. Impulses tick under my skin, flying too fast for me to nail any of them down.

My instincts have been worse ever since Remi's symptoms

ramped up. The sharper and sweeter her perfume gets, the more we are on edge. There have even been a few pissing matches among ourselves; all of us jockeying for position the second she expresses even the slightest interest in sex. Last night, I swore Cass was going to rip Damon's throat out for trying to steal the Big Spoon position in bed after he had already gotten to take a shower with her.

Hopefully, none of this shit will be an issue for her next heat. Archer gave me a comprehensive run-down of exactly what to expect, including all of our Alphas getting more and more territorial. As soon as we bond, those impulses will settle. *Allegedly*.

It's hard for me to picture that when I'm borderline-feral. I haven't gotten any work done all day, too busy imagining what it will finally feel like to sink my teeth into her neck.

I'm nervous. Archer recommended waiting until the end of her heat to bond with her so she'll be lucid. I'm fairly certain I can handle holding off... until I scent her slicing sweetness, swirling around the house. Or from my jacket pocket.

Fuck. This is not going to be easy.

Irene and Julian insist that the only thing I need to be a good alpha during my omega's heat is to pay attention to my instincts. I've been practicing; zeroing in on all the minute nudges I've spent years silencing.

Maybe that's why I notice the way the back of my neck prickles while I loop a tie around my neck. I pause with it halfway tied, listening to Remi's quiet singing voice.

Is that an ABBA song?

My feet carry me down the hall faster than they normally would. I knock on Remi's cracked bedroom door, pushing it open to find her standing at the foot of her bed. There's a pile of sheets on the floor beside her. And she only has half of her clothes on.

Goddamn, she looks good. White heeled sandals and a tight teal mini-skirt make her legs long and lean. The white lacy bra molded to her breasts contrasts with her pretty skin. Her hair is half-curled, the top portion still clipped up on top of her head like she rushed out of the bathroom mid-style to...

...strip our bed?

Oh fuck. The scents. On the sheets.

She's *nesting.*

Stepping into the room, I pitch my voice low, going for soft and affectionate. "Hi, angel. Time to get these sheets into the nest?"

Remi turns, her eyes unfocused. "I—um—I—no. No. I can wait. We have the playoff game tonight. We have to—um—go? We have to go!"

I approach her slowly, reaching over to smooth my hands down her arms. My purr wants to kick up, so I let it. "We don't have to go," I soothe, flexing a solid bit of dominance, layered with lust to soften its blow. "Let's get in your nest. I want you."

Poor baby. She's shaking and burning up. I'd be shocked if she wasn't in pain already. I bet she's been suppressing it all week, trying to force her Omega into submission so she doesn't fuck things up for the guys.

She doesn't know that we've all discussed it over and over, only to come to the same conclusion every time: she comes first. And this heat means everything to us.

Between tips from the Ash pack alphas and my classes, I feel completely prepared. As I step up and pull Remi into my chest, I slide my phone out of my pocket and shoot off the round of texts I've had prepped for weeks, along with a two-hour grocery order I've refreshed daily.

Satisfied that everything we need will be here soon, I pull my loose tie off and nuzzle my face into Remi's hair. My hands already seem to have minds of their own—one skims up her back, and the other dips below the hem of her skirt, cupping her ass to draw her body into mine.

Hot skin sears me through my dress shirt, her rounded cheek burning against my sternum. She tries to scent-mark me through the material. It must chafe because she whines, the sound distressed.

"It's time, omega," I murmur. "Let me take care of everything."

"But I'm not ready!" she cries, tears squeezing out of her eyes. "I haven't cleaned the downstairs or ordered our meals or gathered up everyone's stuff. And the game! I can't take the guys out this week—"

I kiss her forehead, enveloping her in my arms. "I've already taken care of all of that. I did the vacuuming and emptied the dishwasher while you were in the shower. The food is on its way. As soon as the guys see their phones, they'll be on their way, too."

My purr gets louder. "Aren't these bright lights hurting your eyes, petal? Come on. Let's go where it's nice and dark."

The rattle in my chest unwinds some of the tension in Remi's shoulders. She sways on her feet, leaning more heavily on me. When I catch a look at her face, I see that her pupils have eclipsed their blue-gold irises.

It's coming on fast, then. No time to waste.

The next words out of her mouth barely sound lucid. "They'll be mad," she mumbles, hiding against my lapel. "They won't want me anymore. They'll send me away."

Control.

I yank on my internal leash, smothering the snarl that wants to rip from my throat. My rage is entirely directed at myself—she doesn't need to deal with it right now.

I hate myself for ever letting her think that any of us could ever send her away or stop wanting her. But none of this is about me. She needs reassurance, and I need to give it to her.

"No one will ever send you away again," I vow, picking her up. "I'm never leaving you. And soon you'll be able to feel how much I mean that."

The way she surrenders to my care gives me indescribable satisfaction. Before, she might have tried to fight the urge to let me take over, but she trusts me completely now. I feel it in the way her body goes lax in my arms while I carry her to her nest.

God, it really is beautiful in here. All the colors of sunrise glow with the soft twilight seeping through the skylight strips. Knowing it will soon be dark, I set to work, stripping her out of her skirt and heels, shucking my own clothes in the process.

She whines when I have to leave her briefly to gather supplies. The helpless whimpers slash at my heels until I'm running through the house, stacking shit into the laundry basket we've used to collect gently worn clothes for the last two weeks.

Our sheets are the last thing I scoop up, charging back into the nest with piles of fabric, bottles of water, protein shakes, and her toiletry bag. I drop it all by the door and go straight back to where she's curled into a ball at the center of the floor mattress.

"Come here, baby." I pull her into my lap and scent-mark her face. "Does it hurt? Do you want my knot?"

She cuddles into my chest. "I want—my alphas. All of you."

I smile into her hair. Irene warned me about this, in so many words. Specifically, she said, *"Don't be a jealous knot-brained alpha-hole when your omega wants your packmates as much as she wants you. And don't even* mention *it when she starts to lose lucidity and can't remember meaningless specifics like names. She needs your knot, not your name, got it?"*

Got it.

"The others are coming as fast as they can," I reassure her. "I'm going to get you settled and help you build this beautiful nest for us."

She nods, rubbing her lips over my Adam's apple. My cock jerks under her ass. I blow a steady stream of air out of my nose and maneuver Remi to the edge of the recessed mattress, propping her against the cushioned, circular wall.

Snatching her hairbrush, makeup wipes, and a protein shake with a straw, I bend to meet her eyes and send a small pulse of alpha power. "You're going to drink this. The whole thing, omega. *Now.*"

She's already starting to get an attitude about food, which is why it's essential that I get as much energy into her as I can. Her nose wrinkles, but she takes the bottle from me. As she sucks on the straw, I set to work brushing her hair out and removing all of her makeup.

When she's beautifully bare-faced and her curls are woven into a loose coil, I take the empty protein shake from her and replace it with a bottle of water. She sips it tentatively, watching while I haul all of her nesting supplies over for her.

Do we have enough? There are three sheets, the comforter, Cassian's hoodie and four pairs of his sweats, six of Damon's T-shirts. Two weeks' worth of my boxers...

"Alpha?"

I turn to find her staring at me with wide, vulnerable eyes. Our Remi's still in there, for now, but she isn't 100 percent in control. Whatever she wants to say must be something she and her Omega agree on. "Yes, angel?"

Her lower lip quivers while she smiles at me. "You're the best alpha ever."

Just five words.

But they're everything I ever wanted.

And Remi? She's everything I'll ever need.

chapter sixty-one

DAMON

THERE'S a moment at the beginning of every game.

The lights go out. The music swells. And some disembodied voice says my name.

I've lived for that moment for as long as I can remember. But this time? It barely registers.

This should be a big deal. We're in the playoffs for the first time in my career. And I'm playing for my life, so to speak.

None of that touches me. I'm too busy watching the tunnel I just skated out of, waiting for Cassian. We agreed, since he's the last one on the ice, that he would do one final check of our phones before coming out. They've announced his name, but he hasn't appeared.

When he finally shows up, he isn't in his pads or even his skates. He thumps our second-string goalie on the back, practically shoving the kid out onto the ice. With his free hand, he waves me in.

Which can only mean one thing. *Remi.*

I had a feeling this might happen. She practically climbed me in the shower last night. Then she cried when we had to leave for practice this morning. It was torture to leave her. Smith told me the only way he calmed her down was by getting both of them undressed and taking her back to bed for an hour.

Turning to our coach, who's huddled with Gunnar over a clipboard. They both glance up, freezing when they see the look on my face.

I smile at them and take off my helmet. "Well, I guess I'm about to make this way easier for all of us."

Coach scowls, opening his mouth. But I cut him off. "Heat leave. Oh shit, did I not mention that our omega was near her heat? Yeah. Sorry about that. Cassian's going to have to come with me, too. But best of luck to you guys. Really."

I hand my stick to Gunnar, patting his shoulder while I push past them, back toward the tunnel. He may be the guy who's replacing me, but he's still a good teammate and a hell of a player. I don't want any of this drama to put him off his game.

"It's all you, kid," I say, meaning every word. "You've got this."

Coach Rolly sputters, his face turning red. I clap his shoulder, too. "No hard feelings."

The lights haven't even come back up yet, but I'm already skating off the ice, leaving the game behind me.

It's funny; I thought this would be hard. I thought it would gut me to walk away from everything I was before. But now I see.

I'm not leaving my future behind. I'm running straight into it.

chapter
sixty-two

THE STABBING PAIN between my hips tweaks tighter with every passing second.

Everything itches. Tingles. *Burns.*

But the alpha is here, kneeling with me on the floor of the nest. I've arranged it all and dismantled everything more than once. He never questions me. And every time I pause to whine or whimper, he wraps me into his body until his purr unspools the cramps in my core.

It's been a slow process, but his patience never wavers. He helps me roll and stack all of the fabrics until the scents are right. A layer of dark chocolate swirled into even darker bitterness. Cinnamon spice with toasted hazelnuts. Brown sugar to sweeten the earthy coffee.

I mix them in every imaginable way. They all have to *make sense*.

Pretty soon, nothing else will.

This last burst of lucidity before the haze pulls me under is one of the worst parts of my heat. I hate how *aware* I feel, every nerve vibrating in pleasure or searing me with pain.

Even the *air* is irritating. It scrapes my throat, swarms in my lungs, stings my tongue. Every single breath is a reminder that they're not here.

This isn't right.

It's too full of my own torched honey pheromones and sorely lacking the autumn spice and hazelnut chocolate I crave. I try to focus on the bitter, rich coffee, but the more I try not to think about the others, the faster fear inflates my chest. Pumping me full of the unbalanced scents and my pack alpha's tension.

Is he angry?

Will he leave me?

"Petal." The pack alpha's voice sinks through my panic, soothing all of the synapses over-firing in my mind with one simple command. "*Present*."

The bark is quiet, but it connects with the deep, tingling *need* lodged in my middle. My core cinches and gels, slick gushing down my inner thighs.

There are no thoughts in my head as I move, automatically dropping into position. I don't really remember *which* position, but rightness zings through my blood as my cheek lands on the pale silk cushion under me.

My Alpha presses his thighs to mine, his warm skin sending ripples of ecstasy through my entire body. A smooth purr sinks into my back as he bends forward. His tongue traces over my spine, licking patterns between nips of his teeth.

This isn't enough. I need more. His cum, his *mark*. I whine, wiggling against him. Begging for the hot steel pressed into my backside. Begging for his bite.

"Where should I bite you, angel?" he husks, nosing at my nape. "Here? Where everyone will see it when you wear your hair up in those cock-tease buns you love?" His mouth slides down to my shoulder. "Or here? Where those thin straps hold your dresses up?"

I whine bucking back into him. "Alpha, *please.*"

"Mmm," he murmurs. "I think here." His tongue swipes the side of my throat. "Where every single person who looks at you will know *you're mine.*"

He toys with the thin skin, pulling it between his teeth until I'm sure he's going to give me what I want. While he sucks at the pulse pounding in my neck, I whimper, grinding harder.

Large hands trail up my sides, gentling me. "Fucking beautiful," he mutters. "Look at how good you are. How perfect. *My* omega."

"Alpha," I whine again, spreading my legs wider. "I need—need—*Ah!*"

We both cry out as his cock stabs right into the pulsing place inside of me. It should hurt—instead, it's *bliss.* Relief slackens my limbs, every muscle relaxing the second he strokes a secret place inside of me.

An orgasm swallows me up instantly. Slick flesh contracts around his perfect length, pulsing. Frothy waves of pleasure bubble through my veins, the release rolling all the way to my fingertips. I moan, my eyes fluttering shut.

"No more waiting," he orders, gritted. "You need this alpha cock, I'll give it to you."

I barely know why, but I know that he's right. And some deeply ingrained reflex provides the words he likes to hear: "Yes, Sir."

"Perfect. Beautiful. Girl," he snaps out. When he speaks again, his voice is the layered rumble of cool over rough. "Already so slick for me, with honey running down to your knees. You going to come on this knot?"

The edge of his swelling knot presses past the ring of muscle clenching at his cock, popping into place the same moment his taunt sinks in. The effect is instant once again, my core spasming around his girth, throbbing for the hot flesh expanding to stretch me around him.

The alpha fists my hair to turn my head, his teeth striking for my throat while he comes in scalding spurts. Cum douses the fire climbing my insides, extinguishing the pain with washes of warm, tingling pleasure.

Unyielding, his teeth scrape at my heartbeat. With every pulse, my thoughts slip further. A whisper. A distant echo. A fuzzy memory.

A cloudy haze covers my eyes like a veil. Some far-off recollection sends a final fissure of fear through my middle.

This is the part where—when—what—

"Shhh." The deep rumble matches the purr vibrating into my back. Fingers tighten in my hair, the force soothing me into submission while hard, hot ecstasy flexes in my clenching core. "That's a good girl, coming on my cock and my knot. So goddamn good."

I can't understand what he's saying, but it trips some sort of wire inside of me. My stomach flips—the final sensation I feel before a fresh round of slick, slicing need rips through my pussy. My brain blinks offline, leaving me floating. The hot steel impaling me is my only tether to where or what I am.

Omega.

And I need—

"Shhh." It's my alpha. His fingers grip my throat. "You need more knots. And your other alphas are here, omega. Can they come in?"

chapter
sixty-three

CASSIAN

"HOLY FUCK."

Damon's muttered hiss pretty much sums up the desperate urgency lunging inside my chest.

Get to the omega. Fuck her. Knot her. Purr for her. Bite her until she's ours.

The need to be with her is a deep, all-consuming thing, but it isn't frantic or fearful the way my rut felt. This is more... pure. Unadulterated *instinct*.

She *needs*. I feel it in the air. In the crackle at my core. She needs *me*.

Damon feels it, too. We both have all of our clothes off before we even hit the stairs, racing up to the Omega Suite as fast as we can.

I was worried about how territorial we've all been lately. When I'm able to let Damon dart ahead and skid into Remi's room without tackling him to the ground, I breathe a small sigh of relief.

It gets both harder and easier to keep breathing as I approach the nest. This entire room is soaked in the honeyed scent of her sex; the heat perfume sharp in the sweetest fucking way. Carving out my sanity, numbing all doubt. Until I can only feel the way she wants us.

I can tell Smith had to start without us, but it's okay. There's no frenzy here. The energy is too raw. Sacred.

Damon feels it, too, drawing to a halt just outside the half-open door to the nest.

Smith murmurs to Remi. She keens, the gorgeous wail sinking right into my gut. *Fuck.* I'm already so hard, my knot aches, pre-cum seeping from my cockhead. Even before we hear her sweet little cry. "*Alpha—come!*"

D and I look at each other. Then we both lurch into the nest, falling over each other to get in.

Damon knows what to do right away, of course. He drops to his knees, crawling down into the recessed mattress. "Hi, pretty girl," he hums, cupping her exposed cheek while she nuzzles the sheets with the other. "Mmm. You look so gorgeous with our alpha's knot in your pussy. You need more?"

She shifts, pulling off Smith. His knot is already back down to half its full size. It's a clever trick of biology—when an omega is in heat, their alpha's body responds to give them more of what they need, which means knots that release fast and recover even faster.

I read everything I could to prepare myself for this. But nothing could have readied me for the way I feel as I pull the door shut behind me, gazing down at Remi in our sunrise nest. Her wide eyes and blown pupils don't fill me with fear like I worried they might—instead, I'm overwhelmed by a rush of tenderness.

My poor sweet girl. She's in pain. And she looks so lost.

I won't stand for it. Can't.

Part of me has been dreading her heat, afraid of the way I might feel when she doesn't recognize me. Our feelings for each other are so entwined with our attraction to one another—I worried about how I might react when our connection faded to her haze.

I should have known better.

Even if the perfume in this nest didn't make me half-crazed with the need to rut her, I would still be hers. Especially when she looks over Damon's naked shoulder and runs her dark eyes over me.

"Bear Alpha."

The books said it's extremely rare for omegas to recognize their alphas by name once they fall into their heat haze. And this isn't technically my name, but...

It's better.

The words hit my heart like flaming darts, lighting me up. While the others chuckle quietly, I sink to the floor and go to her, lifting her right out of Damon's arms and into mine. "That's right, butterfly. It's Bear. Come here."

I scent-mark her face before I lower myself to the mattress and pull her on top of me. She scrabbles against my bare chest, her blunt nails leaving stripes behind. A small squeak eeks out, telling me she's having another cramp.

My Alpha and I immediately snap to action, lifting her by the hips to tunnel my cock right into her needy pussy.

Fuck.

She's scorching hot—and slicker than ever. Sensation zings up my spine, tightening my abs while she bears down, riding me in sloppy rolls of her hips. Her head falls forward and lolls, her sightless eyes searching.

And I just... know what to do.

"Here," I rasp, dropping one hand to her hips to guide her pace while the other cups her cheek and brings her face to mine. "I'm right here, baby."

With a strangled moan, she burrows into my neck, licking and nipping my throat while she tries to fuck me harder. I grunt, snapping my hips up to meet hers.

Damon appears behind her and sends me a half-smirk. "Here, allow me."

I spread my thighs for him to kneel at her back. He grasps her hips and works her over me, the motion instantly going from sloppy to seamless. With his help, she slides right up and down without a hitch. I groan, my balls tightening as she squeezes me in smooth glides.

He bites her shoulder gently, murmuring encouragement in that sweet voice he saves just for her. "Hi, sweetness. Mmm, I'm so glad I'm here with you. Does your alpha's cock feel good?"

"More," she cries. "More, please, Alpha!"

Smith crawls over, sitting on his knees at my side. He grasps Remi's chin in his hand and squeezes just hard enough to get her attention. When their eyes meet, he speaks to D. "Get her ass slicked up."

Remi gushes over my cock. Damon doesn't even pause, immediately gripping the knot swelling at the base of my shaft, kneading it while he collects her honey-drenched slick on his fingers.

He purrs, and she turns, searching for his lips, moaning when their tongues meet in an open-mouthed kiss. He skates back between her ass cheeks and works his thumb in until I feel it in her pussy. When he feels me pounding inside, he growls.

"Fuck, you feel good, Cass. I want in."

Remi bucks between us, begging. I smirk at my packmate. "You heard her. Get in there."

He's clearly on edge, pupils eclipsing the blue in his eyes as he nestles himself against her ass. A ragged groan tears out of his throat. He pushes into her back hole, instantly making her grip on my cock twice as tight.

My vision goes white, my head falling back on a pant. "God-damn it. D. Fuck."

Smith lays a staying hand on my shoulder and cups Remi's head with the other. "You good, omega?"

She whines, the sound needy. Smith takes her lips, kissing her hard. "My good fucking girl, taking two alpha cocks. You going to come all over them?"

Remi strangles my dick, more slick dousing my groin. *Fuck.*

Damon curses, too, his head falling to her shoulder while he pounds her harder. The friction of him rutting her ass makes me feel feral. I screw my cock into Remi faster, my knot swelling.

Damon's is, too. It bumps against mine as we both batter into her. Smith drops his hand to our omega's clit, stroking for barely two seconds before she starts coming all over both of us. I shove in deep, letting my knot lock into place seconds before she detonates around it. Slick pours onto me, her scent and screams tipping me over the edge.

Every muscle in my core clenches while I fill her. Damon sinks his teeth into her shoulder, groaning around his gentle bite and erupting his own release.

He collapses while I thump back onto the mattress. Smith catches Remi, holding her up while he licks into her mouth. She kisses him back until my knot releases, then flashes her hazy eyes at him.

"More, Alpha."

chapter sixty-four

DAMON

I'M LYING on the floor of the nest like I've just been shot. Cassian might *actually* be dead, for all he's moving.

I could feel how hard he fucked her. And I know I emptied both barrels on that round.

Did our omega really just say *more*??

What did Cass say he read in her file?

She needs "three active alphas, minimum" for her heat.

Thank God we're athletes.

"I know what she needs," Smith intones, speaking into her

breasts while she grinds her pussy against Cassian's pelvis. "Damon, think you can fit in her pussy with me?"

Fucking... ex-*cuse* me?

Well. I thought I was dead, but I guess not. My cock twitches, rising right back up.

Shit, alpha. Say less.

Smith reads my mind, meeting my eyes over her curly hair. He arches a brow. "Think you can handle that?"

Oh, he's going *down*.

"Get her ready for us, Cass," he murmurs. "We're both going to have to be hard as fuck for this to work."

I can tell he's already there, but I need about thirty seconds before I'm back at full capacity. While I manhandle my knot, my teammate rolls Remi over and huddles on top of her, framing her round, reddened cheeks with his huge hands.

"Hi, baby," he mumbles, scent-marking her as she whines softly, bucking up into him. "I'm here. It's okay."

His purr echoes through the nest. "I'll stay with you while your other alphas fill you up, too. I'll always stay with you."

Shit, they're cute together. I may be a sex expert, but Cassian is a *Remi* expert. He's the one who taught me how to connect with her, showed me all of her favorite things.

I'd be lying if I said I wasn't jealous of his foresight. Because he waited, he's hers in a way no one else ever can be.

He's only known her body. Only ever wanted *her*.

"She likes this," he grunts to us, rocking his hips in a C-shape until she keens.

He leans down to nuzzle at her cheek, speaking only to her. "You like that, butterfly? My girl is so good for me."

It's fucking sweet, the way he speaks to her. For her. She may not be able to answer us, but his girl is still in there—and he's making sure she knows that he's not leaving her.

If the way he grits his teeth is any indication, she's coming again. He lets her use him, holding himself deep until she whines for *more*.

Fucking perfect, dirty omega.

Mine.

He rolls off her, and she huffs in outrage, a bratty expression pinching her features. "More," she says again, this time pissy. "Need more, Alpha."

Judging by the dangerous glint in Cass's eye, I'd say she's poking her bear. When she doesn't stop pouting, he wraps her hair around his fist and uses his other arm to lift her onto her hands and knees, putting her mouth level with his glistening dick.

"More, Rems?" he taunts lightly, pressing the head to her lips. "See what we taste like together—your cum and mine. Suck it off my cock."

With a starved moan, she pounces, pulling his entire length into her mouth. He groans, head falling back, gritting, "You two better get in her pussy—*fuck*—before she sucks out my soul."

Smith helps me lift her so I can slide underneath. She instantly presses her palms to my chest, whimpering and moaning while she deep-throats Cass's cock less than a foot above my face.

Hot damn.

This is fucking *incredible.*

Smith spreads our omega's thighs, his knuckles knocking at mine. "Do you mind?"

I shake my head, panting as I brace for what's next. Smith grips my straining dick and positions it, checking the angle before he lines his up beside me.

"Look at this perfect omega," he husks, planting his hands on her hips. "About to take two of her alphas in her pussy. Think you can take it, angel? You want two cocks inside you?"

A shrill shriek vibrates around Cassian's cock, and his knot visibly pulses. "Ah, *God.*" He gnashes his teeth. "Fuck her hard."

Smith and I both thrust at the same time, stretching Remi's pussy wider than any of us ever have before. For a second, I'm not sure I'll last. They feel too fucking *good.*

The hot, hard pulse of Smith's erection beating against the underside of my dick, her wet heat sucking at our heads. When she screams and starts bucking, her smooth, slippery inner walls stroke us both. We're sucked in deeper, both groaning and growling.

At first, we barely have to move. Shallow pulses have all of us clinging to the edge of our control until Smith snarls and shoves deeper. The bottom of his crown rubs into mine, pressing me into the spot where one of our knots will fill her later. She keens, the sound a gorgeous gurgle around the veins rushing up Cassian's cock, tightening his balls.

With his new angle, Smith's knot grinds into mine. And —*fuck me*—it feels so good. The more they touch, the harder they get, until our knots are kneading one another without anyone's hands for help.

He pants, glancing down at the place where we're all connected, then over at me. His eyes are wild, but there's a question lurking in them. If I weren't half a breath away from coming and ending the ecstasy, I might smirk at it. Instead, I flash my teeth on a growl, "Harder."

I keep my thrusts shallow while he roars, plunging in faster and deeper. The motion makes Remi's luscious tits bounce over my face. I stretch my neck and nip at her to distract myself from the delicious friction stealing my sanity, licking the bites off her nipples with soothing swirls of my tongue.

She whimpers and whines. Cass tenses, his knot inflating while his balls draw up. Her hands scrabble at his thighs, and I realize what she wants—but she can't reach without losing her balance. Without thought, I reach up and back, rolling his balls in my hand.

"*Fuck*," he bellows. "Shit. D. Remi. Gotta fill this pretty mouth with my cum."

Smith snarls again, the sound desperate. I reach around Remi's thigh and his to roll his sack, too, tugging on it until his eyes roll back. He remembers himself two seconds later, growling, "Knot her deep, D. I'm going to take her ass while Cass lets her taste him."

The feeling of him pulling out of her pussy, sliding hot and slick against me, is enough to juice my knot. I work the extra girth in, grateful that Smith helped stretch her first when I have to ease the top half of my knot in before popping the bottom into place. The second I do, I feel Smith tunnel into her tight little ass.

Our omega shakes and screams, her body clenching us both so tightly that we may never get out.

Fine with me.

Fuck it.

I'm staying *right here.*

Her slick pussy tugs at my cock and bears down around my knot, squeezing in the most delicious way. She's scorching hot, slippery *bliss*. The sense of rightness that races through my blood, from my throbbing knot to my aching heart, just makes everything so much *more.*

Which is just what she asked for.

chapter sixty-five

WE HAVE the most beautiful little brat who's ever existed.

She's passed out again, snuggled in between Cass at her back and D at her front. They both knotted her that way before purring her—and themselves—to sleep.

It's been four days since her heat started, and each one has been transformative. Other alphas tried to explain this part to me, but I didn't have a prayer of understanding until I experienced it for myself.

We've *grown together*.

From three separate alphas into one unit. A real team. So

much so, I'm starting to wonder if waiting to bond until the end of an omega's heat is really for their benefit, or really for ours.

After years of feeling like everything fell to me, having them here to help keep Remi comfortable has been a revelation. The way they've stepped up would make any pack leader proud.

Damon and Cassian have never let our girl down. Or me.

We haven't always been a picture-perfect pack or the world's best alphas.... But what did Remi say about making perfect the enemy of the good?

I look around at the guys who grew from angry, lost teenagers into men who love our omega so well, and I think...

I did good.

They are good.

And *I* did that.

Built us a life, took them in, made this pack. Somehow kept us together even though we were falling apart.

The whole time, it felt like I was failing. Not being the pack alpha they needed to reach their full potential. But maybe *potential* was never the fucking point.

Maybe *this* is.

They don't need someone to micromanage their lives into oblivion. They just need me and Remi. And a place where they know other people see them. And *love* them.

Remi did that part, just by being herself.

The heat has been life-changing for a lot of reasons, but I think the best one may just be how much I *miss* her. It's odd—I've been inside her body for a third of every day, soaked in her scent, surrounded by her moans, and sleeping with her silken curls strewn around me.

But I miss *her*.

Science never could have done that. No equation in the world would make her the woman who warms my heart like no other. It has nothing to do with her omega or my alpha, it's just.. her.

So when she stirs, cracking open eyes that actually seem somewhat alert, my heart flips. Joy rises right to my face, and I let it show, flashing a smile at her while I arch an eyebrow. "Is that my very naughty omega? Or my sweet little petal?"

She doesn't answer with words, but the beaming grin on her face is enough to tell me that I'm right—she's back from her haze. At least a little bit.

I'm relieved. She's been increasingly bratty about eating and washing. Last night, Cass and Damon had to hold her down in the tub while I spanked her ass and her pussy. Luckily, she didn't notice they were rinsing bubbles out of her hair while I did it.

The food issue has Damon stressed. He's tried to feed her every time she's woken up for the last two days, but she isn't ever up for more than a few bites before she goes back to begging for a knot.

In four days, I doubt she's gone more than a few hours without intense *need*. I'm grateful she'll never have to go through a single heat alone ever again. Enduring them on her own must have been excruciating.

Just picturing it puts me on edge. She feels my scent darken, and her eyes go wide. I make my way over to her, reaching between Damon and Cass to cup her cheek. She feels cooler, but still warm. Which means it's time.

This is the moment I've been waiting for. Aching for.

She's going to be mine. *Ours.*

chapter sixty-six

THE FIRST THING I see when I open my eyes is the alpha who makes my belly flip.

He's lying close but still far enough to necessitate peering through the murky pre-morning gray that's filtering into my nest, somehow. The details are still hazy, just like the edges of my vision. But his face is set in sharp, clear lines, relief and desire bright in his dark eyes.

Pack alpha, my Omega supplies, sounding sleepy and sated for the first time in as long as I can remember. *Bite. Claim. Mine.*

I swear, she just about yawns on that last word, as if she can't be bothered to keep her eyes open anymore. As far as she's concerned, there's no urgency. Nothing to worry about. These alphas are hers, and they're going to bite her as soon as we let them.

The pack alpha does nothing to dispel her smug assumption. Instead, he crawls over and cups my face in his hands. That one simple touch is enough to pull a whine out of me.

The cramp that pangs through my core isn't as wrenching as I expect, but it's enough. My body clamps around the other alphas. They're still inside me, and the motion rouses them both.

My bear alpha grunts into my hair, nestling closer, while my sweet alpha kisses my forehead, muttering. "Mm, pretty girl. Love you, too."

I feel them both get thicker, straining to press deeper. The pack alpha smirks, running his eyes over our tangle. The expression looks so familiar; a name suddenly pings in my brain.

Smith.

Being able to think at all is a relief, but remembering all of them banishes any last bits of trepidation thrumming in my blood.

That's Smith, and this is Damon, and the mountain of bulging, brooding muscle behind me is Cassian.

And they're all *mine*.

Except, not really. Not yet. I've tried to bite them so many times over the last few days, but Smith has stopped each of us every time. His barks were soft and careful, but remembering them still floods my eyes with tears.

Why did he say *no*?

"Angel," Smith whispers, bending over my head to give me an upside-down brush of his lips. "I've been waiting for you. We all have. Are you ready to be ours, now?"

The words swirl around my blurry brain before they sink in. My stomach trembles with nerves, but fresh slick douses Cassian and Damon, who both groan. Smith's half-smile blossoms into a full grin. Even though my head feels fuzzy, I can't resist grinning back.

Grumbling, the alphas rearrange all of us, handing me to Smith. He curls my body in his lap and lowers his forehead to mine. "How do you want us, omega? Separately?"

No.

I never want them to feel separated from each other again. They lived like that for way too long. My Omega and I agree—we know what we need to do.

It takes a moment to find words. When I do, my voice is a scratchy whisper. "All together."

Smith's smile glows with pride. "Perfect." He brushes his lips over mine, murmuring low. "Kneel, omega."

A burst of perfume fills the nest. All three alphas react—Cass growling, while Damon chokes. Smith smooths my hair back and kisses me softly. He pulls back and stares into my eyes, speaking to the others.

"I want her throat."

Damon chuckles darkly. "Mine's a surprise."

Cassian's chest rumbles. "Her shoulder." Green eyes peer at me over his packmate's shoulder while he lifts my arm by the wrist and skims his teeth over my palm. "Is that all right, baby?"

I whine again, trying to squirm closer to him. He smiles—and it's so beautiful my lungs stutter. His big hand cups my head, petting down my hair.

Threading my fingers around his wrist to hold onto him, I reach my other hand out for Damon. He comes to me right away, helping position my thighs around Smith's hips. "Ride our alpha, sweetness," he rasps. "When you're ready to come, we'll all bite you."

My inner muscles clench while a pulse of pain rocks me. When I whimper, Smith instantly lifts me up and slowly lowers me onto his cock.

I don't know how they're all so hard and ready for me, but this alpha is *throbbing*. His knot is already half-full, hot, and swollen where it touches my pussy lips. He groans at the feel of me, panting. "I've been inside you for days—how do you feel so fucking incredible *every time*?"

Urgency clamps me around his length when his head rubs into the place where I want his knot. I keen, bouncing on top of him. My thighs tremble, the muscles exhausted. But Cassian notices and slides his chest to my back, rubbing his dick over my ass while he holds my weight, banding his huge hands around my waist.

"Rems," he whispers into my nape. "There's no rush, butterfly. We're all here. We're all *yours*. Relax and enjoy your alpha's big cock. Is his knot going to fill you all the way up?"

I cry out again, nodding frantically. He's right—there's no *reason* to rush, and I don't *want* to, but the desperation sinking its claws into my stomach refuses to retreat. My hands scratch at Smith's upper arms. Our pack leader leans away to let Damon lower his face between our bodies. He hums as he licks around the top of my clit.

"Alpha!" I scream, fisting his hair. "*Ah*!"

"Shhhh," he purrs into the pulsing nub, rubbing his full lips over it. "Feel this, baby. Focus on how good it feels and let us take care of you."

They do. Holding me up, filling me gently, lapping at my clit until I'm so full of burning bliss, I think I'll slip back into my haze. Cassian cups his calloused palms over my breasts while Damon licks smooth, slick circles around the place where Smith pushes into me deeper and deeper.

No matter how hard I beg, they refuse to go faster, each one clearly relishing every second. They're all working together. A team.

A real pack.

They're ready.

The impulse comes straight from my Omega, along with a rush of slick that has Smith bottoming out, his knot popping into place. He hisses, and I whine as Damon sucks me into his mouth, lashing at the swollen bud with his tongue until I come all over Smith.

"Now!"

The word snaps out of me, and none of them make me wait. Smith lunges up, finding the perfect place on my bare throat and sinking his teeth right into it.

Smith.

The scalding spurt of his seed bathes my insides like a volcano as his essence blazes an unyielding path down my throat. Heat winds its way to a part of me I've never known. Some secret, sacred space in my very middle. Under my air, in front of everything else that makes me who I am.

He's there. A coil of gold silk—or maybe just *gold*. Smooth and cool, but somehow heavy and solid, too.

The tether curls around my soul, waiting. I sob, wanting nothing more than to bite him back, and feel the inside of *him* the way he must be feeling me.

But a set of perfect white teeth flash at my thigh, sinking into the flesh just beside my mound.

Damon.

Like a crack of lightning, his energy zips into my blood and races right for my core. It's bright and bouncy, with a secret bit of sweetness. The bolt hits my pounding heart harder than Smith's cool, thick coil, but entwines with it seamlessly.

The cold metal tempers his heat. The charge of electricity livens the gold. Balanced. Brilliant. Bliss.

Another climax rocks through me, my slick pussy gushing over Smith's knot while he releases another load, along with a serrated growl. Damon moans, his teeth still piercing me, coming all over my side and hip. Their scents swell to fill the nest, stronger than mine, blending into bittersweetness.

And it's every good thing I can imagine, except for...

Cassian.

He nuzzles into my nape, purring against my back while he takes his time finding the right spot. In the end, it's opposite

Smith's, right where my shoulder knits against the side of my neck. Right where he likes to lay his head and hide from the world.

His lips vibrate against my skin, whispering. "Always was," he vows, "Always will be."

My bear winds up biting the softest of all three. And unlike the heavy unspooling of Smith or Damon's quick charge, Cassian's soul comes slower. Like a misty rain, showering my heart in everything soothing. Protection, devotion, promises.

There's power underneath. Rolling thunderclouds that could clap or roil. Strength and depth and a bit of mystery.

But mostly, love. So much, so soft. It blankets my heart, pitter-pattering over the others and sinking into us all.

It's perfect, some delirious part of my mind murmurs. After precious metal is tempered by heat, it's cooled in water. And it comes out indestructible.

Cass releases the soft part of my neck, moaning into my skin while he comes against my back. The warm lashes pump the scent of dark chocolate and hazelnut into the air, turning our nest into the most perfect place on earth.

My alphas move to arrange themselves in a triangle, each of them kneeling and facing each other. Smith hauls me up with him, snuggling me in his arms and licking at the claim he left on my throat. His knot pulses inside me, stretching to fill every last nook. I feel us lock together again and sob while I find the place I want to mark each of them—just above the heart.

It's like plugging in a string of lights. One moment, the tether is loose, and the next, it pulls taut, connecting us as it sparkles to life.

And I can *feel* him.

His pride, his adoration. The solid, serious weight in his center. And underneath all of that, the fear that he won't be able to hold us all up.

I funnel reassurance to him, opening every inner door to let him see inside. Showing him how cared-for and loved I've felt for the last few weeks. Telling him he's the strongest, most competent alpha an omega's ever had.

"Remi," he murmurs quietly, clutching at me while he comes again, groaning. "God, I love you. Can you feel how much?"

It floods into me, a wash of warmth and *gratitude*. He's so, so thankful. For *me*.

The feeling sends tears to my eyes. He kisses them away, nuzzling our faces together. "I've never been more grateful for a gift in all my life. Or more unworthy."

It isn't true. I press my lips into his skin, showing him just how worthy he is with flashes of memory. I feel his mouth curve against my cheek while he listens internally, the connection between us solidifying into an unbreakable strand.

My pack alpha's knot releases. I hear a gasp. The scent of spiced autumn beats at me, like a pulse in the air. Smith feels my pang of guilt for getting distracted and laughs softly. "Is Damon next, angel?"

I nod a bit too fast, and he chuckles again. Before I can think about moving, I'm lifted off Smith and passed to Damon. He envelopes me immediately, impaling me on his rock-hard length while he pulls me into his purring chest.

"Need you," he pants. "Please, baby. *Please*."

My feeble little omega purr starts up, reacting to his distress. He makes a plaintive moaning sound, his cock twitching inside of me as my body vibrates around his length.

Cassian likes the noise too. He presses closer, breathing hard while he fists his knot and watches us with wild green eyes.

I bury my face against Damon's smooth, hard pectorals, inhaling his rich autumn spice, holding it deep in my lungs while I open my mouth and pierce the place over his left nipple, giving him a claim to match Smith's.

Damon chokes on a growl, his knot exploding to fill me so perfectly. His tether pulls tight and lights up, just like our pack alpha's, only his strand flickers with joy instead of shining steadily.

I love the way he feels—so happy and *sure*. We're his family, his everything. And not one speck of him dissents.

Holding him close, I pull up all of my favorite memories of him, lingering on how much happiness he's brought to my life. How many times I've smiled watching him walk out of a room, thinking how lucky I was to get to be home with him. To build a home with him. To be a home *for* him.

I send him all of my appreciation for the days spent on the couch watching Bake Off and nights spent pleasuring me and expecting nothing in return. Shifting through my favorite moments brings me back to that day in the ice rink, his questions about us making a family together, and how excited I am to do that with *him*. To know him like no one else ever has.

By the time I'm finished, I feel his tears soaking into my hair. He swipes them away, grinning. Unashamed because he can feel all of the same emotions swirling through me.

Our damp lips brush and cling. "All in, pretty girl," he whispers, smiling and teasing me with a subtle thrust of his hips. "All the way in."

With one final kiss to my forehead, he hands me off to Cassian.

My bear is out of patience, it seems. Paying no mind to the creamy swirl of cum and slick dripping from me, he lodges himself deep inside, locking his knot into place right away.

I gasp, coming around him in a rush that stuns me. Damon and Smith both feel it through our bonds and grunt. More hot release splatters over my back and my ass while Cassian takes my mouth, ravaging me with a filthy, licking kiss.

"Fucking need you," he groans, pained, while he bounces me on his knot, letting it tug at all the most sensitive places I have. "I've needed you for so long, Rems. I didn't know what the fuck I was missing, but it was *you*."

I let him scrape the words out and give him what he wants, clamping my teeth over his heart, smoothing the sting away with my tongue while his bond stretches and flips on. The glow is softer than the other two—but there's a beautiful tinge to the weak light that reminds me of sunrise.

Smith is steady, and Damon is bright, but Cassian? Cassian is *eternal*.

To the bottom of his soul, all through his fathomless depths, he loves me. In a way no one else possibly ever could. In a way I never knew existed.

He's *devoted*. Unshakable. Consumed with complete contentment just from this. From *me*.

Now it's my turn to cry. As my eyes well, he holds me against his rumbling chest, dropping soft kisses to my brow. *Do you feel how much I adore you?* he says inside. *Do you see how gray my world was before I found you again?*

I do, and it almost destroys me. I hate that he ever suffered like that, so lost and lonely. Never knowing what he needed or how he felt. Buried in a fog of apathy that wouldn't lift, no matter how hard he tried.

My fingers thread into his hair, sinking against his scalp. The pleasure of that simple touch echoes through him like a sonic boom. When my body clenches in reply, his answering bolt of bliss nearly sends me into another orgasm.

I feel his smile against my shoulder and the corresponding flicker of joy inside of him. Both have me grinning like a loon while I hug his neck. "I love you, Cassian."

His contentment swells to fill his whole body. *I'll always love you, Rems.*

A thought occurs to me. I lean back slightly and shoot him a look. *Just because you can talk to me in here, now, doesn't mean you get to stop talking altogether.*

He flashes his rare grin, cocking an eyebrow. *Wanna bet?*

Damon and Smith surround us, both smiling, though our pack leader's expression has a wry edge to it. "You know he hates talking to anyone who isn't us. He'll never have to speak again now that we're bonded."

Joy pings through all four of us. The bonds wrapped around

my middle light up like a switchboard and I know they're all using them to speak to each other without using words.

They're connected, through me. They can all hear each other, show each other things.

I did it.

All three alphas hear my dazed, exhausted exultation. I'm instantly flooded with love, pride, possession, amusement, and soft concern. The lights inside me glow and pulse, but I can't hear anything they say to each other. Some tired, distant part of my mind realizes they're talking *about* me, not *to* me, and I smile sleepily.

Purrs rattle around me. My body feels weightless—like I'm floating on a cloud.

I land on Smith's richly-scented skin, burying my face in his pecs. Cassian curls around my back, pressing his rumbles into my spine until it melts. Damon makes space for himself between my torso and Smith's, hugging my hips and nuzzling his face into my belly.

"Sleep, angel," Smith croons. "We'll be in your dreams."

chapter sixty-seven

CASSIAN

THERE'S a charge thrumming in my blood as I step out of the car.

I can't remember the last time I felt this way. The rush of competition, the thrill of anticipation. It reminds me of playing for our high school team—the way I used to spend the whole day before a game buzzing. Full of restless energy, tinged with aggression.

I'm... excited.

And pissed.

But, hey, a color is a color and nothing here is gray.

Remi feels my nervous anger and puts her little hands on my chest, beaming up at me. I love the look of pride in her eyes and the way it echoes down our bond—but I hate how she shakes when I cup her shoulders in my palms.

It's too fucking soon for us to be back out in the world. Most packs stay nested or nest-adjacent for well over a week after they bond. But here we are, two days out from the evening her fever broke, facing this clusterfuck of a situation.

My protective instincts don't like it. Remi has barely caught up on her sleep, let alone adjusted to having three alpha bonds running through her. Not to mention regaining her strength after eating so little during her heat.

That won't happen again. Now that we're all bonded, it will be much easier for us to coax her through next time. The thought gives me a burst of satisfaction, infused with a vein of heated lust. Remi feels both, giggling quietly and raising her brow at me.

You all ready to go again, Bear? So soon?

I snatch her waist, picking her right up and planting my mouth over hers. *Always, butterfly.*

We can feel Damon's pulse of curiosity before he lopes around the car. In the last three days, I don't think the guy's closed his curtain even once. If I focus long enough, I can always pick up on the thread of his thoughts, playing unobtrusively in the background of our bond like an upbeat pop song.

D snorts a laugh and loops his arms around Remi's waist to hug her from behind. "I wondered what had our pretty girl all happy and horny. Just this big guy, huh?"

She purses her lips to hold back a chortle and makes the absolute worst joke of all time. "Well, he is un*bear*ably handsome."

While she and Damon crack up, Smith's groan can be heard all the way from the other side of the Range Rover. He shakes his head, dusting the navy lapels of his suit and plucking at the pair of silky, blue-striped panties folded in his jacket pocket. "These puns are out of control."

D flashes a wide grin, hooking an arm over Remi's shoulders

and rolling his eyes at us. "C'mon, let's get this the puck over with."

Jesus. Even I have to groan at that one.

Paying no mind to my grimace or Smith's, Damon leads Remi through the parking lot. His mood takes a nosedive once we hit the sidewalk in front of the arena. Apprehension and embarrassment fill the bond, along with Remi's sweet reassurances.

Smith is surprisingly quiet. He has been every time we've discussed Damon and me returning to work.

It's our fifth game of this playoff series and, so far, the Timberwolves haven't totally sucked without us. Our back-up goalie has allowed more points than I ever would, but Gunnar's been channeling Damon, and he's posted enough shots to keep the score even at two games won for each squad.

We're not exactly sure what we're walking into tonight. Standard heat leave procedure calls for us to report to the next team event as soon as we're able, which happens to be tonight. But Coach could tell Damon to fuck off and bench him until his contract officially expires in three games. And I could be looking at some bench time myself, after the way I wordlessly walked out for Remi's heat.

So fucking worth it, I think to everyone, grumbling. They all reply with various blends of fond amusement and annoyance.

Not the point, Bear, Remi snaps.

Totally the point, Damon replies, bending to kiss her head.

Smith mutters something about going to speak to the team managers, straightening his sleeves and fidgeting with his not-a-pocket-square again. We all look at each other when he stalks off, wondering what we've missed.

Has his internal curtain been drawn like that all day? What for?

Remi doesn't know either. She chews on her lower lip, anxiety bleeding into her chest. Damon and I wrap her in a two-sided hug. "He's just stressed about the contract shit," I mumble. "He'll be back soon."

We're here early, even for us. Plenty of time for Damon to indulge his Alpha's instinct to stuff Rems full of food. He gets her a soft pretzel and a pornographically large hotdog, purring and petting her loose curls while he feeds her both by hand.

She accepts his overattentive fussing with sweet smiles and little bursts of bemusement. I keep an eye on our surroundings, grappling with my own impulses. The need to *protect* feels particularly urgent. When I spot the sleezy reporter who tried to corner Remi at her first game, I know why.

He's watching the three of us, a phone dangling from his hand. I'm sure he's already taken a dozen pictures, but none of us react. We already decided, as a pack, that we don't care what the press reports. It won't change anything for us.

So let them take pictures of the marks on Remi's throat and her shoulder.

Let everyone in the whole damn world know she's *ours*.

Smith reappears about twenty minutes later, holding a folder and striding right toward us. He waves a hand over his shoulder, sending us a smile and a beat of impatience that makes no sense. "Come on."

We all batter him with questions while we follow him out of the main, public area of the arena, into the bowels below. There are offices down here, along with our locker rooms, equipment, and medical facilities.

Once we get to the carpeted hallway, I realize there are a lot of administrative staffers here. They usually don't have to come in for weekend games.

Maybe, because of the playoffs...?

But everyone seems distinctly harried while they rush from one office to another, carting boxes or stacks of files. Damon's brow knits. He feels stupid for not immediately understanding and I send him a pulse of *you're not alone*.

"What's, uh, happening?" he asks, releasing Remi to turn in a half circle. "Are people moving offices?"

Smith nods. "Yes, I've restructured some things down here."

D and I both blink at him, each vaguely wondering if he's finally cracked. What makes him think he can come down here and give orders?

Remi figures it out first, of course. Her eyes drop to the folder in his hand and fly back up to his face. "You didn't," she breathes.

But she knows he did.

He bought the team.

Her dazed realization reverberates through all of us. Damon balks. My jaw drops. Smith's features pull into a cringe.

My mind races, recalling odd memories that seemed off at the time, but make sense, now. Like his lack-of reaction to hearing Damon walked off the ice for Remi's heat. The muttered phone calls he made the day we all finally came out of the nest and faced the world—all conducted with his internal walls up. And the way he and Ronan Ash spent over an hour talking at our last gathering.

Is this what they were cooking up? A team takeover?

The brilliant bastard.

"I'm sorry I had to keep it a secret, angel. There was an NDA clause in place for the acquisition process. Until we all signed the paperwork, I wasn't at liberty to say anything to anyone, not even our pack. I never thought I'd be waiting so long; we were supposed to sign last week, but with the heat, things got pushed a bit."

Half of his words don't even hit me. Remi's thought keeps twirling through my head. *He bought the team.*

For her, to keep her alphas together.

For Damon, to give him time to figure himself out.

For me, so I can keep playing now that I can finally enjoy it again.

For *us*. Our pack, our home, our family.

We all start to collapse around him, moving for a group huddle (okay, okay, a group *hug*)—but there's a crash behind me. I whirl, immediately putting myself between Remi and the source of the noise.

It's the weaselly reporter, on the ground, surrounded by gear. He must have been hiding in the open supply closet and fell out trying to record us. His phone lies two feet from my foot, where it landed when he fell.

With a decisive stomp, I smash it under my shoe.

He opens his mouth to protest, but we all snarl viciously. The coward's eyes fly wide as he leaps up, scrambling backward in retreat.

Remi peeks around my arm, watching him run away and letting out an indignant huff, "What a cunt."

chapter
sixty-eight

Five Months Later

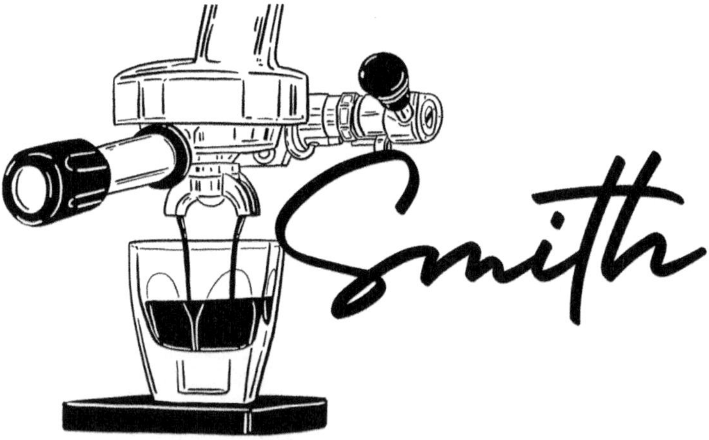

SHE BOUGHT *this thing on purpose.*

The thought makes me smile. I push harder at the lever of the espresso machine, putting more weight behind cranking the damn thing than I'd like to admit.

Damon may have me working out with him and Cass four mornings a week, but we tend to do more talking and bullshit competitions than actual work. Which is fine for them, since the team trainers I hired are some of the best in the country. But maybe I need to get my own weight coach if I can't even make a latte without breaking a sweat.

Of course, there's the fact that this is not an average espresso machine. But one that our omega selected specifically, I suspect, to torture me.

Touché, little petal.

It's French and appropriately temperamental. She chose it on our summer trip to Paris, when she fell in love with the café au lait from a tiny café near our hotel. Remi being Remi, she then proceeded to learn enough French to charm the proprietor into telling her where he bought the damn espresso machine.

Once she saw the price tag, she never mentioned it again. So, of course, I made it my mission to source one for her. A light blue one, to match our kitchen at home, and a sand-colored model to keep here at the beach house.

Now, as I fight with the machine for the fourth morning in a row, I realize my brilliant omega may have played me like a piano.

She knew I would buy this. And she knew it would be impossible for me to use.

Evil genius.

I send the thought through our bond, along with a mental image of the machine. I get a sparkle of delighted laughter back. Sleepy but still full of smug amusement.

I hate that I have to close the curtain between us, but I can't let her see anything else that's going on in the bungalow's tiny kitchen. Most importantly, it's a surprise. And second, Damon hasn't exactly perfected the clean-as-you-go aspect of his budding cooking skills.

"Hey!" he says out loud, feeling my internal wince when I look around at the countertops. "I have a system!"

On any other day, I might bitch about the mess, but not today. And not when he's so palpably excited to bring our girl her breakfast.

He's worked hard on it, I'll give him that. After months of watching Remi's baking shows with her, he started venturing into the kitchen on his own. What started as a batch of brownies here and an omelet there has now turned into him doing just as much in the kitchen as our omega.

Pride thumps in my chest while I watch him bend over the stove, poking at the French toast he's cooking. A lesser man may have taken my purchase of the team as a free pass to go back to the way he used to live. But Damon really took the lesson of nearly losing his hockey career to heart.

The team finished third in the League, but with Gunnar still improving and D back on the ice, we're planning to go all the way next year.

Damon is still applying himself to other ventures, though. Over the summer, he started looking for other hobbies and goals outside of being a pro-athlete. He asked to come on a few rounds with me for Pierson Properties, looking into what being one of our sales directors would entail.

After some coaxing from me and Remi, he also agreed to see a professional regarding his dyslexia. But, in the meantime, he and Cass started an informal audiobook club with some of the Ash pack's alphas and our omegas.

Apparently, Theo is really into monster romances; Declan prefers cowboys.

No matter what life throws at Damon, he comes out the other side stronger. Smiling. And, usually, better off. He still likes to call it luck, but I think Remi's right—it's less about luck and more about him, being the kind of person who spins straw into gold.

I let a beat of pride through our bond while I clap him on the shoulder, peering over his shoulder. "Looks great, Damon."

He smiles, the easy grin masking the internal note of surprise I sense every time one of us is proud of him. "Did you get the candles?"

"Yeah." I reach into the side pocket of my briefcase, where I've been hiding them all weekend. "Here."

Damon rips them open, shaking his head. "I never realized how hard it would be to plan a surprise for her," he mutters. "I haven't even *heard* her yet today."

He means in his head. Of all of us, Damon is the one who can be counted upon to have his every thought available. Going hours without "talking" to Remi must be strange for him.

"She's happy," I report, stabbing at buttons on the espresso machine. "And she bought this thing to annoy me."

"Everyone knew that, Big Hoss," he laughs. "You should have seen her face the first morning you tried to use it."

He slides his mental curtain open just long enough to slip me an image of Remi, rumpled and sexy in one of her negligées, giggling behind her palms while I fought with a stubborn lever. Every time I cursed, she snorted into her hands.

Damon and I stand still, each of us staring internally at her sweet, gorgeous face. Love bursts through my body and echoes in my packmate's. When his is accompanied by a whack of doubt, I turn my head and find him wincing at our breakfast.

"Do you think she'll like this?" he mumbles.

I know what he means. Nothing ever seems quite good enough for the girl who gives us everything.

We could get more flowers. Another present. Some shells from the beach...?

I start to look around for some other idea, my eyes darting across the small living room. When they fall on the sign our omega now has hanging over the front door, I freeze.

Don't make perfect the enemy of the good.

A smile stretches over my face. "She'll love it."

Because she loves us, and we love her. It's not perfect, but it's *good.*

And that's the best of all.

CASSIAN

SHE DID THIS ON PURPOSE.

The quiet thought occurs to me as I lie in the beach house's only bed, facing the wall of windows. Golden pink streams through the tissue-thin curtains framing the view. It's a straight shot through the tiny house's tiny backyard, over a few dozen feet of sand, right to the ocean.

To the *sunrise*, emerging from the aqua blue.

Once Remi decided to dedicate a portion of her summer to making this house exactly the way she wanted it, we all knew it would be beautiful. She surprised us by abandoning the preppy, sophisticated style of our pack house in favor of a kitschier, more bohemian style here.

We all love it, but Smith is particularly enamored. This place has been healing for him, I think. The way the deck slopes slightly, the constant salty musk of sea air, the fine layer of sand that coats the threshold no matter how many times we vacuum. All the little quirks he'll never be able to fix—it's been surprisingly easy for him to let them go.

Remi helps. Her first beach house rule? No one cleans until everyone's been to the beach and had a nap.

Her second rule: no one closes the bedroom curtains.

Because she wanted me to wake up to this, I realize. A sunrise view. The one we spent years chasing.

It's here. And she made sure our bed was oriented right toward it.

My beautiful, brilliant girl.

She hears my thought but doesn't reply, burrowing down into my chest instead, pretending to sleep. She does that, sometimes. And none of us ever call her on it because it's so goddamn endearing.

If acting like she's still unconscious to get more cuddles is the only thing my girl feels the need to pretend ever again, I will die a happy man.

Her leg flinches against mine, confirming my suspicion. The side of my mouth twitches into a half smile while I tuck my face into her mussed curls.

Now that we're bonded, Remi and I rarely speak out loud when we're alone together. We both enjoy the quiet and revel in the feeling of being so connected without ever having to break it. Instead of speaking, I send her a mental image of the sunrise outside our window. Then I send her pictures of a hundred other sunrises. On rooftops, balconies, bridges, from the top of the Eiffel Tower.

That one took some doing.

Worth it, though.

For this exact moment. When her pure, unadulterated happiness lights up my soul. *Good morning*, she thinks, *Bear*.

Her name for me floats through my chest, brushing my heart. So soft. Like a butterfly landing on a branch. The flap of her colorful wings. A flit of devotion.

Never intrusive. Just enough to remind me: I'm not alone.

I hold her closer, completely content. *Happy birthday, butterfly*.

DAMON

SHE'S DOING *this on purpose.*

Pictures flit through my mind. Cassian's hands, working her nightgown off. The view of her bare body in the morning light. The way her thighs part to let him slide between.

I've corrupted you, I send back, every word saturated with satisfaction. *Tell Cass to save room for breakfast.*

She bats back a flicker of impish delight and the image of her knees parting wider. *Whatever you say, Trouble.*

I grin, figuring this is retaliation I deserve, after the way I've tiptoed around the bond all morning. She knows I'm up to no good and feels inspired to make a little mischief of her own.

Naughty, pretty girl.

Her answering laughter gives my insides a glow. I chuckle, too, closing the mental curtain up and turning back to her birthday brunch. Seeing that it's almost done, I send Cass a hard nudge. *Dude, you have* five *minutes.*

He laughs, smug, offering a brief-but-glorious glimpse of our omega, all laid out for him. *I only need three.*

Smith and I both glower at him and at each other. *We know.*

The Bear Formerly Known As Beast is true to his word. Less than five minutes later, he has her propped up against his naked chest, holding her with one arm around her waist.

She put her nightgown back on, but that's probably for the best.

I won't be able to sing Happy Birthday on key if my cock is out.

Smith walks in first, carrying her breakfast tray and the small vase of flowers he chose for her. He also decorated her platter with seashells he collected and cleaned. I come in last, carting the three-tiered pumpkin-spice cake I made, walking slowly, so I don't extinguish her birthday candles.

Remi's golden-blue eyes fill, her bare, beautiful face reflecting all the awe and gratitude flooding her center. We all sing to her—even her grumbly bear—laying the trays carefully over her lap and her knees.

She sways and blinks, crystal tears trickling down her cheeks while she blows out the candles. Her fingers float up to touch the wings of the tissue-paper butterflies Cassian insisted we use as decoration.

I spread them up one side of the cake, their blue wings gradually lifting higher off the light pink icing. All the way up to the one single piece on the top, which looks like it's taking flight.

Just like you, I think to her. *Just like all of us since we found you.*

Remi strokes over the thin wing and whispers, "It's perfect."

Smith pets her hair, purring for her. "*You're* perfect," he corrects. "But Damon's cake is pretty damn good."

Cassian nuzzles at her hair. "We got you a present, too."

Smith has been holding onto it, but he must know how much it means to me, because he hands it to me to pass to our omega. "Here, sweetness."

Remi takes the small box, turning it in her hands with an adorable look of suspicion on her face. "You guys already got me a gift. It's in the driveway—remember?"

We feel her irony in the bond. She's kidding; because of course, no one would ever forget her custom powder-blue Mercedes SUV. Specifically designed to fit all of us, with room for more. Smith surprised her with it a few days ago when we were packing up to come to the beach.

"This one is special," I murmur, resisting the urge to bounce impatiently. "Open it."

She smiles, shaking her head in a totally bogus chastisement. I can tell she doesn't really mean it because she immediately starts ripping the paper off.

The second she gets the little box open, all humor falls off of her face. Her plush pink lips part on a gasp. Her eyes fly wide. "Oh my God!"

Smith designed the piece, modeling it after a traditional engagement ring—one large stone in the middle, with clusters of diamonds around it and a shimmering diamond band. Remi touches the aquamarine at the center, tracing the azure gem lovingly.

"It's gorgeous," she breathes. I feel her delight, along with a wash of guilt. "But you didn't need to—"

We all send her fierce blasts of reassurance. Mine comes with whispered words.

"Yes, we did. We even engraved it."

While she lifts the band to her face, tilting it to read the inside, I send her a picture of us in the ice skating rink. The day she told me why she didn't like her birthday; because it was the day her parents gave her up.

We all hear her read today's date, along with her new name. *Remi Pierson*. A beat of excited confusion melds with a bolt of too-good-to-be-true apprehension.

Cassian fixes it, speaking quietly. "We made sure the paperwork to officially change your name would go through today."

Smith takes the ring from her and slides it onto the proper finger. "So, now, when you think of your birthday, you'll remember that we chose *you*. And you'll always know how much you're wanted."

A dam of emotion bursts inside of our girl. More tears spill over while the guys hug her between them.

But I'm the one she looks right into, her heart touching mine internally. Telling me she knows this was my idea. Spilling gratitude and love through our bond. I multiply it and send it back, doing my best not to give in to the lump in my throat.

She feels that, too, though. And, of course, she knows just what to say.

Still crying happy tears, she smiles and raises a brow at me. "What do you think, Trouble? Cake before breakfast?"

SO MANY THINGS HAVE CHANGED, but I'm still a terrible liar.

Smith tugs gently at my salt-crusted ponytail, tipping my head back into his wide shoulder. "Are you tired, petal?"

I am, but... "Nope."

He tuts, shaking his head slowly. His free hand skates down my belly, skirting my bikini bottoms.

"Omegas who fib get edged until they tell the truth. You know our house rules."

As if the four of us didn't spend half of our afternoon in bed together. But between all the birthday sex, a long morning walk along the shore, and our late-afternoon picnic on the beach, I'm feeling sun-drenched and sleepy.

Of course, that could be due to the half-bottle of champagne I've had with Smith while Damon and Cassian throw the football around. They're determined to beat Theo and Declan in a game when we host the Ash pack for a cookout next weekend. All because Theo met up with them for conditioning one morning and turned out to be a secret hockey star. Ever since he scored a goal on Cassian, my alphas have been fired up for retribution.

Meg and I have a bet going on how quickly "flag" football will devolve into full-tackle.

She thinks six minutes. I give it four.

Luckily, we'll both have our eye protection for any impromptu dick-measuring.

I smile, admiring the way the light refracts off of my new ring when I reach up to pull the teal heart sunglasses from my hair. I perch them on my nose and send my alpha a look.

"What about the house rule regarding work emails on the beach?"

His phone sits off to the side, open to his inbox. He grins at me. "If you must know, I was checking our reservations for tonight. Family dinner at our favorite place, for your birthday."

I don't have to poke at his thoughts to know he's telling the truth. And that makes me smile even wider as I give him his very favorite compliment. "Best alpha ever."

It's true. He really is.

Since he gave the everyday operations of Pierson Properties to his subordinates and stepped up to run the Timberwolves, he's been happier than ever and much less overwhelmed. Aside from a few key administrative changes, the team was already set up to run without much oversight.

Of course, my Type-A alpha still keeps himself plenty busy—but, now, he's home every night for dinner. No matter what. And so are Cassian and Damon.

Most evenings, that means we're all gathered around our kitchen table, in our pack house. But sometimes, family dinner looks like takeout in front of the TV. Or ice cream in our nest. Or dates on the town.

Or, my favorite—sunsets at the beach.

It's funny. I grew up with this ache in my middle. Longing for a real house. A picket fence. My own room. Some *place* to call my home.

It turns out, home isn't a place at all.

But I found mine anyway.

want more?

KNOT HER *Fight*

an

MVP: MOST VALUABLE PACK

omegaverse romance

PRE-ORDER HERE!

a note from ari

Hi lovelies,

Thank you so much for reading Knot Her Shot!

After writing Meg's book, Remi instantly took a special place in my heart. When reviews and requests started to pour in asking for her story, I was absolutely buzzing to write it!

I hope I captured her sweet heart and spirit the way all of her incredible fans deserve. She is one of my favorite main characters ever and I wanted to do her justice.

When I set out to write her story, I reflected a lot on the things we do to feel accepted. I think it takes a lot of bravery to stop people-pleasing and show others your true self, especially if you're someone who has experience rejection like Remi!

I wanted to highlight that struggle; between being true to yourself and longing for the approval of others. So many of us straddle that line, just like Remi.

In the end, I hope you loved her alphas and her HEA as much as I did!

On a personal note, I want to include a note of gratitude for everyone who has read Knot Her Goal. For those of you who loved it, reviewed it, shared it with friends—you changed my life!

The way my career has shifted since releasing Meg's story is my dream come true.

So, to anyone who has been a part of this journey, please know —you are my MVPs.

xo,

Ari Wright

acknowledgments

The team I've gathered around me has been my favorite thing about writing this book. I remember sitting down to do the acknowledgments for Knot Her Goal and realizing that frightfully few people even *knew* about it.

This experience has been so different.

I've had so much support from my fellow authors in our unhinged group chat, gotten a ton of great advice from "real" authors, and found new friendships all over the place.

To my absolute ride or die, Kelly—look at us. Who would have thought? *You* did, which is why we're here. I love you for believing in me when I don't and always knowing what will make the girlies feral. Thank you for coming on this crazy ride with me.

Katie, my amazing editor, friend, cheerleader, and teammate; this book would not exist without you. Thank you for helping me climb every mountain (real or imagined lol) to get here. You are the very best!

To Christina, who got dropped in the middle of all my chaos—thank you so much for going with the flow and becoming a part of this crazy team!

I would also be remiss not to mention my lovely BFF Erin, who hasn't called me crazy even ONCE despite me becoming an unhinged Omegaverse author. Thank you for always supporting me—even if it means getting on a plane and coming with me on some unhinged adventure!

Always last and never least—a huge vat of gratitude for my husband. He makes the rest of my life possible while I write these books and I am so lucky to be his.

about the author

Ari Wright was once entirely sane, but then she realized sanity is overrated and decided to write sporty Omegaverse smut.

Because life is short, you know?

When she isn't writing unhinged romances, she enjoys drinking coffee to the point of excess, kitchen experiments, raising her littles, and trying to keep her plants alive (just kidding, her husband does that).

She loves really embarrassing music, moody weather, and any story where the bad guy gets the girl.

Because what's Happily Ever After without a little (or a lot of) spice?

You can follow her works in progress, favorite reads, and very pink aesthetic on Instagram!

Printed in Great Britain
by Amazon

50674613R00249